Y0-DNM-115

Confrontation with a Terrorist

When Novik and Washinski entered the small room in the back of the *espresso* bar which contained only one table, Novik was surprised to see it occupied by a blond youth, obviously a German. He looked at Stefan, saying in Polish, "I assumed we were having breakfast alone."

Speaking in English, Stefan said, "There's been a little change, Your Eminence. This is Hans. He has something to tell you."

Novik looked from face to face. He liked neither the expression he found on Stefan's face—worry—or that of the German—arrogance.

Novik spoke in Polish. "The Red Brigades?"

The German smiled and answered in Polish, "Yes, Your Eminence. It is. I assume you realize there are many Red Brigades."

"I understand." Novik sat down. "What is your business, young man?"

"Your Eminence, who I am or what organization I represent is of no consequence. I am a hireling. At the moment I represent some highly placed people in Italy who are curious about your meeting with His Holiness yesterday."

Novik turned to Stefan. "Washinski, did you bring me here to be questioned by this mercenary? If so, I am surprised. Horrified, really," Novik fairly shouted.

The German pressed his hand against his breast pocket. Silently he slid his fingers around the outline of a revolver.

"I am afraid Padre Washinski had no choice. Nor do you, Your Eminence."

We will send you a free catalog on request. Any titles not in your local book store can be purchased by mail. Send the price of the book plus 50¢ shipping charge to Belmont Tower Books, Two Park Avenue, New York, New York 10016.

Titles currently in print are available in quantity for industrial and sales promotion use at reduced rates. Address inquiries to our Promotion Department.

THE
VACANT THRONE

◆━━━●━━━◆

DAVID HANNA

BELMONT TOWER BOOKS ● NEW YORK CITY

for Edmund MacIntosh Smith

A BELMONT TOWER BOOK

Published by

Tower Publications, Inc.
Two Park Avenue
New York, N.Y. 10016

Copyright © 1979 by Tower Publications, Inc.

All rights reserved
Printed in the United States of America

PART I

New York—Saint Patrick's Day

When Donald Thaddeus Brady awoke from a night's sleep, a Spanish nap (twenty minutes) or a cat nap (five minutes), there was style about it that never varied. The Brady technique of awakening involved neither yawns, stretching nor scratching. He never awoke with a start—nor did he slither reluctantly out of bed. He simply got up, wiggled his toes into bedroom slippers carefully placed in the same position under the bed and walked to the window to see what kind of weather the day promised. Dressing to accommodate weather meant the start of his work day which could be nine, noon or three in the afternoon.

Donald was a newspaperman and the unpredictability of his profession had nurtured Donald's cool, perhaps fussy preparations, characteristics not especially noticeable in his other activities. He wasn't a snappy dresser; he could even be sloppy. But the trick lay in being ready for whatever the day produced in the way of a story. He might not return to the apartment until the following morning, a couple of days or several weeks. Donald had abandoned operating within the arbitrary framework of twenty-four hours. His private timing mechanism functioned in terms of stories.

For thirty-two of his thirty-three years, Donald had enjoyed the freedom to cultivate his personal and professional habits without interference. At worst, when he was very young, he sometimes had to explain them to his teachers and elders.

But on this particular March seventeenth when he arose and took two quick steps from a double bed to the window

5

that looked out through thick iron bars from the one-room apartment, Donald knew that very shortly he was going to cringe. To have been holed up for virtually twelve months in a basement cheerfully described by the rental agency as a "garden apartment" was a grim confinement indeed. Knowing that his companion was shortly going to close the four walls tighter around him in the cage of an apartment had become a daily fear—like morning sickness.

Donald didn't particularly enjoy his quiet, unhurried, deliberate routine of showering, shaving and dressing and then checking out the tools of his trade. It was part of the job—making sure a necktie had been stuffed into his side pocket, that other pockets contained two pens, three or four letter-sized envelopes if he had to make notes, that his wallet's secret compartment contained five twenties and two fifties, an international travel card, coded address book and a White House press card which had improperly crossed too many police and military barricades to be counted.

As habitual as this daily organization had become, it required a degree of concentration—either that or wear the same clothing every day. Seemingly insignificant items had to be moved from one suit to another and carefully checked out before he left for work. Donald nearly lost one major story because of a forgotten travel card. The coded address book (with a mate in his safe deposit box) was worth a hundred times its weight in newsprint.

Only a year ago Donald slid daily through the routine an untroubled and unattached man. Today it was "a far, far different life" than any he'd ever known before—or expected to know. A glance at the clock told him it was nine-thirty and he tried to mumble "fuck it" when the two yards of sidewalk in front of the window told him the day would be clear and sunny. The Irish had scored again.

The mumble had been a waste. He hoped that in the room's semi-darkness his shudder would pass unnoticed when the sound of a sleepy, feminine voice, attractively accented, came from the tumbled mass of sheets and one thin blanket curled up in the bed; the only visible part of its origin being yards and yards of thick, luxuriant black hair scattered across the pillows.

6

"It is criminal. No man has a right to look as beautiful as you do in the morning, *liebling*. It's not..."

Erika Wald seldom finished her first sentence of the day. But that offered no promise that she'd fallen back to sleep. Far from it. Erika was still dreaming and Donald had lived with the Viennese beauty long enough to know that her private world between sleep and being awake embraced few thoughts beyond sex.

At first, her morning sexuality, reflected verbally, emotionally and physically, charmed Donald who, until Erika, had never shacked up with a girl friend for longer than a weekend. Then he blushed from his neck down to his buttocks as Erika mumbled, "*Liebling*, you have the most beautiful ass in the world. Oh, how I love to look at those cheeks!"

Donald wore only the tops of his pajamas even during weekends of the cold winter when the landlord cut back the thermostat to a thousand degrees below the legal level. In making the short trip to the window, Donald shivered and goose bumps broke out on his behind.

Erika loved them. "Come quickly, come quickly, here to the bed. I want to count them—before they go away." He was happy as a kid who'd discovered that playing doctor beat baseball any day of the week. He plopped down on the bed, all six feet of him, flat on his stomach while Erika sat up, wrapped the thin blanket around her chest and began counting. "*Eins, zwei, drei... un, deux, trois, uno, due, tre—* right through her endless collection of languages, French, Italian, Russian, Spanish. Then in her native German, she'd move into the hundreds, using various dialects, the lilt of Viennese, the no-ending sound of Bavarian and the harsh snarl of Prussian. Donald had read about actresses who could charm an audience by reciting the alphabet. None, he was sure, matched the joy of Erika counting the goose bumps on his butt.

But that was last year when all was enchantment for the handsome pair who invariably drew gazes of admiration wherever they went.

Erika was twenty-four, but the age difference disappeared when Erika put herself together. Donald gleamed with a healthy all-American look (which he loathed) and Erika possessed that uncanny talent of European women to seem any age an admirer enjoyed. Donald was a shade over six feet, sandy-haired with a lean, rugged face, harboring two bright blue eyes, a long, straight nose and full sensual lips that eliminated some of the sting of his perennial boyishness. He owed this to his Italian mother as well as a defect that Donald had scarcely noticed until Erika discovered it.

"*Gott sei dank!*" she cried one evening as Donald came naked out of the bathroom to crawl into bed. "*Puppchen, es ist wunderbar! Du bist nicht perfekt! Du hast eine fehler! Liebling*, you're not a God! Look at the mirror. Your legs are too short for the rest of you. Oh, I am so happy! Isn't it beautiful. Oh! I'm so mixed up—aren't they beautiful? Good legs, *ja*, but too short. Just like Italians and Austrians."

"How about my balls?" Donald flipped, as he looked at himself in the full-length mirror that Erika installed the first day they moved in. "I feel they hang a little too low, don't you? What do you suggest. A tuck here." He touched his right testicle.

"I don't know, *tesaro*. Maybe you better bring them over here and I can make a closer examination."

His balls, his ass, his cock, the fuzz on his chest, the way his nipples hardened when she wrapped her lips around them—these and their long, lazy sessions of lovemaking were dramatic, important and all consuming to Erika. For herself she asked no compliments and when Donald expressed appreciation of her loveliness, she was neither surprised nor grateful. Erika's beauty was part of her. Since she took it for granted there was no reason for her to become *begeistert* by the appreciation of others. "I know I am beautiful. Why must I fall back in enchantment when someone tells me that?" she explained when Donald once asked her about her coolness.

Erika's face was all elegance—a photographer's dream. The way Hedy Lamarr once looked—and perhaps still did. The marble whiteness of her face heightened the air of worldliness in her deep, dark eyes, the long, aristocratic nose and inviting lips. She was the sort of woman once described as small, *petite* in another age, a *Dresden doll*.

Like Parisian women, the Viennese could create the

impression of chic in the way they carried themselves, in the unselfconsciousness of slapping a belt around a garment—whether it was a dressing gown or a working smock.

They understood the art of compensating for shortcomings—like Donald's short legs. Erika was not quite the *Dresden doll* she appeared. Without makeup, her mouth was big—"like a peasant's," Erika described it. "That means I'm sexy, *liebling*," she explained.

Donald often grabbed the Kleenex and wiped away her lipstick after they came home. "You're making my makeup *kaput!*" Erika would scream, scrunching her body close to his, grinding her hips. "You're cruel. A male chauvinist American."

When he was through, Donald would pull back, adjust his hardened crotch and fling his arms out, "There she is folks, the genuine article, a real *Bauerin*, the hottest peasant girl ever to have been exported from Kitzbuhel, Austria! Grab her while you can!"

Donald was enchanted with the idea that chic, sophisticated, cosmopolitan Erika Wald was born in a small Austrian village, the sort of hick town that her countrymen described as a *Nest*.

Stripped of her makeup and her clothes, Erika wasn't the beauty she appeared to be. Her bust was oversized, balanced by an attractive, bulging rump. Donald belonged to the school which pontificated that one wasn't an "ass or tit" man—that the girl was more important. It was a lie, of course, for his track record revealed that women who activated his sizeable equipment invariably were those possessing both attributes.

For a baby who was supposed to be a boy, Erika had turned out an extraordinary handful of woman. Her parents had long tried to have a child and they were well into their thirties when Rosi Waldenheim finally conceived. They prayed for a boy to be named Erich for Hans Waldenheim's brother, Erich Franz-Josef Cardinal Waldenheim, the distinguished Eminence of Vienna, a brilliant theologian who, by virtue of his long tenure in office, had become the Dean of the German-speaking Cardinals in Switzerland, Germany and his native Austria.

When the Waldenheim baby turned out to be a girl, it was

9

still possible to honor their distinguished relative by naming her Erika. As events turned out, it became a happy relationship, both for the child and the elderly man in the Cardinal's palace in Vienna.

At the time he was given the scarlet beretta by Pius XII, the Cold War was at its height and Waldenheim won quiet appreciation from both sides of the Iron Curtain for his patient efforts in easing tensions—a diplomatic feat made possible by his shrewd manipulation of the couriers, spies and counterspies who passed in and out of his diocese.

"All so conspicuous," Erika told Don. "Uncle Erich knew their names, aliases, birthmarks and their plots the minute they reached Vienna. Uncle Erich had arrangements with the hotels and boarding houses so spies were put up in special rooms close to permanent Austrian agents. Economical and practical, don't you think?"

Whenever Erika mentioned Cardinal Waldenheim, Donald was struck by the curious coincidences in their backgrounds. Although separated by age, by miles of geography and centuries of different cultural backgrounds, they shared an influence which, if not uncommon, was still out of the ordinary.

Both Erika and Donald were orphaned as young children; Erika, at four; Donald when he was seven. Both had been named for their uncles, Erika having been the compromise for Erich. Donald had been named for Thaddeus Donald Brady, one of New York's legendary newspapermen.

Like Uncle Erich, Uncle Thaddeus was still very much alive and also a Catholic, not so devout, perhaps, but reluctant to make any waves as he grew older and closer to eternity. "Why take chances?" he explained it. "They may be right about heaven, after all. Who the hell knows?" So Uncle Thaddeus made it to Mass on Christmas and Easter, fulfilled his Easter duty and enjoyed his own quiet way of dropping into favorite churches on quiet afternoons and simply sitting.

"No formal prayers," he once confided. "I sort of give myself up. I know I look so easy to everybody, but to me I'm not. That's my way of settling problems. I give myself up. Try it sometime."

From photographs of Cardinal Waldenheim, Donald saw similarities to Uncle Thaddeus. They possessed massive brows, thick eyebrows and thick gray hair. Thaddeus was neither as heavy nor as tall as the Austrian, but both were husky, broad-shouldered men. Their eyes were blue; the Cardinal's, touched by sadness; Thaddeus' by disarming innocence. One could see strength of character in each man as well as deep intellect and finely honed honesty which they could dispense with in tight political situations. Waldenheim was eighty but his photographs certainly never revealed it.

Whether they would enjoy each other was a point Donald hesitated to contemplate. Thaddeus cultivated prejudices as assiduously as others tried to free themselves from inbred convictions. He viewed fellow Irishmen with deep suspicion and on Saint Patrick's Day he bolted his doors, turned off the television and answered the telephone only if forewarned by an elaborate system of signal rings known to Donald and a few friends.

When Donald and Erika became wards of their uncles, Erika was taken from Kitzbuhel to live in the Cardinal's palace in Vienna and Donald was moved from Brooklyn to Thaddeus Brady's Central Park West apartment.

They had known each other for a couple of months after meeting at a United Nations cocktail party before Donald and Erika were struck by the similarities of their youth.

"Of course, *liebling*, you know that all European Cardinals have nieces," she said. "The difference is that I'm authentic."

"Of course," Donald laughed. "I don't doubt that. But there's always incest."

"Ho! Ho! Ho! And how about all those incest stories you hear about the Irish?"

"Strictly father and daughter."

"No uncles? Not ever?"

"Well, I don't know," Donald said. "I can't imagine Thaddeus Brady buggering a little boy. Put it this way. I can't see him enjoying it. Too untidy. A bit sweaty. Not gentlemanly. A niece? Different. Then, it would be gallantry. You do see the difference?"

"Of course. The Irish are brilliant at semantics. But all

these things we had together as babies is not why we love each other, I hope."

"God forbid! It's sex, *liebling*. That's what it is. Those tremendous knockers, the rest of your equipment."

"And the goose bumps on your behind."

"Let's forget them for the moment," Donald remembered saying one night.

Today Donald wished he'd never been born with a behind. Or that he'd never met Erika Wald, directress and/or executive *person* in charge of the translation department of the Austrian delegation to the United Nations. He even hated Uncle Thaddeus who had never blushed in his life—either on the cheeks of his face or the cheeks of his ass.

Yet the honest truth was that neither Erika nor Uncle Thaddeus had a damned thing to do with his present irritation. All by himself Donald had reached into the grab bag of trouble and come up with a hand filled with so many conflicts that sorting one from the other was difficult enough—much less trying to settle them.

So the sight of a sunny sidewalk became the last straw. "Fuck the Irish and their Goddamned Irish luck," he muttered as he stalked from the window to the bathroom. He raised his voice, "Sure and the Saints be praised for this blessed day. In a hundred years it has never rained or snowed or pissed on Saint Patrick's Day and our beautiful parade has been a continous joy to the sons and daughters of Ireland who live in this great city. Shit!"

Of course it was a lie for the Irish had marched through cloudbursts just to keep the tradition of perfect Saint Patrick's Day weather alive. Reporters, like Donald Brady, had helped pile up the blarney like so much manure.

From the bed there came that small, sweet voice, clanging in his ear like a gong, "Does that mean you will have to visit the parade, *liebling*?"

"Yes, *liebling*," Donald shouted from the bathroom. "That means I have to visit the Goddamned, fuckin' parade."

"Couldn't you do it by television—like last year?"

"Sure . . . sure. With a bomb threat received at the Chancery yesterday. Why not?"

12

"I didn't know that..."

"Not everybody does. I do."

"Then it's true."

"It's true all right." Donald poked his head around the door of the bathroom to make sure Erika got that one.

"Your voice is getting shrill," Erika shrilled.

"It's characteristic of the Irish," Donald yelled. "We warm up our voices early Saint Patrick's morning so we can sing *Mother Machree* and *Irish Eyes* tonight in croaked voices. Otherwise it's not authentic. Remember, we're a fuckin' minority. Christ, we're splitting construction contracts with Jews and Italians. And if that's not bad enough, even the blacks and Puerto Ricans want a piece of the pie. They want to ship us all back to Ireland."

"Where they grow good potatoes, fat pigs and bigoted priests."

"That's it, baby."

"Good, that's what Uncle Erich told me."

"He knew Mother Church all right. If anyone ever doubts what a mortal sin is, let him spit on the sidewalk instead of the gutter and an Irish priest will explain it."

"Which is which?"

"The sidewalk's mortal; the gutter's a venial. Now you can pass that on to Uncle Erich and he'll have another canard to tell about the Irish."

"What is a canard?"

"It's Gaelic for lie."

"Oh, thank you. Every day I am learning more."

"Didn't Uncle Erich ever tell you that Ireland also managed to grow quite a few poets and writers?"

"*Sicher*. He liked Shaw. They met once, you know?"

"No, I didn't. I probably wasn't even born then. How about you?"

"You crazy or something?"

Erika's Viennese accent didn't quite go with her attempts to "get with it" in modern colloquialisms. But Donald was charmed when she tried.

"About those snakes, Donald ... you *are* listening to me?"

Donald's head popped around the edge of the door. "Do I have an alternative?"

13

Erika ignored that with ease. "Uncle Erich always wondered where he drove them to. Do you know what Shaw told him?"

"It better be good."

"He said he shipped one-third to Northern Ireland, a third to the English Parliament and the rest to America."

"Baby, that answer was invented not only before you and I were born but at least a half century before Shaw. Now take that back to Uncle Erich."

"*Danke*, I will." She was quiet for almost a minute.

Donald started to place the razor next to his skin for about the tenth time when the little voice was heard again. "I suppose there will be the usual demonstrators, Women's Lib, the Gay Rights people."

Donald managed to shave the right side before answering. "They're getting to be old hat. Too familiar to rate much attention."

"Donald, why is it that Cardinal Muldoon always stands up when the Puerto Rican girls march by? Does that mean something?"

"You can read whatever you want into that. Last year Monsignor Ryan got caught by the TV cameras poking him to stand up for the black baton twirlers. They've got terrific legs."

Donald heard Erika chuckle. "He's smart—that Ryan!"

Donald's head rounded the corner of the bathroom. "Do you know him?"

"No," she giggled. "Not exactly. I would enjoy it though. *Ach! So ein schöner mann!* He's beautiful. He was with the *Rota* when he was assigned to the Vatican right after his ordination."

"The *Rota*? I didn't know that."

"Well, that's where he was, working on American annulments, I guess. Uncle Erich loves Rome. He hates Vienna. The weather. I think he sent me to study in Italy so he would have an excuse to visit more often. He'd drag me along with him. There was always so much business in the *Rota* section of the Vatican. That's how I got to know Father Ryan. *Ach!* What a lover he would be. Oh!"

Donald roared. No one was sacred to his Viennese chatterbox and the first to appreciate her admiration would be Tom Ryan. Hands down, he was the best looking priest on the Cardinal's staff since anyone could remember. It was a difficult comparison to make for the Cathedral had been famed for generations as home to the best looking Irish priests available.

Even doubtful preaching ability was sacrificed on the altar of male beauty, but anyone really interested in hearing a priestly Cathedral sex bomb display what Italians denigrated as "white Irish voices—not warmed by the sun"— could attend the six or seven o'clock Masses. For some Cathedral parishioners it was brutal disillusionment to see a young god with the physique of a football player, his shoulders so wide he walked sideways up the steps to the pulpit, but when he opened his mouth you'd imagine the *castrati* were back in style.

Erika jabbered away. "Uncle Erich would like to have been assigned to Rome. But he was too progressive when he was younger. *Gottes willen!* He still is."

"How about Ryan? What did Uncle Erich say about him?"

"Nothing much. He was a spy. Everyone knew it. He could see the Pope whenever he wanted. *Nein...nein...* that's not right. He could see the Pope when Cardinal Muldoon wanted him to. When Cardinal Muldoon had some confidential message for His Holiness. Not when Ryan *wanted to.* You see the difference?"

"Yes, baby, I do." Donald finished shaving. Not a cut. That was pretty good—considering the blood that had flowed from his chin the past several days.

Wiping the soap from his face, Donald stepped out of the bathroom, walked to the bed, "So my little *puppchen* from Kitzbuhel knows something the big city reporter doesn't. I wasn't aware that it went that far back."

"What?"

"The Cardinal Muldoon-Thomas Ryan association."

"How could you? You weren't there."

"I'm supposed to know everything."

15

"Pooh! Only the Pope's infallible. You know that." Erika hid under the covers and giggled as Donald pulled his towel into position to snap her with it.

"Has Ryan ever come by the United Nations?"

When Erika appeared she sat bolt upright, her nightgown had been pulled down and her breasts stared at him like heavenly-white mounds.

"Oh, my God, Saint Patrick! Give me strength!" Donald leaned down and held a nipple in his mouth for the longest time. Erika wiggled happily, placing her head on his hand, careful not to muss it. She knew he hated that.

Suddenly Donald stood up, "As I was saying..."

Erika crawled back between the sheets. "Yes, he's been there now and then. I never talked to him. He wouldn't remember. Anyhow, I was afraid to."

"Why?"

"A girl like me? Who knows? I might throw myself at him and unzip the poor priest's pants."

"He'd love it."

"*Ach!* Now you tell me."

"Yes, and now I guess it's too late. He's a Monsignor—the real brains, the *eminence grise* of the boiler room at the *powerhouse*."

"That's funny. They call the Cardinal's Palace the same thing in Vienna—*Das Machthaus*—the house of power."

Suddenly Erika's face turned serious. "Donald, will those abortion women be there?"

He was pulling on his trousers. The question stunned him. He answered quietly, "Yes, Erika, I suppose they will. It is sad."

"Where is the answer?"

"I don't know, *liebling*," Donald said. "I don't think anyone does." He shivered at the words "abortion women" but said nothing. Abortion was a touchy subject.

An abortion had killed his mother. It might have been a secret that Thaddeus Brady could have locked away forever, but that was not his way. Donald remembered how they'd met in Philadelphia, while Donald was in prep school at Malvern. Thaddeus had come down from New York to celebrate the boy's thirteenth birthday.

Much happened that day. Thaddeus called it "Donald's Emancipation Day." He said, "I am setting you free to make your own decisions. Choices, really. You are still my ward and I control the purse strings, but you are going to have choices from now on—where you go to school, what you will study, how you spend your student days. I am not going to decide them for you. Suggestions, yes. But no orders. I have tried to be your friend, a counselor rather than a surrogate father.

"Your own father would kill me for this. But that's his problem." Uncle Thaddeus ordered a double bourbon— which was outrageous. He seldom drank doubles, always stuck to Scotch. "Kinder to the system," he explained.

"I have to rattle some family skeletons. You have no relatives left, Donald, except your great-aunt, Lucia, on the Italian side. You and I are the last of the Bradys. Lucia's older than I am, but she'll probably outlive me. There's the danger that in her dotage she might blurt this out without thinking. You would wonder and perhaps be resentful that I had not told you everything I should."

Donald started to say something.

"Don't interrupt," said his uncle suddenly with uncharacteristic sternness. "I've rehearsed this for ninety minutes on the train and God knows how many years. Let me get it out.

"You have never been told the truth about the death of your mother and father. You must know it and it's my duty to tell it. Your father, Will, was my senior by ten years. Your mother, my junior by ten years. An incredibly beautiful girl and I thought we were going to be engaged and be married. I dated her first. But I realized she wanted Will. Fuck it. I'll give you the whole truth. Her mother wanted Will for Maria. There were three stillborn Brady babies between Will and me. I was an accident, I guess. And that's how Will treated me, the bothersome little brother and intruder. I was going to school and he was already making it big in the contracting business. So Will became the more suitable mate for Maria.

"About a year after you were born he was injured at one of his construction sites. I would never have known that Will had become impotent except that Maria's mother told me. Italian mothers will tell their in-laws everything. Their daughters? Never.

"Donald, your mother was a young woman. She had an affair. God knows who the man was. She got pregnant. She asked no one's advice—certainly not her mother. Why she never came to me can only be explained as shame and fear that I would be disgusted. Irish Catholics have a bad reputation that way, you know.

"To cut it all short, she died as a result of one of those kitchen abortions. Will Brady shot himself the day of the funeral."

Donald never flinched.

"God bless you, son. I was afraid of tears. I couldn't take that. You have only the dimmest memories of your parents. They were strangers in your life. There is no need for you to cry. Or me either. But I did weep then. Not for them. But for the folly of it all. Will Brady may have been an Irish bigot, but he was not a stupid man. He could have faced reality. There were many things we might have done. Maria could have borne the child. There would have been a cover-up. The families could have managed that, partially, at any rate. We wouldn't be the first to live with snickers for a few years. Eventually those things are forgotten.

"It is hard today to imagine a young woman resorting to an abortion she didn't want—but Will amd Maria were products of their times and their environment. I was younger. I could see all the roads open to her. But she chose to ignore me—and, sadly, my sensitivity.

"I dreaded the act of abortion then and time has not changed me. I doubt that it will. I am sorry, terribly sorry for women who must make the decision. For reasons more profound than your mother's fears. I wish I could take all the women in the world with unwanted pregnancies into my home and care for them and their children. I cannot believe that there is not room at the *Table of Life* for all of God's children.

"But I am not God. I can only think as God must sometimes and as the Church does."

He stopped short, "How absurd of me! Catholics still have much to learn. We have no monopoly on God and we have no monopoly on our aversion to abortion. Fine ministers and great rabbis deplore it. So do men and women of no religious persuasion. It is an old moral dilemma. I know I will never live to see it solved. Still that doesn't give me the right to knock on the doors of Congress and hassle the President into supporting my view. But the time is coming when the Church will be forced to abandon its position on artificial birth control. I think non-Catholics who dislike abortion will agree there. Ah, but it's a long way off—you can't expect relaxation of old prejudices from this crop of reactionary Irish priests in America and the Italian eunuchs running the Church in Rome."

Thaddeus paused, "For a thirteen-year-old boy you are marvelously patient with me, Donald. I thank you."

Donald remembered looking at his uncle solemnly and saying, "You're a great man, Uncle Thaddeus."

Thaddeus Brady patted the boy on the head. "That's a patronizing gesture. I shan't ever do it again. But," and he smiled warmly as he kept his hand on the boy's head, then let it slip to his shoulder, "you have spoken a truth. I am great. And now to prove it, we will order some Philadelphia ice cream. This afternoon we are going to the Shubert for the matinee of *My Fair Lady* and tonight we have a ringside table at the *Top of the Belmont* where Sophie Tucker is playing. After Sophie, you're on your own. You can stay at the hotel with me or go back to Malvern. What do you say?"

It was at the same luncheon that Thaddeus Brady said, "I think we can dispense with the 'Uncle' bit. Just stick to Thaddeus. That's a mouthful as it is."

Donald laughed. It was difficult at first, but soon he got used to it, especially after the night club show when Sophie Tucker came over to the Brady table and kissed him square on the mouth. "Call me up in a few years, kid," she said. Then she kissed Thaddeus. "I already know enough about this gentleman to put him away for life. How many years is it, Thaddeus?"

"Not enough, Sophie."

"That's what you call a *goy* with class," she said, looking at Donald. "Christ, he's a handsome kid. Not much doubt he's a Brady. Looks sexy, too."

The headwaiter called Sophie to another table where old friends, as always, were waiting for the beloved entertainer. Her big breasts hovered over Donald like two mountains of flesh as she kissed him.

"You're lucky, sonny," she said, "to have this beautiful person as an uncle. God bless you." A few seconds later a waiter appeared with a photograph, autographed, "To Donald Brady, Love, Sophie."

*   *   *

Donald glanced at the clock. "I've got to go, baby." He leaned over and kissed her, slipping a hand under the sheets and feeling her breast. The nipple was hard. The little minx. Erika had been playing with her tits.

"I ought to be back about three—unless I go into the office. I'll call you."

"And tomorrow we start on our trip."

Donald forced a smile, "You bet, baby. Just as we planned. He pursed his lips in a good-bye kiss. *"Ciao, liebling."*

Outside he felt the rush of fresh air and it was refreshing. Christ, the mornings were getting longer, he thought. Erika was like a pet dog—always in need of attention. Nothing else satisfied her. She could go without food and drink. She could sleep anywhere. This dungeon was good enough for her because it was safe and near the United Nations. Erika wanted no part of the Central Park West building where Thaddeus owned two apartments. He'd bought an extra one years ago at a bargain price, figuring Donald might one day need it. He did. It worked out fine. The two men met by appointment and there had never been any intrusion on the other's life while Donald grew from cub reporter to boy wonder and now to a senior feature writer and investigative reporter at the *Sun-Mirror*.

After the demise of the old *Telegram*, the Whitfield Foundation had snapped up Thaddeus to be their chief writer on historical projects. He was handed a lifetime contract at a salary twice the pay he had ever earned in the newspaper business. Right now he was up to his happy ears in writing the history of old New York neighborhoods.

Donald probably should have gone to Thaddeus when he made the big decision the first of the month—but that wasn't how the uncle and nephew operated. Thaddeus was true to the promise made on Donald's thirteenth birthday. He had been given control of his own destiny. Not that Thaddeus had really ever interfered. The one time he did was dramatic enough.

Donald smiled as he recalled it while walking down Lexington Avenue to Fifty-first where he crossed over to reach the Zenith Room at Madison where he intended having breakfast.

He was an earnest student at a boarding school in upper New York run by nuns. Thaddeus had come to pick him up on Commencement Day when the boy was in the seventh grade, walking off with half of the class' scholastic honors and some sports awards. He was expected to make a grand sweep of the medals in his graduating year.

Mother Superior had taken Thaddeus aside. "I think you should know, Mr. Brady, but we feel Donald has..."

Her voice dropped to a whisper. "We think he has *the call*. You know he's an altar boy and such a devoted one. Why, Mr. Brady he begs us to serve daily Mass. It's years since we've had a boy who showed such piety. Truly remarkable."

Nuns usually kept their eyes averted when speaking to the opposite sex in the years Thaddeus Brady knew them. In speaking of *the call*, their eyes were virtually closed. Mother Superior, therefore, hadn't seen the blood drain from Thaddeus' cheeks.

"Thank you, Mother. I certainly appreciate knowing this. I'll bet God's terribly happy, too."

Before she could react, Thaddeus swept up his nephew, the boy's suitcase, popped youth and baggage into his car and raced into town and the nearest bar.

"A double Scotch for me," he said, "and a ginger ale for him. Where's the men's room?"

The bartender nodded to the rear. Thaddeus pointed to

Donald. "Better get in there and take a leak now, Donald, so you won't wet your pants when I talk to you."

Donald ran to the lavatory. Thaddeus was really laying it on. Why?

Thaddeus looked at his hands. "Well, I'm not shaking. That's a break. This drink is all I can have if we're to drive to New York tonight. Now, young man, Mother Superior talked to me."

Donald shuddered, "Yes . . . and . . . ?"

"She said you have *the call*."

Donald let the straw slip from his lips. "*The call*? *The call* to the priesthood? She's crazy. She's got us mixed up. Chuck Festing's got *the call*. You know . . . the big skinny guy. He says he wants to be a priest. We serve Mass together all the time."

"Ah-hah . . . so that's it. And who asks you to serve Mass with Chuck Festing? Chuck Festing?"

"No, Uncle Thaddeus. Me."

"How come?"

"It's nice. You told me to get on the altar so I'd learn some Latin. I'm only doing what you told me to."

"That's what you say. You haven't anything to add? You like Chuck Festing so much you get up early every day to serve Mass with him?"

"Well . . . not exactly."

"That's better. Whew! You certainly had me worried. Stick that straw back in your mouth. You can relax. I get it."

"Get what?"

"Used to do it myself. Got on the altar. I was head altar boy for a year. Always had a slug of wine before the priest came into the sacristy. Another one, afterward. Right, Donald?"

Donald blushed, "Yeah . . . of course. Wouldn't you know? You catch on to everything. You're like *Superman*. You know what's going on before it happens. And you're not even sore."

"Why should I be?"

"God help me if I was Chuck Festing and *his* old man found out about *the call*—and us. Chuck wouldn't have an ass left."

22

Thaddeus laughed, "I took everything going. Benediction, funerals, Holy Days and during Lent, when other kids were amazed at how easily I gave up candy and sweets, I was knocking off at least two shots of wine every morning. Great days, then. You have to realize the joy was so wonderfully evil. There I was, a little, snotty kid, swilling down legal Sacramental wine during Prohibition. Some memories make life worthwhile.

"You can beat City Hall and I figure God didn't care one damned bit."

*   *   *

Donald never saw the nuns again; he finished grammar school in New York. Donald's high school years began in Malvern, Pennsylvania. After his freshman year, Donald's selections were made from a list of suggestions Thaddeus had prepared. He noticed early on that his choices somehow agreed with his uncle's.

Thaddeus was doing the one thing he felt he knew well—giving his ward the sort of education the older man had been forced to acquire on the job. Will Brady had left plenty of money and Thaddeus gently led Donald down an educational path that would certainly work for him if he decided to become a newspaperman. If he didn't—so much the better. He would have enjoyed a variety of experience and that, in the long run, was what produced the well-rounded man.

Donald sailed through two years at Malvern, switching to a New York public high school to test his uncle. Thaddeus voiced no opposition. "Do you good to get the feel of cement under your feet," was all he said.

Thaddeus was pleased when Donald's interest in sports settled into track and swimming. "Good training, Donald. You need fast legs to run on the beat; good arms to swing your way through a crowd. Of course that is...if it happens...if you become a newspaperman."

Then there was college, broken by two years in Europe where he spent six months each in France, Italy, Spain and Germany working on languages. He became a good linguist, but not until he followed Thaddeus' advice, who arrived in

Italy six months after Donald had gone abroad. He was horrified to find the youth could barely say *buon giorno*.

"Go to the movies, watch television, listen to the radio, get an Italian girl friend, memorize all the stanzas ,of the *National Anthem* or an equal number of pages of *Dante*. Memorize the first act of any play you want. You'll talk."

He took the older man's suggestion and when he started at the *Sun-Mirror* over a decade ago, Thaddeus Brady wasn't the only one who knew Donald Brady was going places.

Writing came easily and naturally to him. Thaddeus had finessed him into one stipulation as the price of his "independence." Donald was expected to write home a three page letter every week, wherever he was. As his facility grew, Donald found himself writing letters that ran four and five pages. At the *Pen and Pencil*, the midtown bar favored by newspapermen, Thaddeus just grinned when his friends asked how Donald was doing. "Just fine. Just fine. For a modern young man, that is."

*　　*　　*

Donald reached Madison Avenue and the Zenith Room about eleven-thirty. It was virtually empty, odd for Saint Patrick's Day. He nodded absently to the bartender who, fortunately, wasn't a regular, thus sparing Donald the usual Saint Patrick's Day chatter about Irish luck and the ever lovin' sunshine. Donald's mind hadn't stopped churning for days and he wondered when, if ever, all the confusion he was suffering would end.

He worried that the shot and beer chaser, seldom a part of his daily routine, would bring on another maudlin retrospect. In view of the day, why not? He ordered another and let his mind slip back to his first days on the paper when he'd gotten to know Ed Muir, a balding pro of twenty years in the city room, who had just been imported from Chicago to take over as managing editor.

Ed Muir had just turned forty. Returning to New York, where he'd come out of Hell's Kitchen, was like a long overdue birthday present. The chain had sent him to Chicago to sharpen his talents and New York was his reward

24

for growing talons that had spread his reputation as a first-rate newsman from coast to coast.

That was exactly ten years ago. Donald had been stringing for the paper about thirteen months while he wandered through Europe and North Africa. Now he was ready to settle in as a reporter. Muir, impressed with his European material as well as the young man's broad general knowledge, hired him as a first-string reporter over protestations of the business department which insisted that, skilled or not, newcomers started out as first year men. Muir reminded the nit picker that he'd been told to build the paper's pool of young reporters and to "ride them."

"You can't kick a kid around these days," he said quietly, "unless he's getting enough bread to make it worth his while. You understand?" That ended the discussion.

Without showing favoritism, Muir shuffled assignments so that Donald switched back and forth between City Council meetings and investigative assignments that often lasted three or four weeks. In both Donald showed a grasp of the essentials of newspapering—looking for the *who*, *where*, *when* and *why* in every story whether it was a two paragraph piece on page eight or a five part feature underscored by a banner on page one.

Five years after he started, Donald was one of the top four byliners on the *Sun-Mirror* news pages. The others were those marvels of the city room, men closer to sixty than fifty, who sensed the pulse of the news with such assurance that they could coax a headline out of a taxi ride to the right address; a lead on a big story from a pair of telephone calls.

They'd seen wonder boys like Donald come and go. They neither cultivated Donald nor ignored him. Their relationship was cool and professional. It was the same with Ed Muir.

Muir and Donald spent hours going over stories in and outside the office, but their relationship remained strictly professional. Muir was disinclined to see his men as intimates. He'd watched too many editors become innocent victims of the friendly, easy atmosphere of the city room, a style that probably worked years ago but had become a luxury in an era when a newspaper's survival depended on the quality and depth of reporting. The flashy journalist who came up with "exclusives" had gone out of style along with the turned-up hat and the nickel phone call. Now, a well-rounded, diligent reporter and news analyst like Donald Brady was the star of the city room.

There were other "Donalds" on Muir's staff and he was proud of how well they'd come along. Except on Sunday. Muir's job required him to spend the morning and early afternoon hours listening to the interview broadcasts which brought national leaders into the television limelight where they stood still for the probings of working newspapermen.

Muir had no quarrel with the grizzled veterans of the nation's dailies who sacrificed Sundays to dip into television's bucket of gold for an hour or so, but he shuddered when the revealing eye of the television camera turned on younger reporters whose inexperience could never be confused with nervousness. Without the guidance of a copy editor's pencil, their questions, laced with four syllable words in long sentences, they were far from the match of politicians whose circumlocution awed even experts like himself.

The exception was Donald Brady. He neither stammered, stuttered, scratched his nose nor wiggled his ears when the camera turned to pick out his handsome, clean-cut features. His looks were matched by sharp, incisive, well-prepared questions. Like his writing, Donald's command of oral English was crisp and lean. Only the soft smile on the man's sensual lips betrayed Brady's satisfaction when a well-aimed verbal assault caused the questionee to squirm.

Muir wasn't surprised when the grapevine told him that Frank Young, head of the News Department at the American Network, was courting Donald Brady, offering him a real Golden Boy deal. He could have the coverage of the whole New York State election scene for months as "an audition."

With the Governorship and a Senate seat at stake, turmoil in the inner circle of both parties and splinter candidates breaking away, it was the kind of assignment a young man of Brady's acumen realized came once in a lifetime. To sweeten the deal, Brady's contract ran for a year at double his newspaper salary for the first six months, and double that for the rest of the contract.

"Cheap at twice the price," Muir mumbled while he waited for Donald to submit his resignation. Although negotiations had been completed in early February, Donald waited until the first of March to give his notice.

* * *

When the day of confrontation with Ed Muir could no longer be delayed, the editor's friendly expression gave no hint that he knew what was coming.

He sat impassively as Donald blurted out his story—taking much too long to do it. He went the long way round to explain his decision, Donald knew it and wished that Muir would cut him off.

Ed wouldn't because he knew Donald needed that long way round to justify things to himself. When finally the young man had finished, Muir's expression hadn't changed.

"Your convenience or ours?"

"Yours, of course. I have almost three months free before I start."

"What are you working on now?"

"The gubernatorial candidates."

"How many are there?"

"Fourteen. Five Democrats, four Republicans, one Socialist, one Socialist-Labor and three Independents. I've finished thirteen."

"Who's left?"

"Just one crackpot who's doing fine at getting signatures. She wants to revive the Townsend Plan."

"Thirty dollars every Thursday? That won't buy *Hamburger Helper*."

"It's different now, Ed. It's a hundred and thirty dollars every Thursday."

"What's this dame's name?"

"Eleanor Roosevelt Streisand Fostini."

"You're kidding!"

"All except the Streisand part. She's an Italian spinster, about forty-eight or so, born on Eleanor Roosevelt's birthday. She added the Streisand to influence the Jewish ladies. She visits all the senior citizen communities, stuff like that. She's got money."

"How come she didn't add Mahalia Jackson to her name?"

"She didn't have to. The Chairperson of her Committee is Ethel Waters Mahalia Jackson."

"Born on Ethel Waters' birthday, no doubt?"

"Exactly. And she added Mahalia. You got it, Ed."

"A good story. When will it be finished."

"Mrs. Fostini is out in California digging into some of the old Dr. Townsend material. She promised me an interview Wednesday."

"OK. Square yourself with accounting and your two weeks notice will begin the day you turn in the story. We'll give you general assignments. They'll be posted. Good luck."

*   *   *

Donald shook his head, looked at the empty shot glass and the flat half glass of beer. That was it for now. Any more to drink and he'd be just another Irish slob crying in his suds. Erika was right about the paper. No one gave a damn about his leaving. The three old men slapped his back and wished him "all the best" and after turning in the series on the gubernatorial candidates, his crummy daily assignments had been posted and the job for today was to pick up the "color" of the Saint Patrick's Day parade.

Donald looked at the clock. Noon. The parade would be just getting underway at Forty-fourth Street and Fifth Avenue. He had plenty of time. There was seldom anything doing before one o'clock when the clergy began assembling on the steps of Saint Patrick's Cathedral; Cardinal Muldoon in the center, surrounded by the Auxiliary Bishops, Cathedral priests, prominent lay guests whom he honored by obliging them to hang on for five hours of marching and in the background there would be the *eminence grise* of Muldoon's staff, Monsignor Thomas Ryan, whose casual way of maneuvering Muldoon—in fact, the entire Cathedral power structure—was one of the wonders of present day New York history.

He slapped a pair of dollar bills on the bar and walked out into the cool air. Crowds were beginning to ascend from the subways and it saddened Donald to notice that most were older people—that block of Americans who suddenly had been grouped as "senior citizens"—a description he'd been taught to loathe by Thaddeus Brady. "Give me a panhandler any day who calls me 'Gramps' but don't lock me into 'senior citizenship.' It's disgusting."

Where were all the kids? Probably knocking off the apartments of the old people who'd ventured out to see the parade. The rest were in the parade, for in trying to make it appear long and full, the sponsors in recent years had been forced to go far afield to collect the essential items—baton twirlers, girls' bands, boys' bands, plain, ordinary marchers. So they bussed in parochial school children from as far away as Philadelphia. There weren't enough of them in New York. The Archdiocese had closed so many. And God bless the *Mummers' String Band* from Philadelphia. They'd been lured from Philly to strut up the Avenue for openers and when you had the Mummers, a parade was guaranteed success.

Donald was in that miserable position of a man who could only be distracted from his inner turmoil for a few seconds at a time. His attention span was about as intense as a cat's. He thought of Erika. Christ, she wasn't to blame for his anxieties. She'd never lost her temper or her sunny disposition during all the dark days that depressed him since the damned television thing began. To his friends Erika seemed a superficial bundle of sex and charm. Sometimes he thought so, too. It seemed to go with her profession—interpreter. They were like singers—gifted with a talent for switching from language to language. And like singers, talent was her *raison d'etre*. He seldom found her with a book in her hands, and all she read in the newspapers were his stories.

Erika was capable of translating that an atomic bomb had just exploded over the Brooklyn Bridge with the same coolness that she could announce that *codfish au gratin* was the specialty of the day at the United Nations' cafeteria. Donald found Erika to be an after-effects person. She reacted to things a day or so after the fact.

Donald considered Erika a very special person, vastly more attractive and interesting than most United Nations' girls he'd met, yet there often arose a nagging suspicion that, in one respect, Erika was no different than the others. They gave the impression of having created superficial personalities to camouflage their real characters. Any red-blooded American who loved motherhood, country and the flag expected this in the working girls of the Russian delegation but, curiously, they seemed the most natural and outgoing of the lot. It was a mystery.

Away from their king-sized bed and the intimacy forced on them by their tiny "garden apartment," Erika came through as a smooth, polished, sophisticated and extremely knowledgeable young woman. She understood the political workings of the United Nations and was way ahead of the press—and sometimes the American delegation—in predicting strategy being contemplated not only by officials within her own working range but of world leaders.

At first Donald never quite believed all she told him but when, time after time, her prophecies turned up in headlines, she delighted in taunting him. "Wouldn't that have made a delicious exclusive for you, *liebling*?" she asked, tugging at his belt to get his trousers off almost the second he stepped in the door.

Lately Donald didn't even know where he was, so it was a surprise to find himself at Forty-fifth and Fifth. Erika had been on his ass again. The goddamned trip!

To get his bearings Donald paused to look at a store window. It was one of those Fifth Avenue linen shops that had been on the street ever since he could remember—places advertising a variety of allegedly cut-rate merchandise that made suckers out of visitors to the Big Town. Everything featured in the window was a come-on. Once inside, yokels were lured into buying genuine "imitation" Moroccan rugs, "hand-embroidered" Irish linen and silverware that was far inferior to the utilitarian stuff one found at Woolworth's. He wondered why the Fifth Avenue Association tolerated the old rackets.

But the linen shops survived—chiseling their way from one "going out of business sale" to the next.

Donald shrugged his shoulders. Ralph Nader could do nothing for him. The goddamned trip! He'd been excited when Erika suggested that they spend her vacation traveling across the good old U.S.A. It was a helluva fine idea. What a thrill to show the lovely girl all the beauties of his country! Especially when Erika turned on all that charm and started taking off her clothes.

"What do I know of this country? This apartment? The U.N. Building?" she complained. "All the good restaurants in town, the Broadway theatres, and of course the sightseeing tours of New York I took at the beginning. It is a wonderful city and I love it. But there's more to America than this."

Donald excitedly told her how much more there was—never believing he would be lured into a diabolical scheme to drive across the land on super highways, spending nights in chain hotels, eating chain prepared food and gassing up at chain filling stations. He figured on flying to key points like Chicago, renting a car to visit the Great Lakes and slipping over to Canada. Then on to San Francisco and Los Angeles where they would follow the same easygoing arrangement.

This was how Donald had always traveled around America—visiting it and knowing it from the lobbies of the finest hotels in the country, in elegant restaurants and the most exclusive night clubs. He'd driven up a few mountain tops, the Hollywood Hills, for example, to smooch with a movie starlet. What other way was there to travel?

According to Erika, they would go by camper. "Dividing the driving, *mein liebling*. I am very good at the wheel. Every Austrian girl knows how to read maps. You know we love going on hiking trips, and I did a lot of mountain climbing when I was a girl. To the top of the *Jungfrau*. Well, not quite to the top—but high enough."

Donald shuddered. But he couldn't bring himself to disappoint Erika. She took it for granted that because they enjoyed everything they did in New York so completely that automatically Donald would share her enthusiasm for camping out, staggering up hills and, God forbid, looking for *edelweiss*—or maybe, four-leaf clovers. Donald remembered finding one in Van Cortlandt Park when he was eight and suffered sunstroke that kept him indoors for three days.

On the other hand, Erika had given him so much—more beautiful sex than he'd ever enjoyed in his life. Admiration that few men enjoyed. She might easily have turned him into a narcissist if there hadn't always been that wicked gleam in her eye telling him that it was all in fun. Erika had wit, humor and an extraordinary talent for getting her own way.

Erika was totally his—yet there had never been a commitment. It didn't seem necessary. They seldom talked about loving each other—as though it were a redundancy, needing no words when there were so many actions between them that demonstrated it. Their relationship was never marred by quarrels. Erika deftly avoided them.

Donald got away from the parade area by going back to Madison. He should have been hungry, but his nerves were jumping and he decided to wait. Suddenly he remembered that he was close to a place where he could sit down and think. It would only take a second, and he'd promised himself a thousand times to drop in and look at a lovely little oasis for prayer and meditation, packed tidily between the skyscrapers of midtown Manhattan. It had been recommended to him by a motley group of people, from shaky old newspapermen who'd missed their commuter trains because of loitering over an extra martini to suburban housewives whose feet weren't the equal of a day's shopping in the city.

It stood in the middle of Forty-third Street between Madison and Fifth, its only identification being a modest wooden sign reading: *The Chapel of Saint Christopher (Catholic)*—the *Catholic* evidently having been added to encourage the Old Guard dismayed by the publicity surrounding its opening more than a decade ago.

Then it was described as ecumenical. It was close to Grand Central Station, hence its name, an international welcome to all travelers in spite of the fact that Saint Christopher had been downgraded in the calendar of Saints. Rudely brushed aside in a Vatican housecleaning of Saints whose existence could not be authenticated by the Vatican. Tut! tut! to that! Donald's own casual Catholicism, shared by millions of others, knew that Saint Christopher was unlikely ever to go out of business and that America's own

Mothers Cabrini and Seton stood little chance of gaining the same affection.

As Donald reached the glass doors to the chapel, noting their simple elegance, they were opened for him by one of those tall, gaunt, thin-lipped Irishmen one sees so often during the day in New York's Catholic churches, quiet, laconic men representing the "silent majority" of New York's Irish Catholics who reject such Irish shenanigans as parades, wearing their Faith on their sleeves and who wouldn't be caught dead at a *Holy Name Communion Breakfast*.

The man nodded in response to Donald's "thank you" and as the newspaperman walked into a small but lovely building, he realized it was unlike any Catholic church he'd known in his long love affair with New York. Missing was the musty air of damp cement and the odor of incense. Saint Christopher's Chapel smelled fresh and clean; its interior was designed almost entirely of polished wood. By habit he learned to ignore the *Stations of the Cross* lining each side of the walls of most churches—those hideous plaster of paris relief panels depicting Christ's journey from His Condemnation to Death to His Crucifixion and Entombment in the Holy Sepulcher. Usually they were painted in ghastly colors, unstinting in their use of painted blood and were not for the faint of heart.

Those in Saint Christopher's, however, were different— unframed woodcuts so simple that the fourteen stations became a feast for the eye. He smiled at the pulpit, raised only a few feet off the floor so that the priest was on a level with his congregation. Attached to it was a banner with the cross, painted on in unconnected sections and the word, *Peace*. One would like to imagine that it had come directly to the chapel as the offering of some hippie artist in the Village.

Donald recalled wondering how a Catholic church managed to be ecumenical. Quite simply, he discovered. The visitor to Saint Christopher's had two sections to choose from—pews which stood before a non-denominational altar, and a second altar to the side to which the visitor was guided by a discreet electric sign announcing the *Altar of the Blessed Sacrament*. In this part of the chapel there hung the eternal red light signifying the Divine Presence.

Like many of her readers, Donald read Ada Louise Huxtable's articles on architecture in the *New York Times* simply to enjoy her impeccable prose, not because of her knowledge of architecture. At Saint Christopher's Miss Huxtable would have been helpful. In her absence, Donald decided that the enchanting chapel was "psychedelic." It certainly described the hippie poster and possibly might apply to the *Stations of the Cross* as well.

He slid into a pew, remembering how Uncle Thaddeus described his quiet visits to church at odd hours of the day and early evening. "I just sit there and turn everything over to Whomever happens to be in charge. I believe it is God. It's wonderful, especially when life beats down on you, and there's no rational way to figure things out.

"'Giving yourself up' is how I describe it. I don't pray. I doubt that I could anymore. At least not in a formal way. I simply ask for help and guidance and I try to shut out the rest of the world. I sit five minutes, ten minutes, maybe longer. But I have to confess that when I leave I feel better. I know that I'm not perfect and I can't possibly live up to my own expectations, much less those people impose on me. I try to leave my problems behind and nine times out of ten it works."

Donald walked to the front of the church, attracted by the poster. He sat down, looked around him and liked what he found.

Saint Christopher's—its warmth, the feeling of security that came over him. The delicious silence, enhanced by the thought of all the noise rattling just a hundred feet away on the street.

Suddenly Donald felt impelled to stand and move toward the altar on the side, drawn to the red candle light flickering before the Blessed Sacrament. Donald genuflected awkwardly and sat in the first pew. He crossed himself and kneeling on the bench that stretched across the pew, he found himself remembering the first words of the Mass as he'd recited them many years ago as an altar boy.

Introibo ad altare Dei. I will go to the altar of God.

And then the response of the altar boy.

Ad Deum qui laetificat juventutem meam. To God, who giveth joy to my youth.

Donald guessed he was praying.

So Donald sat—five minutes, ten minutes, a quarter of an hour. His mind gradually began to clear. The worries he'd been fretting over seemed suddenly unimportant. He knew they'd work out even if he hadn't the faintest idea how. That they weren't bothering him was important—and a surprise.

Then Donald decided he was hungry. He stood up, nodded a "thank you" to the altar, smiled again at the *Peace* poster and tucked five dollars into the poor box on his way back to the noisy city. His stride was brisker as he walked back uptown to the Zenith where he intended to have lunch.

* * *

The luncheon action was just average at Zenith, but, being alone, he was shunted off to a side table set for two. It suited him fine. He ordered an omelette, coffee and toast. He'd picked up the papers on his way and might have remained hidden behind them but he was distracted by the arrival of a party being guided toward a large round table in the rear, usually reserved for businessmen.

Donald glanced across the room and absently brought his fork back to the plate. The gentlemen at the round table were anything but ordinary businessmen. Donald couldn't believe his eyes. It was a crazy group to be assembling at the Zenith just as the Saint Patrick's Day parade was getting underway. Donald was familiar with every one of them, on cordial speaking terms with two.

First, there was Monsignor Thomas Ryan, nattily dressed in slacks, a tailored sports jacket and an open shirt. This certainly wasn't a normal outfit for an important prelate who, by all the rules, should be wearing his cassock and standing behind the Cardinal's chair on the steps of the Cathedral.

At his right sat Archbishop Luigi Poli, the Apostolic Delegate to the United States. To Ryan's left sat Pietro Gentille, managing director of the American Division of the Mediterranean Airlines, a dapper, handsome man of thirty-seven, who had only recently returned from Italy to assume the top post with the company after having served for several years as the Eastern Division Manager.

35

Max Schwartz of the law firm of Sweeney, Sweeney, Sweeney and Schwartz was the fourth important person in the group and the fifth chair was set up for Giuseppe Bianco, Jr. who, like his father, had Anglicized his name to Joe White. They were Cathedral fixtures. For years, Joe, Sr. had been the personal driver of Cardinal Hellman and stayed on when Cardinal Muldoon became New York's Archbishop.

When his father retired a year or so ago, young Joe, personable and attractive, born into the traditions of the *powerhouse*, was the obvious choice to take over. As a confidant of Cardinal Muldoon, Joe ranked close behind Monsignor Ryan. Actually Joe didn't occupy the seat; it was simply there for him to operate from. He arrived with the others, ordered a cup of coffee, cooled it with water, drank half a cup and evidently, on Ryan's instructions, dashed out and down the street to check on proceedings on the steps of the Cathedral.

The men talked volubly and Donald would have given a year's salary if a bugging device had suddenly descended from the gaudy chandelier in the center of the Zenith Room to establish communication between his table and theirs. He seemed so near and yet so far. There were snatches of conversation that he understood, but invariably, when the men got down to the business at hand, they lowered their voices.

There had to be an extraordinary reason to bring them all together. Normally they would use the Cardinal's mansion for any one of the thousands of reasons they had for consulting. What astonished Donald most was Ryan. The good-looking Monsignor simply wasn't where he was supposed to be—that wasn't the Cathedral way.

Donald had to admit the priest had become handsomer as he grew older. Donald figured Ryan was thirty-eight or thirty-nine now. They'd become friends over the years, close enough to call each other by their first names long before they were thrust together professionally when Donald had to hit the powerhouse for a story. As a young priest, Ryan was much in demand as a lecturer and Donald was one of many students who followed him from campus to campus where he held seminars on a wide range of subjects, not always Church-connected.

Pietro Gentille was head of Mediterranean Air Lines—and much more. At social functions he rated far higher than representatives of Italian business, the Italian Trade Council or even the Consul General. He deferred to the last in seating arrangements at dinners and other events when protocol was followed. But Gentille was known as the man to reach if one wanted to make a favorable deal with any Italian organization, either private enterprise, government or the Church.

He was a tall, slim, handsome Northern Italian with blue eyes who'd been considered quite a catch when he arrived to head the New York office in the mid-sixties, a comparatively young man, barely thirty. His roving eye involved him with numerous American women and his name appeared frequently in the gossip columns. He squired young beauties, their mothers, divorcees, widows and blue-haired grande dames with equal aplomb. He was linked with a famous singer at the Metropolitan Opera where he was a boxholder. That coupling ended when the diva's husband-manager announced she was suffering from fatigue and canceled all her American engagements.

Gentille surprised—and dismayed—the names in his little black book when he was summoned back to Italy to survey the company's worldwide operations prior to taking over complete charge of the Air Lines' American operation.

On his return, photographers also greeted the lovely Contessa Lucia Rossi who had become Gentille's bride. They'd been married a month earlier at the *Duomo* in Milan by Daniele Cardinal Rossi, the Contessa's older brother.

For the bride and groom, as well as Cardinal Rossi, the ceremony served as a publicity bonanza. It was covered by Italy's weekly pictorials, France's *Dimanche* and England's racy *News of the World*. The marriage of nobility with a successful businessman couldn't miss as a human interest story. The pair's attractiveness helped considerably. It made a beautiful television sequence.

Cardinal Rossi, a handsome man with a strong, leonine face, had only recently been named to the Archdiocese of Milan which in terms of political stature could be compared to New York State. As a New York Governor automatically slid into the running as a presidential candidate, the

Archbishop of Milan knew that his post offered him a pulpit from which he could expect to garner national and, in the case of his sister's wedding, international publicity. It made him *papabili*, a possible candidate for the Chair of Saint Peter.

Rossi's reputation as a moderate, able to see both sides of the business scene, labor and management, had won him points in the industrial north where there existed vast differences between Italian businessmen and the Vatican. They felt that some of the encyclicals coming out of the Vatican urging the relaxation of tensions between the West and Iron Curtain countries while theologically progressive, could have contained a few references to improving business relations. Executives of Milan and Turin, Italy's business capitals, enjoyed good relations with Yugoslavia, Moscow, Poland and even Czechoslovakia. A kudo from the Pope was always welcome.

Labor unions looked for integration of the migratory Iron Workers into the benefits labor had gained in the Common Market, making it possible for them to move from country to country, job to job, without losing their benefits. Friction between the Vatican and the Iron Curtain threatened their profitable coexistence. A practical Pope like Cardinal Rossi was seen as advantageous to Italy's shaky economy.

Rossi, at fifty-nine, was a shade underage for the Papacy, but there was a widespread belief, perhaps better expressed as hope, that some of the old traditions governing the choice of Supreme Pontiff would begin to fade away with the dawn of a new century. The possibility that the next Pope might be younger than sixty-five was not as remote as it had once been.

Max Schwartz had long been one of New York's most colorful characters. Max was probably seventy, but one would never guess it by the slim, natty figure the brilliant lawyer presented as he slithered through New York's cafe society, political and church circles with grace and charm. Famed as an after-dinner speaker, he identified himself as the surviving partner in the firm of Sweeney, Sweeney, Sweeney and Schwartz. "I was their token Jew," he used to quip and the gag got a huge laugh. The Sweeneys had long since died, but Schwartz kept the firm's name.

Generations ago the Sweeney Brothers had gotten in on the ground floor representing the growing New York Archdiocese and when they needed a real estate expert they sought out the best, Max Schwartz. It took months of negotiating for the night school lawyers to lure the eminent counselor into their firm, but once he was there, he served the firm and the Church with faithfulness that moved Cardinal Hellman to introduce him as his "indispensable Jewish Bishop." Now Schwartz was working closely with Muldoon in maneuvering diocesan properties around to produce sorely needed cash.

Donald watched and wondered. He could see that Tom Ryan was the dominating figure in the group. Whatever was going on, Ryan was in charge. Donald smiled. Ryan had always been in charge.

Ryan had barely been ordained before he was rushed into service as a guest lecturer at Catholic high schools and colleges along the East Coast. Donald was impressed with the young priest's talent for blending blind faith, witty cynicism and abiding optimism in a topic as complex as Church history. Catholic students seldom were exposed to a speaker who could cover whatever point he'd chosen, work around it, inspect it from every angle, positive and negative, and offer a conclusion which he frankly labeled as his own.

Father Ryan had no patience with post-lecture gab sessions, explaining that he'd had his fill of those debates in his days as a seminarian. Pointing to his reversed collar, Ryan would smile, "Now that I've got my credentials as an authority, I can afford to be myself. You ladies and gentlemen are privileged to argue with one another and with me *in absentia*. I not only need my sleep, but there are seminarians all over this diocese I've got to make peace with for all the nasty things I said during those long-winded encounters. Take my advice—argue in muted voices. You'll never regret it."

Donald, curious about Ryan, especially when he was snapped up by the Cathedral talent scouts, discovered that he was the nephew of the Bishop of Buffalo. For a time this devastated Donald because he was all too familiar with Irish Catholic families who made a hobby of raising young boys as candidates for the priesthood and young girls for the dedicated life of nuns.

Thaddeus Brady set Donald straight about Tom Ryan. "Bishop Billy Ryan! The most anti-prelate sonofabitch that ever got accepted by a seminary. Came out of Hell's Kitchen, same as your father and me. He was your father's age. It was the time when Irish kids became cops, priests, boxers or went into politics. Billy Ryan weighed them all and decided to try the priesthood. He told me he went over the wall a dozen times the first year, but got back before he was caught. I guess Billy became a priest in spite of himself. It took him years to become a good one and he only got his Bishop's ring because there was a vacancy in Buffalo and some smart guy figured that was the place to tame Billy down. He's done a great job and could have had Muldoon's spot, but he told the Vatican he'd quit first.

"Billy disowned Tom Ryan and only attended Tom's first Mass in Buffalo where his family had moved because Tom's father, Sean Ryan, got down on his knees and begged him to. He attended, dressed in a suit and dark glasses, and sat in the rear. What sold him on young Tom was his Latin. 'Haven't heard Latin like that from an Irish priest,' old Billy Ryan muttered, 'since I first began serving Mass.' When Tom was appointed to the staff of Saint Patrick's, friends congratulated Bishop Billy who guffawed, 'Congratulate the boys at the *powerhouse*. They need him—desperately.'"

It was true. The late Patrick Cardinal Hellman had been such an authoritarian that the New York diocese had been left not only without a leader, but without priests capable of taking full charge of their departments. They'd been intimidated too long. Muldoon was hesitant about everything. He hadn't sought the promotion, loathed it the first year, expecting things to run themselves. When they didn't, he took over and gradually gained respect as an administrator.

Father Ryan, quickly promoted to the rank of Monsignor, arrived at a time when administration was going well and Muldoon needed a theological as well as a political adviser. It was an election year; the subject of abortion had become an issue in the presidential race and Muldoon was frothing at the mouth, ready to lead marches and hit the pulpit daily, hourly on the hour. On the half-hour he was prepared to rant against artificial birth control.

Ryan led the Cardinal along a more dignified course in which a number of powerful letters emanated from the Cathedral to be read at Mass throughout the diocese and which were widely covered in the press. The views were presented as those of the Archdiocese rather than attitudes exclusively Cardinal Muldoon's.

Ryan cajoled Muldoon, saying, "Gordon Graham, the Democratic candidate, is in the same position you are, Your Eminence. His private and religious instincts are against abortion, ambivalent perhaps about birth control, but let's not make it any tougher on him than it is. He can't cope with the power of a New York Cardinal, whoever he is. And this diocese can't endure another Republican in the White House."

Ryan's statements blew the minds of Muldoon's old buddies who still believed New York City was the province of Irish Catholic Democrats like Al Smith, Jim Farley, Jimmy Walker and it didn't matter much who was keeping store at the White House. They'd been sympathetic to Nixon, devoted to Eisenhower, cherished Herbert Hoover and the memories of Calvin Coolidge and Theodore Roosevelt.

John Kennedy's was a name seldom mentioned inside the *powerhouse*. "A Boston Brahman! That's what he thought he was," complained Monsignor Edward Vaughan, in charge of Cathedral public relations for many years. "Did less for the Church and Catholic education than any President of modern times. The cock-of-the-walk was so preoccupied with his Protestant-lover image that he refused to see the Papal Nuncio except in a private meeting. Imagine it! The representative of the Holy Father himself sneaking in the back door of the White House like a thief in the night! Not even invited to a spot of brandy. Having tea shoved at him by Jackie who talked about interior decorating after Jack paid his respects and went back to the Oval Office. Shameful!"

Ryan grew fond of Muldoon and tried to shield him from

41

the unpleasant duties of his office, at least to the extent that he could. During the presidential campaign whenever newspaper accounts reported how candidate Graham was pushed against the wall by tough women groups involved in the quarrel over abortion and birth control, Muldoon expressed his sympathy. He appeared relieved that he hadn't conducted the violent campaign he intended.

William Muldoon's faith was profound and real. "We will find the right way to meet this dilemma. When? I don't know. The poor think I am unfeeling. The rich don't care. Poor Graham! I wonder if he's aware that we pulled away from the issue."

Tom ignored the questions. Of course Gordon Graham was aware and that was why Donald Brady's last long conversation with Monsignor Thomas Ryan had taken place aboard a Metroliner returning to Washington where Donald had been covering the New York Congressional delegation and their battle for loan guarantees to New York City.

"You couldn't see the Congressmen or Senators for the blasted lobbyists," Donald told Ryan.

"So I gathered."

"I suppose you got your information straight from President Graham."

Ryan laughed. He'd always been open with Donald Brady, figuring that their friendship transcended their positions and it wasn't necessary for him to state "off the record" every time he opened his mouth.

"No, we didn't talk about that. The President offered me a job though."

"I can understand that."

"In the State Department or on his staff. It was quite an honor, but I turned it down."

"Any special reason?"

"Common sense. I wouldn't want to be compared with that priest fellow who became a Nixon apologist, living on a fat cat's salary and whooping it up at the Watergate in a posh apartment when the rule of his order was so rigid about its poverty vows."

"That wouldn't affect you, would it?" Donald asked.

"No, I guess not. A pastoral priest isn't supposed to get

rich. Yet we're paid salaries, enough to get by on. I suppose, in another atmosphere, I might take the job or, like some priests, run for office. That's more honest."

"Trading on your Roman collar?"

"I suppose in a Roman Catholic district you'd call it 'trading,' but how about Louisville, Kentucky?"

"Touché," Donald answered after a second's reflection.

"Anyhow, I've got my work cut out for me for the next couple of years," Ryan said seriously.

Donald wondered if he should ask about it. He figured that since Ryan had volunteered it, he might want to talk. At worst, the priest could cut him off. They knew each other well enough for that.

"May I ask what it is?"

Ryan smiled. "You may, Donald. Not everyone can, though. It's about rumors of the Pope's resignation. Where there's smoke, there's fire. I think Morelli means it although I shouldn't be surprised if *he's* the source of a lot of the speculation. Like any Pope, he would prefer a successor who will carry out the work he's started."

"Why are you so convinced that Morelli will quit?"

"He's human and he's got a phobia about senility. Like any intelligent man who's been in the Church virtually all his life, he's seen the harm incompetence brought on by old age can do. I think this Pope wants to avoid that for himself and to set a precedent."

"How does that affect you?"

"Not me personally. But the American Church. You know we're not overloaded with pious gentlemen or great minds in the American group of Red Hats."

Donald laughed.

"Have you been hearing their confessions?"

Ryan smarted at the remark. "No, and I'm not trying to read their consciences either. They may be deeply spiritual men in their hearts and perhaps I've been guilty of using the wrong word. So let's substitute theologians for pious gentlemen."

"Agreed."

"Anyhow, the American Church has to take a more incisive role in the next Conclave whether Morelli resigns or ends his reign in the traditional manner of death. We cannot forever acquiecsce in the nominees of the Curia and the Italian Cardinals. Not that their choices have ever been inimical to our interests. They haven't. And that's because we bring American politics with us into the Conclave. It's a mistake. But every Cardinal's luggage carries a file of national priorities. So they please us by offering us candidates who won't offend either American Catholics or Americans period. It's too narrow a choice and someone's got to do something about it."

"Someone's got to wake up the American Cardinals, in other words," Donald volunteered.

"That's about the size of it. American Cardinals really don't qualify as Popes—even if one were acceptable. At this moment none is. But a Pope from one of the super-powers would be disastrous, particularly now. But that doesn't preclude our having a candidate, someone whom we believe is worthy of being considered as Pope. That's the man I'm looking for. He doesn't have to be elected.

"He simply has to stand as a choice of the Americans— someone who can invite the Cardinals of the rest of the world to think in universal terms. Not as Rome does—where the Church is bait for tourists, a money-maker for the country, a good place to work and, for the big fish, a power base to battle every theological innovation that threatens their authority whether it originates with the Holy Father himself or the Bishop of Brooklyn whose diocese has become the equivalent of Nevada as a Catholic annulment capital."

Donald smiled, "That makes sense. Why should an annulment cost six hundred and fifty dollars in Brooklyn and be granted in a few months while Catholics elsewhere have to wait years?"

"Exactly. If partners in a marriage that can be legitimately annulled fear they're going to have to wait ten years, what's the use of staying in the Church? None. Yet our American prelates stand up in pulpits shedding tears over their diminishing parishes. It's got to stop, and we can't say that fault is entirely Rome's. We've been the fat cats of the Church for too long. We wanted nothing to do with Vatican II. It threatened the status quo. Our schools were doing fine;

44

the faithful were under control; the kids a bit restive, but weren't they always?

"Then there was that undercurrent of dissatisfaction that exploded in all sections of society. The sexual revolution, the demands for equal rights for women, Gay Lib, and who was so arrogant as to assume that the American Catholic Church would escape it? The Cardinals, of course, and half the Bishops, I guess. But not the young parish priests or even the wise old pastors. They'd seen it coming, but what could they do? Simply mumble over the pastoral letters from the men in the Cardinal's Mansions which they were obliged to read at all Masses—letters complaining about the decline in morals, the indifference of the Catholic layman, bemoaning their loss of faith and urging them to return to the Sacraments. It wasn't enough.

"Paul saw this. He liberalized the marriage of Catholics and non-Catholics. He revised the liturgy of the Church." Here Ryan paused. "That was poorly considered in respect to the United States."

"You can't get an argument there. Wasn't there some talk that the Latin Mass might be retained in some measure— once a month, special occasions ... I forget?"

"Yes," Ryan answered, "there was and, in effect, the rule is still there. The Latin Mass may be said on Feast Days important to some parishes, the anniversary of a church's Consecration; there are numerous options. Pastors seldom avail themselves of the opportunity. They say there aren't altar boys with sufficient knowledge of Latin."

"When were there?" Donald asked.

"Not in my memory," Tom Ryan laughed.

The train had drawn into Newark leaving little time for Donald to get at the meat of Ryan's project. "In other words," he said, "you've appointed yourself the impossible task of getting eight elderly, individualistic, impatient, disillusioned American Cardinals to agree on a Papal candidate in an election you have no idea will happen this year, next year or five years from now?"

"That's the size of it," Ryan smiled.

Donald noticed the smile was worried.

"How do you hope to manage it?"

"Not easily but with less trouble than it might have been ten years ago. Today the Cardinals are concerned by the extraordinary growth of this so-called 'Italian-style Communism.' It's like a brush fire, spreading fast and in every direction. It has seduced priests and bishops as well as politicians. Unfortunately, we have only ourselves to blame. Both America and the Church have thrown so much weight supporting the Christian-Democrats that Italy has been a one-party country from its first post-war election. The results have been predictable. It grew fat, overconfident and corrupt.

"They've not been exactly responsible. How could they be? Not with the largesse they enjoyed under the Marshall Plan. Not with all the help Italy enjoyed in the years when it was called the forty-ninth state. Not when the Church rigged the elections in its favor. Not when Pius XII excommunicated the Italian Faithful who voted Communist. Ridiculous!

"Whew," Ryan said, "I'm talking an awful lot."

"Guess you need to," Donald said. "It's a tall order—pushing the American Cardinals against the Italians. They've been pals a good many years. It's big stuff. You might get defrocked before you pull it off."

Tom Ryan laughed. "Oh, how aware I am of that! Fortunately, Muldoon is with me."

"Muldoon is with you?"

"You're surprised?" Ryan said, and a soft smile crossed his lips.

"Amazed," Donald answered. "Absolutely amazed."

"I suppose a lot of people would be if they knew. But they underestimate 'Granite Face.' Granted Muldoon is no intellectual. You must be aware that he was made a Cardinal over his firm protests. He meant it. But New York requires a Cardinal. And Muldoon was the man who took over when Patrick Hellman died.

"Muldoon was the only prelate close enough to know what Hellman was doing. I read the Pope's personal letter to Muldoon. He can be proud of it. Few people have seen it. The Holy Father appreciated Muldoon's modesty, his desire for a less conspicuous role in the Church and his longing to become a simple pastor again, but he was needed. After meditating at length, Morelli found no way to accommodate

46

Muldoon's private hopes. He did promise that at the proper time he might be relieved of his heavy responsibilities. In a postscript, using the personal pronoun *I*—not the Papal *We*—Morelli said, 'I know you for many years when we were both young men in the Vatican Curia. We foresaw the huge problems then. Now as older men you and I must work together and solve them. Faithfully, Morelli.'"

"Funny, how even the press gets misconceptions. How have we missed that one?"

"Because you only looked for Muldoon's flaws—and unfortunately they stand out like the warts on Cardinal O'Toole's nose."

"They love O'Toole in Boston," Donald said.

"Anyhow, Muldoon's a pastor. He makes the rounds. You know that. There's a lot of O'Toole in him. They are closer to the wrong people than the power wielders in their dioceses would like. They pay too much attention to the other side of the tracks. I have to pull Muldoon away from some picnic with school kids to get him to at least perform a side altar marriage of a prominent non-Catholic with a divorcee. It's not easy. That part. But when I broached the idea of finding our own candiate for the next Pope, 'Granite Face' took it under advisement. Two days later he called me into his office and said, 'OK, get at it.'"

"Get at what?"

"Being a Pope-maker, *the Grand Elector*. But don't tell anyone I authorized it. I promise only one thing—I'll save you from excommunication."

"Did he give any grounds?"

Ryan laughed, "Yes, I asked him how. Poor Muldoon! He thought a long while and his expression became serious. 'Because you're doing a work that should be mine. In more than six decades of living I have come to one delicious conclusion. God has a sense of humor. He names one man a Cardinal and chooses a quiet Monsignor to do His Will. I believe this intention has come to you as a manifestation of God's Will and it is my duty to support and, I suppose, protect you...'"

Then he paused, "But not until they light the fire around the stake."

They were at Pennsylvania Station and the meeting,

Donald felt later, had shaken him up. Being a revisionist did not come easily in the cynical world of newspapering. Bishop William Muldoon assumed the high position of Archbishop of the Diocese of New York under the aura of invincibility left behind by a predecessor who reigned long and wisely in temporal matters, but had left his parishioners spiritually impoverished.

William Muldoon, burdened by learning the complexities of his job, had been at it for nearly five years. In all that time he'd revealed only the superficial side of his personality, the granite-like qualities of faithfulness to his Church and the inevitable comparison to Hellman that had earned him his nickname.

The press cynically believed his parish visits were calculated image-making. His fondness for children was ridiculed. It was used by every important man of power wherever he stood in the pecking order. Muldoon hardly rated as an original.

Although they'd seen each other frequently since that warm conversation on the train from Washington, Ryan and Donald had not talked at length. Finding Ryan huddled with the Cardinal's men brought back thoughts he believed had been eradicated during his little visit to the Chapel of Saint Christopher.

There they were—those nagging doubts about television. Why the hell was he doing it? He really didn't want to. He tried shaking off the thoughts.

That didn't answer the question he really wanted to know—what Ryan was up to, deep in conversation with the Papal Nuncio, Pietro Gentille, an Italian wheeler-dealer, Max Schwartz and the Cardinal's driver on Saint Patrick's Day when there was absolutely no legitimate excuse for them not to be where they should—standing on the steps of the Cathedral showing themselves to the crowd, greeting politicians who dashed from the line of march to kiss the Cardinal's ring and to applaud and acknowledge the dipping of the colors of every high school from Teaneck, New Jersey, to Albany, New York, to hail the Sons of Erin and pay special private attention to the lovely lean legs of the Puerto

Rican and black girls who were, without question, the neatest baton twirlers on the avenue.

The break came when Joe made one of his appearances. He huddled with the four, drank cold coffee, and got up to leave. Joe's was not one of those high Irish voices so familiar at the Cathedral, but one that had been exposed to the warm sun of Naples for hundreds of years.

"God bless him! God bless him!" Donald said over and over again, turning aside, the first attempt he'd made to conceal his presence from Tom Ryan. Donald had stumbled into a story.

Joe stood up and began confirming the last minute arrangements. Obviously it was going to be his final appearance of the day at the Zenith Room. Hence, he summed it all up for Monsignor Ryan. The Musak had blessedly stopped.

"Then it's set. His Eminence and I hit the Newark Airport at six, the charter flight entrance. Monsignor Ryan's coming by cab. Cardinal Novik and Cardinal De Cordoba are already in town and they'll make their own arrangements to get to Newark. As soon as the plane takes off, I telephone overseas and advise Cardinal O'Toole in Dublin."

Joe's voice wasn't loud. But like an Italian singer's, it carried. Monsignor Thomas Ryan had a lot to learn if he intended to crown a Pope!

Donald hastily paid his check and slid out to Madison Avenue across the street to the old Donahue Building where there was a bank of public telephones.

Donald dialed the *Sun-Mirror* and asked for Lily Stein, Ed Muir's secretary.

"Mr. Muir's office," she answered, with the authoritative tone that reflected Lily Stein's extraordinary efficiency. Ed Muir was Lily's second-and-a-half managing editor and, although he'd suffered early doubts about having a secretary ten years his senior, Muir recognized that all that kept Lily from being a newspaperwoman was Lily herself. She preferred executive work. And smoothing troubled waters as she would do when she recognized Donald's voice.

"I'm calling in sick today, Lily. I think I'm due it."

49

"Of course, baby. We figured on something like that. One of the kids is covering the parade."

He started to say something arrogant like, "Why the hell wasn't I notified?"—but why light a fire under Lily? She held too many of his chits.

"And listen, Donald. If it means anything, Ed's sick, too. Not physically. You tied a knot in his stomach and it's still there. You gotta understand. He didn't know how to behave. He's a newspaperman. He doesn't know anything else. He's getting you severance pay. The brass is balking but Ed gets his way."

For a second Donald was tongue-tied. "Thank him for me, Lily. I'll be seeing you."

"Have a nice trip, honey. We miss you."

Christ, that trip! Donald shuddered at the thought. But there wasn't time for more than one solid shudder. He began the elaborate signaling system to get Thaddeus Brady to the phone. It involved ringing once, hanging up, ringing once again. Thaddeus answered the third ring. He'd barely finished the second ring of the code when Thaddeus answered, "Yes, Donald, what is it?"

"*Hurricane type.* I need you."

"Where?"

"Your place. Stay put. I'll be there in ten minutes."

"I'll be here, Donald." The old man hung up. No use wasting words now. They would come soon enough.

Hurricane was an old signal used by Thaddeus and Donald when the younger Brady needed trustworthy outside help. It was newspaper jargon for seventy-two point type—used for big events like hurricanes, wars, the deaths of presidents, great men and women of modern history—bigger than life men . . . like . . . like the Pope.

* * *

Donald hadn't seen Thaddeus Brady's "non-observance" of Saint Patrick's Day in many years. It was quite a ritual. Thaddeus held Patrick in great respect as a Bishop and an educator, a major figure in Church history. He felt that

Patrick deserved more dignified commemoration than was his lot in the United States.

"In the old country, it is a Holy Day," Thaddeus explained to Donald when he was young, "and people attend Mass as they should here." Thaddeus quickly realized he'd gone out on a limb. "Of course, that would apply to those who attend Mass as a matter of devotion." It was an ambiguous sentence. Thaddeus knew it. Hopefully, Donald didn't.

As an alternative, he had created his own elaborate ritual. He drank neither beer nor whiskey but turned instead to Dubonnet which Donald noticed was being chilled in a silver bucket by the side of Thaddeus' working area, close to the large picture windows which offered him a beautiful view of the park and the luxurious mansions along Fifth Avenue and the Plaza to the south.

"Have a drink?" Thaddeus said. "You look as though you've swallowed that tireless canary. Must be a mighty good story."

"I don't know that it *is* a story," Donald said, pouring himself a glass of the French wine. "That's why I'm here."

"Fine. Sit down and tell it to me."

Thaddeus listened attentively as Donald recited the events of the morning, what he'd seen and the very little he had learned at the luncheon gathering. When he finished Donald asked the obvious, "What do you make of it, Thad?"

"Only this. Our priests in scarlet are waking up—but it seems to me they're a little bit late."

"Late? How come they're late?"

"Late in catching up with the Pope. He's eager to resign. He's worried about getting too old for the job and behaving like a senile old fool. If I were Pope, the President of the United States or Chairman of a Neighborhood Committee to Roust Cockroaches, I'd feel the same way. He's smart. He's been leaking rumors, collecting information here and there. He's not going to turn his job over to the first Cardinal that walks in the door—or the first group of Cardinals. Our boys are already way at the end of the line if they're going over in a body to ask the Pope his intentions. Everybody's been there except the Archbishop of Lyons and that's only

51

because his mistress won't let him."

"Come off it, Thad, you're pulling my leg. I'll buy the fact that they're shipping to Rome tonight on a charter to ask the Pope about his resignation, but they've been at this project for months."

"Hey, there, how about that? I didn't know it."

"Well, I did," Donald snapped.

"Don't get churlish. I collect a lot of information. Not everything. I do know that for the past eighteen months Cardinals, Bishops and special representatives have been scurrying around the world trying to organize alignments that would give the Curia and the Italians something to worry about. They no longer hold a majority in the College of Cardinals. They can neither dictate their own choice nor block the selection of another combination of votes. I'm pleased to hear that the Americans have been moving. That means they must be going to Rome with something up their sleeves. What is it?"

Donald volunteered, "Not a something—a someone, Thad."

"Good. That's it. They've got a candidate."

Donald's voice trembled, "But I haven't the faintest idea who it could be."

Thaddeus poured his own glass of wine. "That's the rub. This is a pretty good story. But no one's going to ladle it out to you. With Ryan in civvies, you can expect the Cardinals to be wearing suits, too. Nothing disguises a clergyman better than a sports jacket. So off they go to Rome and, so far, you're the only newspaperman with the story. Not bad. Are you going to the airport?"

"Of course."

"And then?"

"I wish I knew. I'm supposed to start that trip tomorrow with Erika. I don't want to."

"Try telling her that."

Light suddenly dawned. Donald's voice brightened. "Of course. That's it. I'll tell her . . . I'll tell her right away . . . as soon as I get to Rome."

Thad smiled. "You're going to chase this to Rome. Good. Very good." He looked at his watch. "That means by three

52

o'clock tomorrow you'll be back on the *Sun-Mirror* and I won't have to listen to Ed Muir anymore."

"Ed Muir? You mean he's been talking to you."

Thaddeus was serious. "Don't ever tell him this. You don't shame a man. He gave you terrific freedom, great leeway to do your thing. No one else was ever allowed to work your style. Now he's got no one. So what else would he do? Ask old Thaddeus if he had any influence. What could I tell him? Not the truth—that I wouldn't influence you even if I could. So I lied. I said I'd try."

Donald was speechless. "I guess," he finally said, "I'm supposed to wonder why he didn't talk to me."

Thaddeus snorted. "You know what kids newspapermen are. Did Jesus talk to Judas after he betrayed him? Did Washington lunch with Benedict Arnold? In Muir's mind you're worse—you haven't betrayed him. You've actually joined the enemy."

"It's that bad?"

"Of course. You should have expected it. But you've got the solution in your hands, assuming you're still doubtful about this television career of yours."

"What's that?"

"Call in a fairly decent story from Rome—if you go—and you'll probably get a raise and a bonus."

"That's not why I'd be doing it."

Thaddeus guffawed. "Of course not. Not for filthy lucre or the old byline. But because you're a newspaperman and a story *is* a story—no matter what. Suppose you get your balls shot off? How would that strike you?"

"A disaster of unbelievable proportions."

"You're damned right. So be careful. They're not playing penny ante in this Papal sweepstakes. Something's going on that's not especially religious. I can't put my finger on it. I think you'd be doing the American delegation of Cardinals a favor if you shipped aboard.

"Remember, the Europeans have been at it for centuries. They know undetectable poisons that go back to the *Borgias*, potions that even *Isolde* would fall for, and she's certainly a gal who ought to know better. I wouldn't want Kissinger standing toe-to-toe with that silky-tongued Secretary of

State, Angelo Torriani. When I think of poor Cardinals Muldoon, O'Toole and Novik up against even the *Keeper of the Keys* at Vatican City, I think we'd be better off sending Willie Sutton. At least he could get inside."

"You can't mean that the Pope is going to turn them away. After all, Ryan was in conference with the Papal Nuncio. That has to be interpreted to mean that the trip is 'go,' doesn't it?"

Thaddeus came back to reality. "Of course it does. As far as the Pope goes, it's fine. He's no fool. The American Cardinals have a right to ask his intentions. Everyone else has. Moreover, it's their privilege to stand up and be part of a Conclave for the first time, and not just sit there on their fat asses, signaling *Ja* to every suggestion the Italians make. The Pope's going to see this. But what will the Curia do after they've gone? That's the big question. They're the power brokers, and if the Americans do have a candidate he'd better be pleasing to them—or it's no ball game.

"I don't really believe the Curia's so stupid that they believe they can contain the Holy Father in the person of an Italian forever. We're lucky that they've produced generally fine Popes over the last couple of centuries. Not super-fine. Not great. They've all been flawed men. Who isn't? Look at our Presidents. Look at New York's Mayors. They're enough to make you believe the more flawed you are, the more successful you can be.

"But that's a rambling lead. They will accept a non-Italian Pope. They'll buy American pressure. They have to. The American votes count now—almost as much as the money we ship over there every year. The dollar may be down, but the real estate they've bought, the Watergate Apartment-Hotel, for instance, is appreciating. All their holdings in American property have gone up. They've never had it so good. Saved the hide of Paul VI who was suckered into that big bank scandal.

"If you want advice, go elsewhere. If you want a suggestion, go help the poor priests and at the same time you'll be learning a whole new world to write about—inside the Vatican. It's a labyrinth you'll never figure out. And

54

maybe you'll be doing a favor for Muir. Scoot over tonight and see what's happening."

"I will. Thanks, Thad. I think I'd like a whiskey, if you don't mind. I'll drink it in the kitchen."

"No, don't bother about that. Look at it this way. You'll be in Rome the nineteenth for the *Feast of Saint Joseph, the Patron of the Universal Church* and, therefore, the patron of us all. In his honor, we may drink whiskey. And while you're mixing, I'd better haul out your passport. You've got the rest of your documents, I suppose."

"Yes. Everything I need."

"Except a car. Take mine. Leave it at whatever airport you end up. I'll send someone out to pick it up. Just be sure you give them the right instructions."

"Thanks, Thad. You're great . . . but that's not news."

Donald swilled down his drink, waved good-bye and barely heard his uncle's last words, "One thing I won't do is get you out of your trip with that darling Viennese."

Thaddeus closed the door slowly. Seeing Donald invariably refreshed him. It saddened him, too. He saw his own life being relived—but how much better! With style and talent that Thaddeus tried to master, but succeeded no better than any of the newspapermen of his generation. "A crummy trade then—not a profession the way it is now," he muttered. "Which is better? Neither. Each belonged to its time," he mumbled and headed for the whiskey bottle.

His eyes brightened as he poured a shot, "Of course, there's one big difference. *We* knew how to spell."

*   *   *

Donald seldom visited Newark's attractive, modern airport, but each time he did, the newspaperman wondered anew at the idiocy of bureaucracy. Here it stood, the answer to the overcrowding at Kennedy, the long delays occasioned by flights arriving simultaneously and forced to wait in holding patterns for minutes on end; sometimes, as long as an hour. Transportation facilities between Newark and downtown New York were excellent, but there remained a whole catalog of petty problems no one seemed willing or even capable of wrestling with, such as the double fare demanded by taxis which were prohibited from picking up return passengers in New York. Superseding even bureaucratic idiocy, there lay the narrow mind of the New Yorker himself who, at the mere mention of using Newark's facilities, excluded it from existence by saying, "How on earth would I ever get there?"

There the matter ended and while Newark's traffic was gradually picking up, it had nowhere reached expectations. Donald found the charter section with ease. It revealed itself as only a comparatively small waiting room with no facilities beyond lavatories—perhaps a V.I.P. room behind one of the unmarked doors—concealing himself presented a problem.

A small one really, because with little effort he was able to determine that a party was boarding a charter jet for Rome, scheduled to depart at six-fifteen. "Yes," answered the friendly stewardess who was the only person around, "it is the charter ordered by Max Schwartz. Do you have your ticket, sir?"

"No," Donald smiled. "I'm not traveling with the party. Mr. Schwartz simply sent me over ahead to make sure the arrangements are in order." It was a sound lie, for checking out a project this size was typical of Schwartz. If the stewardess mentioned it, it would be days before the clergymen would suspect they'd been watched. By then they would know it anyway.

Donald chose the car to watch his quarry. He simply needed to be sure who was aboard the flight. There was plenty of time to reach a telephone and make his own reservation to Rome. It offered no problem, assuming he was willing to travel first class. A flight at eight o'clock from Kennedy would bring him into Rome at about eight in the morning, approximately the same time the charter landed at Ciampino, the old international airport. He would set down at the Leonardo Da Vinci.

A telephone call to Thaddeus told his uncle that he'd put things together and that the car would be left at Kennedy in care of the Helms Rental Agency where the paper had a friend in the manager.

"Fine," Thaddeus grunted. "It's my guess they'll head for the Palace-International, down by the station. You ought to know it. Old and elegant. There's a side entrance where the 'incognitos' are able to get in and out as well as upstairs to their apartments if they request that the section be sealed off. I presume that's been done.

"Take down this name and address. Angela Nero, Albergo Merline on Via delle Carrozze. The street number isn't important. *The Street of the Carriages* is only about three blocks long. The Merline has been there since Nero fiddled. Angela's no relation, by the way. She's the granddaughter of Nellie Nero, a newspaperwoman of my day. A great lady. Took her name from Nellie Bly who went around the world in eighty days.

"Nellie was a wonder woman right after the war. That's when I was assigned to Rome. We traded stories and did each other lots of favors. She's dead now. I've been told young Angela's a chip off the old block, just as good.

"That's about it." There was a long pause. "Donald, I called the apartment. No answer. You've got that excuse for not calling Erika. OK?"

"OK? Thaddeus, you're wonderful. How come you're so great?"

"Because if I were in your shoes, I'd be scared shitless, too. Erika's a lot of woman. Let's leave it there."

"Bless you," Donald said softly.

"Bless you, nephew. Do a good job."

Donald had barely gotten back to his car when a taxi drove up, decanting Monsignor Thomas Ryan, accompanied by Monsignor Robert "Yes Yes" Pfeifer. Ryan was still in his sports jacket, but he'd changed shirts and was wearing a striped tie of blinding colors. He appeared totally at ease in contrast to Pfeifer, who looked as though he were walking around naked in spite of the good taste and tailoring of a quiet gray suit that fitted his short, trim stature perfectly. Pfeifer's hair bothered Ryan until it dawned on him how seriously Pfeifer was taking his mission. "Yes Yes" was really playing *The Third Man*. He'd switched the part from left to right and, of course, on top he resembled an adolescent straight out of a comic strip. Pfeifer's nickname came from his habit of agreeing with everybody and everything. He was an enthusiastic "yes man."

Ten minutes later Donald was rewarded by the sight of William Cardinal Muldoon looking natty and business-like, carrying a handsome leather attaché case which might be described in a male fashion show as "the perfect accessory for the businessman's tasteful pin-stripe suit of medium blue, with matching dark maroon socks and tie." Donald liked his role of fashion expert. "Notice the rolled lapels, the hand-sewn buttonholes and the polka-dot lining of this creation by Leonardo of Rome."

Muldoon seemed perfectly at home in his banker's outfit except for the fedora which someone must have pulled out of the top shelf of a closet at the Cardinal's mansion. Doubtless, it had been left there by some visitor from Little Italy.

Minutes later a limousine arrived containing Cardinals Juan De Cordoba and Alexander Novik. The Chicago Cardinal, tall and stately, his position as a Prince of the Church evident in his carriage and manner, was the least successful in masquerading. Yet, he'd chosen a conservative, dark brown suit, white shirt, wore no hat and carried a battered briefcase stuffed full. The briefcase gave him away. Only someone terribly important could carry anything so ancient. With his sharp eye, Donald saw that one of the straps was missing.

Those swooning Los Angelenos who adored their Mexican Archbishop, Cardinal De Cordoba, would have been devastated by the appearance of their idol in civilian attire. He'd allowed his Latin taste and flare for wearing clothes to go wild in a baby blue sports coat, gray trousers and a multi-colored sports shirt purchased at the same shop that once catered to Harry Truman. Donald had done his share of writing for the women's page and never sneered at it. There, the word for De Cordoba would have been "ador-able."

Donald presumed "Yes Yes" Pfeifer had accompanied Monsignor Ryan in order to receive last minute instructions and would return in the car with Joe White. If there were any surprises, Donald would meet them in Rome. He turned the key of the ignition and headed for New York and the drive to Kennedy.

Time was running pretty close and Donald's heart beat a little faster as the realization struck that he was chasing one fantastic story. When had three Cardinals sneaked out of the country, intending to meet a fourth in Rome, where they would sit down—they hoped—and ask the Supreme Pontiff of their Church some rock-bottom question? Donald had to give Tom Ryan credit. He had certainly chosen the right day. Who would miss any of the Cardinals, each the spiritual head of predominately Irish congregations, after the Saint Patrick's Day parades were over?

PART II

Rome—The Velvet Curtain

Donald arrived at Kennedy in time to board a nonstop flight to Rome. The stewardess led him to a seat in the last row of the first class section and nodded cheerfully when he asked for a drink.

"I need one," he said in a faint, cracked voice.

"I can see that," the dark-haired girl replied. "After all, it *is* Saint Patrick's Day."

That the stewardess bore no resemblance to Erika seemed beside the point. For the first time since this morning Donald felt obliged to think about the roommate he'd stood up and, what was worse, leaving the nasty business of apologizing to his uncle. It was enough that the stewardess, tall and flat-chested, had black hair to remind Donald of Erika and all his sins. Why, he wondered, couldn't they have logged a blonde on this flight?

An answer to his thoughts, a blonde, arrived at the same moment as his rye and soda. He recognized the girl, an overage starlet, probably on her way to Rome for a movie. She glanced briefly at Donald and the drink, wrinkled her nose in disgust at the sight of both. Her seat was next to his.

After spending an inordinate amount of time arranging and rearranging her carry-on luggage in the compartments above their seats, she sat down and devoted another several minutes to flattening the bottom of her skirt and adjusting her figure to the contour of the chair. Finally satisfied with her body arrangement, carefully keeping a safe distance from Donald, the blonde dug into an immense shoulder bag, fumbled energetically and eventually extracted a pocket-book edition of *Madame Bovary*. Daintily she licked her forefinger to slip through the front matter, settling at Chapter One.

Donald edged his own body closer to the window, slumped way down in his seat, allowing his legs to slither under the chair in front of him. He would have closed his eyes at that instant except his attention was caught by a flurry of excitement on the gangway. Virtually all the plane's stewardesses had flocked to the first class entrance to greet a late passenger—some of them, on a first name basis. Like a conquering hero, the last minute passenger dispensed handshakes and warm smiles to the collection of enchanted young women. Donald recognized Pietro Gentille. If anything, Gentille seemed handsomer this evening than he had at lunch at the Zenith. Then Donald looked up at the plane's lighting and realized how cleverly designers built flattering illumination into the cabins of today's giant planes.

A man with Gentille's looks would inevitably loom in the aisle of a curious cabin of plane passengers as the next thing to a Greek god. Miss Starlet promptly closed *Madame Bovary*. After only a second's hesitation, she shoved it back into her treasure trove.

Gentille moved to the rear with the grace and ease of a man used to being noticed, taking the last row window seat, thus separating himself by one reservation from Miss Starlet. Donald could hear the lady chewing her lips. She could hardly surmise that Gentille's appearance on the flight was as much a surprise to her roisterer of a seatmate as it was a frustration to her. Why in God's name was Gentille headed for Rome aboard a regularly scheduled plane when he might more comfortably have traveled in the charter jet with his distinguished customers?

Donald imagined that if Gentille could have gotten aboard the Cardinals' jet to overhear their private conversations, he wouldn't have hesitated a second. Obviously that hadn't been in the cards, so Gentille chose another road to Rome and, hopefully, information. He'd be there to handle the Cardinals' return trip.

Since Gentille was also the brother-in-law of a Cardinal

considered *papabilo*, Donald chose to see the flight with cynical eyes. Gentille was part of a jigsaw puzzle whose scattered pieces Donald hoped would fall into place in Rome.

The engines were warming up and the stewardesses had begun demonstrating the oxygen apparatus and pointing out the emergency exits. Before taking her station in the aisle between the two last rows, the black-haired girl plopped a "reserved" sign into the seat next to the Italian executive. Donald could distinctly feel, if not hear, over the roar of the engines, the feet of Miss Starlet tapping angrily on the floor.

He fastened his seat belt, pulled down the shade, knowing nothing could be done about anything for the next eight or nine hours. He might as well let his mind churn away freely until he became exhausted enough to sleep.

Among the stories Uncle Thaddeus told of his theatrical friends was the wire Sophie Tucker sent to her manager when she was out on tour and kept hitting the same cities and theatres as a famous troupe of vaudeville entertainers, Singer's Midgets. Wired Sophie, "Up to my ass in midgets. Get me rerouted somehow. Love, Sophie."

Donald guffawed at the old saw and Miss Starlet fidgeted. He'd been up to his ass in Cardinals and the wonder of it all was how simple priests ever became Cardinals in the first place. It was as much a mystery to those inside the Church as to outsiders. There were no set rules.

In a secular sense, the job could be considered a political plum, but no Cardinal ever got his red biretta by running for the office. If it were a popularity contest, the College of Cardinals would be decimated by half its members. Even Popes who in the final analysis named the Princes of the Church, could not always select men of their choosing, much less priests they sincerely believed worthy of the honor.

Yet being named a Cardinal wasn't a hit and miss promotion. A variety of factors, some tangible, others mysterious, went into the creation of a Cardinal. Mother Church, in her infinite wisdom, could circumvent precise explanations by crediting Divine Providence. At the nomination of many Cardinals, both in modern and ancient Church history, Divine Providence often heard mutterings and language from the clergy that an ordinary layman would feel obliged to take with him into the Confessional.

Today's Cardinals all came from the same humble ranks, out of the seminaries that made priests of Catholic young men. In Europe, those with leanings toward theology, law, diplomacy and public relations, found themselves involved in the Vatican's never-ending talent hunt. They became members of the Curia, the management of the Church. They could either connive their way to the rank of Cardinal or hang on so long that their seniority entitled them to the honor.

Americans were more accustomed to Cardinals the Church called "pastoral"—heads of diocesan areas. The importance of New York required that it be headed by a Cardinal, and William Cardinal Muldoon, the incumbent, was fairly typical of the genre. Most American Cardinals came from modest American families and rose in the Church through diligence, hard work and a capacity for managing the finances of their parishes.

Consequently American Cardinals were labeled unfairly as business tycoons with a talent for dipping into the pockets of the wealthy to sustain their fashionable life-style and ignoring the poor. Although the accusation could not withstand close scrutiny, Donald's view was more generous. He could not claim that the Cardinals he'd met ranked as great philosophers, theologians or even brilliant pastors, but he found that most possessed dedication and had made a positive contribution to Catholics and non-Catholics alike. America, he felt, would be poorer without the energy of the men who in a comparatively short period of time had built the American Catholic Church into a powerful and respected institution.

*   *   *

Juan Cardinal De Cordoba offered a lesson in "destiny's handiwork" when Church and the right man met under what the world might call "proper auspices," but which their spiritual brothers attributed to "God's Will."

De Cordoba, a Mexican, fifty-one, and looking ten years

younger, had become the glamour boy of the College of Cardinals thanks to his height, which was well over six feet, his marvelous physique, which even Cardinal's robes couldn't conceal, his thick, luxuriant black hair properly touched at the temples with gray and an aristocratic Latin face which would have drawn attention in any profession. Becoming a Cardinal was simply another achievement in the catalogue of accomplishments this remarkable man had managed. Add charm, a gracious personality and a deep reservoir of faith in his calling and one found a rare and valuable human being.

In joining the older Cardinals on their mission to Rome, De Cordoba was no lamb among wolves. He was not along for the ride. He was a skilled, effective diplomat as well as a popular pastor and capable administrator. The senior Cardinals appreciated De Cordoba's intellect and the profundity of his faith.

Juan De Cordoba was admired as a true servant of God in whom special attributes had been evident from the time he was a small boy to his appointment six years earlier as the temporary head of the Los Angeles Archdiocese. When he was called to Rome and invested as a Cardinal, by De Cordoba's old friend, Francesco Xavier Morelli, the Pope, reaffirmed a promise to relieve him of his duties in the tangled California office and assign him to Mexico where De Cordoba felt he was more urgently needed.

Morelli reassured him, "It will happen, just as soon as I can find a suitable replacement. Be patient, Juan."

Los Angeles, naturally, was reluctant to let him go. The City of the Angels was unique in the United States. In some respects it was like a virgin who couldn't make up her mind; in others, it was as sure of itself as a thrice-married movie star who had already picked her fourth spouse. The city's mayor, police department and the entire structure of city government existed at the pleasure of the powerful business community who ran the town from meeting places in old dingy hotels where they could make their deals out of the public eye. Los Angeles had grown and flourished as the exclusive domain of the Associated Farmers, the National Association of Manufacturers, the City Council and the

Chambers of Commerce, the old boys and the *jaycees*.

De Cordoba's swift ascent to Cardinal at the age of fifty-one was not unprecedented. He was by no means the youngest Red Hat in history, but he'd followed a curious path that began when his mother and father, Mexican wetbacks, landed on the San Diego ranch of the Thorn family forty years ago. The first two years Maria and Juan De Cordoba, Sr. had come alone. The third year they brought their son, Juan, Jr., a sturdy, bright-eyed child of seven.

The De Cordobas, honest, capable workers, captured the affection of the Thorns, an elderly couple whose grown children had shown no interest in ranch life and fled to the city. The Thorns maintained the ranch because they enjoyed hard work and the challenge.

Like most ranchers in the valleys and mountains hidden behind the city of San Diego, the Thorns carried political clout not only locally but with the Immigration Service. The De Cordobas swam no rivers in the dead of night when they traveled between Mexico and the United States. John and Ethel Thorn met their Mexican hands when they arrived and drove with them to Tijuana when they returned to their own land.

The Thorns sought to persuade Juan and Maria De Cordoba to apply for American citizenship and remain permanently. "We love our homeland," Juan, Sr., a strong, husky man, explained, "and we have a responsibility to it. We work here now for the money, but in Mexico we are building. We build decent homes for our family and our friends. We do not make much money, but that is not important. We want our son to honor his Mexican heritage."

De Cordoba, better educated than most wetbacks, held high hopes for his boy. He was shocked but not upset when at fourteen young Juan announced that he intended to become a priest. Maria interpreted his feelings as a *true call* because, in anti-clerical Mexico, the child had met few priests. He'd been exposed to little religious education. Attending Mass was an occasional obligation in the De Cordoba family, reserved for Saints' Days, Christmas and Easter.

65

In Mexico they brought the youth to a priest who questioned him at length. He told the parents Juan indeed possessed the spirit to serve God.

On returning to the Thorn ranch, the senior De Cordobas confided in their boss. John Thorn, a Seventh Day Adventist, was a man of action who decided the only person to contact about young Juan's hopes was the fellow in charge, San Diego's Bishop Richard Teague, who immediately recognized Thorn's name. He agreed to meet and talk to the Mexican youth.

Teague was so impressed with the boy that he invited Juan and his mother to be his guests for several days in order to study him more carefully. At week's end, his conclusion agreed with the Mexican priest's.

He recognized Thorn as a straightforward, decent man, so he spoke to him first. "The boy is bright, close to a genius, I suspect. This devotion to religion could be a childish fantasy, but it is not wise to discourage it. It might be what we describe as *the call*." The Bishop smiled. "It's an intangible. We meet it all the time among the boys in parochial schools. They're usually shy, sensitive types and the appeal of religion generally is their substitute for something missing in their lives. It could be anything. That's irrelevant. Eventually they outgrow it, so we urge them to wait a little longer and pray harder before making so firm a decision. Nine-tenths of them usually forget they ever had *the call*.

"But there's something different about this young man. That intangible I mentioned. You came to me for advice. My suggestion is simple. Help the boy. Send him into town where he can enjoy a Catholic education. He's no farm hand. The boy is someone special. We'll soon discover whether or not God intends him to become a religious. In the meantime, nothing has been lost. A great deal will have been gained. The boy will have the feel of a formal education."

The Bishop paused long enough to allow Thorn a few seconds to prepare him for the next advice, "You can afford it, Mr. Thorn. You're the kind of man who wants to help people—especially kids."

"Mr. Bishop, you're a smart *hombre*," Thorn laughed. "Of course I can afford it, and there isn't a boy I'd rather help than Juan. Whatever you and his parents agree on, I'll accept."

"And Mrs. Thorn?"

"Ethel wants what is best for the boy."

So young Juan's education was paid for by a Seventh Day Adventist. The senior De Cordobas continued in Thorn's employ as ranch hands. Juan first attended schools in California; later, in Mexico. He studied at seminaries in both countries, under the direction and advice of Bishop Teague. Finally he was sent to Rome and the North American College under Teague's sponsorship, nominally a student from the San Diego diocese. But in all recommendations regarding the young man, Bishop Teague respected Juan's desire to serve eventually in Mexico where, as he wrote to his sponsor, "the gifts you have given me, Your Excellency, are needed."

Teague arranged to be in Rome for Juan's ordination and was touched when he was asked to perform the ceremony of bestowing Holy orders on his young protégé. Teague timed the trip to arrange for continuation of Juan's studies in Rome. He knew that Juan needed as broad a background as he could get while a Bishop was around to plead for him. In Mexico he would be pretty much on his own.

After two years of service in the Curia, working in the State Department where Monsignor Francesco Xavier Morelli was his immediate superior, Juan Maria was granted his wish—pastoral work. He was assigned to a poor parish in Morelia, Mexico. Juan proved himself a "worker priest" in the literal sense of the word. What local laborers would not do to repair the broken-down church, he handled himself. Juan's diligence brought young people into the church who eventually persuaded their elders that the young priest, so well educated, was really one of them.

Bishop Teague never let this shining light of young priesthood out of his sight. Juan came to his own diocese where he was made a Monsignor and given another tough job in the Mexican section of the city where he turned around a long neglected parish, making it one of the most active in the city. His bilingual sermons drew parishoners from nearby neighborhoods.

"We're pleased to hear about God," said the Anglos, "and not the collection plate."

De Cordoba never mentioned money as the needs of his parishes from the pulpit. "I leave that to God and the businessmen I invite to help me." This was innovative in America where pastors normally kept a close watch on finances and parishoners seldom saw an accounting of their contributions. When other priests remonstrated to Bishop Teague, he told them to mind their own business. "De Cordoba is as clever a businessman as he is a wise pastor. He tells his people, 'You count the money. I'll count the souls.' It's good advice."

At thirty-five De Cordoba was anointed a Bishop and served with distinction in Mexico City. But the Vatican, recalling his experience in the Curia, kept him on the move— touring South America as a roving observer. He was given no title—thus offending neither the national hierarchy nor the Papal Nuncios. They knew De Cordoba reported directly to the Pope, bypassing the Curia whom Bishops, particularly in explosive Latin American countries, loathed as a matter of principle and experience. Often they arrived in Rome to inquire about matters they had corresponded about for years only to find their communications filed away in boxes, sealed and forgotten.

Then there arose the almost unbelievable situation in Los Angeles when complaints began pouring in about the behavior of Archbishop Peter Astor Haynes, a curious phenomenon in American ecclesiastical history, whose meteoric rise in the Catholic Church was never adequately explained even after his forced resignation and subsequent withdrawal from public view. Haynes was a businessman, a Wall Street tycoon, who converted to Catholicism when he was thirty-five. He studied for the priesthood, was ordained at forty-one and became closely associated with Cardinal Hellman who promoted him to Monsignor and later recommended him as an Auxiliary Bishop of the New York Archdiocese, where he supposedly worked in the financial division, driving Max Schwartz up a wall.

When the Los Angeles post became vacant because of the death of Archbishop Cartwell, a modest, competent but unimaginative man, Cardinal Hellman saw a way of getting rid of Haynes, pacifying Max Schwartz and relieving himself of a case of poor judgment. He prevailed upon friends in the Curia to recommend Haynes for the Los Angeles post.

The Pope acted recluctantly. In considering various Bishops to succeed Cartwell, he ran down the list of those already installed in the diocese. The Holy Father was horrified that the interim custodians of the diocese included only one Spanish name. He thundered to his secretary, "Can you imagine this? One lonely Latin Monsignor of prominence in a diocese that once was predominately Spanish and still contains a vast population of Hispanic-Americans."

Morelli, however, was bound into one of those compromises with his own judgment that he described as "a reminder that Christ carried a cross and I only have to control my temper."

It would not be prudent for the Pope to overrule the advice of a man of Hellman's importance. Hellman had many flaws, but Morelli recognized him as a Cardinal who earned the respect he enjoyed and would be recognized in American Church history as an outstanding leader. Morelli was bound to help him unload Haynes, but he noted in his diary that removing him to such an important diocese as Los Angeles would prove a "grave mistake."

Morelli's predictions were quickly confirmed when shortly after his installation there came a series of reports about the new Archbishop's capriciousness, his lack of sensitivity, his authoritarian ways and high-handedness in dealing with Los Angelenos on both sides of the tracks—the poor as well as the rich.

Haynes assumed personal censorship of the diocesan newspapers which enjoyed an enviable reputation as voices for social justice in California's complicated racial and labor problems.

Haynes ignored the Mexican-American population, refused to meet the city's blacks and arbitrarily suspended priests who disagreed with him. Asked to comment on the

Watts riots, the autocratic former businessman answered, "What do you want me to say? They're over."

Such callowness did not please the city's businessmen who assessed the Archbishop as being inimical to Los Angeles' good name. He was achieving an unpleasant notoriety in the press both inside and outside California. Protestant voices reached the Pope's long ears before those of Catholic pilgrims. Morelli took the more prominent aside and asked their opinion of Haynes. The politest description was that the man was a psychopath.

Morelli dispatched an American priest to visit the diocese incognito. The report the young man brought back was devastating. He described Haynes as a disaster, a man any doctor would certify as manic. His removal was not a matter of choice; it was an imperative and immediate necessity. The investigation had been thorough. His portfolio bulged with statements from prominent laymen, bishops, priests, workers as well as psychological profiles prepared for him on *Psychiatrists' Row* in Beverly Hills.

Morelli rewarded the young priest with a letter of commendation; moreover, he expressed himself as appreciative of the psychiatrist's advice. "I couldn't agree more," he wrote, "and this experience serves as an illustration of the need for our priests to understand the work being done in medical science to better understand the human mind. We have too long turned our backs on this area of research."

Morelli, however, proceeded to forget his acknowledgment of psychiatric profiles and went off "half-cocked" as American churchmen eventually described the fit of pique that led him to summon Bishop Juan De Cordoba to Rome where he was named an Archbishop and given a letter written in Morelli's own hand authorizing him to remove Haynes and assume the administration of the Los Angeles diocese immediately. Wisely His Holiness requested Vatican travel experts to use the polar route for De Cordoba's trip, thus eliminating any embarrassing meeting with Cardinal Hellman in New York. Hellman wasn't advised of the Pope's abrupt action until after De Cordoba had taken off.

The news that the handsome De Cordoba, an authentic Mexican with a genuine Spanish name, was coming to the

City of the Angels to dispossess the hated Haynes spread faster than a San Fernando Valley brush fire. City fathers wondered how quickly they could summon Dolores Del Rio from Mexico to stand at the head of the receiving line. Someone asked if Leo Carillo was still alive. When the answer, alas, was negative, it was proposed that a palomino from the Carillo stable be procured so the new Archbishop could ride into the city in the fashion of his forefathers, the friars who founded the Missions and discovered Los Angeles. No one bothered to inquire how Mexican-Americans regarded the appointment or to note that, in their part of town, horses would be welcome to serve an ancient function, transportation.

Los Angeles drooled at its latest claim to individuality—having a "foreign national" as the head of its Roman Catholic Archdiocese. They chose to ignore the announcement that De Cordoba's tenure was temporary. Few bothered to check how many foreigners were serving American congregations in other parts of the country. It was an old custom and if America's shortage of priests persisted, the program would be expanded.

No matter. *They* weren't Archbishops and if Angelenos were all they were cracked up to be, their *divine* Juan De Cordoba would be wearing scarlet instead of purple faster than you could pronounce the Spanish name of his dominion, *Nuestra Señora la Reina de Los Angeles de Porciunucula.*

Before consenting to the avalanche of proposals to celebrate Los Angeles' first "Spanish" Archbishop, De Cordoba had to accomplish the resignation of the incumbent. Haynes' paranoia had become more serious. He imagined he was the victim of an international conspiracy masterminded by the Pope and the President. He was determined to fight the ouster—even if it meant going public.

So De Cordoba made careful preparations. In a downtown hotel he collected a group of prominent Bishops, priests and laymen in the Archdiocese, as well as two judges and a physician.

Using patience, De Cordoba and his delegation accomplished their mission with such finesse that nasty publicity was avoided. Juan De Cordoba assumed control quietly and modestly, remaining virtually invisible until all the passions Haynes created had died down. When he did emerge, his handsome face and luxuriant black hair dazzled Angelenos who hailed him as the savior of the ragged, harassed diocese. He was embraced with characteristic Southern California enthusiasm, described as a champion of the common man, an attribute to which all the "uncommon men" who ran Los Angeles sounded vigorous "Amens."

Seers and occult prophets, featured on Southern California's TV news broadcasts, solemnly pronounced that the De Cordoba era would shine as a glorious epoch in Southern California's religious rebirth; that there would be gatherings of believers from the far corners of the globe to take part in mammoth outdoor ceremonies—gigantic celebrations in which the new groups and traditional churches would join hands to drive all the evils of the southland into the sea where they would be swallowed up by whales and prehistoric creatures arising from the deep.

Unlike Haynes, who railed at California's faddists as more dangerous than atheists, De Cordoba finessed their predictions by observing that "There is room in God's house for men and women of all persuasions. He blesses each believer in His own way."

Once De Cordoba achieved full control of the intricate machinery of his sprawling parish, the Mexican Cardinal proved an adversary worthy of the smooth public relations men who masterminded the power of the Los Angeles City Council, the influence of the Chamber of Commerce and the comfortable control exerted in the delicate field of labor relations by the National Association of Manufacturers and California's very own Associated Farmers.

As saber wavers, the Associated Farmers of California had few peers. They'd been rattling away securely for half a century, capitalizing on every evil and prejudice from the days of the "yellow peril" to the "Communist threat" inherent in the unionization of farm workers of the seventies. With one hand they lured wetbacks to harvest crops; with the other, they encouraged outrage by California's unemployed. While tempers flared in the City Council, the California legislature and the Halls of Congress, and the press editorialized, the harvest was quietly brought in by the wetbacks as it had been for years. Neither the furor occasioned by John Steinbeck's *Grapes of Wrath* in the thirties nor the tentative victories during the seventies to unionize the farm workers had dented the Association's policy of holding the fruit pickers to a substandard level of existence.

De Cordoba sided with the strikers. He sought to clarify the contribution alien workers made to the American economy, explaining that they were essential to its growth and their status as "illegals" was a cruel deceit played on their human rights by both farmers and the Government. Not a word of De Cordoba's opinions seeped into any California newspaper of importance. However, women's groups adored him and passed countless resolutions supporting De Cordoba's position.

Eventually De Cordoba realized that the office of Los Angeles Archbishop, like the Mayor's office, existed at the pleasure of the business community. His outrage served only to articulate their claim that there was "plenty of honest dissent in the biggest city in the world—and that's why Los Angeles kept growing and prospering." They applauded, they pressed his hand, they slapped his back. Nothing changed.

In anticipation of his eventual transfer to Mexico, De Cordoba prepared an assessment of the problems peculiar to the Los Angeles Church which urged that the diocese be fragmented into little diocesan areas where Bishops and Monsignors might get closer to the people. He stressed the importance of ending the alienation of Mexican-Americans as well as their "illegal" brothers, the wetbacks.

Morelli was impressed with the thoroughness of De Cordoba's report which he submitted on arriving for his investiture as Cardinal—an event that brought not only Los Angeles' Catholic laymen to Rome, but a prominent group of Protestant businessmen as well. They told the press, "We want the Pope to know that Los Angeles owes its greatness to the brave Spanish priests who discovered her and we figure he's honoring their memory by making our beloved

Juan De Cordoba a Cardinal. It couldn't happen to a finer man or to a greater American community. We're still a little *pueblo* in our hearts and we can always spare time to do the Lord's work."

A few weeks earlier, the Vatican announced that Cardinal De Cordoba would leave Los Angeles after Easter to return to Mexico and that Bishop John Teague would come out of retirement to head a task force of priests, predominately Spanish-speaking and blacks, who would work on the recommendations of De Cordoba before a new Archbishop would be named.

Angelenos hailed this as another triumph for their community. TV commentators, taking their cue from the press, applauded this innovative step. The seers cooed that De Cordoba had shown himself much, much more than "another pretty face in the land of beautiful people," but as a priest who had made a major contribution to religion in the Southland. News analysts commented on his six years of service with solemn expressions of praise and prayers for his future to lead-in and fade-out bars from the song, *Ramona*.

*　　*　　*

Donald's mind finally stopped whirling and he drifted into a half hour or so of deep sleep. When he awoke it was in answer to the stewardess' request that he fasten his seat belt for a brief, unscheduled stop at Milan. No further explanation was given.

The stop was brief, but not exactly unscheduled. It was difficult to call it that when the front entrance was thrown open and a short, stocky man with steel gray hair and piercing blue eyes walked briskly aboard and was ushered to the seat next to Pietro Gentille. The younger man rose, embraced the new passenger and as soon as he was settled, the plane taxied toward the runway.

Pietro Gentille had been joined in the flight to Rome by his brother-in-law, Daniele Cardinal Rossi. In rapid fire Italian, they talked in hushed whispers all the way.

Donald never made it back to sleep.

Miss Starlet, however, slumped at his side, snoring with

an intensity that would have horrified *Madame Bovary*.

The instant the gangplank was placed against the door of the first class section, Gentille and his brother-in-law darted up the aisle and down the steps to a limousine waiting for them on the field.

Donald could hardly feel he'd been cheated out of a story. No doubt they were part of it, but for the moment he was better off staying close to his own—the American Cardinals.

* * *

At Rome's venerable Palace-International, Donald registered as D. Thaddeus Brady, which he presumed would mean little to the young room clerk, immaculate in morning clothes, starched white shirt and bow tie, but the name produced immediate reaction results when it was brought to the office adjoining the registration desk where an elderly assistant manager seized it joyously.

He came bouncing out of his hiding place, grasped Donald's hand, "You're Donald Brady, Thad's nephew. Welcome, welcome! I'm not going to tell a man of your age how you've grown, but you couldn't reach the desk the last time I saw you. How's Thad?"

In three years at the hotel the young clerk had never seen such a display of effusiveness. To Donald it came as a surprise. He looked over the manager's shoulders to the youth, "You don't know Uncle Thaddeus. He's better than a passport."

"In this hotel, he is," the manager said, "I'm Ruggero Bulatov. And now, Mr. Donald, what can we do for you?"

"The best you can for a working newspaperman, nothing more at the moment. I'd like the first or second floor if you can manage it. A single is all I want."

Bulatov scratched his chin. "For a few days, the second floor is not possible. But I am going to give you a lovely suite on the third floor, and the rate will be the same as a single. Professional courtesy. There is a twenty percent discount at the bar and restaurant for the press. For our special friends, the discount is twenty-five percent. And, of course, you will be my guest at dinner whenever you can arrange it. Besides

75

myself, there is another admirer of your uncle in the family, my wife, Nadja. Oh! Young man, you are in for some wonderful stories."

Bulatov clapped his hands and an army of bellboys appeared to carry Donald's luggage—one airline bag and one briefcase. He helped them out by offering one his trench coat, another, his hat and a third, a bag of books and newspapers he'd bought for the trip.

His flight had arrived on time. He telephoned Ciampino. The charter was slightly overdue. Was there a limousine waiting? "Oh, yes, Mr.—I didn't catch your name..."

"I'm Donald Thaddeus of the Embassy. Just checking out the Max Schwartz party. The limousine driver knows to take them directly to the Palace-International?"

"If you will excuse me, sir, I shall check."

A few seconds later the voice was back on the phone, "That is correct, sir. Is there anything else? I am going off duty in a few minutes. I can leave any instructions you have with the day man."

Donald chuckled. Saint Patrick, or was it Saint Joseph, was riding with him today—and the winds were certainly at his back. "No, thank you very much. You have been most helpful. There are no instructions."

He tipped the boys a dollar each and at the Italian rate of exchange, eight hundred plus *Lire* to the dollar, it made a nice sounding figure even if it bought only seven or eight cigarettes. He wasn't sure, but Italy's inflation was probably worse than the situation at home.

He was dead tired and the big decision had to be reached. Sleep first or telephone Erika? In New York it was now about six o'clock in the morning. Unless she'd checked with Thaddeus, Erika would be terribly worried. He'd better call. Risking waking her was the least of his problems.

Donald reset his watch. Well, he figured, he could waste an hour or so—stall, to put it more accurately—by having a decent breakfast and bathing and shaving. He rang for room service, ordering rolls, *espresso* and a bottle of German beer.

When the tray arrived, Donald was in the tub. The waiter left it near the bathroom door. Donald stepped out of the tub, reached for the beer, sat back and relaxed. The coffee could wait. Cold *espresso* was better than steaming American any day of the year. He delighted in the huge tub, all the gadgets and the giant-sized towels being warmed up on the hot pipes. America may have been the first country to go wild over indoor plumbing, but when Europe got around to it, they certainly mastered the art of arranging vast comfortable bathrooms.

After an hour had passed, Donald knew there could be no more stalling. The Palace-International had not yet installed direct overseas dialing, but the operator put his call through in half a minute.

A far from sleepy Erika answered, *"Pronto!"*

"Pronto yourself. This is Donald."

"I know," Erika said sweetly, *"comé va Roma? Bene?"*

"Sure, *bene* as hell. Baby, I'm sorry about..."

Erika interrupted, "Darling, *mein liebling*, why are you American men all alike? I thought you were different. Why are you so frightened of women? What could I do if you told me yesterday?"

"Uncle Thaddeus called while I was working and you were out."

"Oh! Well, that was nice."

"Anyhow, it happened so suddenly..."

"Liebling, no harm has been done. I understand. You must be busy. This is a big story. Our vacation can wait."

"What are you going to do?"

"Go on the trip, of course."

"Oh!"

"Yes, it's been planned."

"Alone?"

"Tesaro! Sei nicht verrückt! Of course not! I'm going with some girls and boys from the U.N."

"Some *boys?*"

"Of course, *boys*. Not all girls. That would be ghastly."

"I guess so," Donald said weakly.

"Ah, now you're jealous. Why? Not one of the boys is nearly as *schön* as you. I might tease one or two—but that's all."

"Except I know how you tease."

"You like the way I tease, *monsieur*? *Come wiz me to*

77

Cheegago and I will show you somezing special, werry special."

"Well, at least you're in a good mood. I'm pleased about that."

She was serious. "Stay pleased, darling, and don't worry about me. I will call you every few days. If you're not in, I'll leave a message. All right?"

"Sure. Sounds fine. Do you know where I am?"

"Of course. In Rome."

"I mean the hotel."

"The Palace-International."

"Yes, but how did you know. Uncle Thaddeus?"

"Uncle Thaddeus? No, *liebling*. I had a call a few minutes ago from Uncle Erich."

"In Vienna?"

"Of course, Vienna. Where else would he be?"

"And he told you..."

"He called to ask if I knew why you and a whole bunch of American Cardinals had checked into the Palace."

"What did you tell him?"

"What could I tell him, *caro mio. Niente.* I told him I knew *rien, nichts,* nothing."

"But in Vienna Cardinal Waldenheim knew all about it?"

"Obviously."

"How come?"

"I don't know. Ask Uncle Erich. *Ciao, amante.*"

She hung up.

Now Donald understood. No wonder when American priests traveled to Rome on official business they described it as "Going behind the *Velvet Curtain.*"

* * *

Donald rested for an hour. When he awoke, it was noon. Too early for lunch. Much too early to telephone Tom Ryan. Before dozing off Donald had talked to the waiter and elicited the knowledge, now known in Rome, New York and Vienna, that Cardinals Muldoon, Novik and De Cordoba were very much in residence at the Palace-International.

The *cameriere* had no information in respect to Cardinal

O'Toole, but Monsignor Ryan was also part of the American group. They had taken to bed shortly after arriving by the side door. The waiter added, "You know, *signore*, their section has been separated from the rest of the hotel. They have their own staff, their own kitchen, bar, everything—the works."

When Donald congratulated the young man on his English he volunteered that his name was Cesare and that he'd spent two years with relatives in Brooklyn. He complained, "A little guy like me was always getting ripped off. Today the dollar's not so hot, the country's not so hot, so I decided to come home. Rome's not so hot either, but at a place like the Palace you've got a good deal. Maybe the tips don't flow like wine, but you meet some very nice people. Like you, *signore*."

Donald figured that Cesare couldn't have laid it on the line any more clearly. He doubled his tip and made a mental note to list Cesare as a young man who'd rank as a world leader one of these days.

From his window he could see Rome's warm noon sun, one of the unfailing attractions of the city for Donald. No matter how dreary the day or worse, how dreary one's mood, some time between noon and five in the afternoon, regardless of the season, the sun would make an appearance against a clear blue sky and set everything right. Today would be a good one. He knew it.

With so much time between noon and lunch, Donald dressed slowly and decided to walk down the hill to the Piazza di Spagna where he would find Via Delle Carrozze. Thaddeus had been so preoccupied in telling him about Angela Nero that he'd evidently forgotten that Donald knew the Merline well.

On leaving the Palace-International, Donald almost bumped into Cardinal O'Toole whose arrival, unlike his colleagues, was accomplished with great flourish. He was in his Cardinal's cassock, wearing his biretta and spreading good cheer in a combination of colorful English, fractured French and unintelligible Italian. He was accompanied by two Monsignors who were busy unloading the party's luggage. *Signore* Bulatov hovered over the distinguished arrivals, all smiles and charm.

Obviously this had been Ryan's strategy, to sneak the other Cardinals in while O'Toole, the consummate showman, occupied the main entrance, hopefully serving as a distraction. Donald sighed. It wasn't working if the Cardinal's Saint Patrick's Day journey was already known in Vienna.

From Dublin to Rome was a natural trip for a Prince of the Church, particularly O'Toole who loved the "old sod" and his visits to the Vatican. With Irish perversity they fed his dedication to the Church and his wit.

"Once you have witnessed the supreme performance of Cardinal Angelo Torriani, ushering you into the presence of the Holy Father," O'Toole once quipped, "you have no doubt that Christ walked on the water."

It was unlikely that O'Toole would recognize Donald, but one could never depend on the Boston Cardinal, so Donald, who'd met His Eminence many times, slid out a side door and headed toward the Merline.

The Merline held its own unique reputation among American visitors who cherished it as a souvenir of post-war Rome. The iconoclastic old *albergo* pursued its free and easy ways during the late forties and early fifties when no one was quite sure of who was in charge of the city—American gangsters like Vito Genovese and Lucky Luciano, the Italian provincial government, or the United States Army. Yet there were regulations and laws governing every phase of life that appeared to have been posted on the hour. The Merline ignored them all.

The Italian *Lire* was worthless and even dollars held little value against the barter of items like chocolate bars, Kleenex, cigarettes, American razor blades, American soap, American toilet paper, American anything.

A visible and huge black market sprung up in Rome. No one worried about its evils or considered its discrimination against the poor, or how it fattened the wallets of evil profiteers like Genovese who had ingratiated himself with the American Liberation Forces.

Genovese, unlike some Americans, hadn't been caught accidently in Italy by the "suddenness" of the War. He was already there. For a citizen in his position there was no alternative but to remain. Genovese was wanted in Brooklyn for a gangland murder and for questioning in regard to his participation in Murder, Inc., a kill-for-profit organization that flourished as one of the most energetic arms of the Mafia.

Donald had gone over Thaddeus Brady's pieces dealing with Rome, the occupation, the eagerness with which high Army officials clasped Genovese to their bosom because "he spoke English and knew his way around." Some had been published in anthologies; they were masterly examples of his uncle's wit and humanity. It must have been a colorful city about which to report at the time.

According to the older Brady, the Americans had succeeded magnificently in one area—raising sex to a problem overshadowing any single event in Rome's history, plagues, Nero's fiddling, the burning of the Christians, Mussolini's march on Rome, as well as the Eternal City's most recent heroic efforts to survive the privations and austerity imposed by World War II; the hideous occupation by the Germans and then, the "liberation" by the Americans.

The chocolate bars of the G.I.'s were surely welcome. So were the friendly, smiling soldiers—a warm contrast to the arrogant, haughty Germans. But Italians had not been prepared for America's fear of sex. Military authorities closed the houses of ill repute almost before they set up canteens to feed the hungry. In weeks Rome's venereal disease rate had tripled and the numbers of young women who turned to prostitution on the streets quadrupled. The most visible commodity for sale in Rome was human flesh. A package of cigarettes bought a taste of pleasure; a carton could purchase a whole night of joy. The Borghese Gardens became the busiest outdoor bordello in the world.

Whatever took place elsewhere in Rome, the world of the *Albergo* Merline remained untouched, operating as it had for many years, a home away from home to transients who knew the place as a good buy.

Its central location was wonderfully convenient. Via Delle Carrozze was a narrow, cobblestone street running between Piazza di Spagna and Via Del Corso. A block to one side lay Via Condotti, Rome's chic shopping center. Via Del

Corso housed the main offices of the world's major banks. At the Merline, a guest was literally thrust into the center of Rome—and Roman life. It was a haven for hustlers, male and female, whose life-style had no effect whatsoever on the management or the small, friendly staff. With reason—the Merline, like many small hotels in the area, had once been a legal brothel. Although they had converted into respectable lodging establishments decades earlier, tradition, after all, was tradition. Sex went with the territory.

Donald hadn't visited Rome since the police had barred automobiles from the Piazza Di Spagna area which included Delle Carrozze. It was charming to be able to walk through the lovely square, set off by the Spanish Steps, the fountain dedicated to Mary, where the Pope visited annually on December eighth, the Feast of the Immaculate Conception, to walk along the *carpeted* Via Condotti, which Donald felt was certainly carrying "chic" to the ultimate.

Still he missed the challenge of the hundreds of cars whirling in all directions that once rendered the Piazza virtually impassable. Only the bravest tackled the traffic singly; tourists chose to wait for groups to assemble, creating a sort of platoon as they crossed, screaming "let us through" to the tiny *Fiats* that nimbly skirted around them.

Delle Carrozze had changed little and the same old electric sign hung outside the Merline. As Donald walked up the long flight of steps to the second floor lobby he noticed that, although the pieces had changed, the rectangular room continued to be furnished by unrelated stuffed chairs, one thin couch and a pair of straight chairs. The walls were decorated with cheap prints of Rome staples—*The Forum*, *Tivoli Gardens*, *Saint Peter's*, the *Trevi Fountain* and from Florence, Michelangelo's *David*.

There was no switchboard. One telephone still served all fourteen rooms and the mail box was empty. Merline guests were not heavy in the letter department. There was no one at the desk and that told the whole story—the Merline had made no concessions to today. He rang the reception desk hand bell.

In seconds there appeared from one of the rooms a woman of medium height, indeterminable age, her dark

82

black hair tied in a neat bun, dressed in an extremely conservative dark skirt and white blouse with a high collar covering her neck. Her eyes, deep hollows of black, opened wide as she drew closer to the young man at the desk. Then she screamed, "*Donald! Mamma Mia! Donald Brady!* No possible—no possible. I not believe my poor old eyes."

Donald flung his arms around the woman, Jennie Jacobowski. "It's you! How wonderful! I prayed I'd find you but you know..."

"Ah, *bambino*, I know. No, *caro*, Jennie is not yet *morte*. *Non encora. Comé va? Comé va lo zio?*"

"*Bene*, Jennie. He's well. He'll be thrilled to know I have seen you."

"Lovely. I live here now. I am in retirement..."

Then those deep, dark eyes twinkled, "Well, you know...almost..."

"Good for you, Jennie..."

"I work a few hours at the desk for *Signora* Bella. We are old friends. Not many friends left for us. So we stay together."

"Pacifico?"

"*Si.* He works at night—like always."

Donald sat down. It was true. Memories of Jennie Jacobowski had filtered through his mind on the way to the Merline, but he feared the celebrated *putana* had "moved on." Known as "Hand-job Jennie," the old whore and the *pissoir* at the corner of the building were all that remained of the Merline of his uncle's day and when Donald had been a guest more than a decade earlier.

Camero Numero Uno was Jennie's place of business. Any man Jennie brought to *Room Number One* was indistinguishable from the other. Tall or short, thin or fat, they were mousy figures, emboldened to indulge in their flights from reality with an aging whore for just that reason. She was old. Jennie understood their sexual hunger; in many respects, no different from her own. A society woman, lonely and on her own, would have to pay for sex. Instead, Jennie was paid, but one would be hard pressed to call her clients "quality."

Jennie's nickname originated from a technique of her profession. Jennie was able to accommodate clients virtually anywhere—in any setting—from public parks to cafes. Probably it had been forced upon her by age. But however it came about, she was known as the *putana* who could shift positions at a bar, swing a sweater over a man's lap and perform masturbation on him for the fee of the era—as little as five hundred *Lire* back in the fifties—less than a dollar.

None of her clients and few friends knew that Jennie, Roman born, had been married to a Yugoslav guerrilla fighter against the Nazis. Jacobowski deserted her for another woman after the birth of their son. Jennie turned to prostitution when the boy suffered an attack of polio which kept him confined to a wheelchair in the Trastevere apartment Jennie bought with her earnings. The boy died on the eve of his twentieth birthday. A painting in her possession, stolen by her husband from a home in Piedmont during the war, brought her a finder's fee on which she could live the rest of her life.

But "Hand-Job Jennie" had been active too long to abandon *the scene* completely. Donald knew she had chosen to locate at the hotel as much for the razzle-dazzle, the street action, the noise, the hustle and bustle, as for her warm devotion to *Signora* Bella. At the *Albergo* Merline, Jennie enjoyed a ringside seat at the eternal fascination they called Rome.

"Will you be staying here?" she asked.

"No, Jennie. Not yet. I don't know how long I'll be here. But we'll see each other. I'm looking for Angela Nero."

Jennie tried to stop a dark look that crossed her face. Donald's quick eye noticed it, but this was not the time for questions.

"You must have known Nellie Nero, didn't you, Jennie?"

A smile lighted up her face. *"Una donna! Una donna elegante—grande!* One of Italy's great women." Careful about such things, Jennie added, "In her generation, of course."

"And Angela?"

"They tell me she is becoming an excellent journalist." Jennie had composed herself. "With her heritage, maybe . . . perhaps very much is expected . . ."

"How old is she?"

"Twenty-five. Perhaps a little older." She paused. Jennie always defined her thoughts clearly. "You have to understand. Career women are yet novelties in Italy. Young people lose time—the war. Ah, *non parlo bene, tu capisci?*"

"*Si*, Jennie, *ho captio bene.*"

"*Vero?*"

"She's in town, isn't she?"

"I am not sure, Donald. She hasn't lived here for more than a year. I don't know where she's staying. She comes by once a week to pick up mail and messages—if there are any."

"Any special day, Jennie?"

"No, but she seldom misses a week. I imagine she'll be around in the next day or so."

"That's fine," Donald said. "I'll write down my name and where she can find me in the next day or so. If there's a change, I'll call."

He grabbed Jennie up in his arms and kissed her. When he let her down, Jennie pulled at her bun, flustered but delighted.

"Donald! At my age! You know, you always giving me...what is it? Yes...the hots."

"*Ciao*, Jennie. I hope I always do."

He bounded down the steps and walked briskly back to the Palace-International. Asleep or not, it was time to rouse Monsignor Thomas Ryan out of his slumber as well as his conspiracy and let him know that tomorrow the *Sun-Mirror* would be running the story of the American Cardinals' secret meeting in Rome.

* * *

Monsignor Ryan had barely opened his eyes when the telephone jangled him wide awake. Tom's was the only phone in the party receiving calls. When the caller turned out to be Donald Brady, the priest couldn't make up his mind whether he was relieved or furious that his carefully laid plans had gone awry. At least God had shown great good will in His choice of the man who was about to upset them. Donald Brady was a friend.

"It's Room Twenty-one in the West Wing. The Wing

locked off from the rest of the hotel. I'm just dressing, Donald. I'll call the porter to let you in," Ryan said, after exchanging pleasantries that demonstrated the respect Ryan and Brady held for each other.

Brady had merely said, "Good afternoon, Tom, this is Donald Brady. I'd like to see you as soon as possible."

"Are you in the hotel?"

"Yes."

That was all there was to it. As he dressed, Tom mused how much smarter Brady had shown himself in that brief exchange than the ordinary newspaperman. The fact that he was in Rome told his story clearly. He'd followed the party. In simply asking to see him, Brady eliminated the possibility of an eavesdropper catching the conversation or embarrassing the Monsignor if one of the Cardinals had been with him.

He splashed some water on his face and had just finished combing his hair when Donald, accompanied by a porter, arrived. Ryan assured the porter that he'd brought the right man and embraced Donald with warm Italian enthusiasm. Donald smiled as the thought crossed his mind that perhaps the Pope-maker was probably pleased to see a friendly face after a trans-Atlantic hop with a trio of America's mightiest priests.

"Don't they give you any light in this place? We might as well be meeting in the catacombs." Donald asked.

In his hurry, Ryan had turned on only the bed lamp and the bathroom light.

"Here it is," Donald said. "I've found it. The overhead switch." He flipped it.

Donald looked up at the elegant crystal chandelier. "Not much change is there, Monsignor?"

"I guess they figure Americans never use overhead lights. They're enough lamps around here to open a shop. I'll turn them on."

"Fine, Tom," Donald said, as he walked toward the open door of the bathroom, his eye fastened on the ceiling and the chandelier. He paused briefly as he caught a glimpse of its window side. A frown crossed his face.

Lights began to brighten up the room and Donald heard the shades of a window being opened. He turned on the tap of the sink and the bathtub. "Tom, do you mind coming in here a second? I think I've started a flood."

"It sounds that way," the priest said, entering the bathroom.

Donald was standing with his back to the sink. He held a finger to his lips. "*Padre*, old boy, you're bugged. Go into the room, turn off all the lamps, keep talking little nothings about my health, your health, the Rome sunshine, and I'll show you where it is. We'll leave it for now until we can get a ladder or find another way to remove it. You and I had better go outside. *Capisci?*"

* * *

The Monsignor and the newspaperman found a bench in the mini-park just outside the door of the West Wing. It contained a kiosk where they ordered coffee and a couple of pastries.

Tom Ryan sighed, "Obviously, I am never going to be a Cardinal Richelieu. Why couldn't I have thought we might be bugged?"

"Easy," said Donald, "because you really believed your flight from New York was a secret. I don't know when they found out who Max Schwartz's party really consisted of, but they lost no time in switching chandeliers and giving you one with a bowl-type to accommodate the bug and lacing it with crystal bangles."

Donald glanced at his watch. "Tom, I'm going to have to call in a story. I have most of it. Muldoon, Novik, De Cordoba—the secret flight from Newark. O'Toole's arrival from Dublin. The old man did himself proud. A grand entrance."

Ryan shook his head, "You don't miss a thing. Isn't there some way we can keep this quiet?"

"Hardly, not with your rooms bugged, when the word is already out in Vienna."

"In Vienna? How do you know that?"

"Private sources."

"You're kidding?"

"That's not my style, Ryan," Donald said coldly.

"I'm sorry, Donald," the priest said, "I didn't mean it that way. I'm a little bit shook up, that's all."

"I can understand why. Anyhow, correct me if I'm wrong. You're all going to see the Pope tomorrow and ask him his plans—whether there is any substance to the rumors of his resignation. Then it follows the lines of the conversation we had on the train a few months back; a confidential conversation whose conditions I respected."

"I never found it necessary to say 'off the record' to you, Donald."

"I realize that. Anyhow, I'm here. I have to ask you for more details—either that or make conjectures you won't like and which certainly Cardinals Muldoon and O'Toole aren't going to like. I don't believe Novik or De Cordoba really care. They're not overcome by the *Velvet Curtain* of the Vatican and anything that shreds it a little appears to amuse them. Am I right there?"

Ryan laughed, "Absolutely."

Then he fell silent for a second. "All right. The secrecy of the trip seemed logical. At least to us. We might have made it public eventually. Anyhow, appearances are deceptive. We are not barging in unannounced or unexpected."

"Obviously not," Donald smiled, "you cleared things with the Papal Nuncio first."

"Do you have the *powerhouse* bugged as well?" Ryan asked.

"No, but I have sources."

Ryan's head shook in astonishment. He was beginning to see the absurdity of all his planning and, with his humor, he could laugh, "Yes, yes, Donald, we did. The Pope, we understand, is neither pleased nor displeased. He feels it is our right to speak to him and he will give us his answer in the light of his feelings today. He has suggested that his thoughts of today may not be those he holds a month from now. This is a rapidly changing world.

"Do you have a candidate?"

"I suppose I should go 'off the record' but why? You probably have the Papal apartment bugged."

Donald laughed, "No, not bugged. But I might have a source there."

"Like the one who gave you the information about

Vienna? That intrigues me."

Donald got up, went to the kiosk, brought back two *espressi* and placed them on the table in front of the bench. "Monsignor Ryan, that source I would only be able to identify under the seal of the Confessional."

"Ho! Ho! Cardinal Waldenheim's very pretty niece! How about that?" Then, thoughtfully, "I wish Waldenheim was our candidate."

"You think that highly of him, don't you?"

"One of the great minds of the Church. But his age, his independence. A man as forthright as Waldenheim makes too many enemies. Anyhow, it's out of the question. He's eighty, ineligible even to vote in the Conclave. But there's no doubt that he would make a great Pope.

"Donald, I've gone out of my way to know Cardinal Waldenheim. I've forced myself on him, just to tap his brain. For all that bravado, that crusty exterior and apparent arrogance, he's as humble as a church mouse. He'd be upset even by the courtesy of one of those first ballot nominations accorded old Cardinals of his stature simply as symbols of the respect they've earned."

"With Cardinal Waldenheim out of the running, then, whom do we have?"

"I can't divulge names. I can only say we are considering three men of the Third World. That is where a Pope must originate in the near future. Not, perhaps, at this next Conclave, but eventually. And that, my friend, is your story."

"One thing more. Who will be the spokesman for the group?"

"By unanimous choice, Cardinal Muldoon."

"Not O'Toole?"

"He took himself out. Use it if you like. To quote O'Toole, 'His Holiness has heard enough of my Irish blarney—it's time he listened to Muldoon's Italian.'"

"It's that good?"

"Yes, and what's more, O'Toole insisted that Muldoon make a solemn promise to speak Italian."

"He's a smart one. Would have made a great newspaperman."

"Newspaperman? My foot! He would have made a great

President, a great Pope, a great anything!" Then as an afterthought, Ryan said, "He'd also make a great bore."

Then Ryan realized he'd missed a point. "Donald, let's get this straight. Are you back on the paper? I thought you'd quit and were going into television."

"That was before this story." He looked at his watch. "In about an hour, I'll be back on the paper."

"Where you belong?"

"I figure that's the way it's meant to be."

Ryan's trigger brain was working. "Fine. You've got your story. I guess you're going to make peace with the paper. You'll stay in Rome as long as we do. Right?"

Donald nodded.

"Can you arrange to meet with us tonight—say, about nine?"

"Who's us?"

"Cardinal Muldoon, for sure. How many of the others, I don't know."

"A press conference—just for me?"

"I'll specify exactly what it is when we meet."

"Sure. Why not? What else have I got to do?"

"OK. Then it's settled. Where are you staying?"

"At the Palace-International."

Ryan sighed, "I should have known."

"What are you going to do about scraping the bugs out of your room and checking the others? I don't imagine you want to call the management. They'll simply install replacements."

"No, just cause them to disappear, I guess," Ryan mused. He brightened. "De Cordoba! He can take care of them."

Donald smiled, "I loved his outfit. Would he mind telling me the name of his tailor?"

They walked back to the hotel. Monsignor Ryan entered through the side door and Donald started for the front entrance.

He changed his mind. He looked around to catch his bearings. *Stazione Termine* was a few blocks away—he could see it from where he was standing. Better to telephone New York from the public phone bank there.

He hadn't checked his own room for bugs. A dumb oversight.

Making up with Ed Muir posed no problem, not with
Donald sitting on top of a story that would land in headlines
within hours. Muir accepted the collect charges on Donald's
call without question. There was only fleeting reference to
his top reporter's flirtation with the gold of television.

Muir handled the piece himself and carefully noted
Donald's suggestions. "Under the circumstances, I suggest
we downplay the Pope's phobia about senility. Drop it in
somewhere as something perfectly natural for a man of his
age. We can get more cooperation from the Red Hats by
simply reporting the facts. In a day or so, if there's strong
follow-up, you might want to call in a shrink to do us a piece
on senility—why it affects some men, how it leaves others
untouched and, I suppose, something about the fear of it—
which seems to be the case with His Holiness."

"I get it, Donald. Fine work. I appreciate it. Now about
those television people..."

"I guess I'll write them a letter."

"Are you sure you don't want me to sock them with
something about raiding newspaper staffs? Threaten them
with dropping their listings? That would put the fear of God
in 'em."

Donald laughed, "No, thanks, Ed. I can handle my own
dirty work. When you come down to it, it was my fault. If I
want TV it's always there—those guest slots."

"Good thinking, kid. They like you and there's no reason
why you can't pick up heavier loot than you're getting. When
you planning on coming back?"

"As soon as my friends pull out, I guess. I have a funny
invitation tonight—to meet a couple of them, maybe the
whole slew, after dinner. Ryan set it up. It's puzzling. I'll
know tomorrow. OK?"

"Fine, give them my best. I'm on their side, and we'll
handle the story with taste."

Donald hung up the telephone. He picked up some Italian
and English newspapers and magazines at the newsstand.
Finally he felt fatigue. It had been a long time since the
Zenith Room. He could enjoy three, maybe four hours of
shut-eye before his meeting with Tom. The sun was

beginning to ebb and the orange and yellows of Rome were beginning to take on their sunset glow. Donald smiled. It *had* been a good day—just as he'd predicted. Only God knew what was coming this evening. He was at the front entrance of the hotel. Time enough to think of that later. Right now, Donald was beat.

* * *

Donald had seen two Presidents in shirt sleeves (one of them naked), a Supreme Court Justice and several Governors, but for all this experience at meeting men of power under informal circumstances, Donald wasn't prepared to meet four Cardinals in shirt sleeves and slacks. When he entered the reception room belonging to the suite of apartments in the West Wing, waiters were wheeling out their dinner tables.

The room—one could almost call it a hall—was lighted by three magnificent chandeliers, a large one in the center; mates, on either side. Brilliant tapestries hung on the walls and the windows were covered with rich velvet draperies. The furniture, all period, hand-carved and upholstered with intricate embroidery, stood as sturdy reminders of Rome's elegance and wealth. Donald had met this exquisite, tasteful memory of the past now and then in earlier wanderings through the Eternal City. They were fleeting moments occurring at an age when he attached little significance to things like fine furniture and tapestries.

Then Donald saw little difference between a Louis XIV bed and a backpack. Now his tastes had grown more sophisticated and he was able to marvel at the room's magnificence. It was like taking a step back into time. And here were his hosts, Princes of the Church, completely at home in their opulent surroundings, as though they had been born to the purple.

How curious were the tricks of fate. Each of the Cardinals had earned this opportunity to appreciate an elegant lifestyle through hard work, determination, dedication and some luck. All had come from the humblest beginnings. None enjoyed the advantages that had been his as a boy—

and only De Cordoba, who was considered more than a Cardinal, a meteor really, had tasted the joys of success and acceptance by his peers before reaching forty.

Before introducing him, Tom explained, "We regretted not being able to invite you to dinner. We ordered a buffet spread for you. I doubt that you've done much eating today."

"Truthfully, I haven't," Donald said, glancing at the buffet spread which looked more like a banquet. A silver bucket contained chilled wine and a most inviting pitcher, obviously containing a batch of freshly mixed martinis.

De Cordoba walked across the huge, high-ceilinged room on a carpet that felt six inches thick, extended his hand, saying, "I'm De Cordoba. May I offer you a martini?"

"You may, Your Eminence. I just got out of bed. I can use it. It's been a hectic day."

"Day and a half, young man," Cardinal O'Toole's ragged voice rang out from an upholstered chair with a back high enough to accommodate his stature. "Neat trick—that. Chasing us down. I've met you, haven't I?"

Donald bowed from the waist. He felt awkward. He wasn't about to kneel and kiss the Cardinals' rings. This was business. When De Cordoba put a martini in his hand, he realized that protocol wasn't expected.

Answering O'Toole, Donald said, "Several times, Your Eminence. In Boston and New York. I wrote a three part series on you—five years ago."

Cardinal Novik, in his photographs, appeared to be a man in a perpetual state of anxiety. Photographers, he'd heard, had long given up trying to produce a smile in Novik's stern countenance. "It doesn't work. He looks like a wax mummy. The way he is comes out fine—a stern, thoughtful guy, real intellectual."

Novik enjoyed enormous respect among the clergy and the press. His Chicago diocese might have preferred a more colorful and less austere leader, but they knew they were getting the best of it. Novik's devotion to his flock was intense; his clout in City Hall, enormous, and his humanity touched everyone who met him. Novik was widely admired by churchmen of other faiths as a theologian with a brilliant grasp of modern problems. Novik was a tireless worker in behalf of ecumenism. He'd stirred controversy by agreeing with O'Toole that the Church eventually would deal more realistically with the problems of birth control, priestly celibacy and the right of women to take Holy Orders.

In Chicago, very much a man's town, his views were seen as expressions intended to offset the bad taste left by his predecessor. The late Cardinal Sefner's dogmatic interpretation of Canon Law was acceptable to the city's old-fashioned Catholics, but his reactionary social attitudes had alienated the poor, minorities and liberals left over from the Roosevelt and Truman era.

Seeing him relaxing, looking amiable and friendly, startled Donald. It was his first meeting with Novik and there hadn't been time to visualize what sort of man he would meet.

Novik smiled when Donald bowed in his direction, "Your Eminence, this is an honor."

"Well, it's an honor for us, too," the Chicago prelate responded. "Hell, we were bound to get caught—sneaking around like thieves in the night. But we had to. There would have been terrific pressure on us not to come. I don't know from whom. But count on it, sir, there would have been heat. Heavy heat. So if someone had to catch us, I go along with Tom Ryan, we were lucky you were the newspaperman."

"Thank you, Your Eminence." One more and he guessed he could sit down. To his surprise, Muldoon got up and walked toward him, grasping both of Donald's hands in his. "Did your Uncle Thaddeus ever tell you anything about me?"

"No, Your Eminence. Never."

Muldoon turned to his colleagues, "There you have it. The whole story of my life. 'Granite Face' of the *powerhouse*. His uncle knows more unprintable stories about me than any New York newspaperman alive. You'd think he'd tell his own kin, so at least one of them would realize that I'm not the terror they write about."

Donald laughed, "I'm sure you're not, Your Emminence. Maybe you should authorize Thad to break his silence. You know he's not the type to gossip."

"But he might—with permission?" Cardinal Muldoon asked.

"I think so."

"Fine," Muldoon answered. "I'll get around to that. Now you sit down and be comfortable. Go ahead and enjoy your supper. Tom will do the talking. He speaks for all of us."

Donald turned to Ryan. He pointed toward the chandeliers.

De Cordoba slapped his knee and laughed, "It's all right, Donald. May I call you Donald?"

"Of course, Your Eminence."

"I prefer being called Juan."

"Thank you, Your . . . thank you, Juan."

"I went over everything," De Cordoba said. "Fortunately I brought a bug detector gadget with me. It seems the Cardinals weren't considered worth bugging. Our curious friends—or enemies—evidently don't think very highly of the men in scarlet. Sometimes I agree. Anyhow, we are perfectly safe in this room. Go ahead, Tom, with our proposal."

Tom began, "Donald, first, may we assume that you have rejoined the *Sun-Mirror*?"

"Yes, I telephoned the story exactly as we discussed it this afternoon. No more—no less. I did mention our meeting this evening, saying I had no idea of its implication. I'm sure Your Eminences will appreciate that I asked the managing editor—and he agreed—to sort of throw away—what we call 'write around'—His Holiness' complex about senility. It is, from all we of the press can gather, the motivating factor in his ambivalance about continuing in the Papacy. When it becomes a major topic, and I imagine that won't occur until there is something definite about his resignation, we will use medical terms and psychiatrists to describe the phenomenon. It is common enough and, like many important people who are opening up today about their private problems, those afflicting His Holiness may help other men to identify with him."

"Well put, very well put," O'Toole thundered. "We appreciate your tact."

Donald was beginning to wonder if all this cordiality was a prelude to an invitation to stand for Pope himself. Nothing stood in his way except thousands of years of tradition. Any Catholic male was eligible for the Papacy, just as any

American kid could grow up and become President. All he needed were the votes.

Monsignor Ryan intruded on Donald's fantasy, "We wonder if we could borrow you from the paper for a few weeks..."

"Borrow me? How do you mean?"

"We shall be leaving directly after our audience tomorrow—the Cardinals will be returning to their cities; De Cordoba by way of Mexico City where he will visit his family, and I will be going on to South America for a time."

"But..."

"May I finish, Donald? It will be clearer if you see our proposal in its totality."

"When I say 'borrow you' I mean exactly that. You would be lent to the Archdiocese of New York to cover Rome for us—to keep us alert to things we should know, the comings and goings of various Cardinals or their representatives, to be on top of Vatican negotiations with the Iron Curtain countries. We want to know the rumors, the gossip; yes, all the absurd trivia that is part and parcel of Rome. We are amateurs at this business of Vatican intrigue. You know that—you caught us—well, you caught us with our cassocks down. No trouble at all. A man like you could be of great service to our hopes. That's about it. You simply would work for us for a short time."

Donald realized the Cardinals were making a well-considered and clever proposal. A newspaperman, even one of lesser skill, could perform a valuable service by covering the Rome scene for the American Catholic hierarchy in the guise of a reporter. It smacked of C.I.A., of course. Donald didn't like that. But there was an answer.

"Your Eminences," he said very slowly, "I am flattered. I appreciate your confidence in me. I don't know how far you have gone into this as a situation which might involve me in a conflict of interests. I shouldn't appreciate that. On the other hand, it is not without precedent for a newspaperman to be, as you say, 'borrowed', or to take a leave of absence to accept a job he feels a responsibility toward. Speechwriting, for instance, for a political candidate.

"In that sense, yes, I can accept if the newspaper approves.

But I'd feel like a fool being here and having to pass up a legitimate story. I fear that would place me in an embarrassing half-world of conflict of interest. I would simply have to file."

Cardinal Novik spoke up, "Don't you think, Donald, that a conflict of interest is a problem you could determine on a story to story basis? We respect your judgment. Your paper certainly would. I doubt that you would rush into print with an unsupported rumor, gossip without foundation in the strict newspaper sense. Yet that is the sort of information we would want—material you couldn't ethically print without substantiation, the rumors you cannot confirm."

"Your Eminence, I don't doubt my own capacity for separating gossip and a news story. I just want to be sure that you understand it, that the paper realizes it, and that my colleagues will if my work on your behalf becomes known."

"And you can be damned sure it will in Rome," O'Toole volunteered.

"Exactly," Donald continued. "But there would be my files to back me up. You can't argue with what has been printed." He took a second to put a morsel of food in his mouth.

De Cordoba laughed, "We offer you supper, then we don't give you time to eat it."

"That's all right, Juan, I may as well finish. If these conditions are understood by us and the *Sun-Mirror*, my own experience will protect my reputation. Let me assure you, I intend to protect it carefully. Still, I feel an obligation to accept your offer. It is, if you will excuse the trite expression, my duty."

"I hoped you'd see it that way," Muldoon beamed.

"Of course, Your Eminence, *you'll* have to obtain the permission of the paper."

Muldoon looked around for someone else to continue. It didn't work. All eyes were on him, "Well, Donald, to be perfectly candid, we've already done that."

Donald's sandwich stopped in mid-air, "You've already talked to Ed Muir?"

"Heaven forbid," Muldoon answered. "I wouldn't dare. He'd crucify me. You don't cross swords with a man like Ed

97

Muir when you're only a Cardinal. No, we talked to Mrs. Hamilton."

"The old lady?"

"Yes," Muldoon answered, "*the old lady*. Your publisher."

"And she agreed?"

"Yes. Under certain conditions."

"Yes?"

Muldoon smiled, "That we say nothing to Ed for forty-eight hours. She wants time to send him a memo and head for California to visit her sister."

Donald leaned back his head and roared. "Cardinal, I love you. I love everybody. That's the damned... that's the darndest news I've heard in years. So the old lady is scared of Ed Muir, too!"

Then he poured himself a glass of wine. "You know even Uncle Thad's called him the greatest. That's rare. If he gives someone a 'good' that's like being knighted."

"I agree," Muldoon said. "We need more Ed Muirs and more Bradys—like Thaddeus and you. Now, please, Donald, get at your supper. We need our rest and we have some praying to do. We could get kicked out of the Vatican tomorrow for all we know."

"Maybe excommunicated," thundered O'Toole, rising to his feet to leave.

"Good night, Donald. You and Tom enjoy yourselves. Forget the job. You have plenty of time to talk it over tomorrow while we're across the Tiber in the hot seat."

The Cardinals' handshakes were warm; eventually the two friends were alone.

"You know, Tom, I think you're a son-of-a-bitch, and if you weren't as wily as Richelieu this morning, you certainly sharpened your wits this afternoon. How come?"

"Obvious, dear boy. Obvious. When in Rome, et cetera... and just behave like the Romans. Think of the centuries of deviousness we have to catch up on."

98

PART III

Rome—The Red Brigades

Alexander Cardinal Novik rose early. He showered and shaved in his careful, precise way that he had clocked decades ago as requiring exactly fifteen minutes. The years had not altered Novik's habits. Each day was a full one and in every twenty-four hours there had to exist some challenge to test the priest's right to his Holy Orders. As he clothed his lean, muscled body and combed the thick gray hair, Novik prayed for God's grace to meet the day's test head on. To succeed meant God's Will had been done; to fail implied honorable human shortcomings.

Novik noticed that the morning papers had been slipped under his door, the *Rome Daily American* and *Il Messaggero*. He picked them up, curious as to what they'd have to say about yesterday's audience of the American Cardinals with the Pope. There could be very little information available at this point—but plenty of speculation. Novik was sure of that.

For him, the time spent with Morelli had been rewarding—especially in view of his misgivings about the practicality of the American initiative rather than its propriety. From the very beginning, Novik approved confrontation between the American Church and the Italian power brokers. "Confrontation" wasn't exactly the word. A better description would be "separation" of the American Cardinals from the Italian wing of the College of Cardinals. For too many years the American clergy, Novik felt, had served as rubber stamps of the Vatican Curia.

William Muldoon's decision, to say nothing of his

aggressiveness, in fielding an American-approved candidate in the next Papal election, regardless of the circumstances, the present Pope's death or his long-rumored resignation, represented to Novik a progressive and most desirable step. It mollified some of Novik's pent-up frustration with Vatican hauteur. He would have originated it himself, but as all American Cardinals realized, a Red Hat outside the New York diocese carried the international clout of the mayor of a small town in the hills of Mississippi. The New York diocese was the cornerstone of the American Church, a bulwark of conservatism, the last place one would expect such imagination to blossom.

Novik was aware, as were some others, that Muldoon was vastly underestimated. He'd served so long and so well in a variety of positions that his capacities were taken for granted. Being a modest man made it simple for Muldoon to stand in the shadow of Hellman. He was more interested in his work than ambition. There were many tight spots Hellman got himself into because of his arrogance and thoughtlessness. Muldoon invariably took the heat off his superior. Novik recalled one of Hellman's characteristically imprudent Birch Society remarks about "welfare chiselers" in addressing a group of black Catholics who were celebrating the appointment of a black Bishop to Harlem.

Quietly and without fanfare, Muldoon, who had served in an extraordinary number of New York parishes, many in ghetto areas, had gone from church to church, saying Sunday Masses for the next several weeks. Displaying rare tact for an Auxiliary Bishop, he made no attempt to disrupt the regular Mass schedule or to assume the pulpit in place of the assigned preacher. Instead, he turned to the congregation just before the Last Gospel and, speaking informally, gave a different reading of Cardinal Hellman's tactless slur.

Yesterday the Pope had signaled out Muldoon for special attention, listening carefully to everything he said, interrupting only to ask cogent questions. Clearly, Muldoon held the Pope's respect. His Holiness, however, had warned the Americans that their mission could not expect a cordial reception from the Italian wing of the College of Cardinals.

"Your visit today is going to be misinterpreted," he said. "I see it as a logical desire to seek clarification of a situation that requires explanation. You are my brothers in the administration of the Holy Roman Catholic Universal Church and I have no special privilege that entitles me to keep you in the dark. Your Italian colleagues should not consider themselves a privileged group, entitled to dominate Conclaves and name Popes pleasing to the special interests of the Curia. We know now that Paul VI would have resigned had he been able to achieve changes he sought in reforming the Church's governing structure and, in particular, the method of electing the Pope. Failing to accomplish these, John reigned longer than his health and judiciousness warranted. I bear these things in mind as I pray for guidance.

"You, my brothers, are going to be the innocents, the vulnerable Servants of the Church who will be plucked at and seized by the eagles who fly around the Dome of Saint Peter's waiting for this old priest to make his decision."

Then Morelli paused. "You understand that I use eagles in a figurative sense," he grinned. "There is another bird given to hovering, over tired flesh, is there not?"

As Novik glanced at the first page of *Il Messaggero* it was clear that the eagles and/or vultures had wasted little time. Donald Brady's story had been picked up and used selectively. Even with deletions it came across as a fair, clean-cut account of the American Cardinals' visit to the Vatican.

In bolder type, also on the first page, Novik read the banner: *Vatican Views American Cardinals' Visit With Dismay*. The "Vatican" turned out to be an unidentified source, high in Papal inner circles, a layman who had been asked by the paper to analyze the moves of the American Cardinals.

The piece read: "A wide range of problems facing the Universal Church has brought the American Cardinals sharply into focus as a body whose collective influence will be felt for the first time in history in the next Papal election.

"In yesterday's visit of three major American churchmen, Cardinals Muldoon, Novik and De Cordoba of New York, Chicago and Los Angeles respectively, they have created a situation in Rome which some Italian Princes of the Church last night chose to describe as outrageous.

"They have displayed shocking disrespect for the Papal

101

Throne and the person of His Holiness in demanding to know his intentions before he has chosen to notify the world whether there is substance to repeated rumors that he intends to resign. The meeting was believed to have been welcomed enthusiastically by ecumenically-minded Cardinals of England, Australia and Cardinals of the Third World who point out that in the year two thousand, fully seventy percent of the globe's practicing Catholics will be the inhabitants of Africa and long-neglected South America.

"Curia officers, among them Cardinals Carlo Torriani, Secretary of State, and Antonio Cardinal Nascimbene, have frequently spoken privately of the Americans' naiveté, recalling that in 1908 America was looked upon by the Vatican as a 'missionary country.' Her church leaders, in their opinion, are today no more qualified to debate in Papal affairs than they were then."

Alex Novik had never been a hair-shirt priest. He felt that life dealt man enough blows in the three score years and ten he was supposed to survive and that a priest's duty lay in helping him discover a sense of morality that would give value and importance to his life. To his way of thinking, the sweat that poured from a working man's brow composed a more glowing tribute to the Creator than thoughtless repetitions of the prayers of the Rosary.

Rome bothered him. He deplored the pomp and pageantry of the ceremonies held at the Vatican. He disliked the imperial Papacy. Novik did not envy colleagues like Muldoon or young De Cordoba who had enjoyed the advantages of life as "Roman seminarians." He had not visited Rome until he was anointed a Bishop shortly after World War II. The hauteur, the studied posture and the aristocratic authoritarian manner of Pope Pius XII offended his sense of humanity. Novik summed up his feelings about the Eternal City as "Vatican Comic Opera."

"None of it is real," Novik complained. "They're all running around in fancy costumes trading in jobs and privileges and have lost touch with the common man." He was shocked to find that priests seldom ventured into the homes of their parishioners and that anyone with a problem had to make an appointment with a pastor's housekeeper or curate.

Novik had come from a working class family which migrated from Poland shortly before World War I. They settled in Pennsylvania where his father worked as a coal miner. The large Novik family had pooled their resources to send Alexander Novik, Sr., his wife, Magda, and their son to America in the expectation that eventually they would repay the money and help the others to travel to the New World.

It had not happened and the years had not evaporated the coldness that grew between the Noviks in America and the Noviks in Poland. Cardinal Novik visited his family there many times. His sister, Marta, who had been left behind, older by three years, refused to see him. However, her children, two nephews and two nieces, brought their babies to meet him when he visited Poland as part of a *Silver Jubilee* tour given to him by his parishioners. Shortly afterward, he was named a Cardinal and appointed to the major diocese of Chicago.

Now the children were grown but his sister still bore the grudge of what she called "betrayal." Yet the younger Noviks ignored her unreasonable hatred. They doted on their famous uncle and hoped that one day he could arrange for their migration to America. Just last year the birth of twins to one of the nieces had raised the Cardinal's total of grand nephews and nieces to eight.

On his trips to Poland and Rome Novik had pressed the case of moving his relatives to America, but he met little sympathy from either the Vatican authorities or the Polish church leaders who reminded him of the awkward position in which he placed them.

"My dear Cardinal," said a Monsignor who consented to consider his case at length in a long conversation held in Warsaw only last year, "we are in a most delicate position. You know where the Church stands in Poland. It survives and enjoys an independence unknown in other Communist countries. We continue to press for reconciliation between the Church and the Government. Some say the Government needs the Church more than the Church needs the Government. On the other hand, there are those who believe that if the Government were to accept legalization of the status of the Church, it would dissolve Communism as a political force in Poland. The Church is still regarded as the

103

opposition. We are trying to overcome that resistance. As I said, the Church survives. We are stronger here than in any nation on the continent. We hope someday to build new churches without interference; moreover, we have the faithful to fill them.

"How would it look, dear Cardinal Novik, if we were to press the Government to permit the migration of a large family to America to become the wards of a prominent Catholic prelate? It would be considered an insult, an outrage. It would suggest that Polish Catholics were eager to leave their homeland."

"Well, aren't they?"

"You are being facetious, Cardinal Novik."

"Of course, I don't mean all. You know exactly what I mean. Poles are no different from other nationalities behind the Iron Curtain. That they have persisted in their faith is to their credit, a manifestation of the strength of the Polish character. You can't tell me that on the one hand they loathe the Communist Government, but resist opportunities to leave Poland because they are permitted to enjoy a spiritual life within the Church. If that were true, then we ought to start canonization proceedings for every Pole who attends Mass on Sunday."

"I am afraid you see only your point of view," the Monsignor sighed.

"I'm afraid I do. I always have. My point of view is simple. I think of people as individuals, not collectives serving either a political philosophy or a religious belief."

The Monsignor reverted to the arrogance Novik had become accustomed to in dealing with the Polish hierarchy. "I am afraid your request cannot be granted. That is all there is to it. The Noviks must remain—if for no other reason than your position." He paused to make sure the words had sunk in.

Cardinal Novik shrugged his shoulders. "I wonder how a man like you ever became a Monsignor."

The prelate took the blade calmly. "In the same manner you became a Cardinal. By hard wor . . ."

"Yes . . . yes. I know that line. I worked hard, but work had nothing to do with my being appointed Cardinal. I was the only man around and available at the time. I never considered hard work as anything but my duty whether I lived in a drafty parish house or dwelt in a drafty Cardinal's mansion. People were my business. They still are. I'm afraid you have not seen the last of me."

Novik recalled that untidy, disagreeable meeting this morning as he rushed through his ablutions to get to the Church of Santa Cecilia in Trastevere to say Mass and be back in time to depart for the airport at noon. He had not seen his young friend, Stefan Washinski, in two years. Stefan was one of the lucky ones, a youth who had sneaked out of Poland, made his way to Rome, endured the indignities of being a displaced person for several years while he studied for the priesthood and now enjoyed Italian citizenship. In his homeland he was *persona non grata*, and in Rome he was forbidden to speak out about the snail's pace of the hoped-for reconciliation of Church and Government.

Privately he complained about inept Vatican diplomats who visited Poland with a list of demands they knew the Communists could not possibly meet and maintain their authority. "It's better to accept the use of a town hall for Sunday Mass than to insist on building a church first," Washinski complained. "But once the Vatican decides an opportunity exists to increase its church property, no one seems to care how many souls are lost. Didn't the Irish survive by hearing Mass out in the fields, hidden by trees and foliage? They managed without Churches and their faith eventually became the protector of their independence. It could happen in Poland if the Church diplomats would only stay home."

No one in Rome knew quite what to do with the outspoken Washinski except to make sure that his views were given minimal attention by the press. His sermons were carefully monitored by Vatican spies—or at least they had been until talk of Morelli's possible resignation had surfaced.

Washinski wrote Cardinal Novik that among the "displaced priests" there was new hope for more freedom of expression providing "Morelli succeeds in naming a successor who can enforce policies he's initiated but lacks the vigor to carry out. Morelli, I believe, sees his resignation as emancipating the Church from the tradition of electing old Popes who too quickly find it easier to get along with the Curia bureaucracy than overhaul it—or throw the whole medieval machinery out entirely."

Novik found some truth in Stefan's interpretation of the Holy Father's action in the two hours the American Cardinals had spent with him yesterday. According to *L'Osservatore Romano* the audience had lasted the traditional forty minutes, a white lie intended to diminish the importance of the conference. This was the sort of evasion that drove Novik up a wall.

Of the Popes Novik had served, Morelli came closest to his ideal. He was frank, straightforward and lapsed into the informal "I" to indicate that what he was saying was confidential. There were no other Vatican officials present when they knelt and kissed his ring, feeling awkward without their Cardinals' robes. But Morelli put them at ease. "You are welcome, pilgrims. I know your mission and there is no sense in exchanging pleasantries before we discuss it."

He looked down at his chest. "I am so accustomed to having a microphone here," he pointed to his plain cross, "that I sometimes miss it. But we need not worry. You can be sure there's a microphone somewhere in this room picking up our conversation." Then, raising his voice, "Good morning Cardinal X or whoever is on duty. I give you my blessings and hopes for a pleasant day."

The Pope's eyes glistened with mirth and in Novik's eyes he seemed to suddenly grow from a spare man with fine features, small hands and feet, to a power ten feet tall. He admired Morelli's past and he certainly was impressed with his present activities. The Pope could be a skilled politician when it suited him but like most Popes, the arbitrary positions of the Curia infuriated him.

Morelli possessed a temper and a will of his own. He'd shown it in handling the Los Angeles situation by appointing De Cordoba to succeed the hopeless Archbishop Haynes. The impetuousness of the Pope's action shocked America's Church leaders, particularly Cardinal Hellman who took it as a personal reflection on his judgment—exactly as Morelli intended.

However, the affair De Cordoba-Haynes-Hellman was a minor victory. More often than not, Morelli wearied of the fight, backed down and let the Curia stumble along in its slapdash, antiquated ways, debating endlessly on minor matters of theology and ignoring the real problems of the Church—her loss of millions of the faithful.

In substance, Morelli told the Americans he felt heartened by their interest in the future of the Papacy. "It would not be proper for us to interfere in the future. It would not be proper for us to object to your proposing and supporting a candidate for the seat I now occupy whoever he is or whatever his nationality. The Papacy has been a flexible influence in the world. We seem to forget that. We believe tradition begins where history ends. There have been old Popes and young Popes, royal Popes and peasant Popes. That is the wonder of our Church. We bless your efforts to contribute to the future of the Church. Work diligently and faithfully at the task. Invoke the Holy Spirit. Ask for wisdom. We can never be wise enough—not one of us. We are only men—fragile human beings with normal failings that even the most exalted worldly positions cannot conceal."

Speaking informally, he said, "I cannot say *when* I will resign or even that I *will* resign. I need more wisdom than I now possess to make that decision. But I can say that I believe a Pope should resign and if it is I who sets the precedent, be assured I will have been guided toward that step by prayer and by the Holy Spirit. Younger men should not be deprived of the opportunity to lead the Church in future centuries simply because of a belief that a Pope must reign for his lifetime. I cannot foresee limitations being imposed on the Pope's years of service, but I can see common sense prevailing, particularly in view of fairly recent examples of moribund years when the Church suffered serious damage to its prestige and growth because of a reigning Pope's incapacity. This will not happen while I dwell in this house."

Morelli rose. He waved aside the ceremony of kissing his ring. After shaking hands with each of the four Cardinals, he returned to the first, Cardinal O'Toole, and blessed each man individually.

Novik was pleased. It had been a most satisfying experience. Moreover he was impressed with Muldoon's deftness as spokesman for the Americans. There was an elegant ring to his Italian and Novik felt that somewhere Muldoon had found the quality of authority that had been missing from his mission as America's foremost Cardinal.

He glanced at his watch as he approached Santa Cecelia. He was a minute or two late. Not that it mattered. Novik would say Mass at a side altar, Washinski would serve. Afterward they would enjoy a quick breakfast at the *espresso* bar nearby.

Washinski was standing on the steps as Novik arrived and raced down to meet him. The men embraced and went inside where Mass was celebrated.

Afterward when they entered the small room in the back of the *espresso* bar which contained only one table, Novik was surprised to see it occupied by a blond youth, obviously a German. It was a face he had seen somewhere. He looked at Stefan, saying in Polish, "I assumed we were having breakfast alone."

Speaking in English, "There's been a little change, Your Eminence. This is Hans. He has something to tell you."

Novik looked from face to face. He liked neither the expression he found on Stefan's—worry—nor that of the German—arrogance.

"Does our guest, Hans, have a last name?"

The German, who had stood up, clicked his heels and bowed, "No, Your Eminence. Not at the moment. Hans is the name I use."

Novik spoke in Polish, "The Red Brigades?"

The German smiled and answered in Polish, "Yes, Your Eminence. It is. I assume you realize there are many Red Brigades."

"I understand." Novik sat down. "What is your business, young man? I haven't much time. I am leaving for America in less than two hours."

Stefan left the youth and the Cardinal alone to fetch coffee from the bar.

"Your Eminence, who I am or what organization I represent is of no consequence. I am a hireling. At the

108

moment I represent some highly placed people in Italy who are curious about your meeting with His Holiness yesterday."

"I am not at liberty to discuss that."

Stefan returned with the coffee. "Washinski, did you bring me here to be questioned by this . . . by this mercenary? If so, I am surprised. Horrified, really," Novik fairly shouted.

The flustered young priest remained silent.

The German pressed his hand against his breast pocket. Silently he slid his fingers around the outline of a revolver. "I am afraid *Padre* Washinski had no choice. Nor do you, Your Eminence. You will please listen to my message . . ."

At Ciampino airport after Donald had said good-bye to Cardinals O'Toole, Muldoon, De Cordoba and Novik and Monsignor Tom Ryan, he was just going out the door to the landing steps when he felt a tap on his shoulder. It was Cardinal Muldoon.

"This is quite important, Donald. I would like to know as soon as you can find out where Cardinal Novik celebrated Mass this morning. Most particularly, with whom he spoke."

"Any special reason?"

Muldoon's expression was serious. "I hope not. Communicate with me directly—by telephone. Monsignor Ryan, I imagine, will be traveling quite a bit for the next weeks."

"I'll be in touch, Your Eminence."

"Thank you, Donald."

He waited at the gate until the plane took off while he pondered the significance of Muldoon's request.

There seemed so many questions. So few answers.

* * *

Angela Nero arrived at the Palace-International as Donald was checking out. He'd decided to move to the Grand-Plaza on the Corso, close to the Piazza di Spagna, a twenty minute walk across the Tiber to the Vatican and only

109

five minutes away from *Stampa Estera*, the Foreign Press Club, whose conveniences and contacts with other journalists would be useful.

Angela Nero turned out to be a pretty blonde, fairly tall for an Italian girl. She'd just been to the hairdresser's, her dress looked as though it had been picked fresh from the rack and there was no doubt that her shoes were brand new. Donald wondered if he should feel flattered or surprised that a young newspaperwoman would go to such pains to make an impression on him.

If there was deviousness behind her appearance in a totally new ensemble, there was none in Angela's warm smile and voice as she walked to where he stood at the desk writing down the places where he could be reached—the Foreign Press Club and the Grand-Plaza.

"I'm Angela Nero," she said, extending her hand in that forthright fashion of European women. "Congratulations, Mr. Brady."

"Thank you, Angela." He liked the touch of her hand and it set off a reaction of interest in the girl as he took in the rest of her. Lovely legs. Not too common in Rome. Blonde? Her mother was Sicilian and obviously Angela helped out nature a bit. Her figure was trim; the new dress, decolleté, made it clear that her firm, plump breasts were her own and their large inviting nipples showed through the filmy material.

Just as Donald was organizing himself to solve one set of problems, another riddle was thrust at him. Angela Nero had thrown him off all balance. Donald didn't know why. Only that she had. He hadn't expected a dog, but Angela was not his picture of an Italian newspaperwoman. Too pretty for one thing. But that was the least of it.

Professionals knew better than to put on their Sunday best when meeting one of their colleagues and Donald had been around long enough to know that this held true of newspapering from Hamburg to Hong Kong. From his experience in Italy where professional women went to great pains to dress well, Angela's fresh finery had to mean she owned little else. Donald recalled the critical look in the eyes of Hand-Job Jennie at the mention of Angela's name.

If Angela suspected his doubts, she certainly didn't show them as she blithely plunged on.

110

"Your story really threw the boys at the Press Club into a tizzy when it began bouncing back from New York. It's the first time in years that a fat exclusive has come out of this town. How did you do it?"

Donald laughed, "I did very little. The Cardinals were the smart guys. They came, they saw the Pope, they went. I happened to latch onto the story in New York."

"Did the Pope tell them when he was going to quit? Oops, sorry. I shouldn't ask you that, should I?"

"Why not? Every question's worth a try. To answer, I have to tell the truth. I don't know. The Cardinals did talk to me before they went to the Vatican, but they answered no questions afterward." Donald paused and looked at her curiously, "But I have a question for you."

"Straight on. Fire away," she smiled.

Her English finishing school command of the language was flawless. "What makes you so sure that Morelli's going to quit?"

She shrugged her shoulders. "It's taken for granted in Rome. We've been on this story a long time, you know."

"So I gather."

"It's just a question of when. He has to move soon or louse up Holy Week."

Donald laughed, "I get it. You go by the liturgical calendar."

"Of course. No Pope in modern times has ever resigned and this one certainly isn't going to make more waves by jumping the ship at a time when a Conclave would interfere in a big Feast."

"Like Easter?"

"Of course."

Donald sighed, "Well I admit that I hadn't considered that or any of the angles which you, to quote your words, 'take for granted.' Religion isn't my usual beat. I just stumbled onto this one story . . ."

"And?"

"And what?"

"Are you checking out to go home or checking out to move somewhere else?"

Donald realized she knew damned well he was moving to the Corso hotel, but he'd have to judge the roundabout question later. "I'm switching to the Grand-Plaza. Now that I'm here, I figure I might as well hang around Rome for a while. I was going on vacation when I picked up this lead."

"Good, then I'll be seeing you. Funny we never met. I know we've been in Rome at the same time before, but I guess I was in school. I remember meeting your uncle when I was very young."

"He sends you his very best regards."

Donald noticed the bellboy standing impatiently beside his one piece of luggage waiting for instructions. Donald pointed him out to Angela, "We're holding up the help. How about driving over to the Grand-Plaza and having lunch with me?"

"Sure, why not? Do you have a car?"

"No, how about you?"

"Not with me."

"We'll use a cab. I'll rent a car when I get settled. All I've seen so far in Rome has been this hotel."

*   *   *

Because their luncheon started late, it was easy to stretch their time together through the afternoon and finally to the evening when Donald decided to rent a car and drive to the hills for dinner at Frascatti.

Angela pointed out that it was too cool to dine outside at one of the numerous restaurants whose tables were perched on the edge of the mountain looking down at the beautiful valleys where Frascatti's famed vineyards offered a feast for the eye.

Donald countered with, "No matter. Just breathing fresh air would be a novelty to me."

So they headed for the hills, ate a slow, leisurely dinner by candlelight and Donald wasn't sure whether Angela intended revealing as much as she did about herself or had been deliberately frank to impress him.

It had been quite an evening, however, and Donald might have stretched it into a long night of lovemaking. He was eager and so was Angela, but Donald hadn't let it happen and all the reasons bothered him.

112

About midnight they returned to the garage where they'd rented the car. One of the youths on night duty drove Donald back to the Grand-Plaza and then took off for Trastevere. Donald didn't catch Angela's address. She'd already told him that since she had no telephone, she would call him in the morning.

"Not too early," she promised. "You look tired. Get as much rest as you can." She leaned over and put her lips to his. It was a long, wet, hungry kiss and might have lasted longer had they not been aware of the motor running and the youth behind the wheel.

It took a long hot bath before Donald realized how tired he was—and how horny. Had he been a damned fool in passing up Angela tonight? That was never how it went in the pre-Erika days when Donald subscribed to the principle of the Duke of Wellington's advice as they went into a lavatory, "Never pass up one of these. You never know when you're going to meet one again." The same rule applied to a piece of tail.

But these were different days. He felt Erika would call tonight or tomorrow morning and he knew he couldn't lie if she asked him—and Erika certainly would—with whom he was sleeping. Maybe in a couple of days, yes, he could get away with it. But not tonight.

Moreover, for all that frankness Angela pressed so hard to get across to him, she seemed to be using it to gain his confidence extremely fast. Or was he the one who'd been playing games? Aside from themselves, the only one topic of interest they shared was the expectation that the Pope would resign and how the forces in the College of Cardinals would be aligned when the Conclave to elect Morelli's successor was convened.

Donald was disinclined to play the cat and mouse game. He disliked relationships that suffered the strain of being guarded, but he told himself that this was Rome where everyone appeared to be in business for himself and you worked in a *quid pro quo* world or lumped it. Angela was not going to give away for a couple of free meals and a drive to the country knowledge that she could sell on the floor of *Stampa Estera* to the highest bidder.

Donald let that thought ramble around a bit before he cleared up its ambiguities in his mind. Donald hadn't talked to another newspaperman since his arrival. And, damn it, he hadn't kissed another woman—except Hand-Job Jennie—since he'd kissed Erika good-bye on Saint Patrick's Day, promising to be back within hours. The thought made him shudder. So did the realization that he was paying entirely too much attention to the tantalizing puzzle of a clever blonde Italian sexpot whose body and knowledge were quite obviously open for bids.

She'd cleared up the mystery of the new clothes in what would have been called the old "hard luck story" if there had not been the close relationship between her grandmother and his uncle. Moreover, Thaddeus knew Angela as a child and she'd been on his Christmas card list for years. From time to time he'd answered her requests for information on stories she was working on. This gave Angela an edge in dealing with Donald. He ranked, like it or not, as a "family friend."

Several years ago when Angela was nineteen and given her first assignments on *Oggi*, an important national magazine. According to Angela, she'd sacrificed a future there for a crack at representing an English newspaper chain. She wanted to work in English and hopefully impress one of the American news magazines or an American paper of the caliber of the *New York Times* or the *Washington Post*.

Nothing worked out as it was supposed to in Angela's fantasies. The British syndicate dropped Hand, saying it was retrenching, yet Donald knew the representation was taken over by an American who represented one of the broadcasting networks. He did find out that she was twenty-three, younger than he had imagined, that she sometimes lived in Trastevere "with some other young people" and that she was a familiar figure around *Stampa Estera* where some correspondents paid for her news tips.

"But," she complained, "they never let me do a story on my own. Or handle their assingments when they're on vacation. Sometimes I think I'm just a toy they play around with. God knows they sure use my stuff. It almost always checks out."

By pressing a bit here and a bit there, Donald decided that his Rome colleagues really didn't trust Angela—not because of herself—but her associations—the "young people" she lived with. If they were the invisible sources of her stories, it would be folly for a newspaperman to repose complete confidence in the girl. That was something he'd look into if he decided to break down and tell her why he was in Rome.

It was clear that Angela was out to impress him. And she was doing a very good job. Angela proceeded to give him a blow-by-blow of the in-fighting at the Vatican that he presumed was common knowledge around town but had failed to hit the American press where news of the Papacy came out exactly as it was issued from the Vatican Information Office.

There was little reason for it to be otherwise. Even to Catholics, the Pope was a remote and awesome figure and they were content with the image they were used to. Vatican gossip was not salable until some huge event swept the headlines—the death agony of Pope John XXIII and now the rumors of Morelli's resignation.

But to Angela as well as Rome's more secure correspondents, the Pope and the Vatican provided a constant stream of material; some gained attention in Sunday editions of their papers; the bulk of it, gossip and tidbits, was filed away in the memory banks of some reporters and the files of others to be extracted at the proper time.

"You know," she said as she put her hand over the glass when the waiter started to refill it, "the American press oversimplifies Morelli's thinking. They keep referring to his phobia about advanced senility. That's childish. Like saying that the Pope's afraid to go to sleep in the dark. It's more than a phobia. It's been...what can I say...it's been a serious study of the problem.

"He's been around seventy-seven years and has seen an awful lot. Not only Popes who took stupid positions because they had lost their capacity to think problems through; there have been a lot of heads of state who overstayed their time— Franco, DeGaulle. Churchill, luckily, remained a great name, but not a great power when even his bowels gave out.

"Morelli feels that his mission at this stage of his life is to

115

set a precedent for resignation that future Popes, hopefully, will have the good sense to follow. He knows the consequences, but they have to be risked—the fact that a power bloc could unseat a Pope it didn't like. God knows the Curia would have booted John out overnight if it could have gotten away with it. They became terribly disillusioned by Paul VI, but he held on. His body went to pieces, but not his mind.

"You know Cardinal Waldenheim of Vienna?"

"Not personally," Donald said, hoping Angela would fail to notice the rush of color to his face. He could feel the warm blood in his cheeks.

"Then you know he would have been Pope hands down in an open Conclave, but being an Austrian—and someone who honestly didn't want the job—well—anyhow both Waldenheim and Morelli exchange symptoms of senility. They've studied it like two college kids in a cram course. Waldenheim is Morelli's idol. The way I hear it, Waldenheim agrees with Morelli about setting a precedent, but wishes Morelli didn't have to do it. Waldenheim is worried about the Conclave. It could create a more divisive Church than the one we've got. Anyhow, Waldenheim has begged off advising Morelli."

She laughed, "They limit their conversation now to discussing their hardening arteries. It's sort of wonderful, isn't it? Two great old men with enormous power able to retain it as long as they live who are trying to find the right thing to do. Not for themselves but for the people. My guess is that Waldenheim will step down as soon as Morelli makes up his mind. He hangs on because he feels quitting now would add to Morelli's worry."

For Donald this was all new. He'd neither read nor heard anything in this area from Ryan. Then why should he? It was only this week that he'd gained Ryan's complete confidence as well as that of the whole body of American Cardinals. Suddenly the weight of his responsibility assailed him. He'd done nothing to fulfill Muldoon's request to check out Cardinal Novik. That was a *must*, beginning tomorrow.

Lying in bed, expecting the phone to ring at any moment, he went over Angela's revelations point by point. She'd

116

enlarged on what he had already imagined, that the two power brokers were Angelo Cardinal Torriani and Daniele Cardinal Rossi, respectively the Secretary of State and the Archbishop of Milan.

Angela had said, "Each knows he can't be elected. Torriani's too tough despite his tremendous support. He can't get the majority plus one, especially in the face of the threat of an American-supported candidate. Rossi is too young, but his brother-in-law is Pietro Gentille. He's been involved in straightening out some sour Vatican investments that looked like they were going wrong. As a reward he wants all the money action in the next regime. So you have two visible candidates, three power brokers. Gentille's also the referee. I believe he's gotten an agreement. You probably didn't know he came into Rome the same day as the Americans did."

Donald figured a little knowledgeable truth from him wouldn't hurt. "Yes, I did. Gentille was on the same plane I took. We stopped at Milan and picked up Rossi."

"Hmmm!" Angela flipped, "nice way to travel." She thought it over. "Sure. It makes sense. They want to complete their deal with Torriani. Like it or not they're those 'strange bedmates' you hear about. They have to agree on a candidate, someone who will follow policies they approve of, a quiet fatherly Pope who won't make waves. Someone who will keep them in their present positions and turn over the key to the Vatican treasury to Gentille. Then some day in the future, they can come out into the open and run for Pope—to put it bluntly."

"It sounds fine," Donald suggested. "Just the way it's always been. But now there's the American threat to upset the apple cart."

Angela shrugged her shoulders. "All that really exists is the threat. You can't back up a threat unless you have a candidate. None of the Americans qualify. So?"

"So what?"

"Who have they got up their sleeves?"

"That's what everyone wants to know."

"Yes, everyone would like to get a lead on that. I must say the Americans have been pretty cagey about this one.

Usually they're open books." Then to give weight to her words, "Well, Donald, if you decide to hang around and cover it, I'd sure like to be your *Girl Friday*."

"It's something to think about," was the best Donald could summon. That appeared to satisfy Angela.

It was almost one o'clock and Donald decided he'd been giving too much thought to Angela. There was tomorrow to check her out. Now he'd better start wondering how to retrace Cardinal Novik's movements. Where would Novik have started his morning? Saying Mass, of course. Logically at his titular church, one of many churches in Rome that Cardinals assume as belonging to their diocese during their lifetime. They often collected sums of money to restore these titular churches to their former grandeur. When they died, the Red Hats of their office were hung in the nave of their titular churches in Rome joining those of Cardinals who in centuries past held the title.

Donald shook his head. Muldoon would have known that himself.

The phone rang.

"*'Allo, babee*. You want good time?"

"*'Allo* yourself, where are you?" Donald answered.

"*Caro mio*. I am still here in New York."

"How come?"

"You poop the party, that's why."

"You mean you decided not to go with the 'boys' anyhow?"

"Now...now...let's keep it straight, *liebling*. We were also girls. Anyhow, I switched vacations with another girl so we can go when you come back. How about that?"

"Great. That was nice of you..."

"It was nothing, *liebling*. Who you sleeping with—some nice Italian piece with fat tits, fat ass and thick legs...?"

"No, sorry to disappoint you. I'm alone."

Erika laughed, "*Tesaro*, you know something? I believe you. What a shame! Those girls should pay you."

"I miss you," Donald wailed.

"Well, come home. That's easy enough."

"I can't. I'm back on the paper."

"Good! Congratulations."

"I thought you wanted me to try television?"

"Ah...that was last month. Now I'm changing my mind. I see all those beautiful dumb blondes on the boobs tube and poof!—there goes my Donald. You know you're boobs-crazy, don't you, *mon amour*?"

"Your boobs, baby. Not everybody's."

"So you're watching Morelli. Yes? No?"

"Well...in a way...yes, I guess I am."

"Good, then I have news for you. Morelli is quitting on Thursday the twenty-fifth."

"That's this week."

"Yes. He doesn't want to louse up Easter. That way they elect a new Pope in plenty of time to go around and kiss the feet of all the pretty young priests on Holy Thursday."

"God, if your uncle ever heard you talk like that!"

"*Babee*, he never will. Before him I speak like a Cardinal's niece."

"How do you know it will be the twenty-fifth?"

"Oh, I would go straight to hell if I told you. Uncle Erich's secretary is my cousin. She knows you and I fool around. I told her you were chasing the Cardinals around Rome. So she mentions something about the twenty-fifth being the day the Pope will go fishing. *Bei uns* that means the same as in America. You put it together."

"*Liebling*, there's more to it than that, isn't there?"

"*Ach! Dein Deutsch! Du* speaks so *gut*. Think a *bissel*!"

"I get it. He's going fishing. He was born in Bari..."

"*Wie klug du bist!* Clever like a newspaperman who will find some pretty little Italian girl to go to Bari and watch for some messenger from the Vatican who will visit the local newspaper with the fishing report."

"Very good. Very good. But I'd never make a scoop."

"That's what I think. There are not many telephone lines from Bari. Better just to know the story is breaking up."

"Breaking. Not up, Erika."

"Up or down. Who cares? Unless it's a cock. Oh! Then I care—plenty."

"How does Uncle Erich feel?"

"Sad, I guess. He admires Morelli. But he thinks he is brave to quit while he's still right in the head. We should all do that. I am thinking that way myself."

"But you're only twenty-four."

"I know lots of crazies who're only twenty-one."

"Anyhow, if he quits on the twenty-fifth, I'll be home that much sooner."

"Thanks God for that. I miss you too, *liebling*. But don't be too good. A little Italian piece now and then is good for the health. *Ciao, babee.*"

When Donald put in a call to Tom Ryan, the Cathedral operator said that he was in South America. Donald spoke to Muldoon.

There was a long pause. "It sounds logical to me, Donald. I'll get in touch with Ryan. I hope you can arrange to get him quietly into Rome. I'm not pressing you. But the information about Novik is imperative. Especially in view of this sudden move."

*   *   *

The long rest Angela felt Donald needed came to an abrupt end at eight-thirty in the morning with the noisy double ring of the telephone which Donald believed was conceived by some devilish insomniac who had convinced European telephone manufacturers that its very insistence would double their business. At home a dozen or so rings could lull him back to sleep whereas the European double whammy sounded like the clang of his neighborhood fire house. One was terrorized into answering it.

The caller was Ruggero Bulatov, the manager of the Palace-International who had been away from the hotel when Donald checked out yesterday. He was in the lobby and sounded terribly upset.

"Donald, I am sorry to intrude, but I must see you. May I come up?"

"Of course, Ruggero. I'll order some breakfast."

"No ... no ... no. I have brought a container of coffee for you and some croissants."

Donald laughed, "That's knocking the competition where it hurts. Come right ahead. I'm in Room 917."

"Thank you."

Donald jumped out of bed, into the bathroom, splashed his face with water, pulled on his trousers and slipped into his

120

shirt, deciding that a bathrobe had better be added to his list if this story was going to start unfolding so early in the morning.

A minute or so later he heard Bulatov's knock at the door. He smiled a warm, "Good morning, Donald," but the smile was easily recognized as professional. The round, moon-faced hotel executive was carrying a picnic basket and in a few seconds, it seemed, turned the desk into a breakfast table and poured two cups of steaming *espresso* from a thermos for openers.

He invited Donald to sit and enjoy the croissants, "While they're still warm. Right out of the oven," Bulatov beamed.

Then the hotel manager drew up a chair beside Donald. He lowered his voice, "Donald, I wanted to talk to you after the Cardinals left, but you slipped away before I had an opportunity. I have to talk to someone... but it's so difficult... anyhow... I'm glad it is you."

Donald tried to put him at ease. "If the bugging of Monsignor Ryan's room is bothering you, Ruggero, forget it. I discovered it. Cardinal De Cordoba got rid of it and checked the other rooms. They appeared to be clean."

He paused—searching for the right words. "It is bizarre when you realize it, but electronic intrusion has become so commonplace that even the Cardinals were not surprised. It didn't seem worth the effort to find out who was responsible."

"And that is why you never mentioned it to me?"

"There was no reason to; besides, we were pressed for time. At any rate, the Cardinals were. I certainly never assumed you were involved."

Bulatov seemed relieved. He relaxed, poured himself a cup of coffee and carefully buttered a small section of a croissant. "You are sure? You would never believe I had anything to do with it, would you?"

Donald laughed. "Of course not. The Palace-International is a huge hotel. Even a manager careful as you couldn't possibly be aware of everything that goes on."

Bulatov's face dropped, "You are right, Donald. I should know. But I don't—and I cannot. There was a time when I knew all my employees' names. Now they come and go so frequently, I barely recognize them. As for names, phooey! More often than not they're aliases. Half the identity cards that go through our personnel office turn out to be forged. The Palace-International is no longer an elegant hotel for elegant people; it is the bedroom of every secret agent with business in Rome. On top of that they infiltrate my staff with their spies, an incredible collection of geniuses in all the criminal trades, from riffling dispatch cases to bugging the rooms of American priests."

"Can't you do something about it?"

Bulatov's laugh was dry, "What? What can I do? Nothing. Remember, I am a refugee. I enjoy political asylum in Italy. So does my wife. But we have family in Hungary. Grown children from our first marriages, my father, her father and mother, sisters, brothers, two aunts I care about. It comes to quite a list, Donald, so I am vulnerable."

"In other words, you're being blackmailed..."

"Exactly. I am blackmailed into not noticing a dozen things every day that should be reported to the police." He looked at the ceiling, groping for the rest of his explanation. "But assuming I was brave and noble and did go to the police, what could I accomplish? Nothing. I learn things— but always *after* the fact."

"They certainly have you boxed in."

"Not only me," Bulatov said, "but every refugee in Italy, at least, those who are in a position to be useful to them; hotel managers, bankers, import-export people, travel agents and ... well ... you can imagine ..."

"How about priests?"

Bulatov lifted his eyes and hands in a gesture of prayer. "Priests! At the rate they've been coming in and out of Rome for the last two years one would think that the Pope's resignation, if it ever happens, will be the most important event of the century. And now we have the Americans!"

Donald offered his own interpretation. "In the sense that Morelli may set a precedent, it will be a significant event. I can understand how it has unleashed the energies of those who want a piece of the Vatican pie. Then there are those who see the election of the next Pope as another struggle between the Free World and the Communist Communities. The Third World views it as a chance to bang hard on the doors of Saint Peter's demanding to be heard. In Africa, where the Church is young, in Eastern Europe where it is embattled and in parts of Latin and North America where it is still vital and challenging, there are those who feel that the choice of a new Pope can no longer be entrusted solely to the Italian wing of the College of Cardinals. That, as I see it, explains why the Americans have decided to assume an active role in the Conclave. What is your interpretation, Ruggero?"

A bitter smile crossed his large, round face as Bulatov answered, "Similar to yours, but not nearly as lofty. I am afraid that at the Palace-International I clean up the ashtrays and open the windows on too many smoke-filled rooms to assume that this is going to be a peaceful, orderly, traditional Conclave with, if you'll pardon the polite expression, 'some differences of opinion.'

"That is how it will look, of course, because all the rough stuff will have already taken place. The decision will be made before the seals are placed on the Vatican doors and the keys are turned to lock the Cardinals into their so-called Communion with the Holy Spirit."

Donald laughed, "I'm not naive. I wouldn't question that analysis. Where does the rough stuff come in? I guess the bugging of Ryan's room could be considered from two angles: a desire to know the plans of the American delegation and a warning that American activism is not exactly appreciated here in Rome."

Bulatov beamed. "Your uncle would be proud of you. Exactly. That's why I'm here. Not to interfere or influence you. Not really to warn you. The interested parties are adroit enough at that. Simply to explain a few things. I seldom enjoy the opportunity to put my knowledge about the guests who come to the Palace-International these days to any practical use. Some of it I share with Nadja—merely to get it off my mind. The rest I keep to myself and I'd rather not. But the alternative—being a counterspy—has no appeal either. So, as you so admirably expressed it, I am definitely 'boxed in.'"

"Whew!" Donald exclaimed. "I see your position. Not very pleasant."

"No, but I live with it. Anyhow, to get down to cases. You

Americans have really stirred up a hornet's nest. No one believes you can name the next Pope, but everyone is convinced the American Cardinals are going to sow seeds of discontent. If they do not affect the Papacy, they will certainly undercut the Curia bureaucracy. Remember, there are more than twelve hundred plush jobs sitting in the administrative offices of the Vatican. The Cardinals who head them, like Torriani who is a psychopath, are going to fight pretty low to make sure the Conclave is securely locked up to choose their man."

"Do you know who he is?" Donald asked.

"Everyone presumes it will be Bellafiore of Bari. He's inoffensive. Morelli's from Bari. They can suggest an extension of the present Pope's fairly liberal policies. But that's today. It could be someone else tomorrow. Torriani and Rossi, as you already know, are polishing the crown together since neither can win it.

"As adversaries brought in as a team to protect their interests, both men are functioning with cool, calculated, deadly efficiency. Their names alone are reassuring to conservatives and their capacity for living side by side with the Communists has won them the support of the radicals. So in Italy and in most of Europe, for that matter, there exists the conviction that a non-Italian Pope could neither manage the Vatican Curia nor cope competently with Communist growth in Italy. It's only a matter of time before they will be participating influentially in the national government. For that reason, the Vatican suggests that a non-Italian Pope is inconceivable."

"Quite right," Donald put in. "Their strategy is sound from their point of view. On the other hand, there are many Bishops and Cardinals outside Italy who believe a non-Italian Pope is needed to shield the office from entanglements with national disputes. They feel it is time the Church shed its parochial Italian character..."

"Philosophy is one thing," Bulatov interrupted, "but are your straightforward, honest American priests ready for what's in store for you when Morelli quits and a Conclave is called?"

"A rough time, I gather...from the tone of your voice, Ruggero,"

"Worse than that. Demonstrations, marches, night and day picketing of the usual places, the Embassy and other American buildings. Now they'll throw in the North American College and wherever the Cardinals are quartered—I don't know who your candidate is, but regardless, he's going to be discredited—somehow, some way. And all this will be done *before* the Conclave."

"By whom?"

"By everyone, Donald, by no one. If the Church can live a side-by-side existence with the Italian Communists, don't you imagine that they would make a deal to discredit the Americans? It's obvious. Who will take the blame—not the leaders of the party, not the Communist Mayor of Rome, surely not Torriani or Rossi or Bellafiore. They will deplore the incidents."

"I get it. Terrorists will be hired to do the dirty work . . . the Red Brigades."

"Exactly and you've already been contacted."

"Me? Contacted? By whom?"

Bulatov smiled, "By the very attractive Angela Nero."

Donald leaned back his head and roared. "So that's the game. She's not very good at it, Ruggero. She changed skins too many times yesterday. I was headed out this morning to check on her first thing."

"So I saved you the trouble. You're right. She's not very good and I doubt that she'd be involved with them if they weren't such an attractive lot. Angela's a sexy piece and now she has it bad for one of the Germans, Hans something or other. They seldom use their last names. The terrorists are anything but a scruffy lot of radicals. Not at all what you imagine. Well educated. They come from good families. They have access to money. That's how they can afford to import a specialist like Hans."

"Can you recognize Hans?"

"Of course. He and Angela were hanging around the hotel while you were there. Evidently there is some connection between you and her." He paused. Then it came to him. "Of course. There has to be. Thaddeus and Nellie Nero were great friends."

"That's why I looked her up."

"Good. So you have a contact. Either you will use her or

125

she will use you. She can help you with your job."

"Which job?" Donald said, smiling as he answered his own question. "Everyone in Rome knows I'm scouting the terrain for the American Cardinals. Is that correct?"

Bulatov pretended surprise, "How did you ever know?"

"From the moment you started talking, I guess..." He thought for a second, "It's good of you to help."

Bulatov smiled, "My friend, as I said, I have never before enjoyed the opportunity. For me, it is a chance to feel less guilty when the fireworks begin."

"Haven't they already begun?" Donald asked.

"Definitely," Bulatov replied.

"How does Cardinal Novik rank among the Communist refugees in Rome?"

"A kind man. Generous with his money, but for some reason, he avoids contact with everyone except a Polish priest, Stefan Washinski. It's curious he chose Stefan."

"Why?"

"For the simple reason that Washinski is the noisiest of us all. It's a miracle he hasn't been defrocked; another miracle that the Italian Government doesn't deport him. A fine, outspoken man. I admire him. Maybe he's the voice of Cardinal Novik. Who knows?"

"Where does he live?"

"In a pension near Santa Cecilia in Trastevere. He's one of their priests. An embarrassment sometimes, but highly regarded."

"Ruggero, you certainly have helped me out. I'm grateful. No wonder Thaddeus thinks so highly of you."

"He shouldn't. He did me many more favors than I ever gave to him. But you can do me a favor..."

"Of course, whatever I can."

Bulatov's small eyes lit up mischievously, "They tell me that your Monsignor Ryan is very thick with President Cameron."

"That's fairly correct."

"Good! When the Vatican excommunicates me and the Communists seize Nadja and me, please ask Monsignor Ryan to have our names put on President Cameron's *Human Rights* list. My friend, believe me, we are going to

126

need it. I am going now. The back way. I noticed a couple of familiar faces at the front door this morning and I'm pretty sure they are interested in you. Me? No. I come here all the time. This hotel is being gobbled up by the same Arab group that bought the Palalce-International last year. I am involved in the negotiations."

Bulatov got up and walked to the door. He extended his hand, "Good luck, Donald. Call me if you need anything. All right?"

"Thank you, Ruggero. I appreciate everything."

Bulatov looked Donald over, letting his eyes wander over his body like a buyer at a slave auction, "You're going to be OK. You ought to be able to use Angela—but don't forget. She can only betray a few people, some minor secrets. She's way down in the pecking order, just a good-time girl, really. Too bad. Angela was cut out for better things. *Ciao*, Donald."

Donald poured the last of the coffee from the thermos. It was still warm. No wonder, he thought, correspondants simply sighed when asked how they maneuvered around Rome. There were so many informers it was impossible to separate news from gossip. Bulatov hardly rated as an informer, but his motives in seeing Donald were clear. Eventually, as many other old friends had done, Bulatov would ask Thaddeus to facilitate a visa for him and Nadja to come to the States. In the meantime it was to everyone's advantage to butter his nephew's croissant.

When Donald heard the sharp double ring of the telephone, he simply stared at the instrument and said, "Fuck you!"

Then, thinking aloud, "Not you, Angela, at least not now. I mean the telephone. First, there's Father Stefan Washinski to see." He stepped into the bathroom, pulled the shower curtain closed and turned on the spray. The double ring eventually gave up.

*   *   *

As he dressed, Donald decided to leave conspicuously by the main door. He might discover how they tailed a pigeon in

127

Rome. He knew the technique in New York, but that didn't imply it was the same everywhere.

First, he stopped at the desk of the concierge to pick up a lone message. It was from Angela who had evidently made her call from the hotel lobby. It said simply, "Couldn't reach you this morning. Will call or drop by at five this afternoon. Can I help you with your shopping? *Amore*, Angela."

Angela was taking a lot for granted. Into his underwear already! But he was hers for the asking. There was nothing in the rule book that prohibited him from sleeping with spies. As a matter of fact, it was encouraged. Angela surely wouldn't impose any hardships on his job.

He stopped at the corner kiosk to pick up a street guide of Rome. Walking to the Trastevere church would afford Donald an opportunity to learn if he were being followed. After crossing the bridge and finding himself walking around in circles inside the narrow cobblestone streets of old Rome, he realized that he was not only going it alone, but he'd been a damned fool for not taking a cab. Assuming there were some mysterious characters hanging around the hotel when Ruggero arrived, there was no need for anyone interested in Donald Brady to tail him. Angela Nero knew perfectly well she had him locked up, unless he unexpectedly dropped dead.

Eventually Donald found himself face to face with Santa Cecilia after rounding a corner he'd previously regarded as unlikely. It led into a small attractive square where the church occupied the central position; its facade showing the wear of centuries, giving it an aura of respect that seemed reflected in the apartment buildings that towered above it. They seemed to have absorbed the serenity of the *piazza* with its small but graceful fountain and the old church. It was the first quiet spot Donald could recall meeting in Trastevere.

Of course the church was closed tighter than a drum. Donald knew it was useless to search out a sign showing the hours it was open. They probably hadn't been revised since Santa Cecilia was built. Instead he pounded at all the doors: side, front and rear. At the last he was able to arouse an old priest who peered cautiously through a large wooden door after unlatching what sounded to Donald like seven or eight inside bolts. Donald identified himself as a friend from

America looking for Father Stefan Washinski.

Even in the semi-darkness, Donald saw the old priest's face turn pale. He said very quietly, "We don't know where he is, Mr. Brady." Donald was surprised at how quickly his name had registered. "We have not seen Padre Stefan at this church for several days. He lives down the street at the Pension Garibaldi. If you look directly to your right, you can see the small sign. If he is not there, ask for Father Franco Pollo. He also lives there and perhaps he has learned something." He paused. "Does that help you?"

"Yes, Father, thank you, it does." He nodded and waited while the old priest bolted the doors and started slowly down the street toward the Pension Garibaldi. The priest's speech seemed extremely well rehearsed. He wondered if Polish priests disappeared every day from Santa Cecelia.

At the Garibaldi, Donald was relieved to find Father Pollo was not only in, but sitting in the lobby of the second floor pension close to the telephone. He responded eagerly to Donald's request for information. He showed no curiosity as to why Donald was looking for Washinski. He seemed relieved that someone besides himself was inquiring about the missing priest.

"I haven't seen Stefan since the day before yesterday."

"That would be the nineteenth, the Feast of Saint Joseph."

"Yes. He was to serve Mass for an old friend from America. I don't know that I should mention his name. He was in Rome on a secret visit. That much I know."

"It was Cardinal Novik," Donald said. "The Archbishop of Chicago. It's been in all the newspapers."

The tall Italian priest looked apologetic. "I seldom read the papers. Yes, it was Cardinal Novik. I should like to have attended the Mass, but Stefan discouraged the idea. Because of the secrecy, he said. Also Stefan hinted they had some important business to discuss afterward. That was early in the morning. I went to Santa Cecelia's at eleven, said Mass at one of the side altars and began looking for Stefan. We usually have lunch together. I'm still studying and I guess I look upon Stefan not only as a friend, but as my teacher and guide."

The words had come gushing out of him with more energy

than the lazy little fountain in the *piazza* and Donald realized that Pollo was finding in him the first person concerned about Stefan's disappearance.

"Have you notified the police?"

"Not yet. The priests at Santa Cecelia tell me he hasn't been gone long enough to be listed as a 'missing person.'"

Suddenly Pollo realized he'd done all the talking. "Why are you looking for him?"

Donald thought quickly. "I have a message for Stefan from Cardinal Novik. That is all. Nothing important. It concerns some books the Cardinal wanted him to look for."

"I don't quite believe that, but it doesn't matter. You're an American so I don't believe you're one of them."

"And who might 'one of them' be?"

The priest slumped down in the worn old chair, the only upholstered piece in the lobby. His answer was surly, "I wouldn't have referred to someone as 'one of them' if I knew who 'they' were, would I?"

"Hardly." Donald decided to play it straight. "Very well, I'll be frank. I am a newspaperman. I am also on special assignment—on loan to Cardinal William Muldoon of New York to make some investigations for him. Would you like to see my credentials?"

"Yes sir, I would."

As he handed his New York press cards and passport to Pollo, Donald said, "These are my newspaper credentials. I have none to support my...what shall we call it...my ecclesiastical duties."

"These are quite enough, thank you," Pollo replied. He studied them carefully before handing them back.

"Obviously you are who you say, Mr. Brady," Pollo said. "Will you tell me the real reason why you want to speak to Stefan? Perhaps, then, I can help."

"Cardinal Muldoon has not taken me wholly into his confidence. There has been little time and our most recent communication was by telephone. For some reason he is extremely concerned by Cardinal Novik's movements on the Feast of Saint Joseph. So far you have supplied valuable information. We know that he came here to say Mass and that afterward there was some business to be discussed."

130

Pollo looked around. There were bedrooms at each corner of the lobby. He lowered his voice. "Someone may still be at home. I'm not sure. Let's go outside."

The priest loped across the *piazza* leading Donald to a wine shop where they found seats far in the rear, out of sight of passersby. The choice barrel seats outside in the sun were already occupied by the regulars—those sturdy perennials of Italian wine shops who spend the entire day there playing *scopa* or talking politics. Miraculously they walk home at closing hour with the surefootedness of a high wire performer.

"Perhaps you can fit the puzzle together," Pollo said, after the store's proprietor settled two glasses of *vino bianco* in front of them.

"Are you personally acquainted with Stefan?" Pollo asked.

"Unfortunately, I know very little about him. Not even what he looks like."

"Tall, blond, quite handsome. But that's irrelevant at the moment. He's the supreme Polish patriot and as a consequence he lives in a pressure tank, forever boiling over about the injustice taking place in his homeland. He lives in a state of fury, angry with Vatican diplomats who want to reestablish relations with Poland. He is dissatisfied with the Polish clergy, particularly the Cardinals who proceed so slowly. He loathes and fears Communists. Now that there are so many in Italy he has become paranoid, fearful that his life is in danger. It may well be true. In Italy today one cannot laugh off such fears. Stefan fled Poland under the fire of machine guns or something like that. I don't know. I have never experienced danger."

The priest reached into his pocket and pulled out a message slip with Pension Garibaldi printed neatly at the top. "I received this message and this number for Stefan the night before he was to meet Cardinal Novik. I started to give it to him. He said, 'Never mind, I know. It's Gentille. I've already spoken to him. Thanks.' He was very nervous about it. Without thinking I stuffed the slip back in my pocket. And this is it. Pietro Gentille is a very important man. So is Cardinal Novik."

131

He was silent for quite a while. "Young priests usually aren't in touch with important men. So I *did* attend the Mass Cardinal Novik read, but way down at the end of the church where Stefan could not see me. Later I deliberately passed by the coffee shop—that one across the street." Pollo pointed it out to Donald.

"Stefan and the Cardinal were together. Cardinal Novik wore a business suit. And there was a third man, blond like Stefan, younger, a German. He was doing all the talking. Novik and Stefan seemed to be in a state of shock. I didn't dare to get close enough to hear anything, so I went back to the pension and studied. I haven't seen Stefan since. Last night I telephoned this number. I asked for Pietro Gentille. The number was the executive office of the airlines he's connected with. They said Gentille had returned to New York."

"I'm sure this is valuable information, Father Pollo," Donald said, "but it will take someone else to put it together. I am grateful to you for having been so helpful. I will give it to Cardinal Muldoon exactly as you've related it. Is there anything else you can add?"

Pollo answered quickly, "Yes, there is. My feelings. They might help. For a week or so before Cardinal Novik came here, Stefan was worried. There were strange telephone calls. I don't believe they were from Gentille. But from—well—I guess—from Communists. I had the feeling Stefan was being threatened. And from what I saw at the cafe, I'd be stupid if I didn't also have the feeling that Cardinal Novik was being threatened, too. Stefan sat mute—knowing what was going on, powerless to interfere. You don't have to live to be a hundred and two to be perceptive. I would swear on everything I am that those two unhappy Polish men were victims; Stefan, the tool of some higher-up; the Cardinal, fearful of some dreadful reprisals unless he acted as he was ordered. I suppose we will not know the truth until Stefan reappears. I pray that he's safe."

"So do I," Donald said quietly. He reached into his pocket and found a *Sun-Mirror* card. He wrote down his hotel and phone number. "Please call me if you hear anything."

"And you will do the same, Mr. Brady?"

"Yes, Father, I will."

They finished their wine in silence. Donald asked the priest to telephone for a taxi. It arrived with amazing speed as cabs often do in Rome. They shook hands and Brady directed the cab back to the Corso. There was time for some shopping before the afternoon closing.

*   *   *

By the time he'd finished shopping it was one o'clock and Cardinal Muldoon would be up and stirring. He went to the *Roma Centro* post office and placed a person-to-person call. A minute or so later, Muldoon was on the wire, amazed as anyone involved in trans-Atlantic calls to Rome at the speed with which they were going through these days—about ten years after England, France and Germany had established direct dialing service. No more shouting—no more interruptions with "Can you hear me?" It was like talking to someone in the next room.

Muldoon listened as Donald told of his meeting with the Italian priest, stopping him now and then to ask Donald for repeat of a phrase. "I'm jotting it down, Donald. My shorthand has gotten rusty." Donald was impressed. He'd never met a priest—much less a Cardinal—who knew shorthand.

There was relief in Muldoon's voice when Donald finished. "Thank you, Donald. This isn't good news, but it's information confirming what I privately have suspected. Monsignor Ryan will explain it to you. We shall need your help."

"When is Ryan arriving, Your Eminence?" Donald asked.

"Probably tomorrow night. No need to meet him. He's traveling as a 'civilian.' Ryan will be in touch with you."

The Cardinal paused. "About young Stefan. I wish I could be helpful. I've heard of him. No doubt about his being a firebrand. He could be in serious trouble. We will pray for him—and for Cardinal Novik. Again Donald, my thanks and blessings."

The old prelate's appreciation pleased Donald and it was always handy to enjoy a good priest's blessings, but as a

133

newspaperman he felt there were too many loose pieces hanging out. Too many unanswered questions.

Why was Muldoon so concerned about Novik? What was the relationship between Novik and Stefan Washinski? Why had a young, fairly well-known priest disappeared after meeting with Cardinal Novik and a German youth, obviously the infamous Hans, imported by the Red Brigade? Was Bulatov on the mark in respect to Angela? Presuming he was, and Angela had the hots for the German, maybe he could squeeze some information from her. As he assembled his packages and headed back to the hotel, Donald intended giving it a damned good try.

* * *

That evening, dressed in the suit he'd bought off the peg, too narrow in the shoulders, too tight in the crotch, self-conscious about both, Donald wined and dined Angela at Gino's, a popular restaurant off Via Veneto which was a favorite of the foreign press corps.

The choice of Gino's was deliberate, made over some mild protests by Angela. Both knew what the other was up to. The dinner would begin their professional relationship which Donald intended setting up at the right moment—between coffee and the *Anis* which the management generally offered to returning faces like Donald's.

Donald presumed someone would notice the new "twosome" and if his knowledge of the Roman grapevine was still viable, by noon the next day it would be all over town. By three in the afternoon, friends would have supplied him with a blow-by-blow account of Angela's professional style, her sex preferences, a list of her lovers, what she'd taken them for and a thorough character analysis which Angela could be proud of if it included one favorable attribute—like "she's sometimes punctual."

Angela, on the other hand, would have preferred sliding quietly into view as Donald's sidekick, thus giving her time to line up a few gossipists on her side. But Angela was in no position to overrule Donald's choice of beanery. She could only hope for the best. Anyhow, Donald was unlikely to be

134

influenced by gossip; by now he ought to believe that she held the key to a number of sources he'd give a lot to latch on to.

Gino served a splendid, modestly priced dinner and faintly recalled Donald. This being the case, he didn't mind mentioning his Uncle Thaddeus. The name brought a broad smile to Gino's face and a welcome that would endure through eternity. Angela was impressed. Donald explained, "He's a second passport and I'm not the least bit embarrassed about using Thad. He'd hate me if I didn't."

When the coffee and bottle of *Anis* were served, Donald lowered his voice and gave Angela a selective account of his double assignment. "Actually I am on vacation time from the paper, so there's no conflict of interest. For the hard news they can get along with the wire services. If the Pope does resign and I'm still here, perhaps I'll handle some of the coverage. Most likely they'll send a man over.

"Where you can help me is picking up the bits and pieces of gossip that will help the American Cardinals. Our job is best described as letting Cardinal Muldoon know what kind of nuts he's up against as well as the men who are clever and those who are plain devious. It's a new experience for them; fairly unusual for me. I'm used to dealing in hard facts and tracing a rumor out as soon as it begins to mushroom. In Rome, I gather, you let the rumors gain momentum until they've been enlarged enough that the truth is either totally obscured or crystal clear."

Angela laughed, "You catch on fast."

But as an overall performance, Angela's would never warrant an audition for a bus and truck company of *Roman Spyin'*. "It sounds so C.I.A.," she cooed. "How wonderfully exciting! The kind of assignment that gives you the feeling of making a real contribution."

At another point, her palms cupped her chin, her eyes grew thoughtful and her voice became somber. "I guess we take the Church for granted. We get so easily into the frame of lapsed Catholics. Then something like this comes along and we realize how important the Church is—not only to Catholics but to the whole world." Donald shuddered.

He also nodded agreement and offered her twenty-five

dollars a day and a guarantee of six days' work a week for the time being. "If this thing stretches out, I doubt that I'll be hanging around, but maybe someone else will take over," he said.

Angela's expression was easily read. Who better to take over than *Signorina* Angela Nero? She clapped her hands little-girl style, "Donald, that's fine with me. It's a lifesaver. I can use the money and the opportunity to work with you is like a dream."

Then she giggled, "Do we seal it with a handshake or a kiss?"

"Both," laughed Donald as he proceeded to take her in his arms, pressing his mouth close to hers and letting his tongue slide into her easily parted lips. They clung together until they were breathless as his hand roamed over her body under the table. When they broke, the tight cut of his Italian pants made him shift awkwardly to find a more comfortable position. It didn't help when Angela affectionately patted the bulge and sighed, "Something's got to be done about that."

"You're telling me," Donald answered as he gently removed her hand. "Give me a second. I need to relax or there's going to be a public exhibition that Gino wouldn't like at all."

The bulge relaxed and so did Angela. She drank more wine than she had the night before. She became giddy and giggly. She seemed to forget for a time that she was playing footsies with a bunch of dangerous radicals and trying to palm herself off to professionals as a clean-cut newspaperwoman. In Donald's world that was not how the game worked—not in Rome or any other capital. You bought informers with cold cash—not with your body. And you learned it was a mistake to sleep in both beds.

Maybe something good for Angela would come out of this experience. She was sharp and intelligent. She had a nose for news, an eye for detail. He wondered if she knew how to play hunches.

Regretfully Donald was about to play one. The bulge in his pants was excrutiating, but this wasn't going to be their night.

The door had just been opened by Pietro Gentille heading

a large party of Americans, not particularly distinguished. Donald figured they were minor V.I.P.'s who Gentille was either stuck with or used as a cover to explain his appearance in Rome. A quick look of recognition was exchanged between Gentille and Angela, but it went no further. Gentille arranged the seating of his party at a table close to the window and deliberately sat with his back to her.

So they were in touch! In less than three days, if Erika's prediction held, Morelli would become the first Pontiff in modern times to resign the Throne of Saint Peter. Gentille was one of dozens of uneasy men who would begin pouring into Rome. Ryan would arrive tomorrow and who knew what other representatives of Cardinals, countries, political groups and news organizations would be on hand for the watch?

Angela pouted—and meant it—when Donald asked Gino to call a cab, telling her that he was bushed and they'd have to postpone their night together for the second time. "I'm sorry, Angela, but I know what I'm doing," he said. "You've had a lot of wine. I've done a lot of footwork."

He stood up to leave. Angela had little choice but to follow him outside where they jumped into a cab.

Asked when she should report for work, Donald thought a second. "Fairly early, Angela. We've got to hit the *Stampa Estera* tomorrow and visit the Vatican Press Office. I shouldn't have any difficulty getting credentials, should I?"

Angela laughed, "Of course not. Let's make it eleven. No, ten-thirty would be better. We ought to go to the Vatican first. They take forever. The *Stampa Estera* is always there and what do you really need? Just check what mail pouches you can use if you want to. Meet some of the fellows and get to know your way around."

They melted into a long wet kiss which Donald broke suddenly before he lost control of his intentions. Angela giggled, "Good-night, Donald. Thank you very much. I appreciate this."

He smiled, said nothing, turned his back on the cab and walked into the hotel, wondering what hunch had led him back so early. It was barely eleven.

There was a message from Erika saying she was calling

from Washington where she'd gone to do some work and wouldn't call until tomorrow. Donald understood why. Erika loathed Washington. "So many pretty men, but they don't excite me. It's waste. Terrible waste," she always complained after a trip to the capital. So she seldom stayed overnight, preferring to take a late train or a bus back to New York. When it turned out to be the bus, Erika seemed ecstatic. "So much *kneesies* to play! Wonderful dirty old men! They love me because I don't scream. I *kneesie* right back."

As much as her infinite joy in sex with him, Donald missed that crazy chatter. Hotel rooms were lonely places. His pants were killing him. A cold shower would help, but first he needed a stiff drink. He headed for the large bar with its comfortable, huge leather chairs all placed neatly around tiny tables. For some reason the Grand-Plaza bar was seldom half or even a quarter filled. It was too conservative for the tourists, lacking entertainment or even a piano player.

Luis made a good martini and at night he fixed Donald a tall concoction of *Campari*, gin and a lemon twist which he found satisfying. With a bottle of beer serving as a night cap to the glow he already felt Donald knew he'd sleep well. The booze, he hoped, would get Angela off his mind. Somewhere between the entrance to the bar and his favorite leather chair in the corner, Donald decided he preferred hoods and politicians to mystery women.

Donald waved to Luis who went to work on his drink. Before placing it on a tray he fumbled around in the cash drawer, pulled out an envelope and placed it beside the glass.

When he set the tray down, Luis pointed to the envelope, "A young priest brought this in an hour or two ago. He wouldn't leave it with the concierge. Crazy! But Renato is used to people like that. He asked the priest if there was any special reason why he would not leave it with him. So the priest says, 'I have to give it to someone Mr. Brady trusts.'

"'Ah,' says Renato. 'That would be Luis in the bar. They are good friends.' So here it is, *voila*. Some crazy people, no? Enjoy your drink, Mr. Brady."

Donald took a sip and then opened the envelope. It read:

Dear Mr. Brady,

I have talked to Father W. on the telephone. He is in seclusion in another city and safe. I told him about your visit. That seemed to make him become more quiet. He asked me to say "thank you" for your interest. When he is coming back, as soon as the Pope resigns and the American Cardinals are returning to Rome, he will communicate with you. In the meantime if there is any urgent message you would need to send him, you may telephone or come to the Garibaldi. Father W. has given me his promise to telephone again.

Yours truly,

Father P.

It had been a good day.

A hunch paid off at the finish. Tom Ryan would be in Rome this time tomorrow. He would have something for them to work with.

Donald suddenly knew how tired he was. Didn't people ever take it easy in lazy, old Rome? Or was there so goddamn much intrigue going on that it fed your adrenalin to the point where you kept going out of the terrible fear you might miss something?

*   *   *

When they did make love it was in the afternoon, after Donald and Angela had spent a busy morning at the Vatican Press Office where she introduced him to Monsignor James St. John, an Irishman with an irreverent gift of blarney that was so obvious it couldn't possibly fool a cub reporter with only two hours on the job. "Jimmy," as he preferred to be called by his "brothers" in the press corps, told reporters as much as he was supposed to—and not even the return of the snakes to Ireland could ever pull an extra syllable out of him.

In talking to "Jimmy," Donald wondered how a hundred and fifteen men could ever possibly reach a decision about anything, much less one so serious as the selection of a new leader for their church. They were as ignorant as the Vatican spokesman of who their fellow Cardinals were, where they came from, what their problems were and so many other details that would be at the tip of an American politician's tongue.

"Jimmy" answered this suggestion with a smile. "Ah, but the Princes of the Church are not politicians. They are guided by the wisdom given to them on these solemn occasions by the Holy Ghost." As "Jimmy" could not pronounce the names of many of the Cardinals—in fact he had difficulties with the priests in his own department—his Irish heritage had not yet brought him to the point where he could say "Holy Spirit." He clung to "Holy Ghost" with the zealous persistence of one who had gone down the "Protestant line" in the modern Church about as far as he could. If "Holy Ghost" had been good enough for Saint Patrick, it suited him fine and there the subject was dropped.

Of course "Jimmy" was a faker. Newspapermen who had dined with him discovered that his Italian was impeccable; his French, almost as good, and he could handle Latin verse with more finesse than most of his superiors. "Jimmy" was a closet intellectual which, combined with his corny affability, made him perfect in his job.

As soon as Donald's papers were processed they raced back to the hotel.

They lunched quickly at the Grand-Plaza bar. Minus her elegant wardrobe, in a plain frock with her hair whipped together casually, Angela appeared vastly more attractive than when her major occupation seemed to be making an impression. It was time to quit fooling around. Angela quickly agreed to go to his room. They fairly raced to the elevator. Donald didn't expect any calls. To make sure that Angela overheard nothing she shouldn't, he called the switchboard and told them to take messages.

Once the door locked behind them Donald could feel that Angela was ecstatic. She seemed to be telling him that she wanted him more than she'd ever imagined, more than anyone in her life.

The Eternal City's magic hour of twilight proved what everyone said—that it was made for lovers in Rome.

For a change the Grand-Plaza bar was fairly full and Donald led Angela to a table on the far side of the room, not his usual, but surrounded by the same comfortable leather chairs. Luis had just come on duty. Donald signaled "two" with his fingers and Angela shrugged, "Whatever you order is fine with me. At this moment you can do nothing wrong."

"Did I ever?" Donald asked.

"Not that I know of. But I guess we've got to talk business even if it kills us. Or kills me."

"I'm a little bit wobbly myself, Angela, and I'd just as soon get back upstairs. But . . . yes . . . I guess this is assignment time."

"I don't know what you're hearing. But if there's a resignation, the feeling I get is that it's about to happen. It seems to be on top of us. Do you agree?"

"Somewhat. As I said the other night—Morelli's got to move now in order for a Conclave to be finished before Holy Week. If he doesn't, it won't happen until summer."

"Meanwhile no one's twiddling his thumbs as I find it," Donald said. "When they were here, the American Cardinals discovered they were at the end of a long line of Red Hats who have been bustling in and out of Rome eager to get a clue to the Pope's intentions. As far as I know, the Americans are about the only group that's organized well enough to offer a candidate. It could be someone they're choosing now or a Cardinal they lined up a year ago when Monsignor Ryan stirred them to action."

"He's the *gray eminence* of Saint Patrick's in New York, isn't he?"

"Yes. He's also my good friend and the reason I'm involved in this job—if you can call it that."

Donald heard a note of sincerity when Angela observed, "I think it is a very important job. America's a long way off. No matter how powerful they may be at home, you can't expect men who know the Vatican only from early experience as seminarians and occasional visits afterward to understand the vast complexities of the machinery of the Curia. It takes years to penetrate the *Velvet Curtain*. In their position they need every bit of information you can pick up for them."

"I suppose that's how I see it," Donald said, "except there hasn't been time to analyze it quite so precisely. I haven't the slightest idea of who the candidate is. But I have been told that it really doesn't matter. Whoever he is, he's going to be slaughtered. Something's going to be dug up or manufactured to discredit him before the Conclave opens. That makes it pretty sticky."

"It does. But it makes sense. That's how the Pope-makers would work it. Torriani and Rossi know how a slur can grow into a lie that everyone absolutely believes. They've had enough experience—on both sides of the fence. Torriani's a neurotic and Rossi's wildly ambitious. But the stories you hear at dinner parties or in the wine shops can get a lot rougher than that."

"I imagine so," Donald said. "What I need from you in the next couple of days is a report on everything you hear about the Americans' plans. Who they think is the candidate? Have they an inkling? Are there any plans already in the works to discredit him? How will the Vatican big shots greet the American Cardinals? Will they ignore their activism or do they intend to nullify it by brushing it off as the ambitions of upstarts?"

"Everything you say is possible. The Old Guard wasn't very polite about the Americans attending Vatican II. They snickered behind their backs. Ridicule is a crude but effective weapon. That could be their tactic."

"That's it then, Angela. You have the picture. There is nothing I can add to it. This evening I'll drop by *Stampa Estera* on my own. Tonight I'm having dinner with a couple of the wire service men. Right now I'm going to love you and leave you for an appointment with the barber. If I don't, they might mistake me for someone from the Red Brigade."

He expected a reaction from Angela. There was none. She quickly finished off her drink. "I'll leave with you, Donald. When shall I report back?"

"Why not call me tomorrow—around eleven."

"Fine, Donald. And bless you for this afternoon. I needed you."

"And I needed you too, Angela. It's going to be nice."

He led her to the door and after she'd gone he made his way back to the bar and took a chair opposite Luis.

"Tell me, Luis, what do you know about that young lady?"

Luis shook his head. "Mr. Brady, how do you know my thoughts . . ."

"My genius—that's all. You've seen it often enough."

"Do you want the truth?" Luis asked.

Donald nodded.

"Quite simply, it is this. I see her too many times with too many wrong men. They use her for a little while; then they throw her away. She has to make up her mind whether she's a newspaperwoman like her family or a *putana* who kisses and tells. But I tell you this. From the good men she knows I always hear the same thing. 'Angela Nero's too bright to waste herself.' Maybe you will help her."

"Maybe, Luis. Maybe I will. Right now I'll take a beer."

PART IV

Vatican City—The Pope Resigns

When Donald awoke on the morning of March twenty-fifth he snapped on both the radio and the television set. He was in time for a travelogue about Sicily on television and for a program of Verdi on the radio. He turned off the television, preferring Verdi.

He'd slept late because, if the morning was quiet, the hours of the night had kept him hopping to the telephone from a number of locations around the hotel.

At eleven Erika called from New York. She caught him at the bar and launched right into her message.

"Darling, *tesaro,* my love. I am calling you now before midnight because I don't want to louse up tomorrow. Sometimes I am not good luck. I feel like a black cat. So I reach you before midnight to tell you how much I miss you. I am so hot all the time, I jump around the house like a Mexican jumping bean. But that's not why I call..."

"You want to hedge your bets—change your mind?"

"Oh, no, not that. It is still like I say unless my cousin has been drinking much wine. She does that, you know. What can I say? Do many people over there have any information?"

"No. I'm amazed."

"So am I. I don't understand it. You know they make bugs of the Pope just like they make of the President..."

"Darling, they bug the Pope... not bugs..."

"Is there a difference?"

Donald sighed, "I guess not. Still, it's strange."

"Do you think that maybe the Pope—he goes outside and

144

talks with Uncle Erich from a public telephone like Al Pacino?"

"I don't know, but they've certainly succeeded in keeping this story quiet."

"Maybe it's all my cousin's joke."

"No, Erika. I believe it's going to break just as you say. The Pope and Uncle Erich may have some method of communicating that his watchdogs haven't caught on to."

"CB?"

"I doubt that. But your Uncle Erich knows a lot of tricks, doesn't he?"

"Like you say, he wrote the spy book. He knows everything. Too bad he can't be the Pope."

"A lot of people think that."

"They are very nice and so are you. I am breaking off now the telephone. *Ciao, liebling.*"

Erika, as always, hung up when she was finished speaking. It seldom occurred to her that Donald might want to add a word or two. As he put the receiver back in its cradle he thought, "It's not much different when we're face to face. She is her own talking machine—Erika makes the questions. Erika makes the answers."

Erika had caught him at the bar. Monsignor Ryan's double ring came through when he was in the shower getting ready for bed.

Ryan's call was direct and uncomplicated. He was held up in London and expected to arrive either late the next evening or early the following morning. He offered no reason for his delay. Again Donald avoided mentioning the note from Father Pollo about Stefan Washinski. He feared putting Ryan on a spot. He might have information about Cardinal Novik that Muldoon wasn't ready to divulge.

"You sound tired, Tom," Donald said.

"I am. It's been hectic. I've been doubling up on my schedule ever since learning about the twenty-fifth."

"Well, for your sake, I hope it's accurate."

"It really doesn't matter. I simply did twice the work in half the time. It produced results. That's what counts. Guess that's it. I'll call when I land in Rome."

Donald imagined that Ryan's trip to England involved

lining up the support of the British Cardinals, the majority of whom favored America's blow for emancipation from domination by the Italian power structure.

Then, Donald toyed with the thought that the candidate might be an English Cardinal. At least one was considered *papabilo*, but imagine how an English Pontiff would set with America's Irish! There would be rioting—not dancing—in the streets. Even Uncle Thaddeus, Donald feared, would view that unlikely event with dark Irish suspicions.

Then, there was Angela who called at two, saying she was in the lobby with her report. "I've written it out, Donald. May I bring it up?"

The last person Donald wanted in his room last night was Angela. Any number of calls could still come through—from Father Pollo, Muldoon, who knew? He told Angela he was still dressed and went downstairs to pick up her material in the lobby.

The meeting with Angela was mercifully brief. She was dressed in blue jeans and looked tired. She silently handed him a few pages of notes, sensing there was no chance of getting into his bed. She seemed relieved when he thanked her, saying he'd read them later. She darted off, promising to call later in the day. After glancing at the notes, Donald understood Angela's reluctance to hang in as she usually did. They amounted to a hastily slapped together rehash of gossip, rumors and predictions culled from old newspaper columns and hearsay information available to anyone.

If work was responsible for Angela's fatigue, the pages she'd brought him could hardly have been responsible. He'd noticed dark stains under her fingernails whose origin was obvious to a newspaperman. Angela had been hanging around a printing plant. Working? For the Red Brigades? Probably. Her nails hadn't gotten that way from gardening. He regretted the effort put into making out with her. Angela was a marvelously talented lover and he couldn't deny that she still attracted him—especially in her blue jeans, even with her dirty fingernails. That he still wanted her added to his guilt. Then, there was Erika. In expecting him to fool around, wasn't she really telling Donald that she hoped he wouldn't?

146

Finally, Donald hadn't agreed to remain in Rome to turn around the career, life-style and morals of a mixed-up girl. There were more profound reasons and their validity was becoming more apparent to him hour by hour. He'd begun to sense the cynicism and decadence that afflicted both Rome and the Vatican. An ordinary news story had become a personal mission. Already he could see signs of how totally Church Conservatives and the Pope-makers intended destroying the hopes of the American Cardinals to become a new voice.

He recalled an angry statement made by one of the California Bishops during Vatican II who, weary of the snobbishness of the Italian Cardinals and tired of being patronized by Italian Bishops, told the press: "Some of the Fathers have taken occasion to preach to us as if we were against Peter and his successors. For eight weeks we have been getting lectured especially about the dangers of association with non-Catholics...It is not our people who miss Mass on Sunday, refuse the Sacraments and vote the Communist ticket."

Donald questioned his own usefulness in this critical assignment. What had he accomplished so far? Very little—beyond reporting Erika's gossip about the date of Morelli's resignation and discovering that Cardinal Novik's friend, Stefan Washinski, had disappeared. Donald knew he'd goofed in not reporting directly to Muldoon on the letter from Father Pollo instead of waiting for Ryan to get to Rome. But the damage was done. Another day would make little difference—not in view of Stefan Washinski's determination to stay underground until after the Pope resigned.

Assuming the resignation occurred today, where did he go next? Donald found difficulty in accepting the idea that he would have to ride with events, that he couldn't push what was obviously a planned conspiracy against the American Cardinals out into the open. He was boxed in. He had no idea of how one reached the conspirators believed to be behind it, Papal aspirants Cardinals Torriani and Rossi and their convenient businessman-partner, Pietro Gentille.

How did one go about proving that high members of the Catholic hierarchy were doing business with the Red

Brigades? Were young people like the mysterious Hans and devious Angela actually members of the Italian radicals who wanted Communism's takeover to speed up? Or were they simply mercenaries—activists of minor importance who sold dubious skills to the highest bidder?

If Donald accepted the latter as a premise, then the men at the top were extremely clever. By using marginal people, girls like Angela whose name enabled her to flutter around the edges of the newspaper profession, they were taking advantage of stupid innocents who could be discredited with the snap of an imperious Cardinal finger.

Donald disliked being played for a sucker. He looked at the pages again. Plain crap! He started to roll the sheets into a ball. Suddenly he stopped. It was copy paper, the kind of cheap pulp stock used in newspapers all over the world, common in printing establishments where it serviced the proof press. It came in many colors, different weights but generally, even in a city as large as Rome, cheap copy paper originated from only two or three sources, big paper companies for which it was a low profit "courtesy item."

If they were up to printing something—pamphlets or flyers—anything, really—Angela and her friends would need a shop, some people who were experts if they wanted quantity. Most of all, they'd need a front to buy government stamps—the Italian equivalent of a tax; in effect, a license. It took money to buy tax stamps. It also took money to buy paper, ink and the time of skilled printers.

Donald folded the papers carefully and placed them in his briefcase. They might eventually become useful.

At the moment there was the big story to sit out. He dressed quickly and hurried to *Stampa Estera*.

Donald couldn't believe that, in a sense, the story was still his even if he couldn't possibly chance turning it into an exclusive. Not the word of a wacky but lovely girl three thousand miles away who had picked it up from a cousin in Vienna who might possibly have been inebriated? They'd laugh him out of the business.

Still, his instincts told him that it was on the level. It wouldn't be the first time that Erika had come in with major news way ahead of the best reporters in the world. Donald was not surprised, then, but his blood chilled and his hands started to sweat and shake, when the linotype began signaling the continuing bells which meant a headline story. They must have been ringing for fifteen seconds before the operator of the machine got around to spelling out the story the world had been wondering about for nearly two years: FLASH—VATICAN CITY—POPE RESIGNS.

*　　*　　*

The Pope had evolved an intricate way of announcing his resignation—a means that reporters watching the teletype and television correctly assessed as intended to make clear that the decision to vacate the Throne of Saint Peter was his and his alone. Morelli had avoided the normal procedure for making such a momentous announcement, the Vatican Press Office and publication of his letter of resignation in the official newspaper of the Holy See, *L'Osservatore Romano*.

The Pope had dispatched his Confessor, a thirty-year-old Franciscan monk, to carry his handwritten resignation to a newspaper in Bari, the Adriatic port in the South of Italy, where the Pontiff had been born, an only son, into a fishing family. Of five sisters, two were still alive.

His note read simply: *Because of our advanced age and the uncertainty of our health, we are resigning the Throne of Saint Peter and our spiritual duties as the Supreme Pontiff of the Universal Church. We feel this is the Will of God and humbly beg the Faithful and our millions of friends in the Brotherhood of Man to join us and our successor in our continuing search for world peace.*

It was signed simply: *Francesco Xavier Morelli*

For all the rumors, warnings and gossip, the Pope's resignation caught the Vatican completely off guard. Obviously it was neither judicious nor practical for the Press Office or any other Vatican department to admit being caught by surprise. While they collected themselves and organized facilities to deal with the tremendous news break, the Vatican temporarily cut off all communication with the outside world, closing its telephone switchboards and suspending broadcasts from the Vatican radio station. The blackout was a short one, less than an hour.

At first the telephone lines were opened one at a time and manned by a Japanese Monsignor well-known to the press. His slow, precise English amounted to a play for time. The Vatican radio was ready to acknowledge the story's veracity; operations proceeded with remarkable smoothness. The Vatican was fully prepared to answer all questions about the Pope's resignation as well as historical precedents for it.

The first big surprise from Vatican sources was the statement that "His Holiness has left the Vatican, seeking seclusion during the immediate present. Church authorities are aware of his whereabouts and are respecting his desire for privacy."

As an instrument of personal action, the Holy Father's absence from the Vatican was eventually interpreted as a strong point. It eliminated doubts that the Pope may have been forced to resign or that his action could be construed as anything but a carefully considered move, reached after months of prayer, meditation and reflection.

Reporters turned to the television sets scattered around the buildings, turning on tape recorders to catch the fast-developing news and background material.

Regularly scheduled programs were promptly canceled. Monsignors and Cardinals from the Curia appeared before the cameras, reading texts, prepared months earlier, dealing with the history of Papal succession, some curious instances of Popes who never were crowned in the Holy Office, others who died within three days to a month after their election.

Monsignor Davide Antonio Basillio, a Vatican archivist, dealt with the historical facts in connection with Francesco Morelli's resignation.

In a well-modulated voice, Basillio read:

"The last resignation of a legitimate Pope (not to be confused with the anti-Popes or pretenders whose names have been erased from the nearly two thousand year succession to the Chair of Saint Peter) occurred in 1294 near the end of the French occupation of Sicily. The revolution wrote a glamorous chapter in the Sicilian struggle for liberty, but it proved catastrophic for the spiritual authority and prestige of the Holy See—turning it into a kind of Vietnam for the Papal Monarchy.

"The next Papal Election found the College of Cardinals divided over the succession and grouped around two powerful Roman families: the Orsinis, who favored the French descendants of Charles of Anjou and the Colonnas, favoring the Spanish House of Aragon.

"The deadlock was broken by the strangest occurrence in the history of Papal Elections. Someone shouted the name of Peter Morrone, a barely educated hermit who, nevertheless, was respected for his holiness. Everyone present felt that he was inspired by the Holy Ghost. They enthusiastically responded to the bizarre suggestion. The startled monk was brought from his retreat in the mountains and crowned Pope Celestine V.

"The unworldly, unsophisticated hermit proved totally unequal to the demands of the office. He became the tool of Charles of Naples who practically held him in captivity. Fortunately, Celestine's own faith in the Holy Ghost led him to the realization of the harm he was doing to the Church. He stepped down after less than a year, thus writing his name in the history of the Papacy as the last Pontiff to resign the august office voluntarily!"

After the Cardinals and Monsignors had finished with their statements, Italy's top newsmen had managed to collect themselves and were behind their familiar desks. Among them was Giorgio Scarangello, generally conceded to be the most articulate Italian newscaster. Scarangello glanced occasionally at notes as he spoke:

"Seventy-eight year old Francesco Xavier Morelli abruptly announced his abdication of the Throne of Saint Peter on March twenty-fifth in an unexpected and dramatic fashion, by sending his Confessor, a young monk, to his home town of Bari where a local newspaper carried the text of his brief statement.

"For all the rumors of his desire to resign during his reign, Morelli's resignation took the Vatican completely by surprise. Without modern precedents to guide them, the succession ceremonies will have to be improvised.

"At present Francesco Morelli's whereabouts are a 'carefully guarded secret.' The quotes in the preceding sentence are deliberate since there does not exist in Rome any such thing as a 'carefully guarded secret.' The Pope is believed to have gone into seclusion at one of several monasteries in the Alban Hills.

"For the first time in modern history, Italian Cardinals will not dominate the Conclave. They cannot arbitrarily chose the new Pope without the tacit consent of the United States, the Latin countries, England, Ireland and other English speaking notions which support their choice, creating an overwhelming majority no combination of independent, uncommitted Cardinals could invade.

"There are fears in the Western World that the choice of any of the Curia Cardinals as Pope would lead to extraordinary concessions to Italian Communists. Some believe the authority of the Holy See would be threatened. Yet selecting a militant anti-communist would be equally damaging. Is it not possible, many ask, that the rising tide of Italian Communism might find history repeating itself in the establishment of an unfriendly national government which could encircle Vatican City or terminate its independence?

"Given these woeful conditions, there have also been gloomy predictions that the Pope and his Court might eventually be forced to quit Vatican City and establish a 'place of business' elsewhere. Obviously this is considered unthinkable, amounting to a disaster not only for the Roman Catholic Church, but for Christianity and the Free World. The Church's power as a spokesman for morality may have been dissipated in recent decades by appeasers within the Church and by vacillating Popes, but the power still exists. Hence to non-Catholics the dissolution of the Papacy would be inimical to their own temporal and spiritual interests.

"Any abandonment of the Vatican would fragmatize the Church into national churches. History has shown that fragmentation leads to weakness. No other religious leader in the world can lay claim to the complete religious sovereignty that the Pope has enjoyed for nearly two thousand years. Although the source of his Power does not lie in his long tenancy in the City of Rome, a displaced Pope would be a matter of deep concern. Away from Rome, a homeless refugee, the Pope could no longer address the world with the respect that now resides in his person by centuries of historical precedent and his titles, the Vicar of Christ on Earth and Bishop of Rome."

Scarangello's analysis of the dramatic situation precipitated by the resignation of a reigning Pope was followed by the first news bulletin from America. The dispatch made it clear that the choice of a new Pope would contain far-reaching consequences affecting both Catholics and non-Catholics and was likely to be regarded as the most important ecclesiastical event of the 20th Century.

The American Council of Churches and a number of unaffiliated Protestant denominations urged their congregations to join in prayers that wisdom might prevail at the Roman Conclave. Their action was followed by countless Rabbis and, unexpectedly, by a number of evangelical ministers who expressed support of the action by the American Council, stating that in the continuity of the Papacy lay a strong moral force which modern society could ill afford to lose or diminish.

Angela's arrival at *Stampa Estera* took Donald away from the TV. The commentators were repeating themselves. For that he was grateful. The sight of Angela wasn't exactly displeasing either. She seemed pert and fresh, her eyes sparkling with excitement as she rushed over to him, saying, "Well, it's really happened. It's here. The biggest story Rome has seen since the end of the War."

Donald wanted to remind her of the reign of terror that was the sporadic contribution of the Red Brigades to Italy's turbulent political situation, of the several brutal assassinations and the ghastly weeks of torture Prime Minister Aldo Mauro endured before his bullet-ridden body was driven into Rome's center city and left for the authorities to discover. Evaluating the importance of news stories, Donald always felt, required objectivity that he didn't really care to possess. He thought better of disputing the point with Angela.

Now was hardly the time to fret about the past or give

lessons to a bright but foolish Italian chick who figured the odds favored playing the game of newspapering with a two-headed coin and the attractive piece of tail she offered as a fringe benefit.

The story was here. It was much more than a headline, actually an event in the century's history. It affected the entire world and Donald's capacities would soon be taxed to their utmost. Monsignor Ryan was on his way to Rome; the American Cardinals would be arriving as soon as the Conclave was called.

This was hardly the time for personalizing a relationship. Either Donald used Angela as Bulatov had suggested or he dumped her.

The crowd clustered around the teletype and TV sets had thinned; correspondents with offices in the building were on the telephone; others utilized the phone bank at the central post office on Piazza San Silvestrio. A number headed straight for the Vatican, hoping to pick up scoops or enough color material to compose features worth wiring in. Donald herded Angela toward the bar where he ordered *Campari* soda.

"I knew I'd find you here," Angela said breathlessly, "so I ran over as soon as I heard the news."

The *Campari* and ice-filled glasses were placed in front of them. The bartender squeezed lemon peel and plopped a chit on the bar.

Angela sipped at her drink, "That tastes good." Then, turning her dark eyes on Donald who noticed they looked less tired, she said, "It's funny, but I have a hunch that you knew today was the date—that the Pope was going to choose today."

Donald smiled, "I hate to answer that question squarely. It certainly would have been a great scoop. But when you look at it, it's perfectly logical—today is exactly a month away from Easter. If they convene the Conclave quickly—and there's no reason why they shouldn't—we can have the new Pope selected by Holy Week. You said that yourself—the first time we talked."

Angela nodded, "Anyone who figures logically would consider it that way. But I guess one loses the habit in Rome where the obvious becomes lost in conjecture."

154

She dipped into her purse and pulled out a sheet of paper. Angela opened it and laid it on the bar, "I got my hands on this today. It's going to be distributed as soon as Monsignor Ryan gets here."

Donald looked at the flyer. The focal point was an old picture of Ryan, full length in his Monsignor's cassock and biretta. Stripped across it in bold black type were the words: *America's Gray Eminence—Pope Maker Sneaks Into Rome*. The text amounted to a ruthless distortion of Ryan's travels on behalf of the American hierarchy to find a candidate the American Cardinals could endorse at the Conclave. The language distorted the purpose of the Saint Patrick's day visit by Muldoon and his colleagues to Rome, suggesting that they had threatened the Pope with exposure of a private scandal and that his resignation was literally being forced by "power-hungry American Cardinals who fear worker unity in Italy."

"Monsignor Ryan, far removed from the class struggle," it read, "is the nephew of an autocratic American Bishop who, like the late Cardinal Hellman, is the sworn enemy of labor unions and a spokesman for the huge capitalists of the Northeastern part of the United States. Bishop William Brady maintains his modest position in the Church hierarchy to obscure his real role as a reactionary tool of American business interests locked into tax-free, million dollar businesses with the Catholic Church.

"Like his uncle, Thomas Ryan serves the economic and political interests of his country and was the first prelate to become active in utilizing America's comparatively recent numerical strength in the College of Cardinals and its political influences in Washington to serve the interests of President Cameron, the warmakers at the Pentagon and American munitions manufacturers who stretch from the Delaware of the Duponts to the atomic energy plants on the West Coast."

The flyer included a list of the major countries Tom Ryan had visited in the last eighteen months as well as the names of Cardinals and Bishops with whom he had spoken. It was impressive, including all the European countries, most of Latin America and virtually all the emerging nations of Africa, one continent where Catholicism was growing at a healthy rate. Yet in the face of statistics showing not only the strength of Catholic philosophy and the eagerness of Africans to embrace it, the Vatican persisted in giving only token recognition of its potential.

There was a great deal of truth in Cardinal O'Toole's claim that, to the Curia, America has never been taken off the list of "missionary territories." Against this sterile concept of the Church's function, what hopes could African prelates share with the Establishment? Donald presumed Ryan had pressed a good case for American "intrusion"—as the Italians called it—on the forthcoming Conclave.

"I suppose I can keep this," Donald said as he folded it into squares and put the flyer in his side pocket.

"That's what it's for," Angela said, unaware that Donald was inspecting her fingernails carefully. They still bore the telltale signs of printers' ink.

"What comes next? Do you have any idea?" he asked.

"The usual, I guess. Pickets, demonstrations in front of the North American College—tracking down the Cardinals if they stay outside Rome in villas. It would help if the American candidate were known."

"Help whom?" Donald smiled. "The kids who printed this piece of crap, the moneybags who paid for it, the dummies who distribute it? It won't help anyone. I'm fairly sure that the name of the candidate is a secret the Americans are going to hold onto until the very last minute."

The blood rushed furiously into Angela's face as Donald recited his litany of conspirators. It pleased him to see that she was capable of shame. However, he didn't enjoy matching wits against a kid. He'd rather have squared off with someone his equal—Pietro Gentille, for instance.

"You'll have to catch me on the run," Donald said, "but that shouldn't be difficult. Either here at the hotel and, I suppose, at the North American, assuming Ryan stays there."

"I will. Thanks a lot," Angela said. She leaned over and kissed his cheek. "Do you think we're ever going to get together. It's been a long time..."

"I'm as aware of that as you are, Angela. I'm getting to feel like all these celibates I'm involved with." He couldn't resist another jibe, this one justified, "After all, I don't know where to reach you when I have a free hour or two."

Angela said nothing more than "*Ciao,* Donald," as she patted his hand, slid off the bar stool and walked briskly down the steps to Piazza Silvestro.

*   *   *

New York's Archdiocese preferred its clergy to wear the traditional Roman collar although the *powerhouse* feared making it mandatory. Monsignor Thomas Ryan often forgot to pack his and, in his travels, he made little use of the courtesies extended members of the clergy. He was not burdened by the ambivalence of older priests who worried about being seated next to women on trains and planes. Ryan ignored tradition. Being a seasoned traveler, he chose seats next to the thinnest female aboard a public vehicle, regardless of age, color, nationality or religious preference.

"There's a free current of air," he explained, "that you don't enjoy when you get stuck next to an overweight male. I appreciate the air—and the company."

Monsignor Ryan's little black book would be jumped on by Jet Set playboys any time he decided to offer it for auction. But the priest neither discussed the women he met while traveling nor answered the inescapable question about how he finessed their advances. "There are some occasions of sin," he replied, "that are best reserved for the Confessional."

Fortunately, Ryan had his ticket to Rome twenty-four hours before the news of the Pope's resignation or he might never have managed the late night flight from London to the Eternal City—or meeting the thinnest woman aboard.

She was Teresa Tashman, one of a handful of women on the businessman's flight which usually went out half-filled. Tonight it overflowed with photographers, reporters and the curious. Newsmen who promptly recognized Teresa could cheerfully have killed the tall, handsome, blue-eyed American who so quickly had the glorious lady involved in a warm, intimate conversation.

"Glorious lady" had become the only possible description of Teresa, although she was on the far side of forty, totally honest about every year of her fascinating life, the years she'd squandered as well as those that had proved meaningful.

Teresa entered college as a best-selling author a quarter of a century ago with a sensational but sensitively written novel of the effect of World War II on an adolescent girl whose father had enlisted in the Marines as the means of escaping the responsibility of being a parent and whose mother joined the ranks of *Nellie the Riveter*, working nights in an airplane factory, for the same reason.

Called *The Girl In The Red Bikini* it eventually was considered the forerunner of the genre invented by the late Jacqueline Susann except that Teresa's writing wove truth, literary style and crude reality into a work the critics found "stark and haunting." Teresa became a celebrity overnight.

During four years of college she wrote two books which she abruptly withdrew from publication. The despair of her publisher was matched by his good sense. He agreed with Teresa that the timing for the pieces was wrong, that her stories needed an air of *déjà vu* to preclude charges of sensationalism. They were published when Teresa was twenty-five and for the next ten years Teresa Tashman dominated the best seller list, even if her style and material slipped from "sensitive and perceptive" to "coarse and vulgar." These were the critics' words. She refused to believe them.

Her furies, fanned by gallons of alcoholic, compulsive traveling and a succession of ill-starred love affairs, culminated in her awakening in a blackout to discover that she'd married a nineteen year old Mississippi farm boy after a charter flight from Biloxi to Las Vegas. A week later she was in a Vegas hospital, beaten to a pulp by the youth's father, Jed Rankin, a socially conscious Korean war veteran who had returned to his state to work with government agencies involved in improving conditions in the squalid world of the backwoods.

Horrified by the consequences of his rage, Jed remained at Teresa's bedside until she was conscious and, at her request, longer—until she had become sober and aware of the shame and embarrassment she'd brought to a naive young man and the sort of "poor but honest and respectable family" she read about in novels of the South but didn't believe existed.

She thanked Jed for the beating and would have forced him to accept a check for one of his private charity projects except that the "hillbilly" had read her books, admired the early work and knew that Teresa Tashman had less money in the bank than he.

She was washed up, a has-been in the Jet Set and literary world she once ruled, a two hundred and twenty-five pound heavyweight who had squandered a fortune and a career on booze, pills, fat farms, countless men and aimless journeys from one part of the world to another. She'd circled the globe more times than could be counted on her fingers knowing little of it beyond posh suites in fabulous hotels where she consumed the local booze and wore out the men summoned to her presence by the lure of cash, drugs and other "entertainment."

Jed led Teresa into *Alcoholics Anonymous* and stayed at her side for six weeks, his expenses paid by Teresa's publisher, who realized he was witnessing a miracle. Jed did it *all* at the very beginning. He found a house for her in Los Angeles, small enough for Teresa to maintain without becoming a slave to housework. He accompanied her to A.A. meetings and gradually led her back to the typewriter.

A year later, *Fat Lady In The Red Bikini,* dedicated to Jed Rankin, swamped the competition on the best seller list to critics' raves and a record-shattering price for the movie sale. As a thinly disguised autobiography it was hailed as a triumphant piece of work, as powerful as *The Lost Weekend,* a devastating portrait of a woman caught in the terror of alcoholism.

Six months later, when Teresa had achieved control and felt fairly comfortable in her sobriety, she made her first public appearance—anticipating and relishing every gasp. She was a tall woman, once a striking brunette. As a concession to her years, the only one, she'd lightened her hair a trifle. But the rest was all real. Tone had returned to her creamy white skin, her wasp waist evoked envious admiration from women, men commented that Teresa's legs looked better than ever and that flounce to her behind was a good reason not to take Women's Lib too seriously. Teresa laughed, but she didn't agree.

A steady stream of work poured from her facile imagination and for the past year she had been a distinguished resident of Rome doing research on a "novel in progress."

Tom Ryan was familiar with the name of the thin lady, but not her face. Teresa Tashman introduced herself, "Monsignor Ryan, I'm honored," she said, extending her hand in her easy, friendly fashion. "I'm Teresa Tashman."

"Wow!" Tom Ryan smiled, looking her over with the skill of a professional wolf.

Teresa laughed, "Thank you, Father. That's what they all say. And it proves that everything they say about you is true, too."

"Should I ask what that is?"

"Of course. It's simply that you make everyone feel comfortable and that's an accomplishment."

"I never thought of it that way," Ryan mused. "Thank you. It's a reassuring compliment."

Teresa's sobriety had brought her back to Catholicism, leading to an interest in Catholic charities. She mentioned having met Ryan at a reception given at the North American College. She laughed, "You needn't trouble yourself in trying to recall me, Father. We both get around a great deal and I've stopped using that old cliche, 'You know, I meet so many people that . . .' Now I just smile and mumble. It works quite well."

Beyond observing that the next several weeks would be exciting in Rome, Teresa avoided involving the priest in a dialogue about the resignation of Francesco Morelli. She could see Ryan was tired. Obviously the Papal change was bringing him to Rome.

They were about twenty minutes out of Rome when their conversation suddenly became serious. "Monsignor Ryan, I have a problem. Maybe you can help me."

"I'll try, Miss Tashman."

"Good," she said, collecting her thoughts. "Can you give me a 'for instance' of how a priest would go about circumventing the secrecy of the Confessional if it meant saving a life...no...no." She stopped. "Let's not make it that serious. Suppose it was just to help out someone in terrible distress. A situation that could happen in a small town or a parish where the priest would recognize the person making a Confession."

Ryan smiled, "That's fairly simple, Miss Tashman. It happens all the time. A husband, for example, confesses that his drinking leads to beating his wife, neglecting his children, problems of that sort."

Teresa laughed, "I'm fairly familiar with them."

"So I've read," Ryan said. "And magnificent books, by the way. Anyhow, a priest would not be fulfilling his duty if he didn't attempt to visit the family, talk to the man, see him outside the Confessional and try to help him. Priests are not fools. You cannot persist in granting conditional absolution to an alcoholic on his promise to quit drinking. It goes deeper than that. So you help if you can—right out in the open. The priest certainly hasn't broken the seal of the Confessional. Far from it, he's acted according to the vows of his office."

"Thank you, that takes a little of the pressure off because what you're about to hear concerns you. You know I belong to *Alcoholics Anonymous*. We are not supposed to reveal what we hear at meetings; certainly not the identity of alcoholics whose problems we share.

"A few months ago a young priest began dropping in on the Rome meetings, always drunk. You will identify him without my mentioning his name. Moreover, the secrets he ranted about in his drunken rage may be known to you. He is Polish. He claimed that he was being threatened and persecuted. Not uncommon among alcoholics. In his irrational state it was impossible to separate fact from his imagination.

"Shortly after the American Cardinals came to Rome he showed up at a meeting and demanded that we give him 'sanctuary.' Now that's not our business. We deal with alcoholism. For that matter, I don't think the Church does a big business in 'sanctuary' either these days."

Ryan interrupted with a chuckle. "No, it's not a policy that adapted well to the twentieth century."

161

"All that I heard then was that he considered himself worse than Judas—that he'd betrayed a friend, a Cardinal. He's a Pole. Cardinal Novik is of Polish extraction. I thought no more about it.

"A few weeks ago, a Polish couple got in touch with me. They are refugees, living at Ostia where they work as domestics. This young man has attached himself to them. He drinks heavily and I gather they support his habit—with terrible misgivings—because when he's drunk enough he's at least quiet. They've asked him to leave, but he pleads to stay, saying that he is waiting for the Americans to arrive, particularly one Father Ryan.

"The name meant nothing to the couple. Evidently the priest mentioned coming to A.A. That led them to me. Moreover, they knew me. I've been active in Polish affairs. Perhaps you don't know that my real name is Rosi Danielewski. What could I tell them? Only that if Monsignor Ryan came to Rome, I would get in touch with him. So that is what I am doing. Does this make sense to you?"

"A great deal of sense, Miss Tashman. I hope you can give me the Polish couple's address and phone, if they have one."

"What a relief—and what a coincidence! Of course it would have happened eventually." She shuffled in her bag, found an address book, dug into another section for paper and pencil. She wrote down the Ostia address. Before giving the slip to Ryan, she said, "On the other side I am writing my own address and phone number. I can't promise you a home-cooked meal or anything like that. But if I can help you in any way while you're in Rome, I would be pleased to. I've avoided...well...lousing up your trip...to put it bluntly...by bugging you about things that must be on your mind. But I'm aware of the work being done by the American Cardinals. I pray for their success. Tonight I felt my prayers—not my questions—would be more helpful."

"They have been, Miss Tashman. I appreciate everything—your company, this information and your readiness to help. We need help—all we can get."

They were losing altitude, getting ready to land. Signs flashed their *No Smoking—Fasten Seat Belt* instructions. "I guess this is a good time to shake hands before we separate, Father Ryan."

Teresa Tashman extended her hand. Ryan smiled, held it for a second, giving her his silent blessing. When he'd finished a thought appeared to cross his mind. "Tell me, Miss Tashman. How is it that you are able to work with Polish refugees outside of Poland and yet you are an extremely popular writer in Poland; for that matter, in all the Communist countries?"

"Dear Monsignor Ryan. In Poland I'm like the Catholic Church. I am able to live in an in-between world, getting along with both sides. An ambivalent situation—like the Church position in Poland. I accept it, asking no questions, because you can imagine that it is very useful."

"I can imagine it," Ryan smiled. "You're a clever woman besides being attractive and one helluva writer."

Teresa smiled, "It's as they say. You make everyone feel so comfortable. Thanks again."

* * *

The following morning the Vatican announced that the Pope had returned to his apartment as mysteriously as he had left. Two hours later they showed a taped television program recorded in the Papal reception room. Morelli did not assume the Papal Throne. Rather, he was pictured addressing the members of his Vatican staff and officials of the Curia seated at a large table. The others were either seated at the table or grouped around him. It was clear that Morelli had insisted that they were not arranged according to rank. His young Confessor stood directly behind him while two nuns who had attended him as Cardinal and Pope for years were seated a Cardinal or two to his left. Torriani, however, had not been snubbed. As Secretary of State he was seated at Morelli's right, but the sight of the shy, old Vatican nuns at a Papal conference was irresistible to the cameraman who shifted to them at every opportunity.

He enlarged on his original statement, begged the prayers of the men with whom he had worked over years of change and, hopefully, progress, concluding with the Papal Blessing. He discreetly or deliberately avoided words like "harmony" and "together"—phrases like "common goals" and "spiritual motivation." It was no secret that the Pope

163

had frequently been at odds with his Ministers. Their relationship, at best, was frayed. Curiously, and this was a fact that many Vatican-watchers interpreted as behind the timing of his resignation, the Pope's relations with the Curia had in recent months been more amicable. This led to speculation that a harmonious Vatican might insure a productive Conclave if not one without sharp dissent. Morelli was too much the pragmatist to imagine a Conclave totally devoid of rancor.

Early in his reign, Morelli expressed support of Pope Paul VI who had urged Bishops and Cardinals to resign their offices at the age of seventy-five. He had carried this not unreasonable desire for making room for new blood in the upper echelon of Church hierarchy further by barring Cardinals over eighty from participating in the Conclaves to elect Papal successors. Unlike Paul, who simply issued a directive to this effect without qualification, Morelli explained his views.

"We have the greatest respect for the wisdom and experience of our elder Cardinals, but is it not a fact of history—and of the human character—that the elderly are inclined to favor their own? Just as the young are partial to their generation. Since the high office of Cardinal is never achieved by the very young, can we not respectfully request that it be sacrificed by the very old in the selection of a Vicar of Christ? We believe it right that the Congress of Cardinals find balance in this supremely important task which only they are authorized to perform. We are confident our elderly brothers will be praying for the Holy Spirit to guide their judgment."

It was a pacifying statement even if it did not assuage the curmudgeons who snarled about "upstarts taking over the Sacred College."

As the broadcast finished, Donald was called to the telephone. It was Tom Ryan who explained how late he'd arrived last night and had thought twice about calling Donald.

"You underestimate me, friend. How soon can we meet?"

"As long as it takes us to reach the Cafe Medici, a coffee bar known to Romans and regular visitors as having the best coffee in town. At least that was its reputation." To Donald, all *espresso* tasted marvelous.

"I imagine we'll each make it in about ten minutes."

"Fine, see you then."

* * *

There was time for only one *espresso*. As soon as David heard Monsignor Ryan's account of his plane trip with Teresa Tashman, instinct told him there was no time to waste. He called the number, spoke to Stefan Washinski who sounded quite rational and not disturbed when Donald explained that he'd been given Stefan's number by their good friend, Teresa Tashman. "Monsignor Ryan is with me. He just arrived." He paused to listen to a brief spurt of temper from the priest. "Yes, we have both seen the pamphlets, Stefan. There's no doubt that a conspiracy is taking place. Monsignor Ryan wants to see you as soon as possible. May we come now?"

There was a long pause on the other end of the wire. Donald did not press. He waited quietly for Stefan's answer. It seemed bright, too bright, almost manic. "Yes, yes. How wonderful to have friends with me after these lonely, terrible weeks. Come, come right away. It's easy to find. Right off the beach highway."

Donald walked quickly to the table where Ryan was reading the flyer. He handed it to Donald, shrugging his shoulders. "What can you say?"

"Nothing, right now. We're going to Ostia. Let's get a cab. I don't want to fuss with a rental agency."

They walked to the cab rack at the *piazza*. An old driver was at the head of the line; a young, bearded driver, a new breed in Rome's taxi business, stood behind him against a bright, clean, somewhat larger cab. Donald gave the old man two thousand *Lire*. "We're newspapermen," he said. "We're going to Ostia. We'd like the next cab."

"*Si, signore. Come no? Il ragazzo e mio figlio. Un autisto furioso!*"

The old man's son was everything his father promised—and more—a furious driver who at the sound of the word "newspapermen," drove with a frenzy that would have won him a Pulitzer if one existed in the category of drivers who knew the art of breaking every rule in the book and getting his reporter-passengers to their destination, hopeful that their brains were not as shaken up as their innards.

For all his fury, three quarters of an hour had elapsed between leaving the center of Rome and arriving at the apartment building where Paula and Michael Proser had been unwilling hosts to a troubled young man.

Donald's heart jumped at the sight of the crowd around the front door, the police cars and the ambulance. He hoped but didn't believe that the source of attention was Father Stefan Washinski.

It was. Donald's press card and Monsignor Ryan's repetition of the words, "I am an American priest," broke the ranks of the crowd, permitting them to enter a roped-off area where police stood guard.

A young officer looked at Donald's credentials. "I understand a little of them. If you will wait until Inspector Mattea comes downstairs, I am sure he will be of help."

The policeman volunteered as much of the incident as the crowd knew. There had been a suicide—a dreadful suicide. It was the handsome young man who had been befriended by the Prosers. He'd slashed his throat with a razor blade. Quietly, without a cry, in the bathroom while the Prosers awaited friends of his.

"He is dead, then?" Donald half-asked.

"*Si, signore*. I assume that. *Pacienza, per favore*."

They waited fifteen minutes before the body, tightly strapped in a canvas bag, carried on poles by four policemen, was removed from the building. Silence swept over the crowd. Men took off their hats. Like the people, the police, Donald and Monsignor Ryan made the Sign of the Cross.

Inspector Mattea came down a few minutes later, surrounded by higher echelon officers. The young policeman drew his attention and introduced him to the two foreigners. He inspected their papers, Donald's press cards, Ryan's passport and documents identifying him as a Monsignor attached to Saint Patrick's Cathedral.

Mattea's expression warmed. "I have visited your Saint

166

Patrick's Cathedral, Monsignor," he said in slow, careful English. Turning to include Donald in his next words, "I regret meeting you under such tragic circumstances—the suicide of a priest. So young—so very young."

Donald figured that Mattea still lacked a few years to fifty, but he recognized the feeling, the look in Mattea's eyes, a look peculiar to policemen whose encounters with tragedy aged their thoughts faster than their bodies.

"Yes, Monsignor," he said, although the question had not been asked. "It would be good of you to visit the Prosers. They are desperately upset. Our men will be leaving any minute. There is not much of an investigation for us, but if you care to talk to me or know the results of the autopsy, I am at your disposition." He fumbled in his pocket. "This is my card."

Mattea signaled to the policeman at the door. "Escort these gentlemen, please, to the apartment. They are friends of the deceased."

At the top of five flights of steps they found the Prosers sitting silently, staring out the window at the sea. The living room was immaculate, but a glance revealed that the bathroom and the tiny bedroom occupied by Stefan, no bigger than a closet, really, had been turned upside down. Two policemen had attached hoses to the taps and were washing the walls and floor where the blood had splattered.

"I wonder if they do that for everybody," Donald thought. "But, then, how many suicides do they have in Ostia?"

Monsignor Ryan introduced himself and the Prosers reacted with relief at the sight of someone who could not ease their shock but who might share their feelings. Ryan understood. A suicide leaves behind not the regret of his passing that he may have imagined, but terrible fear by those who survive that they could have prevented it. It was a burden that often took years of prayer to pass.

The Prosers, he knew, were locked into this state of fear. Paula kept saying over and over again, "If only..."

There was nothing to follow it. There were so many "If onlys"—but how could she have recognized the step by step degeneration of a pathological mind to the point where suicide loomed as the ultimate, uncompromising end.

While Donald searched through clothes and papers the police had left behin.', Ryan talked slowly to the Prosers, gradually drawing them out of their silence to the point where they agreed to leave the apartment and spend the night at the home of their employer. They intended to anyhow, since the family was away.

"Let us drive you there," Ryan said.

"No, thank you, *Padre,* we can walk. It is only a few steps. We will leave shortly," Michael Proser said. "I know you must want to talk to us about poor Stefan. He mentioned your name often. Maybe...perhaps...tomorrow or the next day. You have our number. We are always here in the evenings." He scribbled another number on a slip of paper, "This is our *padrone.* Call there if we are not at home. They do not mind."

As they made their way slowly back to the street and their driver *furioso,* through the crowd that filled the staircase, Donald's face had become taut and angry. "Tom, this is hideous business. We have a great deal to go over. Your Pietro Gentille has much to answer for. Once again we find him using a misfit in the world to do his dirty work. Someone no one will miss. Someone no one will ask questions about."

Ryan didn't need to be told that his friend was suffering. His agony was no different from that of the Prosers.

Donald was trying to complete the rest of the words to the tragic sentence that began, "If only..."

PART V

North American College

The suicide of a Polish priest went unnoticed in the Italian press. That it produced a flurry of activity in the Cardinal's Mansion in New York went unnoticed as well. By coincidence Cardinal Muldoon's telephone calls from Rome coincided with a decision by the Vatican not to delay selection of the date for the Conclave to elect the two hundred and sixty-fifth Vicar of Christ, Pontiff of the Roman Catholic Church. Members of the College of Cardinals throughout the world, approximately one hundred and fifteen Princes of the Church, were summoned to assemble in Rome on April eighth, exactly fourteen days after Francesco Morelli's resignation.

In making public the date, the Vatican drew attention to the unusual nature of the Conclave. Unlike those following the death of a Pontiff, this election was being prepared as a joyous religious celebration, a festival of the spirit. Tradition would be followed in the actual Conclave, but preliminary ceremonies would have a far different tone because of the absence of the period of mourning. Moreover, the Vatican news release declared that the Holy See intended inviting suggestions from Cardinals abroad about the style of ceremonies most suitable to this unprecedented event in Church history.

As the news sped around the world, Donald was speaking to Cardinal Muldoon from the Central Post Office. In New York Muldoon listened in horror as the newspaperman and Monsignor Ryan related their accounts of the tragedy, beginning with Ryan's conversation with Teresa Tashman aboard the plane.

When they finished, Muldoon said quietly, "A terrible tragedy. So very sad. It explains many things to me." He was speaking to Tom Ryan. "I have to think this out, make a decision, call Novik. Give me a second." The silence seemed endless until Muldoon came back on the line. "I have it straight now. Call me back in exactly one hour, please. Thomas?"

"Yes, Your Eminence."

"Pray for your Cardinals—all of us."

Donald, standing close to the receiver, grabbed the phone before the connection was broken. "Your Eminence, forgive me, but I'm trying to read your thoughts. I suspect you would like to bring Cardinal Novik to Rome as soon as you can, without attracting attention."

Muldoon managed a chuckle, forcing it, really, to ease the tension on both sides of the Atlantic, "That *is* running through my mind."

"Then whatever arrangements you make, please do not use Mediterranean. Avoid giving any information to Pietro Gentille. Call Ed Bowers at American Trans-Atlantic. Tell him to respect your wishes and remind him that he owes 'one' to Donald Brady. That will do it."

The chuckle was warmer. "Thank you, Donald. I wonder if your feelings about Gentille coincide with mine. God bless you. We'll talk again in an hour."

On their way to a coffee bar out of sight of newspapermen going in and out of *Stampa Estera,* Tom stopped at a church.

"It's closed," Donald warned.

"Are you sure?"

"I haven't tried them all, but show me a church that's open in Rome and I'll show you a synagogue or that lonely Episcopal Church the Vatican permits to operate."

Discovering that Donald was right, Tom asked, "How about the Church of Christ? Didn't they make a landing here?"

"Could be," Donald said. "I haven't tracked it down yet. But I'll put it on my list and let you know."

Both men ordered a double shot of English gin splashed into their Campari and each drifted into his own thoughts. Donald's went to Angela. "This is it, baby," he told himself,

170

"showdown time. That kid better shit or get off the pot . . ."

But thinking tough wasn't in him—not after what he'd seen today. Who was Donald Brady to come to Rome and kick a kid around who didn't know the score and never would unless someone laid it out for her? She was existing—surviving—like so many others in this capital of Church, Government, ruins and tourists. Where were the careers for young women? Were they at airline counters figuring out complicated fares for impatient tourists until they could snare a husband? Or sewing in the fire traps behind all the boutiques under conditions that even that apostle of dawn to dusk work, Richard Nixon, would be repelled by?

In going about the business of naming a new Pope, the Cardinals were proceeding with the arrogance born of ages of belief in the male's superiority to women. Once locked inside the little cubicles where they would be sequestered until a new Pontiff was chosen, Donald thought, they will be symbolical of their disdain for one of the most significant movements of the day, that of women rising.

There will be a male Pope named by male Cardinals. Even the attendants hovering outside the sealed door to the Vatican apartments will, like themselves, be old and male. No wonder pretty girls hustled in Rome. Was there really that much difference between hustling on the streets or, like Angela, hustling in the bar of *Stampa Estera?*

Erika, for example, had no patience with discussion about equal rights for women becoming an international objective. "You think every place is like America? America is not the whole world. In the rest of the world, women are not regarded as equal to men. That's it. *Punkt. Finito.* Close quote."

"Pray," Cardinal Muldoon had urged him. "Right on, old boy," Donald told himself. "The kid's hustling a buck just like I am. Who has time to pray when your belly's growling and you're not sure where you're going to sleep. When you're too poor to make things work out at the Merline."

Donald had to stop thinking of Angela as a nasty kid who happened to be a good piece of ass. They'd both be better off if he faced the truth. Angela was scared, a frightened kid who'd been left on her own for God knows how long!

Somewhere along the line Thaddeus had told him. Since she was sixteen, at least. Not ideal conditions for an Italian girl, brought up by a busy grandmother, to learn the difference between good and evil. Donald wasn't so sure that he knew the difference himself.

The hour was almost up. They'd knocked off two double gins, grabbed a sandwich made of two thin slices of bread with a razor-thin slice of *prosciutto* buried somewhere between. "You only eat these on the way to the guillotine," Donald remarked. "I hope it's not an omen."

Tom touched his arm, "Hold your fears, my brother. I am praying."

"Me, too," said Donald as the sandwich disappeared in a mouthful. There was not even the taste of *prosciutto*.

The telephone call to New York produced information that Monsignor Pfeifer had flown to Chicago to pick up Cardinal Novik. Tom explained to Donald that they were old friends; moreover, Novik was in a terrible state of shock.

Muldoon, Novik and Pfeifer would arrive in Rome within forty-eight hours. Ed Bowers had taken over expertly and rather than risk leaks, there would be no further communication between Rome and New York. Ryan was to sit it out at the North American College and make temporary living arrangements for the three men. Ed Bowers would shepherd them from portal to portal.

Donald beamed, "That will relieve Ed of *Easter* duty for five years at least. *Ciao,* Tom, I've got some dirt to dig. I'll be in touch."

* * *

It was all so easy—after you'd done it a couple of thousand times. That was his trouble and Angela's too. Donald took it for granted, having worked so long with cool professionals, that everyone else was skilled. Angela probably figured that hiding out and being evasive made one a skilled spy, a counterspy, a news source, or whatever the hell she assumed she was.

His address book turned up the name of a sub-editor on *Il Messaggero* he'd met briefly on a junket Italian newsmen made to New York and Philadelphia for the *Eucharistic Congress* a couple of years ago. The office was nearby. He dropped by. Renato Zacardi was not only in, but delighted to be remembered by an American colleague.

His office was in a bull pen which suited Donald fine. He could tell by checking the copy paper at the bull pen desks that Angela's was similar. He needed a sample to feel the weight. He found it at Zacardi's.

After exchanging a few words, Zacardi leaned over and whispered. "You, of all people, will understand, *Signore* Donald. This is the first day of my vacation." He looked at the clock. "Now. It is imperative I get out of here, *now*. And way, way, far away, before I am assigned to this Conclave ... you know what I mean?"

"Very well, my friend, very well. I will call again—if I am in Rome. We can lunch together. Here is my address here and in New York." He scribbled on the top sheet of the pile of copy paper, then asked, "May I borrow a few sheets?"

"Take them, my friend. As you say in America, 'Be my guest.' I like that."

He grabbed Donald's hand, shook it vigorously. "See you soon. Me? I go out the back."

Someone interested in printing and knowledgeable about its artistry can make off with anything from guarded galleys of sensational new books to secret financial reports on the simple pretext of being a visitor to a printing plant from another city, country or outer space. Fine printers love to talk about their craft and accessibility to their plants has become easier with the growth of automation which has reduced an honorable craft to the status of a push button word dispensing machine.

A man prowling around inquiring about copy paper, smooth but not coated, weight thirty-five pounds, could linger long enough to learn the combination of the safe and the telephone number of the office manager's mistress. To men who work with it, paper is a word that needs an adjective—good paper, slick paper, glossy paper, fine paper, bonded paper, newsprint—and copy paper.

A visit to three shops within a ten block radius of *Il Messaggero* was all Donald needed to find what he wanted.

Porters, the equivalent of receptionists, know nothing in Italian businesses. That's what they're paid for. Except in print shops where the magic of their world affects even the dumbest. The porter at *Shop Numero Tre* was excited enough by the sight of the blank side of Angela's page that he wanted to hold it up to the light. Donald politely got out of that one. The porter pondered briefly, "*Momento, signore.* I speak to the manager."

In seconds, Donald was inside the manager's office. The man proved to be a goldmine of information after Donald identified his profession, explaining that he was looking for the source of this particular paper. "I suspect a colleague is receiving direct information from a terrorist group. I keep saying to myself, 'This paper has to be stolen from a reputable house.'"

"How right you are!" the manager exploded. "It's this shop. Look at it—always open in the back—in the alley—for the air. During the last month someone's been slipping in here and carting off the stuff right under our noses. Now we keep it under lock and key. So it's stopped. That's it."

"Have you reported this to the police?"

"Police? Why? What would they do? *You* think it is terrorist. How do I know? You have no proof. Maybe it is some crazy person. What have they stolen? Maybe a hundred dollars of material. Perhaps it is someone inside the shop. There is nothing to report. But I can tell you that it is ours—the way it is cut tells me that. Have I helped you?"

"A great deal," Donald answered. "Thank you very much."

He gave the manager his card and dropped another off at the porter's desk, "If you ever come to New York, perhaps we can have lunch."

The porter wasn't surprised. Why not? The Italian and the American were brothers. They cared about printing.

Donald wandered seemingly without purpose for an hour in the neighborhood until he found himself at the *Trevi Fountain.* Behind him on either side of the *piazza* lay dark alleys containing repair shops, wine stores and, hopefully, a small printing shop with its door closed, secured by a padlock, left hanging and open on its latch.

He looked in the gutters and inside the tiny, green, disposal baskets attached to traffic signals and miscellaneous posts, intended for trash. He counted one, two, three. When he reached six flyers, his eyes turned toward a tiny alley that, of course, had a street name. Halfway down he saw his shop, the door shut, a padlock hanging half-open. As he approached he could feel the quiet inside.

How odd! Clandestine printing was universal in its bad habits. In their excitement to hit the streets with their materials, even sophisticated radicals distributed too much too close to home. They all assumed they were carefully protecting the premises by leaving someone on guard around the clock. It never varied.

Angela Nero was surprised as hell when, neither hearing the half-opened lock being removed, the creaky door opening nor the sound of footsteps, she found herself being awakened by a tall man who pulled a blanket off her and yelled, "Get off that cot, Angela, and let's get out of here."

She wanted to lock the padlock. "Fuck off, Angela. You're either finishing with that crowd now or you'll end up like Stefan Washinski."

"Stefan? What happened? Is he . . . is he . . . is he dead?"

"Quite."

"Murdered?"

"I don't know."

Donald thought a second. "All right, Angela. Go back and padlock the place. Maybe you'll be coming back. It depends."

*　　*　　*

Angela's composure held until they reached Donald's room. She flung herself on the bed and cried, softly, very softly. She was not hysterical and Donald wondered what Angela's feelings actually were; her shame at being caught, guilt because she was playing the game both ways or simply crying because it was all that was left for her to do. When she got up from the bed, her face was a mess, but there had been no tears.

She went into the bathroom and poured cold water over

175

her head with a pitcher. Then she tied a towel into a turban, came out and sat in the easy chair, looking like a school girl ready to be scolded. But Donald didn't scold. He told her he was giving her a choice; either to begin playing square with him or to walk out and play spy games with a group of young pseudo-radicals who were being used by mature men who knew precisely what they were doing.

Angela appeared to need little persuasion to realize she'd been duped. Doubts, she said, had surfaced before Donald asked her to work for him. Angela found herself questioning why she'd been seduced into harassing a group of American Cardinals who intended participating actively in a Papal Conclave. "What difference did it make to me?" she asked. "I'm Catholic, of course. Casual, like a lot of Italians. I go along with whatever part of the Church I need. You know, Donald, it was easier, safer and cheaper to get an abortion before Italy legalized abortions. Now the same doctors who performed them refuse because it's out in the open. They risk losing their appointments at Catholic hospitals. How many hospitals in Italy aren't Catholic? It's like Frankenstein's monster. You've settled one problem and made another one—only the new one is worse.

"You don't have to believe this, but they wanted to include you in the *Gray Eminence* flyer. I talked them out of it."

"Not that it matters, but why?"

"Because I care for you. You've been good to me. You gave me an idea of what it's like to be a professional—not a gossip monger."

Angela started to cry again—but this time with little damage to her eyes. She was able to tell him everything, from the very beginning of her association with a handful of Italian young people who wanted to establish their own Red Brigade, and of Hans whom they'd brought from Germany because he knew electronics. He'd bugged Monsignor Ryan's room at the Palace-International.

"Now," and for the first time she smiled, "Hans is figuring out how he's going to bug the Conclave."

"Does he really believe he can do it?"

"Of course," Angela said, "he's got a terrific ego."

Donald poured himself a drink. "Doesn't Hans imagine that if you add his bugs to all the others that are being planned, they'll probably negate one another and all that will come out is gibberish."

Angela laughed. "Is that possible?"

"I'm going to check it." Then he brightened. "You check it. Ask Hans."

It was all so clever—and obvious—how Pietro Gentille had managed it. Angela was an easy make. Her name made her attractive to his scheme; her failure as a newspaperwoman was easily preyed on. According to Angela he never came out and said it, but there were hints here, suggestions there, that if she did a good job of getting close to the Americans, she would be rewarded with a correspondent's job for one of the big American magazines.

"He got to Stefan the same way," Angela said. "He made Stefan believe that if the Americans turned the Conclave away from the rightful heirs to the Papacy, qualified educated Italians, there would be immediate suspension of the delicate talks between the Communist Government in Poland and the Church. On the other hand, if he split the Americans, preyed on the fears of Cardinal Novik, Stefan could look forward to an improvement in his position. Maybe he might become part of the negotiating team the Vatican maintained to keep open the road to rapprochement with his homeland.

"Nothing was ever put in writing. Nothing was ever firmed up. There were casual payments. Sometimes they received considerable sums; other times, just token payments. All the big money was supposed to start when the American Cardinals arrived."

Angela said that her own contact with Gentille was limited—no more than a couple of conversations—both out in the open—at parties to which they'd both been invited. Mutual friends had asked her. Now she suspected that Gentille had been responsible for the invitation. Gentille's dealings with Stefan were also casual. After one meeting, Stefan had only spoken to Gentille on the phone. No special number. Gentille usually took the priest's calls at his office.

Gentille had covered all bases. He hadn't been devious

about being seen with his informers, not with Angela, at any rate. Payments had been in cash. He maintained no secret headquarters, no private telephone numbers, no mail drop. Donald could not conceive of a starting point to link Gentille with the ragged efforts of a group of malcontents whose aim was to discredit the Americans. Any investigation would hinge on the words of Gentille's recruits. Here the man showed his genius. Who would believe them?

"What was Stefan supposed to obtain from Cardinal Novik?"

Angela seemed surprised. "The name of the American candidate, of course. That's the most important thing. From then on, it seemed simple—at least the way Hans explained it. Then they'd go to work discrediting the candidate."

"With a few thousand flyers?"

"I think they imagined they'd be more effective than that. They believe they can instill doubts in the minds of the American Cardinals. They're sure to reach others. That list of Cardinals in the *Gray Eminence* flyer would be worked on."

"Where did the list come from?"

"Gentille, of course."

"In writing?" Donald asked, hoping he didn't sound eager.

"Oh, no, Donald. He was much too clever for that. It was part of a list that an American research company prepared recording all the trips made by major Cardinals throughout the world. Then there were lists of trips made by Bishops. Another list made by Monsignors. You ought to know about it."

"I do," Donald groaned. "Boy, what a smart-assed bastard he is! Hiring a two-bit publishing company to put together a list from research they slapped together any way they wanted, depending on him to supply the meat. It's chilling. Do you think Novik told Hans the name of the American candidate?"

"Yes—not straight out. He didn't say 'yes' or 'no,' but I think Hans has it broken down to where if somebody on your side—maybe I can say 'our side'—drops the wrong shoe he'll know."

"What makes you think that?"

Angela thought. "Well, Hans is a loudmouth. He talks about a lot of money coming in soon. That we're really going to do a job of sabotage. He's a blowhard, but do you really think he'd be talking like that at this stage of the game if he weren't sure of something?"

"I wish I knew," Donald said. "I've never met him."

Angela thought, "Put it this way. He's careful—even when he's talking big. Does that make sense?"

"A lot of sense. One thing intrigues me. Why did they steal the copy paper?"

"No reason, none in particular," Angela answered. "One of the kids saw it on the loading dock. He stole a few packages. Then he found out how easy it was to sneak inside through the alley. I guess we didn't have to do it."

Angela was unable to supply specifics about Stefan's meeting with Cardinal Novik. She knew that Hans was there and gathered he'd done the talking. "You know, Donald, Stefan disappeared the same day. I never talked to him afterward."

"Where does Hans live?"

She laughed, "I don't know. He's the one who decided no one should know the other's address. I played it with you. I live at the Pension Maria Di Fiore, around the corner from the top of the Spanish Steps. Not far from here. I'm sorry, I've been stupid. What can I do to make up for it?"

"To be honest, I really don't know, Angela. We'll have to see. I would appreciate your going back to them for appearance's sake. Your friends are stupid and that makes them dangerous. You have to protect yourself, I'm afraid. In a few days the American Cardinals will be here. I guess Hans will want you to keep in touch with me."

"I'm sure of that."

"Good. So keep in touch—just as they want. We'll have to improvise as we go along. As to promises, when this is through, I can make you one that will stick."

"You can?"

"Yes, but it depends on just how good you are. Professionally, I mean. There are a lot of stringers and correspondents in Rome—I won't tell you their names—

who hold their jobs because their publications can't come up with suitable replacements. There are spots for you. The trouble is, Angela, you've been so busy walking on both sides of the street that you didn't look where you should have."

"In your position you can afford to be smart."

Donald had hit where it hurt. "In your position, Angela, you start being smart by playing an honest game of pool. It's tough and the money's lousy, but integrity is like an insurance policy. It pays off when you need it most. You've got that chance now. Grab it."

"I shouldn't have snapped. I'm sorry. You're a friend, Donald. Thank you."

He wrapped her in his arms and their lips fell into the kiss they'd both been waiting for. They stripped off each other's clothes in total silence and fell naked into bed where Donald held her so close that she pulled back for a breath of air. Just as quickly she moved back into the safety of his strong arms.

$$* \quad * \quad *$$

Ed Bowers' arrangements brought Cardinals Muldoon and Novik into Rome without a hitch, along with Monsignor Pfeiffer and, by a lucky coincidence, Bishop "Gabe" Hearn, a well-known character in the tristate area. He was an M.D. who took Holy Orders after losing an arm in the Korean War. Now retired, "Gabe," who was seldom called Gabriel, just decided to pack up and visit Rome while the Conclave was being held. "I want to see one Pope installed before I die," Hearn had explained.

Hearn intended staying at the Pension Enrico Caruso as the guest of a retired singer he'd known from a parish he'd served in Yonkers. Bishop Hearn regularly renewed his physician's license. In his retirement he worked harder than ever.

Hearn examined Novik as soon as they reached the College, diagnosing his condition as nervous exhaustion. He dug into his bag and found a mild sleeping pill and assured Muldoon that the patient would be better in the morning.

"Thank you, Gabe," Muldoon said. "I'll expect you here

180

for lunch tomorrow. You're going to be put to work. It's quite a job we have on our hands."

"Whatever you want, Your Eminence, I'm pleased to do."

He left with Ed Bowers whom he had promised a night on the town. "You can come over to my place and hear opera records for as long as you can stand them."

"Thanks a lot, Bishop, but I'll do Rome my way. At the Palace-International in bed with a big bottle of *vino rosso*. I'm bushed."

After they left, Cardinal Muldoon, Ryan and Donald Brady pooled their information about Alexander Novik. Said Muldoon, "I've known for years that he's been eager to move some of his family from Poland to America. He's met resistance from both sides—the Church and the Communists."

Tom Ryan said, "That explains why Stefan felt he'd betrayed his friend. Hans was supposed to frighten him—he probably used some wild tale that Novik's relatives in Poland would suffer unless the Cardinal took orders from him. Obviously they saw Novik as the one Cardinal they could intimidate."

"And get information from..."

Muldoon frowned. "Do you believe that, Donald? Do you think they got information from Novik?"

"I have knowledge, Your Eminence, that leads me to believe they have a fair idea of where to look for your nominee. I suspect Cardinal Novik gave them some possibilities without pinpointing the actual choice."

Muldoon was silent a long time. "Donald, you're going to have to confront him tomorrow. As a newspaperman."

"Very well. A nasty job, but I'll get it for you."

"Will it hurt?"

Donald's laugh was hollow. "Of course it hurts. But, like any confession whether you make it to a priest or a newspaperman, there's a sense of relief when it's over. We all know Cardinal Novik. He's a strong man. Even strong men break under threats to the family."

"It could never really happen, of course. It's impossible. Neither the Communists nor the Church would tolerate it. Gentille would never go that far."

"You're almost right, Donald," the Cardinal said, "Gentille isn't playing a gentleman's game, but that doesn't make him foolhardy. The trouble is that you never know what a bunch of fanatical kids will do. And that's what these young people are. Not fanatical in a political sense. Fanatical in trying to establish their identity. It's the old criminal myth—that by pulling a sensational job—the killing or kidnapping of a Cardinal's grandson on the eve of a Conclave—they will become big shots—world famous—international figures. It's not difficult to accomplish. There's a grapevine from one group to another. Just as we've seen in the States. Maybe this group is punk stuff by tough hardcore Communist standards—but they get around. One crazy idea like this might appeal to a group in Poland or in Germany. You don't know. Because you don't know, you don't take chances."

A worried look appeared in his eyes. "Maybe we should all pull back," Muldoon said. "Perhaps we should get in touch with Gentille and reach some sort of agreement."

Donald was tempted to laugh but refrained. "Cardinal Muldoon. Say that all over again in your own mind and you'll see the folly of it. Mr. Gentille would say that you were crazy. He'd deny knowing anything of a wild plot to use Novik's family as hostages to wreck the American strategy."

After a second the Cardinal shook his head in despair. "Donald, I must sound very stupid."

"Not stupid, Your Eminence. Tired."

"You're right," Muldoon said. "You know, I think I'm going to follow Ed Bowers' example. You'll excuse me, won't you?"

Donald and Tom rose as the Cardinal left the room. He stopped at the door, turned back, "Donald, I am in your debt. Once you get to this 'Your Eminence' stage, too many people are afraid to speak up. A man can only be a true Eminence if he has friends who level with him. Thank you."

Tom looked wearily at Donald, "How about my driving you back to the hotel? I could do with a shot of *vino* myself—but not here."

"Fine, Tom, let's go."

Ryan put on his sports coat and fixed his tie. "You know,

not a soul in Rome has come up and called me the *Gray Eminence*. Have I aged that much?"

"Not yet, *Gray Eminence*. But you will."

* * *

By morning Cardinal Novik felt better. He insisted on telling his story to everyone involved in the American delegation, Cardinal Muldoon, Monsignor Ryan and Donald. He told of the meeting with Hans, how it had been engineered by Stefan. He recalled his own anger with Stefan, of leaving him without saying a word of good-bye. "I didn't even bawl him out beyond one outburst at the beginning of the meeting. Even that would make me feel better than I do now. I should have tried to understand his pressures. Instead, I only saw my own."

Novik showed his listeners how Hans had outlined the gun in his breast pocket. "When Stefan went to the bar for coffee, Hans asked me to use German. That's why Stefan was never sure of what I said or how I'd been threatened.

"Hans said that the parties he represented wanted me to give them information on our plans as we went along. Finally he asked me to identify the American candidate. I refused. He brought out a list of names. He pointed to this name and that name—asking me if this was the one. Was that Cardinal our choice? All I can remember is that I shook my head negatively at the mention of every name.

"Then came the threats. They would kidnap my grand-nephews in Poland unless I cooperated. What could I do? I said I would cooperate, but that they would have to tell me how. As to the candidate, I repeated that we had not made up our minds. At the time, it was partially true. We were not unanimous. I didn't know this man. I was trying to be careful not to reveal anything or allow him to penetrate my subconscious. That's how you give away secrets. So I alternated between rage and fear. I became arrogant. I tried to play the game as well as I knew.

"After we got back to America there were calls, local calls and calls from Italy. They were simply voices reminding me that I'd promised to cooperate. They said they'd be in touch with me when we returned to Rome. Naturally they telephoned on the day Morelli resigned. Then it was a call from Poland. Whoever it was spoke Polish. It was a friendly voice—saying he wanted to remind me of my promise and wish me a happy trip. Can you imagine?"

Then Cardinal Novik's voice changed. It reflected real fear. "My brothers, I don't know what I am going to do. I genuinely fear these people. I ask myself who can we turn to with this story? To the Church in Poland? To the Communist Government? What would they say? They'd laugh at me—produce all the children, my nieces, maybe even my sister who would do anything to make me look like an addle-brained old man.

"I understand that the other Cardinals are coming to Rome and they will be living at a Villa out in the Alban Hills. Have you chosen the villa, Monsignor Ryan?"

"Yes, Your Eminence."

"Well, if it is ready to be occupied, I would like to go there now. William, I am going to resign from the steering committee, as we call ourselves. You will have to replace me with O'Toole. Obviously I am in no position, mentally or physically, to participate further. My loyalty you have. My belief in the ambitions of our colleagues is as staunch as ever. It is a holy work and we will succeed. But for now I must be alone. William, I need to pray. Only God can help my peace of mind. Not your good will, not the medicine of our wonderful Bishop Hearn—I just hope you understand."

"Of course I understand, Alex. And I respect your wishes. You can drive to the Villa whenever you like. Monsignor Pfeifer will go with you. Nominally, I am supposed to be living there, too, but this is more convenient. They have arranged accommodations for us and we propose to call in Cardinals De Cordoba and O'Toole—when they are needed."

There was a flash of the Novik wit, "O'Toole will pray with me and I can use his prayers, but he won't be sorry to replace me. He's been itching to get a bigger piece of this action ever since we started. Enjoy him."

On April fourth, Donald and Thomas were summoned into the room that served as Cardinal Muldoon's combination study, bedroom and sanctuary. It was situated deep inside the building of the North American College so as to spare Muldoon from hearing the sporadic demonstrations occurring outside the walls of the seminary.

Silently he showed them a letter that had just come from Cardinal Novik at the villa.

Your Eminence,

In order not to surprise you and make your role in the Conclave more difficult, I am advising you at this time of my plans. I intend attending all the preliminary ceremonies of the Conclave and will indeed enter the Conclave itself or, at least, appear to.

I have made arrangements to leave through a side entrance of Saint Peter's and drive to Ciampino where I have chartered a private plane to fly me to Warsaw. I have no alternative but to present my person to our enemies, whoever they are, as the only means I know to protect my family. I hope this does not embarrass you. If it does, I can only express my regrets.

Obviously my gesture may serve to nullify the Conclave if the Americans are treated with the same arrogance inside the Sistine Chapel as they have been before the Conclave begins.

I will not hesitate to announce to the world my reasons for abandoning my duty to attend the Conclave for the higher duty of protecting those who are near and dear to me. In my present frame of mind I cannot distinguish between the two responsibilities. So I have chosen to protect people—not a political nightmare.

Yours in Christ,

Alexander Cardinal Novik.

"The man's gone stark raving mad," Donald exploded. "He's got to be stopped! This is crazy! He's simply gone ape!"

"Donald, Donald, what's come over you?" Muldoon snapped.

Donald stopped short. "What's come over me, Your Eminence? What's come over Cardinal Novik? He's gone crazy."

"Are you sure?" Muldoon asked serenely.

"I'm afraid I don't understand your reaction...it doesn't..."

"My son, it doesn't make sense. That's what you are trying to tell me. I'm sorry to disagree. It makes a great deal of sense to me. Cardinal Novik has been afflicted with a terrible problem. His family has been threatened. You were the first voice to warn of the reality contained in the threat—even thought it came from some stupid...some stupid commando or militant. Whatever, that doesn't matter.

"Now Cardinal Novik is acting according to his conscience. That is all God asks of any of us. It may affect the Conclave. It may hurt the American ambition. That does not matter, does it? Not compared to human life."

"But Your Eminence, a telephone call to any of the head men in Poland would get protection for his family. It's inconceivable that a group of kids can drive an American Cardinal to Warsaw to stand in the streets shouting that his family is in danger—all because of the Conclave in Rome. He'd look like an idiot."

Cardinal Muldoon's face grew taut. His voice was cold, "Mr. Brady, would a telephoned promise from a Communist country satisfy you that your family was safe in the face of a threat you genuinely feared?"

Donald backed down, "No, now that you mention it, I guess I wouldn't be very comfortable."

The silence was deafening. Donald's face flushed.

"I'm sorry. I apologize. You've got to understand this ecclesiastical beat is new to me. You don't expect hoodlums in the Church, but here they are. You take it very calmly. You wait for events to happen. We don't. We push, we pull stories out of dark holes. I guess I have something to learn."

"You could begin with your Church history, Donald, and

I'm not being facetious. Applying pressure of the vilest sort during a Papal Conclave is not unusual.

"Placing a Pope on the Throne of Saint Peter to represent the special interests of a king or an emperor was commonplace in the Middle Ages. The Papacy was often sold to the highest bidders. Murders were committed and wars were fought to corrupt the Papal Office. But one really doesn't have to look back five hundred years in history to find arrogant interference in Papal Elections. Our own century brought Pius X to the Throne when the Archbishop of Cracow, Poland, Cardinal Puszyna, according to the orders of Franz Josef, Emperor of Austria-Hungary, vetoed the election of Cardinal Rampolla, the Secretary of State. Emperor Franz Josef claimed the right of veto because Austria had threatened in the past to intervene by force. This was in 1903.

"Who presented the beloved Pope John XIII with his Cardinal's Red Hat? The atheist President of France, Vincent Auriel, acting under an ancient Vatican concordat with the Government of France. That was a warm, friendly tribute to Cardinal Roncalli who then was Papal Nuncio to France. But what about Spain? In the years of Franco's dictatorship the Church was unable to name Cardinals of whom the Franco dictatorship disapproved. The treaty has since been modified, I believe.

"The Church has survived centuries of scandal, intrigue and political skullduggery. Why should we assume that in a more sophisticated age it would cease being the target of ambitious, greedy, power-hungry people? Perhaps they cannot buy the Papacy today, but they can buy modern weapons—slander, discrediting new voices in the Church like ours and the African states, ignoring the needs of Latin America. Our beloved Cardinal Novik has become their victim. Charitably we may hope that this terror was not intended to go as far as it has. But we are face to face with facts. It is out of our hands. We must respect Cardinal Novik's wishes, however absurd they may seem ..."

"Unless," Tom Ryan interrupted excitedly, "we can come up with an alternative, some way to pacify him, some move that would make him believe that neither the Communists

187

nor the Church in Poland would harm his family." There was a long pause. Suddenly Tom spun around in a circle, "Your Eminence, I think I have a solution."

"Let's hear it, Tom."

"Forgive me, it's as mad as Cardinal Novik's terror—but just as real. Suppose we were able to bring some of Cardinal Novik's family here to Rome—the grand-nieces, the grand-nephews, maybe his nieces. Wouldn't that reassure him?"

"I should imagine it would, but how do you expect to accomplish this miracle?" Muldoon asked.

"Through a 'Glorious Lady.'"

"The Blessed Virgin? Is that a new title for Our Lady?"

"No...no...not Our Lady," Thomas laughed. "Just a lady in my little black book. Let me ask her first—and then if she'll try it, I'll tell you all about the 'Glorious Lady.'"

Donald laughed, "Your Eminence, he's right. I know this lady. She's very much you. She's got a mind of her own. Hop to it, Tom, if you need any help, call me. I'll come running."

"Thanks, but no thanks. This job I prefer to do on my own."

*　　*　　*

Three hours later, Tom was back at the College, looking pleased as a Monsignor dared who had enjoyed tea with a beautiful woman and had obtained her consent to go to Poland and intercede with the Government to permit some of Cardinal Novik's family to attend the Conclave and visit him in Rome.

"We hesitate to go through the Church, Miss Tashman. So I thought of you."

"I won't lie and say that was very kind of you. It wasn't. But I am a lady of my word. I said that I would help if I was needed. I see where I might be useful. This sort of thing could take a day, a month or a year. You give me three days. I hope you believe in miracles."

Monsignor Ryan beamed, "In my business we have to."

Before he left, the efficient "Glorious Lady" had booked a flight, packed her bags and made appointments to meet with high officials in Warsaw. One of them had promised to meet her at the airport.

"Did I sound imperious?" she asked after the calls to Warsaw.

"Most."

"That's how to handle the Communists. They still long for Czars—they'd love Catherine the Great to be reincarnated and come back and scandalize them all. Crazy, isn't it?"

"Sometimes I think the whole world's crazy and then someone like you comes along and I see how wonderful people can be," Ryan said.

"You know, Monsignor Ryan, there's something you ought to know. Your 'Glorious Lady' had a pretty bawdy reputation when she was drinking. If you think all that bawdiness disappears overnight when 'Glorious Lady' sobers up, you're wrong. It's like this, Monsignor, an alcoholic's traits linger. They even surface now and then. Not his drinking, mind you. I'm talking about his traits."

"Traits? Like your bawdiness?"

"Exactly. I'm sorry you're a man of the cloth."

"Glorious Lady, you have no idea how sorry I am."

They grabbed each other and Teresa danced the priest to the door.

"I'll call you, Monsignor, the minute I have news."

"I'll pray for you, Teresa."

"You do that, Thomas. *Ciao*."

PART VI

Rome—Cafe Cinque

The Conclave began with a Votive Mass to the *Holy Spirit* celebrated by five Cardinals and the brilliant French theologian, Monsignor Pierre Cashin, who pronounced the homily. The co-celebrants represented the six continents of the world.

The *Votive Mass* to which the public and throngs of distinguished guests were invited, carried out the joyousness with which the Church hoped to imbue the Conclave. Normally the *Votive Mass* was said in the Pauline Chapel, attended only by the Cardinals and their aides.

Saint Peter's Basilica provided a glorious setting for the Mass. The magnificent music and colorful pageantry was televised around the world. Loudspeakers carried the Mass into Saint Peter's square. The crowd, estimated at a hundred thousand, carried their own portable radios and television sets—creating a sound that seemed to reach straight to heaven.

Besides the Cardinals, Saint Peter's overflowed with Bishops, *Monsignore,* simple priests, nuns, brothers as well as all Ambassadors to the Holy See, Rome's diplomatic corps, the international press, Italy's government officials, members of the Papal Court and the creme de la creme of the Vatican's press department invitational list.

For everyone it was a once-in-a-lifetime experience, a magnificent pageant of pomp and splendor, a truly Roman spectacle. It was emotionally stirring—the music, the Swiss Guards (in their Michaelangelo uniforms) standing at attention, carrying the Papal colors, dipping banners to salute the Princes of the Church wearing their ermine trimmed scarlet robes, carrying the Bishop's staff, and youths in cassock and surplice holding their trains. Then there were the Papal Knights, the Knights of Malta, the diplomats—all in colorful regalia that signified their office.

There was a flurry of confusion at the steps when Juan Maria Cardinal De Cordoba of Los Angeles arrived on foot wearing a simple scarlet cassock. For a brief few minutes it appeared that the tall, handsome Southern California Archbishop might have been mistaken for an imposter. But the Vatican was prepared for all emergencies—the fragility of old and sickly Cardinals as well as the insouciance of younger Church Princes. A scarlet cape was located and De Cordoba was permitted to enter.

The crowd shrieked its approval of De Cordoba whose dark Latin looks and comparative youth—he was fifty-one—had made him the "glamour boy" of the Conclave. De Cordoba seldom wore his biretta, the better to display his gloriously thick black locks with just the right touch of gray at the temples. De Cordoba's smile—which he flashed often—revealed white, even teeth and his dark eyes suggested a mischievousness that one didn't expect to find in a Cardinal.

*   *   *

Cardinal Muldoon and Monsignor Ryan returned to the North American College elated by the magnificence of the beautiful Mass.

They had barely entered their working quarters when the telephone rang. Ryan fielded it, whispering to Muldoon, "It's Monsignor Metaxas. He's calling for Cardinal Desvargo of Braziliana."

Muldoon signaled Ryan to find out what it was about.

The Cardinal rose and began pacing the floor as he heard a flood of heavily accented English words pouring out of the receiver into Ryan's ear. Finally Ryan looked up. "Excuse me for a few seconds. Let me go over this with Cardinal Muldoon now. He is right here." He covered the receiver.

"Your Eminence, Cardinal Desvargo says it is of the

utmost importance that he see you today, alone if possible, on a matter of great urgency. It is, in fact, so urgent and the matter so discreet that he would prefer meeting you at some convenient place in business clothes out of sight of the press and certainly of the other Cardinals."

Muldoon let a wry smile cross his face. "I sort of expected a last minute upset like this. Obviously, I must see him. Does His Eminence speak English?"

Ryan asked. Muldoon could hear the voice answer "no." There was a pause.

"Does His Eminence Cardinal Muldoon speak Italian?"

"Yes, Monsignor, fluently," Ryan answered.

"Very well, then. Would you ask His Eminence, please, if the *Cafe Cinque* on Via Sistana would suit him at any time in the afternoon; best, during the siesta when it is quietest."

Muldoon, sharing the receiver with Ryan, nodded affirmatively.

"Now, tell the good Monsignor to hold it a bit. I need to think. Either hold on or we'll call back."

The Brazilian Monsignor preferred to hold.

Muldoon paced rapidly up and down the floor, muttering, waving his hands, stopping, thinking—a process familiar to Ryan—which he knew would terminate with a decision and directives coming from Muldoon's mind that invariably proved the right ones. "Granite Face" had a talent for seeing a problem through to its end.

"Now, tell the good Monsignor Metaxas that I do not recommend any Cardinal walking the streets of Rome *alone* either in his red cassock or in business clothes. I, therefore, will bring you along. Cardinal Desvargo may choose his own method of movement. We will speak privately, without you being present, if that is desirable. It doesn't matter. You, Monsignor Ryan, and I will be wearing simple black cassocks with the narrow brimmed biretta of the average Roman priest. I know the cafe—and its reputation."

Muldoon smiled, "Ignore the last remark. Two-thirty will be fine."

*   *   *

"I used to have to crouch down when I got into one of these," Muldoon said, as he slipped the loose-fitting black cassock over his head, and wrapped a black cord around it. "I'm not sure this is the right cord to go with the cassock. Maybe it should be white. But I've used this before and no one seemed to think it odd. Priests in Rome appear to be pretty free in their choice of habits; no one seems to care as long as they wear their cassocks."

The Cardinal placed a pie-shaped black biretta on his head; the masquerade was almost complete. He seemed indistinguishable from any of the hundreds of priests and monks who scampered through Rome day and night by foot, on bicycles or on motor scooters.

From his attaché case, Muldoon pulled out three or four handkerchiefs. He stuffed them loosely into the pocket of his cassock. "There are more of these in the case, Tom," he said to the Monsignor who was getting into a woolen cassock. "They give you something to hold onto. Roman priests always keep their hands in their pockets, wrapped around whatever they're carrying. Could be a sandwich or a wallet. It doesn't matter. It's something to concentrate on. That way you just forge ahead and get through the crowds. Not that people will be much of a problem this time of day."

Ryan foraged through the case and came up with a handful of bright blue and red handkerchiefs. Muldoon looked him over. "You'd better crouch, Tom. You tower pretty high even though the Italians are taller now than they used to be. Vitamins, you know..."

Muldoon peered into the case, dipped in and came up with a pair of wire-rimmed glasses. He put them on, looked for the mirror over the sideboard, turned right, then left. He nodded. "That does it."

Looking at Ryan, he cocked his head, "That's fine, Tom. When we get outside just zip along with me. Keep your eyes straight ahead. Don't look right or left, up or down. Think that you're headed for a urinal and you'll look like every monk in Rome."

"Si, padre. Capisco bene."

Muldoon looked at the grandfather clock that probably had been in the library of the old College when he was a seminarian. It was about to strike two. "We'd better start. We'll drive the car down the hill and then walk. Ring for Willy; we'll go through the back."

Willy led them through the garden to the tiny back gate, barely wide enough for thin men like themselves to squeeze through. "Good luck," the seminarian said. There was a smile in his voice when he added, *"Padres."*

* * *

Via Sistina is part of a collection of little streets, alleys and sharp turns that lead from the Via Veneto to the top of the Spanish Steps from which tourists can swoop down on the American Express during its morning and afternoon hours. At this time of day Cardinal Muldoon and Monsignor Ryan found it fairly deserted except for the second story offices of Rome's "quiet men"—the money speculators.

Muldoon and Ryan knew that anyone visiting the buildings during the siesta was reasonably sure to be a Mafia bag man, the representative of a bank from any part of the world. They also were aware that some *Cambio* offices belonged to the Vatican.

Cafe Cinque was one of those Roman bars that wore many faces. In the morning it served *espresso* to Roman businessmen who seldom took breakfast at home. At noon and in the afternoon it catered to tourists and after dark the *Cinque* was the spot where ladies of the evening spent their "coffee break" and shoveled hard earned *Lire* into a jukebox that played loud enough to be heard up and down the street. At night, too, information was exchanged between male visitors from the Embassies, visitors quartered in the numerous hotels nearby—or between Mafiosi reporting the details of a shipment of narcotics to Marseilles by way of Naples. For all these reasons *Cafe Cinque* was not "off limits" to priests who sometimes had their own hands in the cookie jar of the underworld.

There were no passersby to notice the two Americans as they walked through the beaded curtains that served as the entrance to the *Cafe Cinque* for most of the year. Muldoon and Ryan found their Brazilian friends waiting for them—

194

sipping quietly at *Campari* soda. Dressed in business suits, they rose to greet the priests and pulled back the two empty chairs at the table.

Muldoon and Desvargo were not strangers. They'd met many times in Rome and New York. The two Monsignors introduced themselves and in turn were presented to the Cardinals. It all appeared very casual and since Monsignor Metaxas made no attempt to leave, Ryan felt he was entitled to become part of the conference.

After amenities were exchanged and *Campari* ordered, Metaxas put a few coins in the jukebox. Then Cardinal Desvargo reached for a briefcase and pulled out a large manila envelope.

"This, unfortunately, is what I have to present to you, Your Eminence." His voice was barely audible. "Let me be as diplomatic and tactful as possible. Everyone is aware that the Americans intend nominating their own candidate to succeed Morelli. Obviously the Cardinal is not going to be one of your own. Hence, there has been much speculation as to whom you have chosen."

"How aware I am of that, Desvargo!" Muldoon said. Ryan was pleased that his superior had dispensed with formalities.

"It must be a trying experience for you, no?"

"In a way, yes," Muldoon answered.

Ryan was astonished by his Italian. Muldoon's sounded far more fluent than Desvargo's, yet the South American's mother tongue, of course, was Portugese, fairly similar to Italian, except for its gutteral sound and the surprising appearance of so many German-sounding words.

"I am not going to presume to ask you the identity of your choice. Most of us in Latin America believe it is Cardinal Riccordi."

Muldoon lived up to his nickname. There was no change in expression. He was every bit the "Granite Face" of legend.

Desvargo appeared to be waiting for a reaction. With none forthcoming, Tom detected a slight shrug of his shoulders as he plunged right on. "If your selection is Riccordi, you have made an interesting one. He is Italian born. That is good. Moreover, he is a Roman. That settles a great many problems arising when speculation centers around the possibility of the Church choosing a non-Italian Pope.

"Moreover, he served in the Vatican diplomatic department when he was still in the seminary. That was during the War and manpower was at a premium—even at the Vatican.

"He has been a progressive leader of the Church in South America, widely respected by his colleagues; yet his tact and diplomacy have enabled him to get along with a variety of governments. That is a special talent South American pastors are noted for."

Muldoon interrupted, "Like every Cardinal attending the Conclave, we are aware of the qualities that have made Cardinal Riccordi an outstanding member of the College. We are short of time."

He paused. "I am also short of patience. If there is something in these documents that you want to tell me about, then let's hear it. Are we to inspect them now? Do we take them with us? Whatever it is you have brought us here to explain, I'd like to know as quickly as possible."

Ryan could see the color rising in Metaxas' face. He wasn't accustomed to hearing brusque language spoken to his superior. The sudden offensive by Muldoon apparently didn't faze Desvargo.

"Forgive me, Muldoon."

Ryan wanted to laugh. Desvargo seemed to swallow on saying only the American prelate's last name.

"These documents are copies—made for you to peruse at your leisure."

"That means today," Muldoon snapped. "Tonight—so that they can be digested by tomorrow morning."

Desvargo's shoulders shrugged—just a trifle. "My good friend, I arrived in Rome just forty-eight hours ago. These documents were given to me only a day or so before I left Braz¨."

"Agreed. What's in them?"

The Brazilian was on surer ground. His voice raised slightly. Metaxas hastened to the jukebox to feed it more *Lire*.

"They show the somewhat cloudy past of the distinguished Cardinal Riccordi. True, he is Roman by birth and he was ordained at the age of twenty-three—a fact which his supporters attribute to his superior talents. Not quite, Muldoon. Not according to affidavits in this envelope, the sworn statements of those who knew him when he was working in the Vatican. Actually he was one of the wheeler-dealers in the Curia who made a fortune selling passports to Nazis, moving their money for them, working hand in hand with Cardinal Shuster whom we all know used his high office as Archbishop of Milan to assist major Nazis, who could afford it, to sneak through the Brenner Pass and down to Rome where documents were manufactured and forged as readily as Papal blessings.

"Riccordi's early ordination had nothing to do with his genius. It happened at the order of Pius XII, acting on advice from his aides who feared the youth was getting too reckless in an office that needed discretion and, frankly, secrecy. Pius had suffered enough because of his handling of the German situation and he could not tolerate an underling who might further undermine his reputation."

"And place in history?" Muldoon asked.

"Perhaps. I don't know. At any rate, Pius was reduced to coming to terms with Riccordi who had close relatives in Chile. Riccordi agreed to clear out provided he was ordained immediately and sent to Chile on an official mission where he would settle. He also demanded and got the promise of a Bishop's ring within five years."

"And Pius kept his word, I suppose."

"Riccordi gave him no alternative. He continued to work with the Germans who settled in South America after the war, assisting them in changing their names, finding new occupations and, mainly, in transferring their wealth from Swiss banks to real property which, as you know, is the strength of the sleeping continent of South America. Personally, he became a rich man."

"Thank you for the history lesson," Muldoon said drily.

"I am sorry. I get carried away."

"And all this information is contained in these documents."

"The largest part of it—enough to warrant your inspection."

197

"Then I may take them with me?"

"You may, Car . . . *Si, signore.*"

Muldoon picked up the manila envelope, rose, shook hands and smiled with more warmth than superficial politeness warranted.

Ryan followed his example.

Wordlessly they left *Cafe Cinque,* walked up the hill to a cab stand situated at the top of the Spanish Steps and stepped inside the one at the head of the line. It took them back to their car.

Muldoon's face had reddened. His hands shook with rage. "What a cheap shot! Even if it's true—to wait until this moment to throw it at us."

He pointed to the envelope in his lap. "This is not the inspiration of our oily friend from Brazil. He was only carrying out orders."

* * *

It was four o'clock when Cardinal Muldoon and Monsignor Ryan returned to the North American College. Muldoon headed for the library, locked himself inside and for an hour or so remained closeted with the papers.

At five-thirty he called Ryan and handed him the telephone number of *Dottore* Luigi Lalli. "Apologize that I am not calling myself, but tell him I need him immediately and to bring as many experts as he can. Tell him I need to test the authenticity of some documents. Let me see now . . . they range in age from thirty-five years to a few that are forty or fifty. They're written in Spanish, Italian, German and Portuguese. Some are affidavits that even I can tell were originally written or made in Portuguese, then translated into Italian. It's crazy! They're signed by Italians who ought to know their own language.

"Shuffle around the College and see if someone can come up who knows some Portuguese—not much—enough to help me until Luigi and his men get here. The damned fools!"

Then he let out a laugh the like of which had never come from "Granite Face" in all the years he'd been at Saint Patrick's. "The damned fools. They've shuffled affidavits around as though they were cards in a deck. One part translated by a kid who thought he knew the vernacular; others by some old priest who hadn't used his Italian for twenty years.

"Tom, get on the telephone and tell De Cordoba and O'Toole to get here as soon as they can. They've got a big night ahead of them. Let them know the crap's hit the fan."

Ryan gasped.

"Don't look so shocked. If you're sensitive about using Anglo-Saxon, try Latin—or make sure you talk to O'Toole. He'll understand."

*　　*　　*

The Cardinals arrived singly, spaced fifteen and twenty minutes apart, as they'd agreed in the case of sudden emergencies. The *paparazzi* were on their trail and it was astonishing that the pickets in front of the College had failed to discover the tiny gate that led from the garden to the street behind the walled villa.

When *Dottore* Lalli arrived he chose a delivery truck as transportation. Muldoon roared. The adventure was putting him into great good spirits. "You're a wonder, Luigi! No one has to tell you to be careful."

"I read the newspapers. You're looking well, William. I want to make sure you stay that way." He introduced his colleagues, four of them, all experts in languages, forgery, differentiating paper quality and authenticating watermarks.

Muldoon turned over the library to them and with O'Toole, Ryan and De Cordoba, he retired to a small parlor where he recounted the details of his meeting with the Brazilians. He interrupted his account to speak to Ryan, "Tom, I think we ought to get Donald Brady over here. Do you think you can locate him?"

"Shouldn't be difficult, Your Eminence. We've got a system to keep in touch."

"Good," Muldoon said, "make another call to the villa. Tell 'Yes Yes' Pfeifer he'll be going into the Conclave with me instead of you."

Ryan burst out laughing. He'd never heard Muldoon refer to Pfeifer as "Yes Yes."

Roman intrigue seemed to agree with "Granite Face."

*　　*　　*

For hours a curious collection of lay and religious authorities in Spanish, Italian and Portuguese languages, forgery, calligraphy, paper quality parchment, watermarks and handwriting analysis gave their years of skill to assessing the authenticity of more than a hundred documents, a pile of papers consisting of copies of passports, identity cards, travel permits, old photographs, airlines passenger lists, school and university records, birth and baptismal certificates, copies of naturalization papers and newspaper clippings. Each piece was intended to touch a section in the life of an individual and each was important, but the real significance of the collection lay in the texts of nearly two dozen affidavits submitted in English, German, Italian and Portuguese.

As *Dottore* Luigi Lalli, Chief of the Identification Bureau for Interpol, assigned for many years to duty in Rome, shifted his magnifying glass from one affidavit to the other, he continued to exclaim, "Impossible! Impossible! It makes no sense. One writer—two at the most—has created all this mischief.

"Look," he said over and over again, handing two pieces of paper to a colleague, "Can you believe this? Documents made years apart, in different languages, attested to in widely separated parts of the world—yet the words of one are virtually identical to the other. It is a madness! What we have here is the work of a systematic character assassin. All this reads like a novel—not a very good one—dedicated to the destruction of a single individual."

Lalli put the affidavits aside and started on a new batch. "Incredible. I cannot believe what I read. There is no consistency; the time periods overlap. It is a mishmash, is it not?"

A colleague held the papers against his infrared light to examine the watermarks. "*Si, Dottore*. A mishmash. To what purpose? It cannot fool an expert. Perhaps it was not intended to. Without a professional opinion, someone could take all this seriously, don't you agree?"

"Of course. That's the riddle. But why? They do not deal with an ordinary John Doe, but with a very important man; in his field, a world figure. And this collection of amateur forgery and childish affidavits has not been handed to little babies or even to recruits in the Police Academy. They have been offered to a Cardinal, an American Cardinal, who was supposed to swallow all the nasty implications we see here without question. Ridiculous!"

"What led Cardinal Muldoon to question the documents?" the watermark expert asked.

Lalli laughed, "His Italian. It's virtually flawless. He writes and reads extremely well. He saw at a glance that some of this stuff was obviously translated from Portuguese—most ineptly. That's why he sent for us. It must have something to do with the Conclave. It starts tomorrow. You know the Americans have come with their own candidate. This Cardinal must be the man. Look here . . ."

Lalli picked up another batch of material. "At a glance I'd say this early stuff is authentic, it goes deeper into the man's past, another twenty-three years in the life of Giorgio Riccordi, born in Rome, as you can see. This certificate is genuine. We have his baptismal certificate here. I've seen dozens like it. It's when Riccordi leaves Italy in 1945 that the trouble starts; then it all stops. And at present we have His Eminence Giorgio Cardinal Riccordi, Archbishop of Santiago, Chile.

"I've heard a great deal about him—a good man. The kind of leader the Church needs, someone willing to come to grips with modern problems and not sweep them under the carpet hoping they'll disappear. He's a survivor. I guess one has to be in one of those Latin American countries with their Juntas, dictatorships and the Communists trying to offer them more than the United States. Evidently our friend Riccordi has walked a pretty narrow tightrope politically without sacrificing his religious integrity."

Lalli glanced at the clock. "Nearly ten. I don't know what more we can conclude without making a more comprehensive laboratory investigation. Excuse me, gentlemen, I'll fetch Cardinal Muldoon."

Dottore Lalli opened the library door and walked across the hall to the parlor where he found that Cardinal Muldoon had been joined by other Americans. Muldoon introduced Cardinals De Cordoba and O'Toole. Lalli had already met Monsignor Ryan. A youngish man in a sports outfit came forward to shake hands with Lalli and introduce himself, "I'm Donald Thaddeus Brady. I am honored to meet you." Donald had arrived a few minutes earlier.

"Lalli's gray eyes lighted up, "That nephew Thaddeus always talked about? And now we finally meet." He paused, "I wish the circumstances were different."

Then, turning to the group of churchmen, "Will you gentlemen come with me, please?"

Muldoon held up his hand as Lalli's associates arose. "Thank you, gentlemen, for flying to our rescue. We appreciate it."

"We all agree, Your Eminence," Luigi Lalli said. "Virtually all of these documents are spurious, especially the affidavits. As you suspected they are translations—and not very good ones—of claims and charges that originated with one mind—maybe, two persons. No more. That's certain. It is apparent in the style of the language, even when it's read through translation. As you suspected, several hands had a crack at translating, but even their work could not obliterate the sameness of the language pattern. I'd say offhand this was the work of a psychopath. Either that or someone who did a rush job simply to...to...what is the American expression...ah, yes...to throw someone off balance. To create a momentary distraction, to intrude, however briefly, on something well organized. That being the case, it wouldn't matter if the sum total of his work turned out to be the efforts of rank amateurs. Does that help you?"

"Very much, Luigi."

Some, he conceded, were copies of authentic documents: Riccordi's birth certificate, his school diplomas, documentation supporting his years at the seminary and the certificate of his ordination.

Things began to go astray when the papers purported to

tie him into the traffic in Nazi bodies and booty to South America. There were inconsistencies in the affidavits supplied by people on both sides of the Atlantic—Riccordi's alleged conspirators in the Vatican and the Nazi runaways in South America.

There were some references to the American Army of Occupation and/or Liberation, depending on your point of view, indicating that Riccordi had been in touch with them about emigrating to America. There were also references to dealings in the black market.

"I regret I am unable to give you specifics, a page by page analysis of this material." He raised his hands in the hopeless gesture of one who was a victim of time. "Perhaps in a week...five days, maybe...we could trace the origins of..."

His voice trailed away as William Cardinal Muldoon stood up and put his arm around the old man's shoulders. "Thank you, *Dottore*. Your efforts tonight have been heroic and I am grateful to you and your colleagues. You have performed an important service."

"An honor, Your Eminence. He started to kneel to kiss Muldoon's ring. "No ceremony tonight, my friend. You are all tired. Thank you again. You have all our blessings."

The experts had gone, leaving six tired, troubled men to interpret their findings.

Against the files on Riccordi collected by Ryan, nothing seemed to jibe. Dates differed—even that of Riccordi's consecration as Bishop was different in the Brazilian-supplied documents than that which Ryan had found at the Vatican and which he supported with newspaper clips, photographs and the like. As a smear job, it was sloppy and inept—even an innocent could see that. The question that remained unanswered after hours of examination by Lalli and his team was why such clumsy character assassination should have been attempted at the last minute.

"It's easy," Muldoon explained when Ryan brought up the question. "It doesn't matter that it's clumsy. It's the timing. They've cast doubt. That's all they needed to do. We've spent a year lining up support for our position. We don't care if we win or if we lose. That is not the point. We came here hoping to establish a beachhead for the future—so that the rest of the world could be heard and listened to. That is all.

"There are powers that don't want even this tiny step to take place. Perhaps they are afraid. Maybe they overestimate our influence and our power. I don't know. All I know is that they want to discredit us.

"They want the Americans to enter the Conclave tomorrow uncertain of our choice. What can we do about it? Nothing, of course. We shall be locked in. If we cast a ballot for Riccordi, then this vile collection of lies will be gossiped about in the halls, in the parlors and at every free moment the Cardinals have to do their electioneering. We cannot risk that—nor can we use a good man like Riccordi simply to take a stand—to thumb our noses so to speak at the powerful men in the Curia. At this moment we are deep into a dilemma. And if anyone has a suggestion, I would like to hear it."

Muldoon nodded to Monsignor Thomas Ryan, "Thank the seminarians outside the door and tell them to go to bed. No one's going to learn anything by eavesdropping on us at this hour of the morning."

Ryan rose from his chair at the highly polished library table where he had started assembling the documents into some sort of order and went to the double door. He glanced at the clock, it was almost midnight. The Cardinals were to assemble at the Vatican between ten and noon. It was beginning to be a tough game that the Princes of the Church had decided to play. The Cardinals, shocked and horrified by what they were learning, sat silently.

The stillness was broken as the grandfather clock chimed the half hour, automatically causing the men to shift their positions to look at it. An unnecessary gesture. They were well aware of the hour—as well as the few hours that lay between the present and the late morning when the Cardinals, vested in their scarlet robes, would be driven to Saint Peter's to enter the Conclave.

Muldoon sat up in his chair. "May I have your attention, please, brother Cardinals, Tom and Donald. The hour is late. I am going to have to make a decision. I would gladly divide this burden with you and with the other American Cardinals, but you have chosen me to act in your behalf. It is too late to enter into consultation and reach a concensus as to how to proceed in view of this extremely damaging material we have seen tonight."

He paused. "Forgive me. I must modify my words. The material is damaging, but as the experts have told us, it appears also to be spurious . . . there is then even more need to join with me in prayer. Silent prayer." The Cardinals began to straighten up.

Muldoon managed a gentle smile, "You are like horses at the starting gate, dear friends. I'm sure God doesn't expect us to get on our knees or to recite any formal prayers. Let us stay as we are. Let us ask the Divine Guidance of the Holy Spirit who, in the final analysis, will be the Author of this Conclave. In five minutes or so I will give you my decision."

Turning to Donald the Cardinal said, "It's been a long night for you, Donald. If you'd like to go out in the garden for some fresh air . . ."

Donald interrupted, "Thank you, Your Eminence. I would prefer to remain . . . that is, if I may."

"Of course, my son."

William Muldoon sat back in his chair. He made the Sign of the Cross. He clasped his hands, closed his eyes and bowed his head.

For Donald it was a touching experience. It had been a grueling evening, a cruel climax to a year of painstaking methodical work by these men of great power who now humbly turned to *their* Higher Power. For them there was no alternative. Donald noticed that in prayer, fatigue vanished from their faces. Their expressions were quiet, confident and serene. The faith of these men, he suddenly knew, was real. In their affirmation, Donald found himself believing too. Their mission would prevail. It hurt his newspaperman's cynicism to be so certain of an intangible. This wasn't how it should work. But faith, he'd been told, could move mountains. Now he was going to see it happen.

*   *   *

205

Slowly Cardinal Muldoon raised his head and unclasped his hands. "My brothers," he said, "we have turned our problem over to the Holy Spirit and there is no more to be done here tonight. I suggest you go to the villa, get what sleep you can pray." The Cardinals embraced in the *Kiss of Peace*. "Monsignor Ryan knows his way well enough through the garden to the back gate. I presume your cars are parked nearby."

Ryan escorted Cardinals O'Toole and De Cordoba to their car. When he returned Donald was sitting quietly staring into space—and so was Muldoon. His presence seemed to stir them back to life.

"You know, Tom, I have two ideas. The first is this. I feel this matter of Riccordi is important enough to bend my vows a little. I might just take it on myself to get sick on, say, the second or third day of the Conclave. That is if I get the feeling that there are documents in Rome proving Riccordi's innocence. It would be comparatively easy to send them in with Bishop Hearn.

"Breaking a vow won't come easy to me, but I've got to do something. So my second idea is this. Tom, I imagine you're going to drive Donald back to his hotel, and you'll probably stop at the *Messaggero* Bar.

"Do me a favor and hang in there for a half hour or so until you hear from me. I'll either call or, perhaps, send a message.

The Cardinal rose, stretched. "I'm tired. It's been a difficult day. Good night, thank you both. You'll be hearing from me."

He extended his hand to Donald, clasping Donald's hand firmly, "I won't be seeing you until after the Conclave. Maybe it will come out fine. Pray for us."

PART VII

Via Delle Scala 72 Bis

Francesco Xavier Morelli was enchanted with his new home, hidden away in the pile of ancient churches, *piazze, fontane, palazzi* and *appartamenti* which appeared to grow out of the old cobblestone streets and narrow, crooked alleys of Trastevere. This was the world of his years as a seminarian, of the church where he had served as a nervous curate, and where he had found lasting friends.

One was Inspector Luke Monzelli, the quiet, soft-spoken official of the Rome police department whom he had prepared for his First Holy Communion. Morelli had never forgotten the serious, stocky, little boy whose memory was letter perfect but who, unlike others in his class, carefully thought out every sentence he recited or extemporized to fully understand its meaning. Morelli appreciated Luke's perception, his eye for detail, the enormous physical strength he cultivated by participating in every sport available to a child whose parents lived in modest circumstances. The priest watched the boy grow into manhood with interest, knowing he was cut out for special accomplishments.

Their friendship as adults began in the fifties after each had made his mark in his vocation, Morelli, as a priest; Monzelli, as a policeman. Monsignor Morelli baptized the Monzelli children and several years later attended ceremonies naming Monzelli a Police Inspector, head of a special unit whose duties would cover the whole spectrum of police operations. Monzelli's cases ranged from jewel theft to narcotic hauls, crimes of passion, riots, and in recent years, the rash of kidnappings by mercenaries, the bloody trail left by terrorists and the political mayhem of extremists. In Rome, Monzelli's feats made him a legend.

Morelli's easy camaraderie with Luke Monzelli became more important after Morelli entered the walled world of the Vatican. Shortly after his election Monzelli visited his old friend. The Pope permitted the stocky, gray-haired detective to kneel, kiss his ring and receive the Pontifical Blessing. "Now, Luke, that blessing is the official one. You know I bless you in my heart every day. My name is Francesco, you are still Luke, and if there is going to be any change in our relationship, if you're going to start averting your eyes from me like the pathetic browbeaten nuns in the Vatican, I might have to issue a *Papal Bull* ordering you not to."

"Very well, Francesco," Luke said, rising from his position of genuflection, his gray eyes brightening. "I would find it difficult to change, too. If a cat can look at the King, a policeman ought to be able to look at the Pope."

"And a Pope, my dear Monzelli, needs a friend whose eyes he can see."

Under these informal arrangements, the friendship continued through the years. They met at least once a week, either for dinner or, if Luke was on a case, late in the evening when they shared a glass of wine or played chess. Luke realized the Pope needed his presence. Luke possessed qualities that he could not find within the walls of Vatican City. Luke's friendship, freely given, involved no favors, no special privileges, only the pleasure of the older man's company.

For the Pope, Luke became his link to the people of the parishes he had served a half century ago. "When one rises in the Church," Morelli often said, "one forgets those cold, wet mornings when a priest wonders how loud the coughing will be after the Consecration. Does this mean he lacks proper concentration on the Mass? Not quite. It usually made me remember that I had vowed to serve God. People were made in His image and likeness. I was their servant, too."

True, the head of the Roman Catholic Church was no longer a "Prisoner in the Vatican"—that had been changed with John XIII and more dramatically with Paul VI, the Pilgrim Pope.

Like Paul, Morelli had visited the far corners of the globe, embracing Patriarchs of the Eastern Churches, shaking hands with Presidents, enjoying the hospitality of royalty. But there was little continuity to these pilgrimages. One was like the other, a protocol-arranged ceremony, the exchange of gifts, gracious speeches and a few minutes of rest.

Where were the people? Way out there—far removed from his presence, a hazy mist of thousands of faces who behaved as they were supposed to when a Pope appeared in their midst. They applauded, they cheered, they listened to his words. But did they understand? Morelli was never sure.

"It is a show," he told Luke, "a performance. I should be looked at because I am the Pope. Alas, how quickly my visits are forgotten. But they must go on. The Pope affirms the Faith, the Pope begs for peace—whoever he is. So he travels, carrying his message, repeating it over and over like the Hail Marys of the Rosary."

Luke became more than a shoulder to lean on. The Pope valued the detective's intelligence, his understanding of Italy's political problems which inevitably touched his Pontificate. Morelli and his immediate predecessors would go down in history as the Pontiffs who reigned during the great upsurge of Communism throughout the land. True, they called it "Italian-style Communism," but how long would it sustain its national character? When would it bend to the will and power of Moscow?

Monzelli was more optimistic than the Cardinals of the Curia who appointed obscure priests to prepare position papers for them, carefully documented and annotated, to which they affixed their seals in their magnificent villas, filled with art treasures, often containing cellars overflowing with vintage wines. Morelli quipped, "Meeting a poor Cardinal is as remarkable as knowing a poor banker."

Luke Monzelli believed Italy's aristocracy, the Church, and its political leaders thrived on fear. That was their technique for protracting Italy's financial alliance with the United States. "There's big money in anti-Communism," Luke said, "but politically Moscow is spread very thin. Moreover, Russian Communism has grown flabby and overconfident. In Africa, where vision is clearer, they've discovered that exchanging Colonialism for Communism is like returning one stale loaf of bread for another. This has not been lost on the Communist leaders of Italy. They are not going to divide the prize of this peninsula with Moscow. We are safer with coexistence than the old weapons of exhortation and excommunication."

"Popes pass; the Curia remains." It is an old Vatican proverb. No one knew its truth more keenly than the Popes and Bishops who had attended Councils of the Church since the ninth century. Repeatedly both Pontiffs and Bishops had sought to break the suffocating power of the bureaucracy. Their best efforts were unavailing. Rather than fight it, Pius XII embraced the administrative arm of the Vatican as long as they allowed him to practice his profession of diplomat. Pacelli served as his own Secretary of State. Privately he referred to them as "little Bourbons who learned little and forgot nothing." Eventually they smothered Pacelli with so much detail that his hope of working directly with Cardinals and Bishops, hand-picked and devoted to him, proved useless.

Paul VI sought to reform the Curia and succeeded only in changing the name of a few offices. John XXIII shook up the Curia briefly when he summoned Vatican II. But once Vatican II went to work and complaints against the stodgy Vatican bureaucracy piled up, the Curia began flexing its muscle. As the executive body in charge of "assisting the Pope in administering the affairs of the Church," no Council could accomplish more than offer suggestions.

It remained for the Curia, the body of Cardinals and their mysterious, uncounted assistants, clerks, archivists and public relations officers, to carry them out. As the history of Vatican II has shown, they chose to ignore all but the most obvious needs for reformation. John XXIII summed up his feelings with, "I am trapped," echoing the words of Pius IX who a century earlier told a Cardinal who urged him to undertake Curial reform, "I am too old." In times past, the Roman Curia often gathered so much power that it made the Pope a *de facto* prisoner of his own bureaucracy.

If nothing else, Vatican II accomplished an examination of the Curia by those who were charged with its day-to-day operation. There were admissions that the Italian-dominated administrative office failed to provide either justice or efficiency. Paul VI loaded the College of Cardinals with non-Italians, some penetrated the offices of the Curia; among them, a highly regarded American Cardinal. But even this influx of new blood failed to stir the Curia to the point where it sought to repair its damaged reputation.

By the time Morelli ascended the Throne of Saint Peter, the Curia had regained its old autocratic, arbitrary and obstructionist character. Like Paul, Morelli maintained balance in the College of Cardinals, calling consistories at which foreign Cardinals outnumbered new Italian Red Hats. Those who managed assignments to the Curia found the choice posts occupied by Italians, sitting on many simultaneously, living permanently in Rome and ruling the amalgam with the skill of an international business cartel.

Morelli chose a middle course during his reign as Pope. When he was certain of Curia support, Morelli exploited it to the limit, heaping praise on Cardinals like Torriani and Silvestri, thrusting them into the limelight as few Popes of modern times had dared to do. On the other hand, when he felt doubt of Curia reaction, he withheld certain Papal obligations. His Holiness, for example, wasn't quite certain that this was exactly the year to canonize new saints pushed into the calendar by the Congregation of Rites. It stood to reason that no one but the Pope could perform a canonization. To pacify Morelli, the Cardinal involved would twist a few arms in other Congregations of the Curia. Sometimes Morelli got his wishes.

The Pope decided early in his reign to count neither his successes nor failures. Circumstances and world events invariably boxed Popes into political positions. Morelli often felt the pressure of world opinion. Unlike other Pontiffs, however, he did not seek the heat of confrontation with immovable forces. Cardinals who once called the mild-mannered Morelli "Topo Gigio" (Mickey Mouse) began referring to him as "The Snake."

Within Vatican City Morelli saw a vicious example of the reasons Italy lived in a world of nagging labor problems, persistent strikes, constant discontent. "We set a bad example," he confided to Luke Monzelli. "This is a medieval island, envied by industrialists who marvel at our ability to persist in shabby paternalism as an instrument of labor relations. We don't bargain with Vatican workers; we depend on Jesus Christ to slap them back into line when they ought to go on strike. How can a Pope speak honestly to the working man when he lives in a palace surrounded by underpaid laymen and nonsalaried nuns? Wasn't it John who talked to a gardener and discovered that gardeners' wages hadn't been raised in a hundred years? Their privileges and benefits may have gotten better, but again that's calling work service to Christ.

"I don't believe Christ expected his Vicar on Earth to live like a medieval Emperor at the expense of the working man. But try and get that through to the tightfisted Vatican treasury. To negotiate proper working conditions for the Vatican City, I'd have to abandon my responsibilities as Pope."

Although neither pretended to be an economist, Monzelli and the Pope fretted about the flight of capital from Italy, spurred by fear that a Communist Government might appropriate all individual wealth, nationalizing what major industries were left to seize. Morelli sighed that the Vatican itself had erred seriously. Paul's financial advisers had mismanaged finances so irresponsibly that some Vatican financial wizards had ended up in jail. "The press has been delicate," the Pope said, "in handling the mess. They have minimized the Church's stupidity. Paul trusted the wrong people. We are still in a financial bind."

On a visit to New York, Monzelli became ill. He was treated by Samuel Broslowsky, Max Schwartz's nephew. When Morelli complained that he'd like an unprejudiced report on his health, the police officer suggested Broslowsky who had made a deep impression on him. "I haven't needed them often myself, thank God," Monzelli said, "but I believe I've worked with enough doctors to recognize an outstanding one when I meet him."

That was how, in the last years of his reign, Morelli acquired another friend who, like Luke, was neither awed by his position nor afraid to look him in the eye. The ice was broken on Broslowsky's first visit. After examining the

212

Pope's feet, Broslowsky, a handsome, young man with deep eyes and a seriousness that made him appear older than thirty-five, looked at them with admiration. Without thinking, he said, "Those crazy red shoes must have something. Your feet are marvels for a man your age."

The Pope roared. It took seconds for Broslowsky to realize his *faux pas*. "My son, I'd forogtten there were Pope jokes. How wonderful! Wonderful to know they still call his red shoes 'crazy.'"

"I didn't mean to offend, Your Holiness," Broslowsky stuttered.

"Don't apologize. And just call me *Padre* or *Father*. You can't manage Your Holiness any better than American Presidents. Even Kennedy, I'm told, stumbled."

"That's fine with me, *Padre!* I like that one. It's got a ring to it."

"Dr. Broslowsky, how is it that you didn't change your name as so many American Jews do?"

Broslowsky laughed, "My father said 'make them spell it.'"

"Smart man."

"I thought so—and so did he. He died poor, but his life was rich. That's what counts."

Broslowsky enjoyed his mission to the Pope. "I hope, *Padre,* when you quit this job you'll continue calling me. You're a fascinating patient besides being a fascinating man."

Morelli had confided his fears of senility. "I won't spell it out for you, Samuel," he said, proud of the modern English he'd acquired from the brash New Yorker, "you can read it in any book on the Papacy. Our history is riddled with dreadful mistakes made by Pontiffs too old to reign, physically or mentally; sometimes, both. I've seen enough examples in my fifty years of priesthood to be concerned."

Broslowsky was serious in responding to the Pope's worries. "Physically, you are eight years younger than you should be, considering the pressures of your work, even considering the normal deterioration of the body by age. Your prostate, for example, is extraordinary. I guess you take care of yourself."

Morelli shrugged.

"How come Paul VI bothered with that diatribe against masturbation, *Padre,* when there are so many real sins in the world to condemn?"

Morelli laughed, "I am not always my brother's keeper." His eyes grew serious, "I see you've been reading up. Pretty well, too. I thought we'd buried that one."

"Wasn't John Paul going to haul it out all over again?"

Morelli sighed, "So they tell me." To change the subject, he asked, "What have you read about me?"

Broslowsky answered quickly, "I agree on almost everything. Tough on abortion in words, but discouraging zealous priests from keeping it in politics. You've made it a moral issue where it belongs, so you have more respect from people like me who agree with you. You would like, I suspect, science to find something between the Pill and the rhythm method that would give Catholic family planning a break."

The Pope nodded silently.

"I like your respect for women. I agree that you can't force social progress. There are some places it has to grow. All our laws haven't guaranteed equal opportunity for America's minorities and they never will. They grow from need, experience and the adjustment of society. So His Holiness has not stuck his neck out. He just smiles and says, '*Pazienza, bambini.*'"

"Your Italian is improving, Samuel. That's a fairly good grade you've given me. How do I pass on celibacy?"

"Great—if you can ever sell it. Local option, like we have in our drinking laws."

"I don't quite understand," the Pope said.

"We still have Prohibition in some parts of the country where people have voted against the sale of alcohol. Is it bad or is it good? I don't know. The people decide. That's the way you see the problems of the priest shortage. If Bishops have to turn to married men, isn't that a logical answer?"

"I think so. You know the Church is not married to priestly celibacy. That's an inheritance from the thirteenth century."

Morelli was taken aback by Broslowsky's next remark. "Personally, I think you're great on *Maryism.*"

214

"*Maryism?*" the Pope roared. "That's Protestant—I thought you were Jewish."

"Mine is a mixed marriage. My wife is a Baptist. Since I started visiting you, she's been reading, too."

"Well, the proper Protestant description of the Catholic devotion to Mary is *Mariology*. Protestants see it as a barrier to cooperation with the Roman Church because it is not rooted in Scripture."

"My wife and I have noted that you invoke the Blessed Virgin only on traditional occasions. May I be fresh?"

"You may be fresh," Morelli laughed.

"You seem to duck her. You've also canonized fewer saints than any modern Pope. That can't be an accident."

Broslowsky was right on target in two sensitive areas of Morelli's duties as Pontiff. Like many priests, Morelli had been dismayed in 1950 when Pope Pius XII promulgated as doctrine the *Assumption of the Blessed Virgin into Heaven* which, heretofore, had been a "pious belief."

That it occurred during the first post-war *Holy Year* strengthened Protestant belief that Catholics worshiped Mary. Catholics have argued for centuries that they simply venerated the Mother of Jesus. To Protestants this amounts to quibbling. To less polite critics of the Roman Church, Pius acted without any scriptural authority for the miracle of Assumption and that it was a money-making device to boost the year-end take of the Holy Year. The dogma of Assumption was asserted in November 1950.

Beyond this new dogma there exists the elaborate system of shrines based upon the sixteen most notable appearances of apparitions of the Virgin in various parts of the world— from Lourdes and Fatima in Europe to Guadalupe in Mexico. All are profitable tourist attractions. As one skeptic observed, "There's big money in the Virgin Mary. She deserves the respect the Church gives her."

The Pope measured his words. "Your wife's observations are incisive. Perhaps in my actions as Pope she may see the validity of the Catholic claim that we venerate Mary; we do not worship her. As to the miracle business and saints, I leave that to history. For myself, my devotions have centered since childhood on the Holy Spirit, the third Person of the Trinity.

215

He is the Patron of wisdom. The higher the office a man holds, the more need he has of wisdom, the more aware he becomes of his own inadequacy."

Morelli was silent, searching for the words, "I sincerely believe the Holy Spirit sent you to me."

"That's a compliment," Broslowsky grinned.

"In my profession," the Pope smiled, "we would call it a 'grace.' No matter, I have found the wisdom to trust you, knowing you are talented in your profession and believing in your honesty. So now let's get down to business."

Broslowsky leaned forward in his chair. "*Padre,* you are past three score and ten, the Biblical Age. You are in remarkable health, but you know you are more susceptible than a younger man to all the body's ills. A stroke, a heart attack, any number of things could put you out of commission the minute I leave this room. Mental instability can follow any sickness at this stage of your life.

"I think you want to resign to set an historical precedent. You haven't expressed this to your own Church, so I don't expect you to confide in me."

He looked around the Pope's sitting room. "I think Cardinal Torriani even has me followed to the Bronx—and that takes following."

Morelli nodded, his eyes laughing.

"I think you should set a timetable for yourself. Finish what you consider your duties, establish the political climate you feel will achieve an orderly succession, polarize Torriani and Rossi so neither can..."

"You certainly read the newspapers, don't you, my young friend?"

"Obviously, when I have a patient of your importance."

"That's neat! Clever sidestepping! Worthy of a Cardinal. Congratulations."

"May I continue?" Broslowsky asked.

"Please do."

"Your timetable will tell you if it is right to retire. Without some sort of fixed schedule in your mind, you will agonize yourself into a state of such indecision that you *will* become sick. Not mentally. Physically ill. Does this make sense to you?"

"Great sense, Samuel. I am grateful to you."

"My pleasure, *Padre*." Broslowsky rose to leave.

"By the way," Morelli asked, "do you have a colleague who's a heart specialist?"

"Of course. But you have your own..."

"Not for me. For the Cardinals—all those old fools hanging around to see the expression on your face when you come and go. They all rush to heart specialists at the sound of your name. Now if a friend of yours could get that business..."

"*Padre,* your friend, the Holy Spirit, certainly had a lot to do with your being in this job. I hope the world does as well when you move out of this palace."

"Thank you, Dr. Broslowsky." He rang for his secretary to escort the American out. "Smile," he whispered, "smile broadly. That will upset them."

*　　*　　*

When Luke Monzelli agreed with Doctor Broslowsky's suggestion, the apartment on Via Delle Scala, 71 Bis, became part of the Pope's plan. His Holiness had no intention of entering a monastery, whether that was the secret hope of his enemies or the honest desire of his friends. He had no need of the communal world. Other Pontiffs had spoken sadly of the "loneliness" of their lives.

"How could they have been lonely?" Morelli asked Monzelli. As usual, he answered the question himself, "They're surrounded by people from morning to night; the only respite they get is the few hours they sleep. Decisions are lonely, yes. But thank God, you don't have to make one every minute of the day.

"I've lived in the magnificent community of the world. In retirement I want to be alone, but close enough to the world to go out and take a look at it now and then. I'm sure that it is going to get along quite well without me."

Monzelli acquired the apartment on Via Delle Scala. It consisted of two floors which had been arranged to insure complete privacy by a relative, an artist, who would be in America for the next two years on a mammoth municipal project somewhere in California. Morelli was never sure about America when knowledge went beyond the purview of crime of cities like New York and Chicago. He was aware of Washington, since it was the headquarters of the F.B.I.

The Pope would occupy the top floor, a penthouse arrangement with terraces on two sides, offering him an earthier view of Rome than seen from his apartment overlooking Saint Peter's. Here he would see the Roman sunset over clotheslines, chimneys and terraces where fashion models might be sunbathing; others, filled with hundreds of plants.

"A typical Roman view," Luke explained.

His staff would be quartered in the apartment below, under the "dictatorship" of Sister Mary Matthew, the Irish housekeeper who had been at Morelli's side since he was anointed a Bishop. Her Italian was hair-raising, so were her interests. She loved God, the Church and Frances Xavier Morelli, in that order. In no particular order she adored pop music, having swung with all the trends from boogiewoogie to rock. Her vacations were timed to appearances in London of the Beatles in their prime, the Rolling Stones in theirs and, in years past, to old favorites like Frank Sinatra, Judy Garland, Sophie Tucker and Lena Horne.

Sister Mary Matthew was the first to approve of the premises. She was delighted. An outside, private elevator led from a rear alley to the penthouse; Mary Matthew suggested an exit on the staff floor. She adored Inspector Monzelli and was always on her good behavior in dealing with him. Noticing that the alley was wide enough to accommodate a small car, Mary Matthew suggested that Monzelli start parking in there now so that when His Holiness moved in, there would be little attention paid to new occupants. In the months preceding March twenty-fifth, Mary Matthew let herself be seen by neighbors as she put the place in order.

After addressing the Curia on the taped television meeting, Morelli was able to slip away from the Vatican in a small car with Luke Monzelli at the wheel for whatever "monastery in the hills outside Rome" that suited Cardinal Torriani. For himself, Monzelli enjoyed moving into his penthouse in Old Rome.

Cardinal Torriani wrote the principal article about

Morelli's resignation in which he pointed out the fragile nature of man, philosophizing that, in a modern age, with so much responsibility on his shoulders, a Pontiff should not be expected to carry the burden beyond the limit of his endurance.

Torriani noted a fact of history never mentioned officially before. Pope Pius XII was restrained from making many injudicious decisions in the last years of Pontificate when he had been afflicted by advanced senility.

Torriani commented: "A wise path has been opened to the Church by the resignation of the Holy Father and the world will remember this day as one of many he has illuminated with wisdom, strength of character and the total dedication of his spirit to the Universal Church. The world will miss one of the profound spiritual leaders of our age. We shall miss him as the Supreme Pontiff, yes, but we will still enjoy his grace and spirituality for many years to come. His Holiness' health has been described by physicians to the Holy See as remarkable for a man of his age, far better than it was several years ago. We pray for his continued good health and the tranquility our beloved Father hopes to enjoy in his retirement."

The references to Pius XII astonished Francesco Morelli. They could be interpreted in two ways. Torriani, prominent among the *papabili* and the leader of the conservative wing of the Curia, might have been inferring that criticism of a deceased Pontiff was not out of order, but that it would be wise to refrain from taking on a live Pope who had chosen resignation rather than death to end his Pontificate.

The references to Morelli's health were clearly intended to warn Cardinals coming to Rome for the Conclave that the former Pope still had his wits about him. His reputation as fair but short-tempered would not tolerate any slurs on his reign now that it was over anymore than he appreciated them while he was in power. It might have added that Morelli, a brooding introspective man, knew his flaws more intimately than his critics. But as the Spiritual Leader of millions of Catholics, admired by much of mankind, he learned to ration his mistakes as well as to consider the consequences of admitting those of which he wasn't proud.

"After all, I'm only the Pope," was a favorite exercise in

self-effacement cannily employed by John XXIII. Only a round, jolly Pope could get away with that one. As the good Dr. Broslowsky would have put it, "That wasn't Morelli's *bag*."

In some respects Morelli once reminded people of Pius XII. Quite soon in his reign they realized the difference in the characters of the two men. They shared austerity, elegance of language and manner. Pacelli, however, was the total aristocrat, a saintly man, detached and aloof. A northern Italian who found it difficult to communicate on the working man's level. Morelli, from the south, possessed greater understanding of social problems. He understood poverty although he'd never experienced it. Still his eye was keen and his mind open. Morelli's integrity was more finely honed than Pacelli's. Still, his reserve was often mistaken for indifference; his lack of decisiveness, interpreted as ineptitude. However, once he made a decision, he was firm about carrying it out.

Morelli had gone as far as the times and the nature of man would permit. He had learned when to move, when to pull back, when to stand still. His reign would go down in history as uncontroversial, pragmatic, intellectually more profound than that of his four predecessors. Spiritually, Morelli had planted seeds. Like the ecumenical spirit, time would test their strength. His resignation could be interpreted as the first test of the Morelli Papacy.

His reign had not been scarred by the financial scandals that haunted Paul VI virtually from the beginning of his Papacy. It was improbable that his death would reveal tragic flaws of character that sadly diminished the stature of Pius XII, hailed early in his reign as the greatest Pope of modern times. Eugenio Pacelli, alas, had lived too long. In his last years, a victim of senility, the autocratic, elegant man was maneuvered physically and mentally like a puppet by the Vatican power blocs.

His audiences were reduced to the equivalent of theatrical appearances of an elderly man who'd been given a statement to read and was capable enough to get through it without stuttering or falling off his throne. The aged Pontiff had performed his linguistic routine so many hundreds of times at audiences in the Basilica and in the Pope's Summer Palace at Gandolfo in the Alban Hills that he'd become an aging actor who knew his part so well he played it from habit rather than conviction.

Death brought the most tragic exposure. Pacelli had fallen victim to a Swiss doctor who circulated among nobility and Europe's wealthy people performing a revitalization cure employing injections of the urine of pregnant women and a diet of goat's milk. He gained favor at the Vatican and, in the last years of Pacelli's life, he became the Pope's personal physician.

The doctor was allowed to supervise the embalming of the Pope's body on his death in 1958. Incredibly, none of the wise men of the Vatican, although aware that the doctor was a charlatan, questioned his ability to embalm a human body. A physician's license or background is not considered necessary to the profession of mortician. The man performed such an inept job that Pacelli's body had barely been carried to Saint Peter's to lie in state before it gave off the odor of dead flesh.

In the middle of the night, reputable morticians were brought in, but it was too late to repair the damage done by the unskilled embalming. The odor became stronger. Each evening during the days of mourning, the crimson-trimmed bier, surrounded by the Papal Guard, was raised several feet and tons of flowers had to be carted into Saint Peter's to diminish the stench.

Like many leaders and spokesmen of the era, Pacelli might be most charitably accused of being myopic when it came to Hitler and Italy's dictator, Benito Mussolini. He considered them as the lesser of two evils. Communism was Pacelli's arch-enemy and it is not fanciful to assume that, as Pope, Pacelli saw Hitler as a bulwark against the domination of Europe by Russia. As Secretary of State to the fiery Achille Ratti, Pope Pius XI, he dissuaded his Holiness from excommunicating Benito Mussolini. Obviously this was the better part of wisdom. It would have made little difference to *Il Duce.* But at the same time, he was able to hold back a second encyclical condemning Hitler's Nazi movement. Pius XI died shortly thereafter, but his reputation as a powerful

221

anti-Fascist had already been secured by notable documents—one being the papal letter, *Non Abbiamo bisogno* showing the impossibility of being at once a Fascist and a Catholic.

It was smuggled out of Italy by an American priest after Mussolini had cut the Vatican's telephone wires and incapacitated the radio station of which Ratti was particularly proud. Although relations between Mussolini and the Holy See were cool ever after, the Vatican's independence was respected and there was no further diminution of services required from the City of Rome.

Pacelli had negotiated a concordat for all Germany in 1933, the year Hitler came to power, but the Nazis never pretended to observe the treaty. In 1937, after interference of every sort by the Nazis in Catholic life, Ratti denounced the government and the National Socialist theory in a second powerful encyclical denouncing dictatorship, *Mit brennender Sorge*.

Ratti also took on Russia when he issued a definitive analysis of Communism from the Roman Catholic point of view with *On Atheist Communism*. But that was only part of the now forgotten record of the feisty Milanese (his hobby was mountain climbing) who denounced in turn: persecutions in Russia, Mexico and Spain. He spoke out against nationalism, racism, totalitarianism and anti-Semitism. He was also highly critical of capitalism.

Obviously Ratti died none too soon to suit the dictators. Pacelli became Pope in 1939 and in his first encyclical, Pius XII attacked totalitarianism, but afterward it was all downhill. Apologists explained that Pacelli believed the Vatican could best work to achieve peace by maintaining formal relations with all the belligerents. This led to criticism for his not speaking out against the Nazi persecution of the Jews and of not doing enough to protect them within Italy.

Pacelli's entire career in the Church had been spent in the Vatican diplomatic service. One of his posts had been Papal Nuncio to Bavaria where he developed an affection for Germans and things German that intimates felt unduly influenced his attitude toward the Hitler reign of terror. His private experiences in Germany conflicted with the authoritative reports he continually received from responsible anti-Nazis—reports that came to him firsthand from prominent German Catholics whose integrity lay beyond dispute. It was believed Pacelli personally silenced Michael Cardinal Faulhaber, the Munich archbishop who preached resistance to Nazi ideology long before Hitler's rise to power. Pacelli, either out of stubbornness or ignorance, chose to close his eyes to the Nazi terror in the pious name of maintaining that the Catholic fold embraced Germans as well as Italians, Americans, French and nationals of every country on the globe.

After the war Pius was alarmed by the resurgence of Communism in Italy and fostered the growth of Catholic Action groups to strengthen the Christian Democratic Party. In 1949 he excommunicated Italian Catholics who joined the Communist party. In the same year, in retaliation for political persecution of the Church in Communist Eastern Europe, Pacelli excommunicated the political leaders of Yugoslavia, Hungary, Czechoslavakia, Roumania and Poland.

Yet this was the same spiritual leader who maintained cordial relations with Hitler during World War II, who granted audiences to Nazi leaders like Admiral Karl Dönitz and who sent the Führer a telegram congratulating him on his escape from the bomb plot by German Generals to assassinate him.

Even the beloved Pope John XXIII turned out, ultimately, to have been not quite what he seemed, the gentle patriarch, the kindly father who waved such a liberal breeze across the stormy sea of Catholic rigidity that John was virtually canonized while still alive. Greater love had never been poured out to a reigning Pontiff of Rome than that which swelled the heart of John, love that sprang not only from members of his own church, but from men of good will representing every conceivable religious and philosophical pursuit.

How real was the John XXIII legend?

Far from being the dark horse who emerged miraculously from the Conclave following the death of Pope Pius XII, the election of Angelo Guiseppe Roncalli had been carefully orchestrated by powerful Cardinals outside the Curia who desired an interim Pope at a time when the most prominent candidate, Giovanni Battista Montini, was Archbishop of Milan. Montini, who eventually became Pope Paul VI, may have been eligible technically. A Pope does not necessarily have to be chosen from the College of Cardinals. But Vatican power brokers were not in favor of Montini and it was simply their good luck that a break in his long relationship with Pius XII had delayed his appointment as Cardinal.

Roncalli, except for his advanced age, was an ideal model for an acceptable Pope. He was of peasant stock which gave him human interest value. He was ordained in 1904, served as a chaplain in World War I. After the war he held posts in Rome and eventually was made an Archbishop and sent on diplomatic posts to Turkey and Greece. In 1944 he was named Papal Nuncio to France where he acted as mediator between conservative churchmen and the more socially radical clergy.

Roncalli was a *bon vivant* and the ambiance of Venice suited his *soigne* life-style admirably. In Venice, Roncalli lived among people he knew. It was a favorite playground for wealthy French families. Couturier Christian Dior maintained a villa in Venice. Because he was fond of the old Patriarch, Dior created the elaborate hand-embroidered, medieval vestments Roncalli wore as Cardinal and later as Pope. They were charitably described as "quaint."

When Roncalli's name first was mentioned as a Papal possibility, a newspaper article declared that it was not possible because of Roncalli's advanced age, his "background" and his "exterior." The witty Cardinal observed, "The Conclave, after all, is not a beauty contest."

When the chips were down, Roncalli delivered himself to the Curia as Pius was stricken with his final illness. They dispatched a young Monsignor to advise Roncalli that they would be willing to give him their vote if they could be assured that Roncalli would not nominate Montini as Secretary of State. At the time Montini was considered a radical because of his support of the French Worker Priest movement. As Pope Paul VI, Montini was not considered radical enough!

To the question of Montini's selection, Roncalli answered, "Please tell my brothers that I could not give such an assurance because it would mean that I would be propagating my election."

These sibylic words convinced the Conservatives that they had chosen the next Pope, a prophecy that turned out to be correct. Montini was not chosen Secretary of State.

Roncalli's career in the church had been friendly, cautious and orthodox, qualities he carried into the Vatican as Pope John XXIII. Examined closely, John's reputation as a liberal was seriously flawed.

Although Pope Pius XII once horrified a group of visiting pilgrim nuns by telling them their long habits were "unsanitary," religious women found little comfort in a letter sent to them by John shortly before the opening of the first sessions of the Council. It advocated Pauline obedience, the "constant sacrifice of your ego" and the "annihilation of self." It deplored the "search for small comforts" by nuns and suggested that the "thorns of poverty must be loved in order that they may become roses in heaven." Obviously, if women were looking for emancipation from the new Pope, they were better off going backward and listening to Pius XII. In another adventure in personal advice, Pius told the Cardinals that the trains of their ermine capes were too long, dust collectors and a waste of material and money.

Although the Council John had summoned was intended to "let new air into the windows of the Church" and grant more autonomy to local pastors and Bishops, he imposed regulations on the Roman clergy that listed *seven hundred and seventy* articles regulating their conduct! Priests and brothers were forbidden to drive automobiles and motor scooters without written permission from their religious superiors. A priest living alone could not have a television set. A priest could stand up at a bar for an *apertivo,* but he could not sit down to drink it. American seminarians could not attend the Olympic Games of 1960 without specific authorization. Among the events from which they were summarily barred were all swimming events in which women participated!

These were petty, even medieval restrictions, unimportant in themselves, but they contained clues to John's character which the media chose to overlook in their emphasis on the more acceptable conception of John as the Father Figure.

At his death, John XXIII was given one of the most impressive funerals in the history of man. He had already become a legend and it was not then—or now—fashionable to carp at the old man's "wisdom."

But nagging questions remain also as to whether John, as the father of Vatican II, really intended "opening windows" as the tall story tells us—or was he simply attempting to shore up the faltering foundation of his own Church and that ecumenical and other innovations attributed to him were simply the natural byproducts of an inevitable need for reform.

For all the inconsistencies in his character, John XXIII was the Pope this century would remember most affectionately. Morelli knew that it had taken him years to escape the popular old Pontiff's shadow. He wondered what the reaction would be as the impact of his resignation began to be analyzed. At the moment, Morelli noted, somewhat bemused, he was enjoying the accolades most leaders never get to read—previews of his obituary.

*   *   *

Francesco Xavier Morelli remained close to the television set for most of the day, watching with interest the Votive Mass which he found spiritually moving, a beautiful event. He approved of the homily and of Monsignor Cashin. The French priest enjoyed a warm spot in his heart. He had hoped to raise him to Cardinal, but there were so many others ahead of him. It took considerable effort to keep the College of Cardinals balanced.

He met no more success in making the electoral process more democratic—no more than Paul had. But he'd managed to suppress the ambitions of Torriani and Rossi. That was comparatively easy. He fed snide suggestions to their enemies that they watch them closely. Little more was necessary—not in Rome. Torriani's compulsive nature

226

became apparent. Vatican-watchers realized that Morelli was his own Secretary of State. There was substance to the rumor that the Pope held Torriani in high office for fear that in another position he might do damage to the Church. Men like Torriani had no trouble attracting supporters—conniving, ambitious men like himself.

Rossi revealed himself, under scrutiny, as a Cardinal way beyond his capacities as the Archbishop of Milan. He lacked administrative ability and his popularity with the businessmen was strictly accountable to his office. They would dump him in an instant were it not for the fine hand of Pietro Gentille.

Gentille's appearance as the *gray eminence* of the Conclave, an outsider who united Rossi and Torriani, had not been foreseen by Morelli, but he believed it would be balanced by the activity of the Americans—even if the Americans appeared now to be in trouble.

How deeply they had been wounded, Morelli wasn't sure. He could not assess the situation until all the facts were in concerning Gentille's smear campaign. So far it had been limited to Monsignor Ryan and Cardinal Muldoon. It would have to toughen substantially if Gentille was to discredit their candidate.

When the telephone rang, it was Luke Monzelli.

"Francesco, we have problems."

"That's hardly surprising. We've been having...pardon...*they've* been having them for weeks."

Monzelli laughed ever so slightly. "It's the Americans. I've had a desperáte call from Cardinal Muldoon."

"Muldoon? Desperate? I can't quite imagine that. If the College of Cardinals had any brains, and if the Curia would go on vacation in Siberia, they'd elect that wise old turtle Pope."

"I know Cardinal Muldoon, not as well as you. Two boulders have landed on him this last week. You know about Cardinal Novik and the Polish situation."

"Yes, and from what I understand it is being handled expertly by Miss Tashman. Church officials were as horrified as the Government that a group of would-be terrorists would create such a crisis."

"It takes only one madman to hijack a plane with three hundred passengers."

"Yes, Luke. I realize that. Terrorism, far from diminishing, seems to be accelerating. There is no way to distinguish the amateurs from the professionals, Communists from mercenaries, madmen from the emotionally disturbed.

"At any rate, I understand that *Signorina* Tashman is flying to Rome tonight with two of Cardinal Novik's grand-nephews, two grand-nieces and their mothers. That certainly ought to pacify the poor man."

"Now another problem has arisen—the discrediting of Cardinal Riccordi."

"Ah! That has been moved on! I expected it! It wouldn't have mattered whom the Americans had chosen in South America, the tactics would have been the same. I suppose it involves charges of collaboration with the Nazi war criminals hiding out in South America."

"Exactly. Riccordi's record, according to Muldoon, has been checked and rechecked. He believes it can be confirmed in Washington by old records of the O.S.S. I consider it highly improbable that they could be uncovered in time. On the other hand, they might. Assuming 'Wild Bill' Donovan's men kept records."

"Some did. I remember the Riccordi case well. He suffered because he was the informer who exposed Curia corruption and their Nazi ties at the time. That case would be on record, I'm sure."

"Muldoon requests that you call President Cameron and ask for them. He would like you to obtain a signed letter from Cameron attesting to whatever he finds in the records. He claims that only someone in Cameron's position would convince the other American Cardinals. His troubles start there."

"I can imagine. I don't think Muldoon enjoys the unanimous support he'd like to have. I think maybe one or two would like to forget the whole thing and go along with whomever the Pope-makers of the Curia select. But I know they're mistaken. Yes, tell Muldoon I will call. I don't doubt that President Cameron will cooperate. I should have some news within forty-eight hours—at the outside."

"The Conclave will have been started. How will the information get to Muldoon?"

Morelli laughed, "Give Cardinal Muldoon my greatest regards and my respects. That's something he will have to figure out."

"Thank you, Francesco."

Among the privileges of his new freedom, Morelli took keen delight in making his own telephone calls and enjoying the presumption that they were not being overheard.

He put in three calls in quick succession, to the White House, to the Cardinal's Mansion in Vienna and finally, to New York.

His Holiness had absolutely no trouble with the first two calls. New York, however, presented a problem.

When the operator in New York explained that Cardinal Francesco Morelli was calling, the voice accepted quickly, laughing, "*Liebling,* don't be silly. You shouldn't play games like that with the Pope's name..."

*　　*　　*

Besides improving Italy's railroads and persuading the trains to run on time, a "miracle" that tourists interpreted as justifying the excesses of Benito Mussolini, there remained another legacy of *Il Duce* warmly appreciated by rank and file newspapermen. Traditionally the profession attracted men with zest for the highly competitive business of reporting the news. Their preoccupation with bylines and scoops blinded them to the reality that newsprint was inedible. While salaries of other professionals rose after the Great Depression, newsmen remained boxed into a wage scale that showed no inclination to budge.

Mussolini, a former newspaperman, established salary standards, working conditions and tenure regulations which made Italy's press the best paid in Europe. Among the attractive features of the *Il Duce* inheritance was triple pay on Sunday and an assortment of political and religious holidays. The test of a reporter's ingenuity was how many triple pay days he could land in the course of a year.

Enjoying a fringe benefit of the profession's life-style was the prosperous coffee bar opposite *Il Messaggero*, a few steps from the Trevi fountain, nestled comfortably behind Piazza Barberini. Open virtually twenty-four hours a day, it was always packed, overflowing with busy, noisy men, indifferent to stragglers who snapped up the few available tables.

The bar was fairly quiet when Donald and Tom slid into a table in the rear, close to the telephone. The early edition was just moving out to the airport and *Stazione Termine* whose planes and trains would carry the Roman daily up and down the Italian boot. The pressmen were back in the plant working on the next run. The only face Donald recognized belonged to a young Englishman, a stringer for several British and Australian papers. He nodded at Donald and was about to turn his back to watch a television replay of the *Votive Mass* when he spotted Tom. A puzzled expression crossed his face. Donald realized he was trying to put the priest together with a name. It had happened before, thanks to the *Gray Eminence* flyer and some sneak shots the *paparazzi* caught of the Monsignor which had run in Italy's lurid weeklies.

They'd played eagerly into the hands of the Curia power structure, at the same time blasting Cardinal Torriani as a modern Machiavelli and just as stupid. Italians had little respect for politicians and Cardinals whose deviousness was recognizable by the man on the street.

Publications of the Right castigated Torriani for seeking a compromise with Leftist Cardinals in Italy, France and a few in Spain simply to stifle the American influence. Scandal sheets of the Left screamed a "plague on all your houses," urging Torriani to press on with his determination to seek a moderate who would make no waves and who understood the immediacy of coexistence with the Communists. The same papers branded Muldoon as the tool of President Cameron and Pentagon warmongers who "intended seizing the Vatican in a last ditch stand to maintain its stranglehold on Italy."

Moderates rejected this interpretation, insisting that it was all bluff. The Americans, they claimed, were no match for the shrewd policy makers of the Vatican or the foreign Cardinals who owed their Red Hats to friends in the Curia.

230

They called the American Cardinals "eight lonely, isolated men in search of a way to recapture prestige and power they'd lost at home."

Inevitably the wilder the story, the wider it circulated— particularly in the English press, the tabloids represented by the young stringer at the bar.

They ordered gin and tonics and settled back to wait for Muldoon's telephone call. If there wasn't much to say, there was much to wonder about. Donald toyed with the blithe idea that there was really no need to worry. The Conclave would turn out as the Cardinals always predicted—a miraculous choice nullifying the wild predictions and "unfair charges" of Vatican intrigue and politics—because it would emanate from the Holy Spirit.

A glance at Monsignor Tom Ryan's grim countenance told Donald that this wasn't quite the hour to bring up the Holy Spirit. It would place an unfair burden on the priest's faith. Ryan had come so far with his grand scheme—and now where was it? Shattered by forged documents which, if they didn't appear in the scandal sheets tomorrow, were certainly being circulated tonight inside the Vatican as well as in the hotel suites and villas of the foreign Cardinals.

Ever so discreetly, of course. In deft hands, documents were not really necessary. It was so easy for one of Torriani's plants to say "Riccordi? Oh, yes, the candidate of the Americans. Mixed up with Nazi war criminals in South America, wasn't he? Very sordid. Imagine if all the old scandals were dragged out of the sewer! A lot of good people would be hurt..."

Little more was necessary. A suggestion here, a touch of innuendo there. That's how it went. No direct accusations. That remained the dirty work of the press. The College of Cardinals consisted of exalted gentlemen, noblemen, really, Princes of an ancient institution, the oldest in the world, who would never soil their ermine robes with blood. They used more subtle daggers.

When the phone rang, Tom reached for it. This drew the attention of the English newspaperman. The conversation was brief. If all Donald could make out was "Yes, Your Eminence" the English reporter certainly was straining hard

231

to catch absolutely nothing. He was, however, rewarded with an expression of complete astonishment when Tom hung up and said to Donald, "We're to stand outside in five minutes. Inspector Luke Monzelli is picking us up."

"Well, I'll be damned," Donald said.

"So will I," Tom echoed.

They finished their drinks, counting five minutes. As they walked outside, a car slid up to the curb. Luke Monzelli waved the men in and quickly sped around the corner. Donald paused a second to nod good-bye to the newspaper-man who was absolutely right in assuming that a good story had disappeared into the night before the Conclave's opening.

*   *   *

Both men had met the taciturn, low-keyed police inspector on previous visits to Rome. They knew of his close friendship with Francesco Morelli and could understand the Pope placing his trust in Luke Monzelli. His very presence assured confidence.

He drove a few blocks before stopping the car. "Gentlemen, Cardinal Muldoon spoke to me about requesting His Holiness to get in touch with President Cameron. This has been done and the President has consented.

"It is probably suspected that I know where His Holiness is staying." The detective chuckled quietly, "Of course I do. It is my duty to protect every person in Rome and the Pope is the most important guest in our city at the moment."

"Then he's not in one of the monasteries outside Rome?" Tom sounded terribly surprised.

"Obviously not," said Monzelli. "Or he would not be within my jurisdiction. For security reasons, I am his courier. Cardinal Muldoon will enter the Conclave tomor-row and will be out of touch with you, Monsignor Ryan. So when the documents arrive in Rome, I will let you know. His Holiness and President Cameron made arrangements for their delivery. It is the President's recollection that they will be most favorable to Cardinal Riccordi. The President was a Naval Officer, you may remember, stationed aboard a carrier during the liberation of Sicily.

"In any event, when they've arrived I will be in touch with you. I presume you can be reached at the North American College."

"Of course," Tom said. "I will stay there and wait until I hear from you."

Directing his remarks to Donald, Monzelli said, "An aide to President Cameron told me that His Holiness' request for the old O.S.S. material was the third in recent weeks. The President did not mention it to the Pope, choosing not to upset him. Not that the President understood exactly why the old World War II data on Riccordi was important. At any rate, it was easy to locate. The O.S.S. records are fragmentary, but there exist numerous references to Riccordi, identifying him as what you would call a 'gang buster,' a young priest who exposed higher-ups in the Vatican who were aiding Nazi war criminals to escape to South America.

"They traveled a carefully protected route, sneaking through the Brenner Pass to Milan where they went underground with the help of Cardinal Shuster. He then made arrangements with Rome. It was well organized, thanks to the camouflage supplied by the Church. There was plenty of money in it for everyone—especially Riccordi's colleagues. He was shipped to South America to silence him. Being a good priest, he obeyed. Now he is being made a scapegoat for old scandals."

"You'll have to forgive my ignorance, Inspector," Donald said, "but the O.S.S. didn't figure in my dossier on the Cardinal."

"There was no reason for it. That was William Donovan's counterspy organization. They called him 'Wild Bill' Donovan. He parachuted Americans behind the lines as your forces marched up the peninsula to Rome. He'd been active in espionage right from the start—appointed personally by President Roosevelt after Pearl Harbor."

"The Office of Strategic Services was the beginning of the C.I.A.," Donald volunteered.

"I was aware of that, but I'm amazed that their records survived and were so detailed. I really doubted President Cameron could help."

Monzelli said what Donald didn't dare. "Evidently, the Holy Spirit had something to do with it. I gather that locating the information was no trouble at all. It's neither classified nor especially confidential. Mr. Brady, you may be interested to know that the whole section on that immediate postwar era depends heavily on confidential information given to the O.S.S. by your uncle, Thaddeus Brady, who also supplied them with notes and supporting documents."

He chuckled again, "I gather that Thaddeus Brady was a one-man intelligence agency. We have met and I would vouch for anything he said no matter how far-fetched it might sound."

"Thank you, Inspector."

"I must urge you, Mr. Brady, to be careful. Anyone close to Cardinal Muldoon is going to be watched. Since there have been other requests for data on Cardinal Riccordi, those opposed to his nomination will assume the Americans have it as well. They will also assume that it will be produced inside the Conclave."

Donald muttered, "That's really an *assumption?* How in the devil are we going to get it inside?"

Monzelli answered, "I'm afraid I can't help you there. All I can suggest is *pazienza.* Stay close to the telephone, Monsignor Ryan. And you, Mr. Brady, be very careful. The terrorists—or whatever they are—who've been harassing the Americans may want to talk to you...privately. My men will keep an eye out, but we are not magicians, only policemen. Now I will drive you back to your car."

After thanking Monzelli, Donald and Tom got into the little Fiat and drove to the Grand-Plaza. There was little to say. Monzelli had laid it out clearly. At this point, Donald agreed that prayer and patience represented the sum total of their usefulness.

Donald promised to call Tom as soon as he finished covering the opening ceremonies later in the morning. It was now well past two.

*   *   *

Donald wondered at the night porter's raised eyebrow when he asked for his key. It was neither friendly nor unfriendly, merely odd and unexpected. He read curiosity into the look. It surprised him. Night porters in first class Roman hotels were chosen, he believed, for their hauteur. Curiosity was beneath them. Their *buon giornos* and *buona serras* were uttered with weary tolerance of their guests if, indeed, they were uttered at all. Roman hotel clerks possessed an uncanny faculty for recognizing a guest by his shoes or the buttons on his coat. They seldom felt a need to look him in the eyes.

Donald took the elevator to his floor and walked down the thickly carpeted hall, enjoying the wide corridor of the old hotel. He rounded a corner, passing the laundry closet. It was lighted. Donald stopped at the sight of a familiar figure seated there on a straight chair, her hands folded primly in her lap.

"Donald!" the figure whispered.

"Jennie! What are you doing here?"

"Waiting for you, Donald."

"How did you get in?"

Jennie smiled, "Donald, there is no hotel in all Rome that would forbid me to sit in a laundry closet if I make the request. Who would dare?"

Donald stifled a loud laugh.

"Shh! Be quiet. You no in danger, but peoples are looking for you. They want to kidnap you."

"What?"

"Not long—not for ransom or killing. Leave here now. Come with me to the Merline. I explain everything."

"But . . ."

"Donald, trust me. I know things. You know I do. No time to talk now. You have anything important in your room?"

"No, nothing. Just a feature story I intend delivering to *Stampa Estera* tomorrow—or today, I guess."

"Get it Donald and come with me."

Donald darted in and out of his room. "You take the elevator," Jennie said. "I go the back way. I meet you in front."

Within minutes they were both behind the locked and bolted door of the Merline, just around the corner from the Grand-Plaza.

Jennie guided Donald into a room on the first floor opposite hers. She locked the door and began to speak in a whisper.

"It's Angela—and those young men she plays with. She was here last night with that German. They were with narcotics—I know little from drugs. They talked much, loud and crazy. I hear much. She has been working for you, *si*?"

Donald nodded.

Jennie sighed, "I should have warned you..."

"Don't worry, Jennie, I've always had my doubts. I just hoped..."

"That you would change her." Jennie shook her head. "Angela's smart, intelligent—pretty, too. You are not the first newspaperman to be fooled by her." Jennie paused. "I'm afraid she likes the wild life too well... young men like that Hans."

"Did you hear anything?"

"Enough to warn you that they want to get their hands on you. But they do not know when. Are you expecting information?"

"Yes."

"About getting inside the Conclave? No, don't answering that, Donald, I want not to know. But they are wanting it. You should stay here now."

Donald thought. "You're right, Jennie. If they are waiting for the right moment, this isn't it. I don't have the information they want." He laughed, "I'm not very good to them—or to myself. An odd situation, isn't it?"

"Who knows. What is that big song you make out of Italian? *Si, Che Sera Sera*."

Donald looked longingly at the bed. Lumps and all it seemed inviting. His eyes were beginning to close on him.

"Donald, you sleep now."

"Thanks, Jenny," he yawned. "I've got to. I can't think anymore tonight. It's too much..."

Jennie closed the door as Donald slipped off his outer clothing and fell to the bed in his shorts and socks.

Donald Brady was not the first man to know the depths of Hand-Job Jennie's friendship.

Donald was one of many.

PART VIII

The Conclave

As he crossed the Tiber at Castel Sant' Angelo, the tired blue eyes of Donald Thaddeus Brady feasted, as they always did, on the lifesize Bernini statues decorating the bridge leading to the ancient fortress. And, as always, he wondered if the castle, once the mausoleum of the Emperor Hadrian, really contained a dungeon full of mysterious doors opening into secret passages that would lead one to other mysterious doors inside the walls of Vatican City.

If the legends passed down through the centuries were true, now was certainly the time for some intrepid adventurer to test them. There wasn't a reporter alive who wouldn't risk digging through the tunnels and sewers of Rome to penetrate the Apostolic Palace where for the next several days the Sacred College of Cardinals would participate in an unprecedented Conclave to elect the two hundred and sixty-fifth Pontiff of the Roman Catholic Church.

Throngs making their way to Piazza San Pietro slowed the long, steady stride of the tall, lean American, allowing Donald's thoughts to shift gears—from Hadrian's tunnels to another mystery of Castel Sant' Angelo. It was the often asked question, "How in heaven's name did Tosca manage to kill herself unless she took a swan dive from the parapet of the castle?" One of the terraces of the multi-leveled tower would surely have broken her fall. At worst, Tosca would have suffered a few broken bones. It was an old riddle among opera buffs, admirably disposed of by concluding that Puccini's music could compel the listener to believe anything.

After crossing the bridge, Donald sensed that the crowds were thinner than they had been yesterday; but still it was hard going, requiring all of his New York training before the lanky, handsome American found himself on the Via Della Concilliazione, that fabled triumphal avenue to the glorious Piazza San Pietro and the magnificence of the cathedral, Saint Peter's, the mother church of Catholicism.

Not even the jostling and pushing or the noisy chatter of the crowd diminished the excitement Donald felt when his eye looked up the broad boulevard to the architectural whole of Saint Peter's. It was indeed one of the world's wonders— the double colonnade surrounding the square, consisting of four rows of columns which dramatized the simple, ageless grace of the red granite obelisk imported from Heliopolis by Caligula, the two Bernini fountains and finally the great dome of Saint Peter's. Here was a symphony of stone made more awesome by one's awareness of the centuries of the history that had created it. It stood as a monument both to God and the mind of man—Emperor Constantine, Pope Nicholas V, and Urban VII who commissioned the Cathedral, the piazza and the Via Della Concilliazone as well as the artists who fulfilled their own and their patrons' dreams, Rafael, Bernini and Michelangelo.

Speculation to the contrary, the Conclave would be held in the Sistine Chapel which had become the fief of Michelangelo who covered the ceiling with his marvelous frescos, focused in the center by the *Creation of Man* and on the end wall by *The Last Judgment*. In this chapel, a crowning jewel of Italian art, the Princes of the Church had crowned Popes for hundreds of years.

The Vatican announced that with minor deviations, tradition would be observed. There would be no televised announcement of the identity of the new Pope nor would there be a voice announcement of the day-by-day balloting.

Smoke issuing from the Vatican chimney would still advise the world of the progress of the Conclave; smoke, produced by burning the Cardinals' ballots; black, if no majority had been achieved; white, when a Pontiff had been chosen. The first view of the new Pontiff would occur on the balcony of Saint Peter's—just as it had in the memory of all living men, back to their great-great grandfathers.

Donald's skill at maneuvering New York's city pavements and squeezing through groups of people without suffering anything more serious than a few snarls brought him to a vantage point where he might see the last public ceremony of the Conclave—the entrance of the Cardinals into the Vatican Palace.

Like yesterday's Votive Mass, it represented a departure in form, if not in substance, from tradition. The Cardinals had been asked to enter the Conclave through the main entrance door to Saint Peter's and to wear, according to Roman custom, their scarlet cassocks. Inside the Basilica they were invited to celebrate Mass at altars of their choice. As young priests many Cardinals had traveled to Rome simply for the privilege of saying Mass within the walls of Saint Peter's. So this arrangement was the first to be greeted with universal approval by the Church elders.

Donald had seen New York's Cardinal Muldoon's eyes brighten in surprise when the schedule for the first day of the Conclave was delivered. "Praise be to God!" he said. "They've finally done something right. I'd like to say Mass at Saint Peter's tomorrow." Turning to Donald, he smiled, "Like to be my altar boy, son? I'll read it in Latin if you like."

"No thanks, Your Excellency. I've still got work to do."

The crowd today was quieter than it had been yesterday. With reason. This marked the start of a fateful event. It was D-Day in a sense. Now there was no turning back. The Conclave was here—a reality. Not something to be gossiped about, speculated over, debated or, as happened in some small nooks and crannies of the world, to be prayed for.

Yesterday had seen a joyous innovation, again within the limits imposed by custom, but made possible because the Church was not in mourning for a deceased Pontiff. The Basilica of Saint Peter's had been chosen to celebrate publicly the Votive Mass of the Holy Spirit which began the Cardinals' deliberations. Usually, the Votive Mass was said in the Pauline Chapel, attended only by the Cardinals and their aides.

Things were not always what they seemed. Not until hours after yesterday's Votive Mass had the world become aware of the extraordinary security precautions taken by the Italian government, collaborating with the Vatican, to prevent demonstrations which had been threatened by a wide variety of pressure groups—left wing radicals, rightists, monarchists, Church dissidents as well as "pilgrims" from outside Rome and Italy who fully expected they could use the Papal Election as an opportunity to propagandize their causes.

Knowing these ominous facts had not quite prepared Donald for the extent to which the authorities had gone to contain the hordes crowding into Saint Peter's Square. The *Carabiniere* (Italy's national police) were everywhere, conspicuous in their three-cornered hats, black uniforms, red sashes and swords hanging at their sides. Roman police and troops from the Italian Army were posted at the outer edge of the Square.

Yesterday Donald had occupied a seat in the press section inside the Basilica. Today he noticed that a squad of riflemen had been detailed to each column of the double colonnade. Looking up to the rooftops and restaurants along Via Concilliazone, Donald saw poorly camouflaged machine gun nests.

Nothing had been left to chance. A few minor scuffles might occur. They would be tolerated, possibly precipitated deliberately by the police to make the public aware of their presence. They would serve notice that *Big Brother* was everywhere.

Indeed he was. Donald's investigation revealed that known radicals attempting to enter Italy at her borders were denied entry. There had been spot checks of out-of-town cars entering Rome and more than a hundred "undesirables" had been shipped back to Turin and Milan in the north, to Naples and Bari in the south. Rome's airports appeared as armed camps, the gangways and passages were lined by soldiers carrying rifles with bayonets affixed.

Italy's most famous prison, *Regina Coeli,* stood only a few hundred yards down the road from the Vatican. Once host to American gangster, Lucky Luciano, and more recently to Italian film stars involved in drug cases, it now overflowed with members of the Red Brigade who had been unable to disappear into the murky underground that hid the modern radical. Donald's experience as an investigative

240

journalist had brought him into contact with the radical fringe and he'd found them to be an extraordinarily disciplined group whose skill at self-preservation and protecting their "comrades" reduced the Mafia code of *omerta* and its blood vows of loyalty to the innocence of a Boy Scout oath.

In the three days preceding the opening of the Conclave, a curfew had been imposed on the area surrounding Vatican City. Each night a systematic inspection of the Papal States had been made by Bomb Squads (Italian as well as foreign) to ferret out possible explosive devices and to make notes on the already exhaustive list of locations where incendiary devices might be concealed.

Since the Italian government controlled radio and television, foreign broadcasters were barred from on-the-spot coverage of the Conclave—an edict that produced enormous agitation around the world. Prominent press lords in England and America threatened to take this "outrageous abridgement" of a free press to the floor of the United Nations.

Inspector Luke Monzelli, in charge of the huge chain of protection, replied in his usual courtly fashion, "I am sorry, gentlemen, but the rules stand. The United Nations has no jurisdiction in Rome. We do not want cameras revealing our protective ring. Since we cannot prevent 16mm. cameras from operating, you will have ample coverage within a few hours of each day's ceremonies. We could censor this material, but we will not. We ask you to refrain from photographing our mode of protection or explaining it too graphically. We do intend to change the deployment of the police and military each day, but only so much variability is possible. I know I can count on you.

Monzelli's diplomatic handling of an explosive situation mollified news reporters on the scene even if their seniors huffed and puffed in the network offices about the high-handedness of the Italian government. "Might as well be back in the days of Mussolini," they fumed. None had been around in jobs of responsibility in Mussolini's era, but that evidently had not occurred to them.

Not all the Cardinals chose to say Mass at Saint Peter's.

Many foreign Cardinals enlarged on the idea of making the official opening of the Conclave an occasion of joy. They decided to read Masses at their titular churches, thus celebrating the beginning of a new epoch in Church history in all parts of the Eternal City.

The Americans were to arrive as a group at Saint Peter's. Once they had entered the Basilica, Donald intended leaving. They arrived as promised at eleven o'clock, but the cavalcade of limousines was far from the staid procession he expected. Two Cardinals, Duncan of Saint Louis and Winkler of Detroit, arrived first in a car that was also packed with their aides. When they piled out, instead of going directly into the Cathedral, they waited for the next car, also carrying two American Red Hats, O'Toole of Boston and Donovan of Washington. This car also overflowed with secretaries. The new arrivals made no attempt to mount the steps and Donald shortly realized why.

The third and fourth cars were like the Toonerville Trolley, disgorging, besides Cardinal Novik and a beautiful, tall blonde, Teresa Tashman, a collection of small children and two women. Quite clearly they were the nieces and grand-nieces and grand-nephews of the Chicago Cardinal. From the bright smile on Novik's face no one could have believed the ordeal the Polish-born prelate had been through. Donald breathed a sigh of relief. One major crisis had been averted.

A final pair of limousines arrived bearing Cardinals De Cordoba, Muldoon and Quinlan. The Philadelphia Cardinal appeared to have arrived in solitary splendor until Donald noticed he was the "baggage man"—a curious sight as he stood at the foot of the steps carefully checking suitcases and attaché cases against a list.

The Americans weren't the only Cardinals who'd invited friends and relatives to attend their Masses at Saint Peter's. A number of Italians had done the same—creating quite a different atmosphere from the solemnity one expected at the start of a Conclave. But hadn't that been the intention of the Papal Chamberlain and the *Camerlengo* (the presiding officer of the Conclave) from the very beginning? The steps of the Basilica appeared to be filled with the gaiety and good will of Sunday in a village square. Donald wanted to believe that, for a few hours at least, the animosities of the past weeks had been put aside.

How long the truce would last was far beyond his powers of projection. What mattered now was that the eight American Cardinals were all present, looking far healthier and exuding more confidence than events of recent days warranted. A group of Polish children clearly had made a difference and, for the moment, Donald believed he could risk the luxury of feeling exhausted.

Suddenly his shoulders sagged with fatigue. He would have liked to have found a seat, but where? Or settled into a cab and been driven back to his hotel. But like the rest of the crowd which was rapidly breaking up, Donald would have to walk. He glanced at his watch, then looked up at the darkened Papal apartment, his eyes automatically sweeping across the dome of Saint Peter's. Without thinking, a gesture that had not come naturally to him for years occurred. Donald blessed himself and quietly said the only two prayers lapsed Catholics remember, *Hail Mary* and *Our Father*.

As Donald started again to glance at his watch he felt his arm stopped, firmly gripped by a hooded monk in black who had slipped up beside him about a quarter of an hour earlier. Turning toward him, Donald realized he wasn't going to identify the man for his hood had been arranged to totally cover a face that had no intention of turning toward him. The monk was shorter than Donald by five inches, but his body was chunky. Donald could tell by the grip on his arm that he was a strong five by five. Whether or not he was actually a monk was obviously irrelevant under the circumstances.

"Mr. Brady?" the hood asked.

"Yes, I'm Brady. What's up?"

"You will accompany me and my friend," the hood responded. Turning to his left, Donald found another hooded monk flanking him. The man, somewhat taller, whose face was also carefully shrouded, moved closer and Donald felt the unmistakable contour of a pistol in his side. Not *cold* steel—not through the layers of the monk's habit and his medium-weight suit. But Donald, having felt a

243

revolver in his side before, was unlikely to confuse it with a popsicle stick. Once you meet a revolver in your ribs, you don't readily forget it.

"Whatever you say," Donald said, "let's go."

"You won't make any moves to annoy us," the speaking monk said. There was an inflection in his voice that sounded unmistakably German even if the English pronounciation was good.

"I know better, thank you." He was tempted to say *danke schön*, but Piazza San Pietro this September afternoon was not exactly the place to make jokes and spoil his captor's good disposition.

"Thank you. We appreciate your cooperation," the chunky "monk" said. "It's not far. Just around the corner. About fifteen minutes' walk."

Donald knew better than to break loose. That could invite a wide variety of unpredictable problems. To run would cause a riot. His captors could easily disappear in the crowd. Moreover, Donald hadn't been in Rome this long for his health. He'd learned that long ago. He'd been lured into the most fascinating story of his life—the resignation of a Pope—and if being hustled by two hooded hoods opened another window on the crazy pattern of intrigue he'd found since he started working, it was his job to offer no resistance and to discover what he could. Even if it meant disappointment or the closing of a window on the only viable plan the Americans had come up with.

No one had ordained him to save the Roman Catholic Church or spare the Papacy a scandal of world-wide implications and God knows what kind of a future, but this was how it had turned out. A newspaperman knows better than to turn his back on the unexpected.

As the men in black had promised it was a short walk, up the hill to that part of old Rome behind and to the side of Vatican City where the poverty of Rome becomes more visible. The crowd thinned out with each few steps they took and they were quite deep into the old city when they reached a blind alley. It was occupied by a car and a driver whose face was shielded by the sun visor.

The talking monk said, "We will have to blindfold you.

244

Do you mind?"

Donlad's laugh was hollow. "Do I have a choice?"

The monk chuckled as he placed the blindfold on the young newspaperman. Once it was securely in place, he said, "I'm afraid I must ask you to lie down on the floor of the car. We did consider your height, Mr. Brady. We picked an American sedan."

"Thanks a lot," Donald said as he folded himself on the floor of the back section. The chunky monk got in and sat behind the driver. "Are you comfortable, Mr. Brady?"

"Indeed. I prefer traveling like this."

"You are a good hostage, Mr. Brady. We will enjoy our time together. You have humors. That's more than I can say about the Italians."

You have *humors*. The plural? He had to be a German. "That's nice to know."

The car started up and Donald felt it speed out of the alley and turn up a sharp hill. That was all he remembered. Just as he was enjoying the thought that he was important enough to rate souped-up wheels, Donald Brady fell asleep.

* * *

At three o'clock, Angela Nero, slim, pretty, with a saucy look to her intelligent face, dark-eyed and titian-haired, walked briskly through the revolving doors of the Grand-Plaza Hotel, nodding "good afternoon" to the doorman and headed straight for the elevator, asking for the ninth floor.

She glanced through the sheaf of papers, an expression of disappointment crossed her face. "Another merry-go-round. Says lots! Tells nothing!"

She'd about finished when she picked up the telephone, dialed a number. A voice, sounding far away from the receiver, answered, *"Ja."*

"Angela here. I've got the story."

"How does it look?"

"I'm afraid it's the usual straightforward reporting. I can't see any clues."

"Better read it anyhow. Hang up, I'll call you back."

Angela made herself comfortable, fixed the story on the desk and waited for the call. It came in seconds.

"Ready?" she asked. "Good, here goes."

In Rome last week, one hundred and fifteen Cardinals of the Roman Catholic Church assembled in a solemn and secret Conclave behind the locked and sealed doors of the Papal Palace inside Vatican City to choose the two hundred and sixty-fifth successor to the Throne of Saint Peter. They have gathered in a tense atmosphere both within the body of the Cardinals, representing millions of Catholics throughout the world at a time when, in the minds of some, the ancient Faith stands in peril of extinction, in danger of schism, according to others. In the opinion of more optimistic Catholic leaders, the Roman Church stands on the threshold of a great spiritual upheaval in a most positive sense that, having already broken with many of its medieval traditions, beliefs and superstitions, it has survived the purgatory of change and will emerge in the next decades as a more forceful voice of morality and integrity than at any time in its history.

In spite of clear signs that the American Cardinals intended acting in concert at the Conclave, none was willing to make a firm statement before leaving for Rome or on their arrival in the Eternal City. However, they did issue statements, each phrased differently, of course, making it clear that the American voice intended to be heard at this vital meeting of Church leaders. They left no doubt that they had abandoned their previous position of being above debate or the election process. "We were damn fools in the old days," O'Toole said, "I shoved in a vote for myself at the last Conclave on the first ballot just to show the snobs that I was there."

In the past year American Cardinals have traveled abroad extensively in an effort to meet and know their colleagues. Back home they pooled their information and by common consent, Cardinals Muldoon and Novik are serving as co-chairmen and policy makers of

246

the American delegation of Cardinals. They enjoy the valuable support of Monsignor Thomas Ryan.

Here Angela stopped in her reading. She said, "He's crossed something out..."

"Can you read it?" the voice at the other end of the telephone asked.

"No, Brady always goes through his corrections with a soft lead pencil, covering the sentence completely."

"Try holding it up to the light. Maybe you can read through the pencil marks."

"OK. Just a minute."

The pretty young woman took the piece of paper over to a floor lamp where she'd installed a strong bulb for Brady to read by after tiring of his complaints that Italians all wore glasses because they skimped on light bulbs.

Holding the paper up, she smiled, said the words to herself and returned to the telephone.

"Hey, that works fine! Here's what it says: Monsignor Thomas Ryan, known as the *eminence griese* of the Archdiocese of New York, a talented youthful priest who has been at the side of Cardinal Muldoon since he was named to head the most important diocese in the United States, if not in the entire Western World. Monsignor Ryan has been a most articulate advocate of active American participation in the Conclave. Ryan was one of a minority of American priests who, firmly convinced that the Pope would resign, urged Cardinal Muldoon into forming a unified block of American voters at the Conclave.

"That's where the marked-out part ends. Shall I go on?"

"Yes. He's hinted at a lot of things, but I think he's wound up now and going to stumble somewhere along the line. Let's hear it."

Although controversy over the Americans dominated Roman gossip since the Cardinals began arriving, there has been no dearth of speculation about the several Italians, two Europeans and two South Americans who rank among the *papabili*. Only Italians are taken seriously, at present; the others are not even considered as dark horses, just players in the game.

The favorites are:

Luigi Cardinal Trentini, Archbishop of Naples, 60, undisputed favorite of the radicals. Fiery, hot tempered, in trouble with Church and civil authorities from the day of his ordination to the present. Achieved promotions through sheer brass and the love he has inspired among the poor of Naples. Still he is no friend of the Communists.

Angelo Cardinal Torriani, 60, Secretary of State. Long diplomatic experience, an avowed conservative who would not tamper with changes already made, but would hold the line. Independently wealthy through his family, his Church career has quadrupled their fortunes. A canny politician, cultivated, intelligent, a linguist and an opportunist. He enjoys the support of the Curia, the senior Cardinals of Spain, some Latin American countries, Ireland as well as isolated support among traditional Cardinals from France and Germany.

Daniele Cardinal Rossi, Archbishop of Milan, 55. Too young to be considered *papabili* under normal considerations. In the present crisis, Rossi, a middle of the roader, appeared an acceptable choice to the conservative wing of the College, palatable to the progressives who wanted church changes to continue, but at a slower rate. Rossi is not acceptable to the radicals who expect more sweeping innovations and immediate rapproachement with the Iron Curtain countries lost through the arrogance of Pius XII. Rossi's flaws lie in his arrogance and abrasiveness which his admirers feel could be cured once the man escapes the yoke of diocesan duties. O'Toole once said, "All parish priests die 'crusty' even if they were born as 'angels.'"

After all the Conclavists had entered, the doors were closed and sealed. Besides the Cardinal-electors, there are many others: the aide each Cardinal may invite to accompany him; in some cases, particularly among elderly Cardinals, two aides are permitted. Then there are the doctors, a surgeon, several nurses, three barbers plus kitchen help, waiters, porters and maids. An accurate estimate of the number inside the Conclave is not possible. More than three hundred is a close guess.

Dark horse Italians include Roberto Cardinal Bellafiore of Bari, Mario Cardinal Silvestri and Manuello Cardinal Nascimobene of the Curia.

European *papabili* include Hans Cardinal Wilhelm of the Netherlands assigned to the Vatican diplomatic corp and Francois Cardinal Lamark of Marseilles. Both are priests whose names have become prominent through endorsement of Leftist activities and their support of acceleration of change by the Church, particularly in respect to priestly celibacy and the easing of the Church's position on divorce.

Finally, there has emerged in the last couple of weeks a flurry of interest in two South American Cardinals, Giorgio Cardinal Riccordi, Italian-born who migrated to Chile in 1945 after his ordination in Rome. Little is known about him at this writing. Despite considerable speculation about his *papabili* in the press as well as the Vatican, Cardinal Riccordi succeeded in slipping in and out of the two public appearances of the Cardinals at Saint Peter's without meeting the press. It is believed he arranged his flight to arrive in Rome in time to proceed directly from the airport to the *Votive Mass* at Saint Peter's.

"Angela," the voice said, "would you read that again?"

"Sure," she answered, as she went over the paragraph dealing with Riccordi.

When she'd finished, the voice snarled, "Brady's got to be kidding. He knows everything about Riccordi, down to his birthmarks. We'll have to check this against the other copy to America. Any way you can lay your hands on the material?"

"Maybe, maybe...yes. I'll try. At least I can ask at *Stampa Estera*."

"Do that. What comes next?"

"The Peruvian, Enrico Gonzales."

"Good, read it."

"It's pretty much the same thing. Enrico Gonzales, native Peruvian, started as humble priest—that stuff—rose to Bishop and then Cardinal. Exiled several times by Junta governments. Age sixty-five. That's about the same age as Riccordi although Donald didn't use it."

"Well, all I can see is that he's tipped his hand in this bit."

"He didn't know that," Angela said defensively.

"Of course, he didn't. He sure as hell didn't expect us to be reading his copy while he's tied up."

"Tied up?" Angela exclaimed in a shrill voice.

"Oh, oh! You like the guy! No, Angela. Brady's not tied up—not so it hurts. He's too smart for that. He's going to cooperate. He was so damned tired, he fell asleep in the car. Maybe he's still sleeping. What comes next?"

Angela picked up the final pages of the manuscript.

With the doors closed on the most-important Conclave of modern times, security precautions have been unprecedented, but in this electronic age one wonders if old-fashioned locks and keys, or even the sacred oaths of Cardinals, will be enough to prevent communication between the Cardinals and the outside world.

There are abundant reasons why the electors would be eager to communicate with associates outside. The very possibility of a dark horse candidate gaining strength would test the nerves of the entire Conclave. They would be eager to learn more about him than is possible from an interview, a speech of intent by the prospect in the Sistine Chapel or even the endorsement of respected colleagues.

The electors in this Conclave are deprived the luxury of an easy way out—choosing an interim Pope. Nor can the differences between conservative and radical be so easily resolved as in the past by choosing someone known to the Italian leaders of both sides and binding him to mutually acceptable compromises.

The Conclave is no longer an Italian family affair and this will be made crystal clear when, as they promise, Cardinals representing the Third World, will demand to be heard if only because of the importance their congregations hold in the future of the Church. Hopefully, benefits will come to them as the result of this Conclave. But most important, they will go on record as a voice, a viable part of modern Catholicism.

Finally, the new aggressiveness of the American Cardinals will be a factor whose importance cannot be underestimated. Like good poker players, they have held their cards close to the chest. When it's their turn to deal, the Europeans expect the shock impact to be enormous. Few Cardinals agree with Torriani that Americans are unskilled in parliamentary maneuvering. Particularly not at this point of the Conclave when the intentions of the American Cardinals remain as mysterious as they were at the time of the Pope's resignation.

When I saw Cardinal O'Toole just before preparing this story, the crusty old parish priest took my arm and said, "Don't be too cynical in your roundup. Give us a break. Cynicism is a disease and terribly contagious. While I'm holed up there, you can tell them all the old O'Toole stories, but tell them to pray for me, too. Ask them to pray that God be with us and between us and all the empty places we must walk."

"That's it," Angela said.

"Well, he covered it pretty thoroughly. Funny he didn't mention Ryan again. I thought they were going to say he'd flown back to America."

"I don't know," Angela said. "Donald didn't say anything about that. Of course I haven't seen him. I figure that Ryan's an 'in' figure. His name wouldn't mean much to the general public—even in a New York newspaper. I gather he's managed to stay pretty much in the background except when women latch on to him at parties."

"I guess that's it. Pretty comprehensive. I made some notes. Funny, he buried the security bit. The English boys are going after that hot and heavy. Somebody's going to get into that Conclave—you know that."

"I don't know that. But if you say so, why not? Who?"

"I don't know, but our friend Brady does."

"Are you sure?"

"How come there was no mention of an English speaking doctor? No. That's not what I mean. An American doctor. You know how Americans are. I checked. Last time around, they had an American doctor with them. This time they don't. Why not?"

"Well?"

"Because they're going to bring one in?"

"That's impossible."

"Not quite. I checked the records. In 1939 a doctor got in. He was a specialist. Only stayed a few hours. It was a one day Conclave. It's like a *cul de sac*. You can get in, but you can't get out—until they're through. Anyhow, thanks a lot. I'll see you later."

"Certainly. Around nine. One thing . . . please . . ."

"Yes?"

"Oh, never mind . . . just . . ."

"Just take it easy on Brady, is that what you're asking me? Why not? He's not our enemy. We want information. He's going to give it to us. And when he does he'll go back to his hotel or to your *pensione*—whichever he wants, OK?"

"*Si, caro. Ciao.*"

Angela put down the receiver slowly, rearranged the papers as she found them, turned off the lights and looked around the large room where she'd spent so many hours with Donald. She sighed, turned the knob of the door handle and stepped out into the hall.

Angela turned the corner to go toward the elevator when out of a dark corner of the hall there appeared two men; one, tall, burly and young; the other, portly, middle-aged and gray at the temples. A warm smile crossed the latter's face.

"*Signorina* Nero, I believe."

The older man pulled a slip of paper out of his coat pocket.

"Angela Nero? That is the full name. *Si?*"

"Yes, why do you ask?"

"I simply wish to be sure. Now, my name is Luke

Monzelli, *Signorina*. Inspector Luke Monzelli. I am in charge of all the security arrangements for the Conclave."

"How exciting!" Angela said nervously, trying to move around him toward the elevator.

"Please, *Signorina. Per favore,* stay as you are. Now you have been working as an assistant of sorts to Donald Brady, the American newspaperman, have you not?"

"Yes, I have."

"Good. Then you are the right young lady. I am sorry, but we have our mix-ups. We overlooked you a few days ago. Funny... your name was on the list. Anyhow, better late than never. You will accompany this gentleman to headquarters. I will see you there later. Meantime, I must have a look around Mr. Brady's room."

"But he's not there."

"I know that, *Signorina*." The inspector's eyes darkened.

He turned his back on the girl. "Take her in, Franco. Hold her on pickpocketing. Look inside her jacket pocket. You'll find my gold cigarette case. It's gold, unmistakably mine, monogrammed and half-filled with *Gitanes*."

Monzelli walked quietly down the hall to Brady's room.

* * *

Donald's captors nudged him awake with their feet. The German's politeness was apparently part of his routine. "Would you mind waking up, Mr. Brady? We've reached our destination. We can all get more comfortable."

Donald sat up and cooperated in being removed from the car into a street floor building which his nose promptly recognized as the gang's printing shop near the Trevi fountain. Angela had overlooked spilling his knowledge of that hideout. Score one for him; one demerit for his captors. Imagine carting a newspaperman to a printing plant!

Donald cancelled the German's demerit. "You must feel at home here, Mr. Brady. Sorry, but we shall not be here long. We might make several stops today. It depends."

"On what?"

"*Ach!* That would be giving you information. It's us who wants to know. *Nicht wahr?*"

"If you say so."

The German ordered his Italian hoods to tie Donald up. They used an awful lot of rope and while they were doing it, Donald tried to remember the layout of the shop. Not that it was important. When he heard a door slam and a telephone ringing, Donald knew there was a back room. He could hear the German's voice, but the words were beyond him. Donald yawned, slid to the floor and fell asleep.

When he awoke Donald's kidneys were bursting. The German was still mumbling on the telephone. He sensed the presence of the other captors.

"Where can I take a piss?" he asked of no one in particular.

He stood up as a hand touched his shoulder. "Come this way." The voice was muffled.

He led Donald a few steps to his right. When a gust of fresh air followed the sound of a lock being turned, he figured a door had opened onto an alley. The muffled voice said, "Go ahead. You're aimed outdoors." He loosened the rope around Donald's wrists.

When he zipped his fly, he asked, "Is there someplace I can sit? I've had an awful lot of floors."

He felt a chair pushed under him. His hands were tied again.

When the door from the back room opened, it was the German. He was surprised at his excellent Italian. "We don't need Mr. Brady anymore. I've got the information."

"What shall we do with him?" It was "Muffled Voice."

"Put him in the car. Drive him around for an hour or so. Then let him go."

They led Donald back to the car. Two hours of driving later he prayed that "Muffled Voice" and his silent pal were as bored as he was. He longed to make a deal; anything to get out. But playing it their way was the rule of the game.

Finally the car stopped. "Muffled Voice" asked, "Hey, newspaperman, what would you like us to do with you?"

"Let me out, of course. What else?"

"Are you going to cause a lot of trouble?"

"I doubt that I can—not right now."

"All right. One of us is going to take you for a little walk. Time to get the car out of sight. Then you're on your own."

The pair of legs got out of his way. He stepped out of the car and took Donald's hand. "Just follow me." As soon as they were out of it, he heard the car pull away.

His captor pushed him roughly—flat on the ground. Donald heard him running to catch up with the car. It was a neat job. The fall knocked the breath out of him.

Minutes passed before normal breathing resumed. More time was involved in getting rid of his blindfold and the mess of rope. Before he was pulled together, Donald knew where he was—on a side road between Rome and the airport.

Like all roads leading in and out of Rome, Donald knew it was being patrolled more frequently than usual. All he had to do was wait for a police car and hail it.

So far so good. His own condition didn't bother him nearly so much as the fact that his captors had gotten the information they wanted.

Donald had nothing to show but a mess of rope, some sore joints and a wasted afternoon. His hosts lifted his watch, but they hadn't taken his wallet. Donald had no idea of the time. It was close to sunset.

So they'd obtained their information. What? And how? His mind traveled over everything that happened last night—the meeting with Monzelli, being surprised by Jennie, dashing into his room for the story which he'd delivered to *Stampa Estera* before setting out for Saint Peter's.

Then it hit him—the carbon copy. If Angela had gotten into his room and read it, it was just possible that his story contained a clue that led the German to some conclusion. Using this as a premise, Donald went down his piece line by line in his mind trying to read it from the viewpoint of Hans and Angela.

They weren't acting stupidly. Damned clever, actually. Someone with their particular skills looking for information from someone they knew well—and Angela knew him well—could literally read between the lines. Hell, he'd done it hundreds of times in researching old pieces. Newspapermen often gave away everything from their own opinions to off-the-record remarks they really intended protecting. Sometimes you could read meaning into what a reporter neglected to say by running into an omission that stared at you so boldly it was hard to imagine how the writer missed it.

But damned if he could find one in his own story.

Not after an hour of steady concentration that ended when a police car rolled by, stopping in answer to Donald's signals. His identification produced a warm reception. "We've had a call out for you—nothing serious, Mr. Brady. Inspector Monzelli would like us to bring you to his office."

It was an amiable trip into town. The sun was setting. The preliminaries would be over at the Vatican. They'd start balloting the first thing in the morning. Time was running out fast.

*　　*　　*

The confrontation with Angela had been painful. It was mercifully brief and for that he thanked Luke Monzelli.

Monzelli happened to be in his office when Donald and the patrol arrived.

"Glad to see you, Mr. Brady. I was worried about you. My men saw you getting the hook this afternoon, but in the crowd we couldn't do much about it. Not even follow the car...

"But I count on luck, the Holy Spirit, all the other intangibles to help me out. Sometimes everything works—sometimes, not. But here we have you safe and sound. I'll bring in the reason for your distress in a second. But first, did you write anything in your story about an English-speaking doctor, an American doctor, anything like that, someone to attend the American Cardinals?"

"No...no, I didn't. I thought of it, but I left it out deliberately."

"Your lady is shrewd. Either she noticed it or the German did."

"And?"

"They went after Bishop Hearn..."

"Oh, my God! Of course, they would. He's an M.D.—just got into Rome from Nairobi. He's close to Cardinal Muldoon."

"Oh, don't worry. Angela told us in plenty of time. We

picked him up and he's staying at my house for the moment. They assume they missed him. They'll try again.

"I dislike asking you this, but we're pressing a number of charges against Angela Nero. I caught her in the act of entering your room illegally. She claims you gave her permission. Even if that's true, I will not be able to drop the charge. Right now I need your identification of the woman."

He pushed a button, "Bring in Angela Nero, please."

For the first time Donald was face to face with the real Angela or, at least, the Angela she wanted to be—surly, defiant, arrogant. It was like a scene out of a poor, made-for-TV movie about terrorists. Angela appeared to be acting a role, trying so hard to be tough, staring at Donald with hate and contempt on her face. She said nothing. When he looked in her eyes, Donald realized there was nothing there, no sign of the girl he assumed he knew. Obviously she was high on something—and that could explain her condition. On the other hand, you don't become a second-rate mob girl overnight. Angela had done her homework.

Monzelli asked the questions.

"Mr. Brady, do you identify this young person as Angela Nero?"

"Yes."

"The same Angela Nero who has been working for you."

"Yes."

"She has been paid for her services?"

"Yes."

"Has she ever been in your room?"

"Yes, several times."

"For professional reasons?"

"Yes, and personal."

"I gather that. But personal reasons do not imply that a visitor is entitled to enter a hotel room at will, Mr. Brady. Did you give her that permission?"

Donald took a long time to answer, "No, I did not."

"Thank you, Mr. Brady," Monzelli said. "That takes care of everything. Miss Nero used a key she had made from a wax impression. Hotels don't care for that. She would have been charged in any event."

"And the others? What about them?"

Monzelli smiled, "Each client in his turn, Mr. Brady. You know there's a big difference between American police methods and ours. We seldom make an arrest without complete evidence, strong enough to hold up in court."

"That's amazing."

"Not exactly, Mr. Brady. We deal with a known quantity, the Italian mentality. We haven't the wide variety of ethnic groups that complicate police investigations in America. Sometimes you arrest a half dozen people before you get the right one. Heaven knows how many you interrogate. We deal with a criminal mind vastly more predictable."

"That sounds like a good story."

"There's a hitch."

"Too bad. What is it?"

"That's how it used to be. Now the terrorists are making detective work more difficult. You find foreign faces involved—like the German. He fits a pattern, but it's cut in a different mold. In short, crime in Italy has become more cosmopolitan, more sophisticated. We can't rely on old thinking anymore.

"Anyhow, to answer your question. We intend to immobilize the others tomorrow. We're baiting a trap and I daresay we'll collect them all, including Hans."

"Well, good luck, Inspector, and thanks for having your men on the watch for me."

"Not at all. I am grateful to you for the identification of Angela Nero. She's tragically mixed up and I'm afraid I've permitted too many serious offenses to slip by, hoping she'd come to her senses."

He paused. Donald knew what was coming.

"I suspect that she made you think she was eager to change her life-style."

"I'm afraid so."

"It's *her* special talent. Quite Italian. That—and using her name. I'm afraid I was guilty of remembering what Nellie Nero meant to Italy—not how her granddaughter was making me look foolish."

"Wouldn't you call it 'human.' I would."

"Perhaps," Monzelli said. "Policemen are still people. Now, can I have someone drive you to your hotel?"

"No, thanks, I'll find a cab."

"Will you be returning to the Grand-Plaza?"

"No, I don't think so. I like the Merline fine."

"Good. I'll be calling you there when we have some news from Washington. I imagine you'll be speaking to Monsignor Ryan."

"Of course."

"Give him the same message. I know he's anxious."

Donald laughed, "I suppose he's been on the phone a dozen times today."

"Not quite a dozen. But you're close."

Monzelli started back to his office, stopped, turned around and said, "By the way, Mr. Brady, do you recall ever seeing Angela cry?"

Donald answered, "Yes, a couple of times. I found her in the print shop, for example. She was hysterical."

"Did she shed any real tears?" Monzelli asked.

"No, she didn't. I wondered about it at the time."

Monzelli laughed, "Quite Italian—that—you know."

* * *

Aboard an Air Force Jet bound for Rome, Erika Wald felt far from uncomfortable on the crowded plane—not when most of the passengers were male and the few women aboard had grouped themselves far in the back, leaving Erika with a virtual monopoly.

Erika had been warned by Uncle Erich to dress demurely and sensibly. She'd have no time to change between her meetings with the President of the United States and Francesco Morelli. She rather regretted the pale blue suit she'd selected and the high-necked blouse. Still, for duty's sake she could afford to appear less sexy. Being "demure" had its problems. There was a hat to worry about; gloves, too. Well, the gloves were in the attaché case firmly affixed to her arm. It was a small, ladylike case, not really uncomfortable. Moreover it was a conversation opener. Erika thoroughly enjoyed being a mystery woman among this glorious collection of American marines, sailors, State Department personnel and other officials returning to Italy after home leave.

Meeting world leaders wasn't exactly new to Erika, but

being ushered into the Oval Office to be greeted by President Cameron who got up from behind his desk to welcome her was a thrill she'd never forget.

The President was a little taken aback, she noticed, when Erika mentioned that she'd "had him" in February. Her English got awfully mixed up when she was nervous, away from her job. What she'd been trying to say, and eventually got across to the President, was that she'd "had him" as his *translator* into German when he spoke at the United Nations shortly after his inauguration.

At least, he laughed, Erika thought. He wasn't angry.

That was improbable in view of the fact that he'd chatted with her about everything but the documents she had sped from New York to pick up. A young aide coughed discreetly every so often. Erika knew the signals. In another situation she might have offered him a cough drop, but this was serious business.

Through South American connections Erika was aware that a Chilean Cardinal, an Italian by birth, was high on the list of Papal candidates being considered by the Americans. She knew, too, from the Rome dispatches that a strong campaign had been mounted to make Cardinal Muldoon, Monsignor Ryan and her own Donald look like high school sophomores involved in a mock Papal election.

Being confident that the ladylike dispatch case was essential to their mission, Erika figured that her selection as the courier made sense. Cardinal Waldenheim could vouch for her; it was simpler to utilize someone "in the family." The fewer who became involved the better. An outsider, someone from the Church, even Donald's uncle, Thaddeus, would attract attention. In the diplomatic world, women couriers were not unusual. They *distracted* attention.

When the jet landed at Ciampino, it was boarded by a handsome, gray-haired man of medium height with sparkling gray eyes. He introduced himself in a quiet voice as "Inspector Luke Monzelli. I will drive you to His Holiness."

"Am I dressed properly?" Erika asked.

"Yes, quite nicely. This is not an audience or a ceremonial visit. You have done His Holiness and Cardinal Muldoon a great favor. They appreciate it."

*   *   *

It happened so suddenly that neither Tom Ryan nor Donald Brady had time to get accustomed to the idea that they had been summoned to visit the Pope before Luke Monzelli had arrived on their doorsteps to pick them up.

He explained the protocol. Morelli was no longer the Pope. He was living in retirement as a simple priest. One might address him as His Holiness, yes, but this visit involved no ceremony. The Pope would be wearing a black cassock; he no longer wore the ring of Papal authority so visitors were not expected to genuflect.

"His Holiness," said Monzelli, "will greet you with a handshake. That's all there is to it."

Monzelli parked in the narrow alley. They entered the outside elevator and were received at the top by Sister Mary Matthew who led them up a flight of stairs to the penthouse where Morelli and Erika stood as Sister Matthew announced, "Your Holiness, Inspector Monzelli with his friends."

Monzelli had coached Donald well, but he'd neglected to explain how he might avoid fainting when Donald saw his roommate standing, cool, serene and perfectly beautiful, beside the Pope.

When he tilted to one side, Tom grasped him. Erika rushed forward, "Am I surprising you, *liebling*?"

"A little," Donald said weakly, recovering in time to accept Morelli's hand and an invitation to be seated in the circle of chairs Sister Mary Matthew had arranged. He even noticed the spare, tasteful furnishings, the Pope's chapel to one side and closed double doors to what was probably his private quarters. This room was handsome—large with picture windows at two sides, French doors leading to different terraces. The view was close to Donald's idea of Rome—its rooftops and terraces.

Sister Mary Matthew had also arranged breakfast. From a serving table she brought coffee, tea, orange juice, croissants, milk; before Donald she placed a glass and a bottle of German beer.

"For me?" he asked.

Morelli smiled, "Yes, Donald, that's yours. Your uncle calls it 'the newspaperman's breakfast.'"

"Thank you, Your Holiness. I do enjoy it. Not every morning. But today it helps. Lots! I wasn't aware you and my uncle were so well acquainted.

"We were close friends, Donald. I was a Monsignor. I wanted to improve my English. Your Uncle Thaddeus was a revelation. I'd never known many Americans. He seemed to know everything: Latin, Greek, Italian—he was well versed in Church history. He taught me poker. I taught him to play *scopa*. As Pope, I enjoyed only one visit from him. Now, I hope, he will come to Rome and we can spend a long evening together. I look forward to seeing old friends again in a simpler world than the Vatican."

Tom was astonished by the sight of the old man whom he'd spoken to more than a year ago on his own secret visit to Rome. Then it was to sound out the Pope's reaction to American activism. It was a delicate discussion. Tom felt like that obituary editor on the *New York Times* who started the policy of interviewing great men while still alive for material to be used in their death notices. In Morelli's case, the Monsignor's situation was easy when the Pope evidently shared the same thought. "I've already seen the *Times* man. An interesting experience. You should try it."

This man, Donald realized, had shed years. His voice had found its old vibrancy. His shoulders were straight; his back, ramrod straight. Morelli's eyes were clear, his skin, fresh. And his vitality! Like Muldoon he seemed to relish the battle of wits going on between the Old Guard of the Vatican and the upstarts.

After breakfast, Sister Mary Matthew whispered to Erika.

"Thank you, Sister. How kind!" She turned to the men, "Excuse me, Your Holiness, but Sister has suggested I go downstairs and rest a bit." She looked at her watch. "Hmm! I've been going for nearly forty hours."

Tom murmured sympathetically.

"Oh, that's nothing," Erika said, "Sixty hours is my record." Gracefully she withdrew, following Sister Mary Matthew to the downstairs apartment.

On a desk in the corner, Donald and Tom could see the papers Erika had brought from the White House. Morelli pointed to them. "Tom, take Donald to the desk and look at the documents as well as President Cameron's letter. They completely vindicate Riccordi."

He rose to turn on the television set. "It's time for the signal."

Luke Monzelli rose. "You will excuse me, Francesco. I have to get to the Square. I will drop by this afternoon."

As they shook hands, Morelli said, "I am always saying 'thank you' to you, Luke, am I not?"

"A man who is merely doing his duty takes pride when it involves you, Francesco."

He walked to the door and called to Donald, "May I see you for a moment, Mr. Brady?"

In the hallway, Monzelli jotted down a telephone number. "His Holiness is not yet ready to discuss the papers from President Cameron. They present a problem..."

"Damned if they don't. Getting them to Muldoon..."

"Ah...yes...that *is* a problem. Well, for now," Luke Monzelli said, "I need your cooperation. We can't have you people moving around. It's a question of security. Miss Erika will stay with Sister Mary Matthew. You and Monsignor Ryan will leave shortly. Suggest that Monsignor Ryan say nothing about the papers beyond appreciating the Pope's efforts in obtaining them. Call this number. A taxi will draw up in the alley. Its driver is a police officer who will take Monsignor Ryan to the North American College and you to the Merline. I beg you to stay there—until I tell you otherwise. Tomorrow I will call you at about four in the afternoon to confirm arrangements we...I mean...I am making."

Donald wondered at the slip. He pulled back from asking questions. Morelli felt it.

The detective smiled. "I know it's not easy to tie a newspaperman down, but cooperate with me, please. It is going to be worth it."

Monzelli appeared to be running down a list in his mind. "That's all, I believe. Beg Monsignor Ryan to get some sleep. He looks tired. And both of you pray. That always helps."

He opened the door of the elevator, "Until tomorrow—at four. Good-bye."

*   *   *

Robert "Yes Yes" Pfeifer didn't mind his nickname. He was a short, rugged, red-haired man, a lone German in the Irish dominated Saint Patrick's Cathedral. He felt drawn to the Irish, feeling that, like the Germans, they were an emotional people. They controlled themselves better than Germans, however. Yet when they exploded the results were fearful. To sum up his conclusions about the Irish, Pfeifer once confided, "They are looney—just like they say. So I agree with them. It's easier that way."

He was pleased that he'd been chosen to take the place of Monsignor Ryan as Cardinal Muldoon's aide. He'd been close to Muldoon until Ryan was assigned to the Cathedral. Pfeifer realizing what Ryan could do for the Cardinal, stepped aside, allowing the relationship between the two men to develop into the splendid working arrangement that existed today.

Pfeifer was no hero-worshipper. He'd been around too many of the Church's wonder boys to be impressed, even if he *yessed* them all. Muldoon was different. He'd picked him as "someone special" long before the Cardinal himself became aware of his destiny. Ryan had supplied Muldoon with the confidence Pfeifer couldn't. He had drawn him out of his conservative shell, breaking down the barriers of his conditioning to reach the real Muldoon, a sensitive, intelligent, progressive man who had matured slowly but well. That explained the skillful leadership Muldoon was showing as head of the steering committee. If the other American Cardinals were amazed, O'Toole was speechless. If Muldoon accomplished nothing else, that would have to rate as incredible.

Pfeifer served Cardinal Muldoon's Mass at Saint Peter's. He said it slowly in Italian. Pfeifer, inspired by the drama of the event, made the responses in German. Monsignor Ryan, kneeling just outside the side altar, smiled. He was aware how Pfeifer had sacrificed his own position on the Cathedral pecking order to make room for him. They both, evidently, had been drawn to the unlikeliest of Cardinals. And now he was a leader whose name was on everyone's lips in Rome. The man least aware of his stature was Muldoon himself.

One's first impression of William Cardinal Muldoon was that the Church had made a ghastly mistake in selecting him to govern the second most important Archdiocese in the Roman Catholic Church. New York ranked next to Rome as a seat of Catholic power, wealth and influence. Whoever he was, the Cardinal who resided in the handsome mansion house on Madison Avenue behind Saint Patrick's Cathedral, automatically became the symbol of the American Church. His views might range from outright reactionary to dangerously progressive, yet whatever his thoughts and however sharply they disagreed with the other Cardinals who composed America's Princes of the Church, his was the voice that commanded attention. There was little about Muldoon that touched the imagination. If ever there lived an ordinary man, he was it.

William Muldoon claimed only a slim resemblance to the common conception of how a Cardinal should look. He was fairly tall, close to six feet. His waistline had stayed trim thanks to an energetic exercise program and habit of walking wherever he could that began when Muldoon was a curate. His white mane was thinning but still impressive. His carriage was erect and his pale blue eyes reflected kindness, but they were tired eyes—eyes that had worked too hard for too many years and seen too much tragedy for one man to absorb. Yet his faith was boundless and Muldoon's wit, sharp and incisive, never failed to surprise those who knew only the public side of His Eminence.

Worry, curiously, had not creased his pale Irish skin. His face, unlined and fixed in a single expression of determination, appeared to have been hewed out of an odd piece of stone hanging around the workshop of a cutter of tombstones.

Accustomed to the effort involved in making his sermons heard in New York's huge churches before the installation of sound systems, Muldoon's reedy voice sounded sonorous even when involved in such ordinary use as "Good morning."

For language, both written and spoken, Muldoon

appeared to have rummaged among the cliches of the thousands of Sunday sermons he'd delivered in the old days when he'd been a simple parish priest. It typified a style that could only be defined as "American ecclesiastical," phrases spun from the Baltimore Catechism and Bible Histories, required reading in the parochial schools of his youth.

In the scarlet vestments of his high office, Muldoon suggested a new altar boy trying to accustom himself to the feel of a cassock around his ankles, fearful that his arm movements might tear the starched surplice. Minus his clerical collar, in grey flannel with a striped tie, Muldoon was *Everyman*—the branch manager of a chain bank in Flatbush, the court stenographer, the weary night clerk of a deluxe hotel or one of those eccentrics, peculiar to New York, whose very plainness concealed a shrewd manipulative mind, making him the self-made millionaire who walked to work, brown-bagged his lunch and lived in a small apartment on the East Side where for years before the power crunch, no light bulb ever exceeded twenty-five volts. One met him regularly in the weekly tabloids where the banner and the art work never varied. The latter consisted of a face minus features, and the blurb would read: *The World's Third Richest Man That Nobody Knows.*

Muldoon's personality had some characteristics of *Everyman,* but his flock had chosen to identify him as the wily miser; hence his nickname, "Granite Face." It made co-existence easier for them, if not for Muldoon whose outward serenity camouflaged a deeply emotional personality. "If they ever knew how old 'Granite Face' was suffering in this job," Muldoon often complained to his aides, "they wouldn't be so flip. What do they want in a Cardinal? Robert Redford? Blond, handsome, rich, and a champion of ecology? Or, God forbid, the resurrection of Barry Fitzgerald?"

At least the name tag endowed Muldoon with some sort of personality. Few loved him but nobody hated him. That was rare for a man in his position. His sixty-five years, forty-two of them spent as a priest, had taught Muldoon that as nations elect presidents they deserve, the Church finds Popes, Cardinals and Bishops to suit the needs of the time.

Even if he found little enjoyment in his Red Hat, Muldoon knew he was the right man in the right place.

Presidential candidates courted the favor of the New York Cardinal, a responsibility Muldoon was not equipped to handle. Fortunately, Monsignor Thomas Ryan had come into the Cathedral elite two years before the last campaign and, as Muldoon's advisor, he'd proven astute and more capable of assessing delicate situations than any priest Muldoon had ever known. Ryan was a modern political animal—exactly the kind of young man Muldoon needed at his side.

Through Ryan the Cardinal was somewhat chagrined to discover the whole truth behind what he already knew, that he was the second choice of the Pope to succeed Patrick Cardinal Hellman who had ruled the New York diocese for almost a quarter of a century. As Auxilliary Bishop Muldoon had been Hellman's right hand for a decade, but Bishop Kevin Birdie seemed a shoo-in. He was handsome, witty, a good preacher and a fine fund-raiser. Muldoon hoped that the appointment would go that way.

Ryan, who was in Rome at the time, told Muldoon of a late night call from Bishop Birdie. "He was in his cups and crying, Your Eminence. He told me to get to the Pope and tell him that his health was precarious. He said, 'You know, Tom, this church can't afford two Archbishops' funerals in two years. I haven't got that long. The doctor is sending you a letter. Muldoon was Hellman's choice anyhow. He'll do great.'"

Cardinal Muldoon was the celebrant of the Requiem Mass for Bishop Birdie who died six months after Muldoon's installation as head of the New York diocese.

That was five years ago. But it seemed like a hundred. So much had happened, and now Muldoon was again being thrust into a role he had no taste for—Pope-maker.

"That's for the Italians to handle," he told Thomas Ryan when the young Monsignor brought him up to date a year or so earlier on the probability that Morelli fully intended setting an important precedent by resigning the Papacy. "We've always been able to live with their choice. We're above the politics of a Conclave. That's for the Europeans.

267

It's medieval, an old game they enjoy playing. No American can ever become Pope, we're too big a power. No American Cardinal today is qualified to become Pope."

Ryan argued, "Your Eminence, these are different times."

Muldoon put up his hand in despair, "How many times a day do I have to hear that?"

Ryan persisted, "Your Eminence, I can't change facts. Nor can you. Everywhere in the Western World the Church is losing its credibility. In Latin America where ninety percent of the people are Catholics, only about one in twenty practices the faith. It's the same in Northern Europe. There's a universal shortage of priests. In France last year only one hundred priests were ordained.

"Look what's happening here. We're losing priests every day. Some resign formally; others just walk away. The seminaries are a shambles. No one understands what the Church is saying any more. We need clear directives, clear lines for dissent. We can't get away with insisting priestly celibacy is sacred. It isn't. It's a thirteenth century invention. In Africa, I understand, where the Church is growing, celibacy is admired. In Latin countries, priests who take mistresses are considered to be exercising their normal prerogatives as men. Why all this unrealistic adherence to tradition in the United States?

"I'll tell you why. Because we are like the Italians. We enjoy the status quo—and as long as we persist in thinking along the lines that what's traditional is best, then we are contributing to the decline of the Roman Catholic Church.

"Paul VI didn't increase the number of American Cardinals to nine as a caprice. You know that. There was a motive behind it. To give Americans an opportunity to exercise the leadership the world expects of us. We must become a voice—not an echo in the Conclave. We must lead and not follow. This doesn't mean we intend to dislodge the Italians or that we are opposed to the tradition of an Italian Pope."

Muldoon interrupted, "Then what does it mean?"

"It means that we must have a candidate. It means that when Morelli resigns we will go to Rome with a nominee, someone we consider worthy of being our Pope, someone

268

with the moral fibre to assert leadership and implement at least some of the recommendations of Vatican II. The seeds were sown at Vatican II for a more democratic church, the diffusing of power, the right of Bishops to autonomy in their own diocese, the modification of the monarchial Papacy and the centralizing of power in the Curia."

Muldoon put up his hand to stop the torrent of well-rehearsed words, "You realize, I hope, that it would require a concerted conspiracy by the non-Italian Cardinals to force through a non-Italian Pope."

Ryan persisted, "I am not excluding Italians as candidates. But assuming we choose a non-Italian, it doesn't matter whether our candidate becomes Pope or not."

Here he paused, "Certainly not if we believe that the choice of Pope comes solely through prayer and through the Divine Guidance of the Holy Spirit."

Muldoon chuckled, "Let's not get sticky. I, for one, believe in prayer. Prayer helps in any situation. Don't knock it."

"I'm not," said Ryan, "but prayer doesn't mean eliminating action. What is important is that Americans go into the Conclave as a body with their own choice in mind, their own opinions to voice and, hopefully, in voicing their choice of man and philosophy they will come closer to the expectations of mankind than the self-serving prejudices of those political Cardinals whose medieval games you deplore."

Muldoon's hand signalled another pause. "I know you're right. I hoped I'd be spared the responsibility. I'll get in touch with Cardinals O'Toole and Novik. After I've talked to them we'll take up the matter and work out some way to implement it."

"Thank you, Your Eminence."

"Don't thank me. Thank the Holy Spirit. He's been keeping me awake for nights lately with this very same problem. I'll get at it. You can be sure of that."

From "Granite Face," that amounted to a commitment. More important—from Monsignor Ryan's viewpoint—it meant a prompt commitment.

* * *

And now they were on the last steps of this extraordinary voyage. Pfeifer was confident Muldoon would triumph. He had to. The odds were all in his favor, beginning with God himself and extending through the man's spirit, his faith and the air of confidence he breathed into everyone around him.

Muldoon was one of the few Cardinals with nothing to complain about in the spartan living quarters where he'd been located—not the best cell he could have drawn in the lottery, far from the worst. They were allocated by a drawing for numbers.

Pfeifer, quartered in a different section of the Apostolic Palace, finished washing up, slipped into his pajamas. He put on his robe and slippers and walked to Muldoon's cell.

Pfeifer found the Cardinal sitting on his bed, reading his office. Not that he had to. He'd read it three times already. "Not sleepy, Your Eminence?" Pfeifer asked.

"Yes, Robert. I'm just about there. Glad you dropped by though. I haven't the strength to pray. The strength, yes, but no will to concentrate. I'm beat."

"Me too," Pfeifer said.

"You too, Robert? Let us both pray to the Holy Ghost. We need all the wisdom He can spare us."

"I will, Your Excellency."

Pfeifer closed the door behind him and paddled down the hall to his own quarters where, like the other aides, he would sit up all night, sharing gossip and the excitement of being on the inside of one of the biggest events of the century.

PART IX

Urbi et Orbi

Teresa Tashman understood emotion. She'd lived the whole gamut, from depths of despair to happiness that bordered on the manic. In Teresa's dark days of alcoholism, her range of behavior switched abruptly from lows to highs, from quiet and composed to wild and frantic. She could look and act like an angel one minute; appear and shriek like a vixen the next.

Understanding Teresa was far from easy for those exposed to her either personally or professionally. As her drinking worsened, Teresa's mercurial moods became more unpredictable, her tendency to violence more pronounced. Teresa sometimes wondered herself if she'd not crossed the border between normality and insanity. Old and new friends wandered in and out of her life. Some may have loved her. They could never be sure. Teresa offered them little opportunity. Love and admiration turned to pity. In turn, pity became indifference.

"I was a standing up drunk," Teresa said, at the end of her decade-long ordeal. "I seldom passed out. With the help of pills I could hold court twenty-four to forty-eight hours at a stretch. It was quite a show. I was, in turn, quarrelsome, suspicious, angry, rude, frequently vulgar. I was a nuisance. But the only person who didn't know it was me. I was filled with self-pity. When friends turned away, I decided they were traitors.

"I assumed everyone close to me was a hanger-on, someone who sought me out to bask in my reflected glory, to bring color into their drab lives. What nonsense! It was drunken fantasy. Now I know that I am still in debt to the companions I paid. They got the worst of a bad bargain. I still 'owe them'—as much as I owe 'the brave ones'—my publisher, some members of my family, newspapermen who respected me and finally, the simple man who opened my eyes to reality, Jed Rankin."

Teresa described her present life as "the years of light"—years in which her professional life had flourished and the problems of her private life had been sorted out.

"I can pull a blouse over my head and fix my make-up. But I'm not yet ready for big responsibilities beyond my work," she told friends. Teresa was selective about speaking engagements, choosy about her social engagements. "I need time to reflect, time to get back into the swing of things I once enjoyed, time to renew my acquaintance with my religion."

On the second morning of the Conclave, Teresa sat alone in her fashionable Parioli apartment for the first time since she'd been visited by Monsignor Ryan and been projected, as she described it, "by some supernatural force" into the sort of activity she couldn't imagine herself undertaking.

Her huge apartment, of which she'd written friends, "contains a dozen more rooms than I need," had been overflowing with Noviks ever since their flight from Warsaw. There were so many, all with different surnames, it seemed, that Teresa gave them Numbers, *Novik Numero Uno, Novik Due,* and so on. At the moment they were out sightseeing. Teresa enjoyed the solitude. It afforded an opportunity to reflect—to realize how far she'd come.

Monsignor Ryan would never be able to imagine the shock she felt when he asked—ever so coolly—if she would help. She could not possibly have refused. Then and there the control had come from out of the blue. The good Monsignor had been so impressed with her efficiency as she put everything together—arranging for transportation, making calls to Poland, communicating her purpose before she arrived. Oh, how her palms sweated and her stomach churned!

Now she knew how she'd survived. Monsignor Ryan had arranged Teresa's meeting with that most wondrous of emotions—pure joy.

Nothing had been easy in Warsaw. Teresa ran from office

to office, from friend to friend, persuading one bureaucrat, antagonizing another. Yet she held on. The answer was never "no." Never quite "yes." But as long as the door remained open, Teresa pressed on. Finally the authorities pondered the significance of sending a delegation of Polish children and a pair of elders to Rome and a Conclave of the Roman Catholic Church to meet their uncle, an honored son of Poland—it began to carry a message.

Abruptly—the way things happen in Communist countries—everything was fine. The barriers were broken and the Polish authorities could not have been more helpful. Like a Fairy Queen Teresa and all the Noviks were whisked off to Rome in plenty of time to end the tyranny that had been imposed on Alexander Novik. The Cardinal was beside himself with joy. Tears filled his eyes. He held Teresa's hand, saying over and over, "Bless you, 'Miss Glorious Lady.' You are a miracle..."

When the doorbell rang and the maid announced that a young priest was at the door, Teresa assumed Monsignor Ryan was calling. She went to the foyer. The caller was a young priest—but not Tom Ryan. He was a short, smiling Italian, so fresh and youthful that Teresa figured he couldn't have been more than six months out of the seminary. He spoke in halting English, "I have been asked to deliver this letter to *Signora* Teresa Tashman personally. You are *Signora* Tashman?"

"Yes, I am."

Teresa smiled. Maybe the young man was a priest, but he was also an Italian. She noticed that he'd begun at her legs and was working up to her face and when he reached it, *his* face was as bright as a cherub's. He handed her the letter saying, "It is from our beloved *Papa,* Francesco Xavier Morelli. I am waiting for an answer."

Teresa invited the young man to take a seat.

"From the Pope...My God!...Oh...My God! ...Good heavens...Anna, come open this for me...get the young priest a drink...take a seat, Padre..."

When Teresa became excited, she spoke in *italics.* She tore open the envelope, saw the signature, sat down, read it silently, then aloud to Anna and the priest. It read:

My dear Signora Tashman:

How happy you have made our beloved Cardinal Novik by making it possible for him to be united with members of his family on this joyous occasion, the election of a new Pontiff to head the Church which Cardinal Novik and his family have served with so much honor and devotion.

Yours was a generous impulse. My heart is filled with love for a gallant daughter of the Church.

I should be pleased if you and your brood of Noviks, the little ones as well as the adults, would be my guests tomorrow afternoon at one o'clock. Father Alberni will give you the address on your gracious acceptance.

Yours in Christ,

Francesco Xavier Morelli.

"Accept! Of course I accept—and so do all the Noviks."

"The Pope will be very pleased," Father Alberni said, as he rose from the chair. He reached into his pocket, pulled out a card. "*Signora* Tashman. This is the address. It is, of course, confidential, alone for your eyes. I know you respect His Holiness' need for privacy at this time."

"Thank you, Father. Be assured I understand. I will be very careful."

"Thank you, Signora. I will be at the entrance to guide the Noviks and yourself to His Holiness' apartment."

Father Alberni let himself out, glancing at the next address on the envelopes he was carrying: Madame Jennie Jacobowski, *Albergo* Merline, Via Delle Carrozze.

"Not too far," he muttered, "by motorcycle."

*   *   *

On the second day of the Conclave, the morning signals from the smokestack of the Sistine Chapel had been unmistakably black. The throngs gathered at Saint Peter's interpreted this as a pessimistic tone for the day. Why? Because the *fumato* had come forth with such force that there was absolutely no excuse for confusion. Moreover, the ballots had been burned in the stove so close to the scheduled balloting hours of nine and noon that self-styled experts interpreted the punctuality of the vote as indicative of the wide split in the voting.

Saint Peter's Square had become a mine of information for collectors of phrases and superstititions connected with the Papal Election embracing the oldest of them all, "He who enters the Conclave as a Pope will leave it as a Cardinal" as well as the prophecy American racing fans brought to the Eternal City, "No champion ever wins the triple crown on speed alone; staying power is what counts."

However in the "secret council" of the Conclave, "secret statements" issued in "secrecy" to the press revealed flaws in the Americans' handicapping. Staying power seldom played a part in the final stretch. Cardinals chose to switch from respectable "shows" and "places" to the front runner or by dropping a new name into the field. As for the Cardinal who enters the Conclave a Pope leaving with egg on his face— that was exploded when Lord Cardinal Giovanni Batista Montini, the Archbishop of Milan, an odds-on favorite, became Paul VI in 1963.

Speculation, being free and the privilege of all, the consensus, when the afternoon smoke signals were black, gave the coalition of Cardinals Torriani and Rossi a decisive victory in the early rounds. Obviously the Old Guard had routed the Americans and their Third World constituency, and now it remained whether the European Cardinals would accept Cardinal Roberto Bellafiore, the Curia favorite, or drag out another Italian dark horse whose name had not even figured in the most comprehensive analyses of probable candidates.

Those leaning to this line predicted the Conclave's end within twenty-four hours—that being as long as the elderly Cardinals could endure the discomfort of Vatican facilities. The Princes of the Church were bedded in tiny cubicles, barely large enough for the more corpulent members to turn around in. Lack of lavatory facilities revived the old-fashioned chamber pot. As far as amenities were concerned, no one seemed to care. The Cardinals had the distinct impression that they were bothersome guests in a community that hoped to be rid of them as soon as possible. The idea of a lengthy Conclave horrified the citizens of Vatican City as much as it did the Cardinals.

At the *Albergo* Merline, Donald Brady was kept advised of all the possibilities, the handicapping, the second guessing as well as a vivid account of the Cardinal-electors' discomfortures by a wide variety of television reporters—ranging from Vatican aides to visiting reporters and skilled local men, accustomed to living in the high voltage worlds of Italian and Vatican politics.

Donald talked frequently to Tom Ryan who, he knew, was having a difficult time keeping himself under control. Donald realized that Tom felt "left out"—but, at the moment, so was he. There had been no call from Inspector Monzelli; not the slightest hint that Muldoon intended making a move. They had read the documents clearing Cardinal Riccordi; the letter of President Cameron clearly stamped the accusations against the Chilean priest as outrageous, unsupported slander. Muldoon and Ryan had proved their case, but the documents remained in the possession of a resigned Pope.

What was protocol? Could one pick up the phone and casually ask Francesco Morelli about his intentions? Not likely. So nerves rattled and tensions grew. Even Bishop Hearn's calm appeared ruffled; he called frequently to Donald and Tom to assure them he was standing by—keeping open the lone telephone line at the Pension Caruso.

For Donald, tensions broke at five o'clock when Luke Monzelli called, saying that he would pick Donald up at the corner of the Corso and Delle Carrozze at five. Although he'd been dressed for the appointment since the crack of dawn, Donald chose to change his clothes and was in the bathroom when Erika made her one and only call. Jennie tried to pin her down to a time when she would call again, but Erika said she couldn't. "I must keep the telephone line open. It's very important..."

276

At six o'clock, Donald stood on the corner of the Corso and Via Delle Carrozze, but twenty minutes went by before he recognized Luke Monzelli's Fiat weaving in and out of the heavy traffic. In spite of his position, the Police Inspector had mastered all the worst habits of Roman drivers and employed them with the zest of one who knew he ran no risk of ever being obliged to tear up traffic tickets in this paradise for scofflaws.

Donald jumped in as the car stopped briefly, before moving on to Piazza Colonna, executing a U turn that would have brought Rome's traffic police swooping down on anyone else. The police, however, recognized the Inspector's car and were acquainted with his eccentric driving style.

When Donald turned to the quiet man in the rear, he gasped, "Your Holiness! Your Holiness! Yes. Good evening!"

"Good evening, Donald, how are you?" Morelli asked serenely.

"Oh! Well, very well, Your Holiness! A little confused, that's all."

"Is this your first trip with Inspector Monzelli at the wheel?"

"Yes, Your Holiness, it is."

"I pray that you are in the State Of Grace, my son," he said.

Monzelli, navigating his vehicle toward the river, appeared not to hear the conversation. He was growling at other drivers on Viale Lungotevere who were trying to move along in accordance with the law.

"Don't growl, Luke. Simply drive. I know you have your own Guardian Angel. At my age, what is there to worry about? Think of Donald now and then, if you will."

They drove along the river to the Bridge of Sant' Angelo, the same route Donald had walked to attend the two days of ceremonies preceding the official start of the Conclave, the moment when all the Cardinals and their aides were locked behind the walls of the Vatican Palace and sworn to secrecy. All communication with the outside world had been turned off and the penalty for breaking the secrecy of the Conclave was assumed to be excommunication.

At Castel Sant' Angelo, the car stopped; Luke parked to the side of the road. Donald looked back and saw Morelli pick up the attaché case Erika had brought from the White House and place it on his lap. The wily old man was grinning.

Donald pointed at the Castle, "My God! You're going into the Conclave yourself! The Pope!"

"Yes, I am."

"My God! Forgive me, Your Holiness."

"Forgiven. I'll grant that all this is very unusual."

"You're not kidding. I'm not going to ask any questions..."

Morelli interrupted, "Except whether we're going to enter the Vatican through the secret tunnels."

"I guess that's it."

Morelli smiled, "I suppose it could be done, but it would make us awfully dusty. We stopped here in order to explain the reason for your being with me and what I intend to do. That and to time our arrival at the Sistine Chapel for the right moment.

"No, I'm sorry to say, we'll drive in the main gate and you'll have to find your own tunnel route. You know, Benvenuto Cellini was supposed to have used it.

"But that was yesterday, and this is today. You may know enough about the regulations of the Conclave that it would be extremely difficult for Cardinal Muldoon to break a vow and feign sickness. He would have good reason, I realize, but I could not permit a fine man to suffer the agony William Muldoon would endure. So at the last moment I told him I would find a way to bring these documents into the Vatican and to the attention of the Conclave.

"A reigning Pope makes the rules for the Conclave that will take place on his death or resignation. Paul died without significantly changing the thousand year old system. He barred Cardinals over eighty from voting—a sensible procedure. He failed to enlarge participation to include Bishops or to lift somewhat the secrecy that surrounds the selection of a Pope.

"In resigning I set a precedent that I pray will have far-reaching consequences; first, enabling younger men to lead the Church if they are qualified, making it possible for aging

278

Pontiffs to put down their burden when their hearts and their minds tell them to. God has ways of sending signals.

"A living Pope, standing aside from the power struggle, brings it out in the open, as we have seen. Out of the viciousness and the calumny we have witnessed in the past weeks there may come some good. Perhaps our more wordly Princes of the Church will realize they are being watched more closely than was possible before. A Pope who is free to resign will feel freer to reign in the style that suits him best; hopefully, as the Good Shepherd of his flock.

"But this is not the time to philosophize or to contemplate the future. The present is our business. In the rules I established for this Conclave there exists a passage entitling a Pontiff who has resigned to address the Conclave in the spirit of joining them in prayer to the Holy Spirit or to be the conciliator in cases of divisiveness.

"The Cardinals know the passage exists as does the privilege. Nevertheless they will be surprised. You, Donald, are to report my visit, exactly as it happened, but not until the Conclave is over and a new Pope has been named. I am visiting the Cardinals during their hour of prayer. I am not intruding on the Conclave."

The elderly man paused, "I think that is all. Luke, let's get started. We are going to open some more of those windows Pope John talked about."

Monzelli volunteered his first words of the evening, "Francesco, I think you're going to smash windows."

*   *   *

As far as attracting attention was concerned, Donald Brady might have been the *Invisible Man* as Francesco Morelli strode through the Apostolic Palace, his carriage unmistakable despite the unfamiliar sight of the former Pontiff in the simple black cassock of a priest. All eyes were on the former Pope. No one even noticed Donald. Morelli smiled and held up his hands in that gesture of greeting and blessing that falls so naturally into the nature of a Pontiff. Vatican workers dropped to their knees.

Cardinals hurried out of the Sistine Chapel to watch him

mount the wide, marble staircase. There were cries in different languages—*Il Papa,* the Pope. His Holiness—he is here. He has come to the Conclave..."

Cardinal Angelo Torriani raced from a conference to greet Francesco Morelli, his face pale, his voice faltering, "Welcome, Your Holiness. Had we but known..."

Morelli raised a hand to quiet him. "Dear Eminence," he said, "this visit is a sudden impulse, an exercise of my privilege to pray with you at this critical hour. Do beg the Cardinals to take their seats. I suppose I am one of you—a Cardinal again."

He was about to introduce Donald, but saw that he was far back in the crowd of Cardinals and attendants; it was just as well not to draw attention to the newspaperman's presence. However, the thought did occur, "Can this be what they mean by the most stringent security ever?"

Morelli's warmth and smile reassured everyone that he had not come only to scold. Gradually the Cardinal-electors took their seats. The thrones of years past could no longer accommodate the large number of Red Hats who'd assembled in Rome.

Morelli waved aside a chair, preferring to stand as he spoke. "My Brothers in Christ," he began, "I wonder if this is not the last of the secret Conclaves." He waited for the embarrassed laughter he anticipated to subside.

"Our Church is experiencing the joy of change. As we stand on the threshold of a new century, the two thousandth anniversary of the birth of Jesus Christ, the Pope you select to lead the world's millions of Catholics and inspire the hopes of fellow Christians may well celebrate the Mass of the Nativity on that extraordinary occasion. Our Church will herself be a few years short of two thousand years of age, then as now, the oldest institution in the world.

"The world is scrutinizing the Catholic Church more closely than at any time in her history. Humanity is asking questions of us. We must answer them. Are we inspiring their respect with displays of jealousies and rivalries, rejecting the intentions of those who long to serve more actively in the government of the Church, who want their voices heard in the high councils of Rome? Have the prelates of one nation abrogated to themselves the right to define our faith in an era when the dominion of the Church has seldom been as broad or as strong? Paradoxically where she is weakest today is in the land that houses her Mother Church.

"I am here on a personal mission—to vindicate the good name of a son of Italy, of the Church and of his adopted country where Cardinal Riccordi has served with honor and distinction. I am turning over to His Eminence, William Cardinal Muldoon, authenticated documents; among them, a letter from the President of the United States, which will effectively clear the callous slanders heaped on him and which, unhappily, would have been tailored to any Papal candidate threatening the monolith that is Rome. To be truly Catholic, truly universal, truly worthy of the confidence Catholics expect of us and non-Catholics turn to as affirmation of their own Christian faith, this Conclave must forge, out of a perilous beginning, an ending that will illuminate, not darken, the decades that lie ahead.

"Supplicatory prayer in the sense that we beg specific favors of God has always seemed to me to be a negation of the intelligence with which He has chosen to endow man. May we then bow our heads and pray for the wisdom to guide us in their quest for a man who will give us a strong Papacy that will emerge as truly representative of the universal Church? Without such a voice, beloved brethren, believe me, there will be no listeners."

*   *   *

As the Cardinals prayed Francesco Morelli slipped quietly out of the Sistine Chapel, Donald Brady close behind him.

Before they had time to digest the words of their former Pope, the Cardinals' attention was attracted by the presence and voice of a tall, handsome member of their group who stood before them—not in the vestments of his office—but as a man working long and hard at a difficult job, his sleeves rolled up, his eyes flashing, his words, insisting on being heard.

"I am Juan De Cordoba, today the Archbishop of Los

Angeles; tomorrow, assigned to return to my native Mexico. I speak for the Third World. To do this I must acknowledge our debt to the Cardinals of the United States who chose to assume an unaccustomed role in this Conclave—to seek out, nominate and work for the election of a Pontiff sensitive to the problems of today, a man who has not isolated himself from the restless Catholics of his diocese. They, like the citizens of the Third World, Latin America and Africa, are indifferent, if not critical, of politics-as-usual at the Vatican. They believe the Church can no longer afford the luxury of trading on history and tradition to satisfy the spiritual and human needs of thoughtful Catholics who want to hear less about the personalities of the Church than the relevant, larger questions—ecumenism, world poverty and overpopulation, human rights and the Church's reaching out to Eastern Europe's Communist governments.

"As head of an international Church—and, in a sense, a wider pluralism that includes all Christians—the Pope has concerns larger than the ties that link Italy and the Vatican. In recent years the Italian Parliament has enacted an abortion law and Italian voters returned a thundering 'no' vote to a church-sponsored resolution to repeal Italy's divorce code. The Catholic Church of Italy has been working side by side with Communist mayors and leaders. The argument that Italy's political security requires an Italian Pope is, therefore, no longer valid. In Italy, separation of Church and State seems the desired goal of the people—if not of the Vatican power-brokers.

"The United States has been a glittering example to the world of the truth that religion flourishes where it grows out of its own soil, independent of the State. Because the American Catholic Church had no ties to European politics or historic involvement in old Vatican concordats with countries like France, Spain, Italy and Portugal, Cardinals attending past Conclaves remained aloof from the 'horse trading that took place in incense-filled rooms.' They were able, in true conscience, to accept the decision of their brothers—the European Cardinals. In this century, the Church has been blessed with Popes who have worn the *Ring of the Fisherman* with honor. Among them were Pontiffs of great vision who questioned the ability of the Church to sustain her moral leadership unless her leaders were prepared to come to grips with a changing world.

"Outside the locked doors of this Sistine Chapel six hundred million Catholics are waiting for the signal of white smoke proclaiming a new Pope. Will he lead them in the same philosophical direction as Pope John and Pope Paul, or will he return to the more rigid conservative, ideology of their predecessors?

"America's Cardinals began asking this question over a year ago when speculation centered around the possible resignation of our beloved Francesco Morelli. They felt the time had come when they could no longer neglect their obligation to the Church and to the world. They could no longer pursue their traditional course of deferring to the European wing of the Sacred College to choose a Pope for them. Had they asked their congregations for approval of the decision to select a Papal candidate far removed from the traditional Italian Cardinal-diplomat, I doubt they would have received much encouragement. They did, however, find support far, far away from their own land—in Africa, behind the Iron Curtain in Poland and Czechoslovakia, and in Latin America.

"In Chile they found Cardinal Giorgio Riccordi, Italian-born, a pastor of the people, a leader who had survived political upheaval, appropriation of Church and his personal property, censorship of his letters to the faithful, house arrest and all the indignities honorable men endure when Governments fear them.

"No one among the United States Cardinals foresaw—or could imagine—the hostility their activism would create in Rome. One is not supposed to speak on behalf of brother Cardinals within the walls of this Chapel. That is an arbitrary rule and I am rejecting it now because it does not pertain to our deliberation or to our profound belief that ultimately the will of the Holy Spirit will touch us all.

"I am speaking because the Americans were discouraged from participating fully in the pre-Conclave discussions. Oh, yes, Cardinal Muldoon, their spokesman, received many telephone calls, personal visits from German, French and

English Cardinals. The African Cardinals were boldly supportive. South American Cardinals feared making their position known because of pressure from old friends in the Curia.

"The antagonism spilled into the press and, at the last moment, into an awkward, childish campaign to discredit Cardinal Riccordi by labeling him a power in the mercenary underground that permitted Nazi criminals to flee to South America, protected by the Vatican. Cardinal Muldoon now holds the documents disproving this malicious accusation.

"For my part, I am indifferent to the accusers, to the plotters, to fellow Cardinals hungry for earthly power. My heart tells me that this Conclave will reject their stumbling parochialism.

"We will find among us one who has no fear to pull away from preoccupation with the national politics of individual countries, a man who, as Pope, will recognize the truth that socialism has embraced all the continents and that the philosophy of Communism is going to be with us for many years to come. We will find a man born of a new Papal generation, born out of war and revolution, nurtured in struggle, aware that his pastoral burdens overshadow all political considerations, a man who is realistic in method and a conciliator in spirit.

"On the question of sexual morality, a shambles exists. Whoever sits on the Throne of Saint Peter must grapple compassionately with the problems of birth control, clerical celibacy and women's rights to a voice in the Church. He must understand the hopes of the poor, know that social justice pertains to all men and that religious freedom is not the special province of the Roman Catholic Church. In ecumenism lies the continuance of our own moral leadership and the strengthening of Christianity throughout the world."

One by one the Cardinals had taken their seats to listen to this quiet discourse from the tall Latin whose simple appearance in ordinary clothes made them self-conscious about the scarlet cassocks of their office.

Then it happened—a strong burst of applause. The Cardinals rose as a body and clapped their hands. They cheered. They sought out the Americans, embraced them warmly. A group clustered around Cardinal Riccordi, tall, aesthetic, a sensitive man whose face had been brightened by this dramatic exoneration by the Pope and now a tribute from a fellow Latin, Cardinal De Cordoba.

Riccordi raised his hands, begging for silence. After some minutes of confusion, order was restored. Cardinal Riccordi, a quiet smile on his face, began to speak, softly at first, the Cardinals strained to hear his words. But confidence overcame his diffidence and his voice rang out as it had many times in the Cathedral of Santiago and the simple churches in the villages of Chile.

"Brother Cardinals, Your Eminence, Cardinal De Cordoba—My heart is filled with joy at this remarkable outpouring of confidence in my person and my office. Not that I ever doubted that it would occur. Truth is the enemy of intrigue; falsehood is the handmaiden of despair. I did not despair. Those who spread lies about me evidently did despair. They despaired because they feared they could not corrupt this Conclave. How right they were! We have not been corrupted. Rather, we have been enriched by this experience. How wise were those words of our own Francesco Morelli, 'This may be the last secret Conclave.'

"Brethren, I permitted my nomination to be offered in this Conclave, not from any personal desire to occupy the office of Pope, but as a symbol of the importance of the Catholic world that lies outside the orbits of Europe and the United States. For me, being identified as *papabilo* reflected the aspirations of the Third World, its eagerness to be heard, to be known, to be loved and respected.

"That has been accomplished. Now I must respectfully withdraw my name from the roster of *papabili*. A shadow has fallen across my path. True, it has been erased in this historical chapel by the extraordinary events we have just witnessed—the appearance of a living Pontiff to clear my name and a letter from the President of the United States as well. This night I am the most blessed of men.

"Still, a shadow remains a shadow. The Church must live its tomorrows in the bright light of sunshine, unafraid of shadows. Adolf Hitler boasted that his *Third Reich* would endure for a thousand years. True, the *Reich* of his promise no longer exists. But we live with its legacy—its shadow—hatred, bigotry, terror.

"Yes, almost a half century has passed since the doom of Adolf Hitler was foreshadowed by World War II. But his legacy still endures. This speaks poorly for civilization, does it not? And the Church, too, I fear. In invoking the Holy Spirit in our quest for a new Pontiff, let us pray for a man who will lead his flock across this shadow into a world of tolerance and respect for God's supreme creation, mankind."

*   *   *

Inspector Luke Monzelli found Pietro Gentille in the V.I.P. Lounge at Leonardo Da Vinci hidden behind a copy of *Der Spiegel,* the German news magazine, an item which German commuters admitted they carried for effect or to help them doze.

Monzelli, whose usual rising time was seven, had pushed it back to six in order to land his quarry at a time and place when the pieces of their mutual interests might be fitted together with a minimum of difficulty on Monzelli's part and embarrassment to Gentille.

An executive carrying a half million dollars in Lire out of the country illegally would never choose a last-minute boarding of a plane to elude customs officers. That was for hoodlums. A man in Gentille's position, on a first-name basis with every authority at the Rome airport, would arrive early to sew up convivial meetings with these gentlemen whom he knew would chalk-mark his baggage and attaché case without question.

But did Gentille *really* have to hide behind *Der Spiegel?* To Monzelli, it reinforced a conviction that Gentille was far from the smooth operator his handsome exterior suggested. A cool con man knew that the safest piece of newsprint to hide behind was the sports page. Well, Monzelli figured, Gentille was pretty much the capon, more heft on the chest, less where it counted.

Gentille was seated in a far corner when the Inspector entered, picking him out without even looking at his shoes, the detective's usual starting point of identification. He saluted him halfway across the room, "Good morning, Mr. Gentille. How surprising to see you here! Of all days! You know, everyone's saying the vote will come this morning—in the afternoon, at the latest."

Gentille put down *Der Spiegel* and forced a smile, "Inspector Monzelli, how good to see you!"

An attaché case lay on the floor beside him. Gentille glanced to make sure it was still there as he rose to shake Monzelli's hand. "Well, I have to get back to New York, you know, and we *do* get the news even in the mid-Atlantic."

"So you do," Monzelli said. He took a step forward after the handshake and appeared to stumble. Gentille's hands reached out to support him. "Are you ill, Inspector?"

"No, no, no . . . simply tired. There's so much extra work involved in this Conclave. Thank heaven they don't happen every year. Then, this morning. Up so early in order to talk to you."

"Talk to me? You could have done that so easily. On the telephone, in town, anywhere."

"I must have overlooked that possibility, Mr. Gentille." He glanced at his watch. "I have so little time. We must talk. Your office or mine?"

"I don't understand. I can use the ticket manager's office, but I have no assigned space here."

"Very well, then, it will be mine, Gentille."

"You have an office?"

"Yes, if you look out the window, it's there, on the second floor of the control tower, the police bureau. Will you come with me, please?"

"I don't understand. My plane leaves in fifteen minutes. Can't we talk here?"

"I don't think so, Gentille. Either come with me immediately or I'll arrest you as a common pickpocket."

"You're mad."

"You have my monogrammed cigarette case in your side pocket. I can call a police officer to search you if you'd prefer."

Gentille's hand slid into his coat pocket. "It's a plant. It's a plant. I can prove it."

"Why bother, Gentille? That takes time. Please follow me."

He picked up the attaché case. "I'll carry this—with your permission."

Gentille wiped his brow with a white, silk handkerchief. His hands were shaky. Monzelli loathed them when they got that way. It usually ended with tears and pleas for understanding of "what will this do to my wife and my children?"

Remembering that the Gentilles were childless, Monzelli figured that would cut several minutes from the eighteen he intended giving Pietro Gentille.

* * *

The handsome *wunderkind* of the airlines, the wheeler-dealer for Milanese businessmen and a *Gray Eminence* of sorts in the Italian wing of the College of Cardinals had begun to behave like every businessman who'd ever been caught with his hand in the cookie jar. The trouble with so-called respectable crooks is they seldom timed it well. Being inexperienced, Monzelli grumbled silently, "They don't understand the knack of switching from righteous indignation to groveling."

Having retrieved his cigarette case, Monzelli offered it to Gentille who refused, squirming nervously, looking at his watch, sputtering, "I can't imagine what this is all about, Inspector. I'm a busy man and I've a plane to catch..."

Monzelli spoke quietly, "I, too, am busy, Gentille. I have to get back to Rome and consider the security, the lives and safety of a whole city—a city you've put under a great deal of pressure with your ugly campaign of hate and character assassination."

"I don't understand."

"You don't have to," Monzelli replied. The Inspector could pack the simplest words with anger and disgust, yet never raise his voice. "Since I understand, I will explain it to you."

He reached into his pocket and pulled out an envelope on which he'd written a list.

"Please, let's not waste each other's time with interruptions. I am going to go down the list of some associates of yours and explain how we've disposed of their cases. You will want to say that you never heard of these people. In a court of law, I would be obliged to listen. Since this is an informal meeting between friends, I have to please only one person—myself. So be quiet and listen.

"Angela Nero. You chose her to begin your attack on the credibility of the American Cardinals because of her name, her short career as a newspaperwoman and easy access to the Foreign Press Club. She had a reputation as a radical, an associate of known members of the Red Brigades; as they say, a mixed-up kid.

"Angela lured two college youths with only minor involvements with radicals to help her; Franco Bertoli and Luciano Casselli. They were big and strong, capable of any rough stuff, if required. Casselli knew Hans Buchmann, a German radical, self-styled, somewhat older than Angela, himself and Bertoli. He could be hired at a price, and they needed his skills. He was a good planner, knew something about electronics. He bugged the hotel rooms of the Americans when they came to Rome last month and I found one in the room of Donald Brady just a few nights ago.

"You paid them cash to print and distribute a scurrilous flyer about Monsignor Thomas Ryan. Your money enabled them to kidnap newspaperman Donald Brady, to attempt the same on Bishop Gabriel Hearn. Therefore, in law you were and are a co-conspirator in criminal charges involving kidnapping, threatening bodily harm, illegal entry, distributing unlicensed literature, maintaining an unlicensed printing plant and harassing prominent members of the Roman Catholic Church while guests of the City of Rome, pursuing an important duty consistent with their high office and responsibility. I'm not sure of the statute here, but it might simplify it in your mind by equating it with the charges police would press against a mad bomber who threatened a session of Parliament."

Monzelli's quiet voice droned on, despite Gentille's sputtered denials of everything.

"Please don't sputter. So far I've only dealt with the minor

289

issues. I have not yet codified my data on your blackmailing a Brazilian Cardinal to do your dirty work in Rome because I am uncertain of the dates you supplied young boys from the back alleys of Trastevere to certain Brazilian clergy on past visits. Of course, I have names, places, statements, definite photographic evidence showing your complicity. But that's an investigation in progress. You'll know more about it in due course. Not complicated. Simple case of moral turpitude involving minors. *Ballet Verde* stuff. The tabloids love it.

"Ah ... yes. This one. This is finished. The nastiest of them all in my mind."

Monzelli turned the envelope over. "Here we have the tragic case of Stefan Washinski, a Polish priest, whose entire life was spent in fear of persecution, real and imagined. You were able to seek him out fairly easily, perhaps through your brother-in-law, Cardinal Rossi. The young man had achieved a certain notoriety by his outspokenness, his eagerness for his Church to come to terms with Poland, regardless of the conditions demanded by the Communists. He was a young man in a hurry, too much of a hurry.

"How easy to capitalize on his fanatacism, on the instability of his mind, on his alcoholism! Any fool could have done it. But, alas, fools judge others by themselves.

"Stefan Washinski, for all his flaws, was a brilliant man. He held himself in high esteem—even at his maddest. He hoped to go down in history. He imagined himself as the savior of Poland. So everything he did, every sermon he preached, every act he performed in behalf of Poland was written in his diary. Moreover, when it was possible, his own opinions, deeds and actions were supplemented by evidence. Washinski would have been a superb policeman.

"Finally, every conversation with you—seven in all on the telephone—one, face to face—was recorded. I gather your language was guarded in dealing with Angela. She had the reputation of being bright and intelligent. Washinski did not, so you treated him accordingly, as an inferior; someone you could push, flatter, threaten or cajole, depending on what signals he gave you.

"Your words were so undiplomatic. Here's a sentence, for example. 'Threaten Novik any way you can—tell him the terrorists will kidnap the little children in his family in Poland. He's an emotional man—the battle to bring his family to the United States is an old one. He's vulnerable there, Stefan. Don't be afraid. Write it all out for Hans. Make him memorize it...'"

Monzelli wheeled around in the swivel chair. He loathed sniveling men.

"We have the tapes. They were in a package in Stefan's room, addressed to Cardinal Novik. We appropriated them. The Cardinal will never see them. Hans Buchmann has confirmed that Stefan coached him in dealing with Novik. There are also tapes recording Buchmann's conversation with the erratic priest.

"So there you have it." He wheeled around and faced his man.

"Now, Gentille, pay attention. This is your one chance out. You won't get another."

"Whatever it is...whatever...I'll pay, Inspector...I'll pay," Gentille sobbed.

"How easy to say—after the fact!" Monzelli shuddered.

"My duty as Special Assignments Inspector is to close nasty cases like this on terms that meet my own standards of justice. They cannot, of course, and never will. I have to compromise with my private sensibilities every day. But it is either that or force victims to spend years in courts reliving horrors perpetrated by creatures like you—hoodlums in high hats, blackmailers without balls.

"I am disposing of the case this way. First, Angela Nero is being held on a number of charges. Hopefully, prison will accomplish what her friends have failed to do, bring the young woman to terms with herself and reality. If it doesn't, then I will press for trial.

"Buchmann was trapped while attempting to kidnap Bishop Hearn, identified by records supplied by you as a doctor. Conceivably he might penetrate the Vatican and bring documents to Cardinal Muldoon which would clear the name of Cardinal Riccordi.

"By the way, Gentille, did you know the Conclave was penetrated last night? That the whole College knows the truth?"

"My God! No! How did it happen? Who got through?"

"That's all I know. Now, to continue. We're shipping Buchmann back to Germany. He's wanted there by the police of several cities, so that's one less problem for Italian jails.

"I have been in touch with the families of the Italian youths, Bertoli and Casselli. Neither boy has a criminal record. They are being granted probation and will return to college. Your company will give them part-time work. I will send the young men to your personnel manager next week."

"Of course, of course, Inspector. He's Tonio Magnani. I'll talk to him myself."

"Of course you will. Now about this attaché case. May I have the key?"

Gentille fumbled in his pocket. He placed it on the desk.

When he opened it and saw the stack of fresh fifty and hundred thousand *Lire* notes, Monzelli expressed surprise. "Hmm! There must be half a million dollars in *Lire* here..."

He glanced at his watch. "We could play cat and mouse. But let's look at it realistically. You have not boarded a plane with this money, have you? For all I know you are carrying it around as a good luck piece. Am I correct?"

"I guess so."

"Fine. Then you'll call a car when we're finished here, drive to Rome and put your good luck piece back where it belongs. Perhaps some other day you'll be able to move it. But not today... not today, my friend."

He spun the case around toward Gentille.

"I don't suppose, Mr. Gentille, that in your zeal to blackmail Cardinal Novik you were aware that he is active in a number of organizations to aid refugees from the Communist countries. Not necessarily Polish. He's quite broad-minded. I should imagine that if you counted out twenty thousand dollars from that pile, the good Cardinal could be talked out of pressing charges against you..."

"But this is not my..."

"Of course it isn't your money. It never is, is it? You are carrying it around for a friend. If you don't tell me who your friend is, I might deliver the tapes and Stefan Washinski's diary to Cardinal Novik.

"He's very hot-tempered, I'm told. An emotional man. Weren't those your words?"

The silence was so profound the men could hear the click of the electric clock on the wall as one minute, then two, passed without either saying a word or making a sound.

Finally, Gentille reached into the case, counted out packages of bills, adding them up with his lips, five, ten, fifteen, twenty.

Monzelli reached into his pocket for a pen and pad. He scribbled a few words, signed and dated it. "This is your receipt, Mr. Gentille. Cardinal Novik will send you an official one when he receives your gift."

Gentille closed the case and locked it.

Monzelli rose from behind the desk, "If you will excuse me, sir, I am already very late. I'll have the officer at the desk arrange for an escort to the limousine stand. *Buon giorno*."

At the door, he turned, "Ah, how fortunate! You will be in Rome for the voting today. It will be quite an afternoon. White smoke! I can promise you that."

* * *

Sister Mary Matthew beamed. "I never had such wonderful help at the Vatican. I love you all." Beaming back at her were Erika Wald, Bishop Gabriel Hearn and *Padre* Alberni who had been up since dawn preparing a buffet luncheon. Francesco Morelli had invited so many guests that his old housekeeper had given up counting. "There's going to be quite a crowd," she said, "and that's the best way to calculate instead of counting heads."

Bishop Hearn had arrived early, accepting an invitation to serve Morelli's daily Mass. On its completion, Morelli knelt at the foot of the altar and became the server for Bishop Hearn's Mass. Then the Pope and Bishop both served a Mass celebrated by *Padre* Alberni. Erika and Sister Matthew, attending the third Mass of the morning, were terrified that *Padre* Alberni would faint from nerves and excitement. But faith prevailed. The young priest made no mistakes and his Latin was impeccable.

By noon the priest's piety of the morning had evaporated

and Erika felt the all too familiar Italian game being played as Alberni's large, brown eyes roamed up and down her body, still encased in the same light blue suit she'd travelled from Washington. She hoped Alberni wouldn't tire before Donald arrived. The idea of her being ogled by a priest would certainly stir his adrenalin.

Rumor, instinct, experience and hunches had drawn huge crowds to Saint Peter's Square; they'd begun to arrive early in the morning. They were not surprised that black smoke announced the first balloting of the day. Romans are not early risers; business men do not breakfast at home, preferring the ambiance of a coffee bar and the *espresso* that hissed from the large machines. Why would Cardinals behave any differently from Romans who avoided serious thinking until nine-thirty or ten thirty?

At noon, the arrivals began. In the first contingent were the Noviks, six of them, firmly in charge of Teresa Tashman who had spent the morning coaching them on etiquette. They were to bow or curtsy and announce their names to the Pope who would probably lean down and kiss the children, shake the hands of their mothers. She wasn't really sure that this was how it would go, but Teresa had faith in Francesco Morelli. He would handle any situation well—even if the youngsters jumped all over him in the excitement of meeting a Pope. For herself, Teresa simply prayed that she wouldn't faint.

Padre Alberni stood in the alley, greeting guests and directing them to the elevator which led first to Sister Saint Matthew's quarters. There the nun and Erika made up the receiving line. Once all the Noviks were inside and checked out by their parents, Sister Mary Matthew led them upstairs; Erika, remaining behind to welcome the next guests.

Monsignor Thomas Ryan was next. He'd come alone, having been unable to locate Donald. Erika assured him that Donald was fine, that he was writing a story and would be along eventually. Next came Inspector Luke Monzelli and *Signora* Monzelli, a handsome, titian-haired woman, as outgoing and jolly as her husband was reserved. They were accompanied by one grown son who was living in Rome, his pretty wife, and two children.

In their conversation late last night, Donald had asked

Erika to take special care of Jennie Jacobowski. Erika instantly put Jennie's formal name together with her nickname and reputation. She was curious and a trifle concerned.

She needn't have worried. Jennie, in basic black and a single strand of pearls, immaculately coiffed, was completely poised and carried herself with the grace of royalty. Later, Sister Mary Matthew told her that "His Holiness embraced *Signora* Jacobowski like a sister, saying, 'We are of the same generation, Jennie, those quiet people who suffered the Depression, the war and then the after-effects. How happy I am to see you again, dear Jennie!'"

Finally, Donald arrived and when Erika caught sight of him in the elevator, she gasped. Her young man was positively luminous. He was dressed in a perfectly tailored suit with accessories and shoes that fairly cried out *Gucci*. His blue eyes sparkled and a halo appeared to surround his immaculately combed hair.

"*Liebling, du bist wie ein Engel*. I'm afraid to touch you," Erika said as he swept her up in his arms.

"Then, kiss me, *tesaro mio,* and you'll find out that I'm anything but an angel."

Their kiss was warm and somewhat restrained—a courtesy to their surroundings. Erika pushed Donald away to take a good look at him. Donald delighted her.

"I don't know what it is. But all of a sudden you are different. More beautiful than ever—you know—more beautiful inside..."

"I wouldn't count on it being a permanent condition, Erika. It's very exciting—but temporary I assure you. May I go upstairs?"

Sister Mary Matthew reappeared in the lower apartment. Erika said, "Take Donald upstairs. You stay there now. I can handle everything..."

"But..."

"No buts. Go upstairs. The signal is late. Everyone's getting excited. You shouldn't miss an experience like this." Sister Mary Matthew put a generation of service to Francesco Morelli into her next sentence, "It will never happen again—never."

Tears filled her eyes as Donald and Erika climbed the

carpeted steps to the penthouse. The Pope's resignation had answered Mary Matthew's prayers for herself. She had never been happy at the Vatican. So immense, so overpowering! The informality she'd known with Morelli had never totally disappeared, but his being the Pope *had* made a difference. Neither wanted to admit it, but there it was.

Mary Matthew was ambivalent about his resignation. She believed it was a loss to the Church and to the world. But as a man he would be spared much. She read Church history; she talked to old employees of the Vatican. She knew the old saying, quiet and cynical, "When one Pope dies you simply elect another."

In the old, enfeebled years which would come to him, the Pope would still be Pope—but not his own man. That was not for Francesco Morelli—nor for Mary Matthew. She could not have endured his being pushed here, shoved there, made to preside at audiences, wheeled to his throne and placed on it like some helpless child, asked to wave and smile, handed papers to read whose meaning he no longer comprehended. A feeble Pope was regarded as a bother. These were the indignities old Popes risked.

Morelli refused them—as Mary Matthew knew he would. But the struggle between his duty and peace of mind was one she'd watched and understood. She sometimes felt Morelli's torment was what they meant in the expression "wrestling with the devil."

Sounds from the alley below ended Mary Matthew's few seconds of reflection. The "spectacular" was on his way up— Mary Matthew knew the excitement he'd create. An overwhelming man. She felt his presence already.

A few seconds later, she opened the lift doors on Erich Cardinal Waldenheim, his niece, Gertrud, and the eighty year-old prelate's faithful secretary, Monsignor Franz-Josef Hoffman.

Waldenheim wrapped Mary Matthew in his arms, "Hello, old girl! You get prettier every year."

The giant's voice reached upstairs and Erika came sailing down, right into his arms. *"Onkel, wie wunderbar! Ich habe nicht gewusst . . ."*

"You weren't supposed to, *liebling*. It's all a surprise."

296

Erika embraced Gertrud and finally Francesco Morelli's friends were all together, overflowing the large room.

There was silence as the two old men embraced. Even Waldenheim had no banter for this historic moment—two great men of the Church meeting quietly in a Rome apartment; one, a former Pope—the other, the Pope who might have been—except for the accident of birth.

Then one of the children screamed, "The smoke—it's coming out—see—there it is."

"It's white," yelled another. "Look at it, Mama. It's white."

White it was. The cameras turned on the crowd which reacted with cheers and applause, eventually quieting down to await the announcement which would be forthcoming from the balcony of Saint Peter's.

When the children wanted to know "how soon" the new Pope would appear, Morelli explained that it took quite a while to get everything ready. Once the new Pope has been chosen, Morelli explained he is asked if he will accept the canonical election as Supreme Pontiff. Then he is asked by which name he wishes to be called.

Then, while the ballots are placed in the stove to be burned and announce that there is a new Pope, the papal master of ceremonies takes him to the sacristy where three papal *mozzettas* are laid out. Three sizes have been prepared. After he has changed, the new Pope returns to the Sistine Chapel, sits before the altar, and one by one, the Princes of the Church approach, kiss the new Pontiff's hand and are, in turn, embraced. Finally the *piscatorial ring,* with the image of Peter the Fisherman, is placed on the Pope's finger. The *Te Deum,* the hymn of thanksgiving to God, is intoned. The balcony is prepared, the announcement made and the Pope comes through the French doors to bless the people.

It was an average wait, fifteen or twenty minutes before the glass doors of the central *loggia* were opened. With great deliberation, the purple papal tapestry was spread over the balcony. Finally there appeared the Cardinal-Deacon to pronounce the old words.

"I have tidings of great joy. We have a Pope."

The crowd cheered. The Cardinal-Deacon stretched out

his arms. His voice was loud but one could sense the emotion as he spoke the name of the new Pontiff.

"*He is the Most Reverend and Lord Cardinal...Juan Maria De Cordoba.*"

First there was shock. Then the roar of the crowd began to grow stronger and stronger. De Cordoba was theirs. He was the handsome Prince from Mexico who had captured their imagination by being one of them—the fellow who forgot his scarlet cape—the tall, young-looking one who smiled and seemed always to have time to stop and chat with people as he was ushered in and out of the ceremonies.

It was some time before the *piazza* was quiet enough to hear the Cardinal-Deacon say: "He has taken the name of *Francesco the First*."

If ever Francesco Morelli doubted the people's affection for him, this was the moment to dispel it forever. The noise was deafening, mounting in intensity as De Cordoba stepped forward. He towered over the others on the balcony.

Then, every window on the loggia was thrown open, and the Cardinals, themselves applauding, looked down at the crowd. They knew their choice had been wise.

Pope Francesco I was in white except for the red stole embroidered in gold. He smiled out at the sea of humanity, his arms outstretched. The faithful dropped to their knees while his musical voice began the traditional Latin formula of blessing—*Urbi et orbi*—to the City of Rome and to the world.

He recited the Litany of Saints and finally, the blessing, "May the blessing of the Almighty God, the Father, the Son and the Holy Spirit descend upon you and remain with you always."

Those familiar with the Liturgy knew the new Pope was born, in the words he had used in his speech to the Cardinals, "of a new Papal generation." The form of blessing *Francesco I* had used was not the elaborate one reserved for momentous ceremonies but the short form used by priests.

The Cardinals who had answered the Litany stepped back. As *Francesco I* moved forward on the balcony to speak to the throng, he casually removed the red stole, held it casually in his hand until a Cardinal stepped forward to take it from him.

Speaking in impeccable Italian, De Cordoba realized the silence that had descended on the *piazza* was, for him, the moment of truth. Juan Maria De Cordoba, son of Mexican wetbacks, was the new Pope, the Vicar of Christ, the Bishop of Rome, and it was to him and his leadership that the world would turn in moments of grave crises. He could not solve them, but he could speak the truth—and he could pray.

That was what *Francesco I* said, "I belong to no one but to God and to you, His children. The voice of the Holy Spirit was truly heard inside this Conclave—and what happened within the sacred walls of the Sistine Chapel will soon be made public. The *Secret Conclave* now belongs to the past.

"Our beloved American Cardinal, William Muldoon, came to my cell this morning and said, 'Juan, they are considering you. Some of us have held your name in our hearts for many years. We believed in your spirituality, in your devotion to your Church and to God and to your willingness to undertake any task, however menial. But there was your age. By the standards the Sacred College measures Papal candidates you are too young. Now, with great courage, Francesco Morelli has opened the doors for leaders of all ages, of all nations, of all backgrounds. If we place your name into the chalice, will you accept?'"

"Beloved friends, I did not hesitate any longer than I hesitated to sweep the floors of the tiny parish I was sent to as a young priest in Mexico. Those who walk with God cannot turn back. I know I am not worthy of this honor. But it is here—and so are the symbols of this high office—the Crown, the Fisherman's Ring, the Mitre, the Papal Throne.

"They are only symbols. I hope to walk among you and to pray at your side. The Supreme Pontiff can no longer separate himself from the people. He must be one of them and they must join him in searching for the answer to the question that haunts us today—not 'Where is God'—we know where God is. He is visible everywhere in the momentous *Act Of Creation*. The question we need answered now is this—*'Where is man?'*

"At his Coronation as Pope, the first of the simple ceremonies, our beloved Francesco Morelli dedicated his reign to the Holy Spirit. I remember the words he said then, found in the *Tract* of the *Votive Mass to the Holy Spirit:*

"Send forth They Spirit, and they shall be created and Thou shalt renew the face of the earth."

Then, as simple parish priests have done for centuries at the conclusion of their sermons, *Francesco I* blessed himself. Once more he blessed the crowd. Finally he said, "I must go now. I am very hungry."

They loved their new foreign Pope—the handsome Prince from Mexico.

To those gathered in the apartment of Francesco Morelli, the emotion of that moment was one they would never, never forget. Tears glistened in the eyes of the former Pontiff. For months thereafter Donald would claim that crusty old Waldenheim had brushed a tear away from his tired but still piercing blue eyes. Erika insisted. "Never! Not Uncle Erich!"

It was an argument Donald never won and at the moment he didn't care. He went to the telephone, after a smile from Morelli, telephoned New York, reached Ed Muir and said quietly, "It's all right now. You can run the story of Morelli's surprise visit to the Conclave."

"Congratulations, Donald. It's a hellu... it's a fine story. And thank His Holiness too."

"He said it was a reward to the paper for lending me to Muldoon."

"Did you really do anything, Donald?"

"A little bit, Ed, just a little bit. Between you and me, I think we were all puppets in *Padre* Francesco Morelli's hands."

"Do you think you could prove that...?"

"Never. Not in a million years."

"It would be a great story, Donald, a great...."

"You tackle it." Erika stood beside him, making pleasant noises.

"Ed, Erika's here. I think she has something to say—as usual."

"Hello, Ed. What do you think of my roommate? Oops, sorry. We shouldn't talk that way on this phone..."

"Why don't you marry the guy, Erika?"

"I have been thinking about it—but now it's all over."

Before Ed had time to ask why, Erika was babbling away, "You don't know it, Ed, but I have been living with a nun, Sister Mary Matthew, *Padre* Morelli's housekeeper. You know I have been thinking about becoming a nun too. Maybe the new Pope—he wants a housekeeper..."

Donald grabbed the phone out of her hands, "I wouldn't put it past her," he said.

"No, Donald. She's all yours. I'd sew it up before much longer. Anyhow, take a week off. Don't call me until you get back unless you run into that story."

"What story?"

"Morelli pulling all the strings."

"Oh! That one. Well, I figure I'll be whistling in the dark a long time before that happens. See you."

The ceremony was over, the television had been turned off. Erika, Teresa and Sister Mary Matthew were serving lunch—buffet style—every man for himself. Waldenheim, Morelli and Tom Ryan were huddled in a quiet conversation, punctuated now and then by roars of laughter from Waldenheim.

Clearly, it was a conversation Donald couldn't intrude on. However, Waldenheim's hearty voice didn't adapt easily to whispering. Donald couldn't help overhearing, "*Ach!* You're a sly one, Francesco, who else would have thought to have a second choice standing in the wings?"

Morelli smiled, "Erich, it is one thing to flip through the pages of past history and come up with a new look to an old idea. But what would have happened if our Monsignor Ryan had not considered the appeal of De Cordoba and convinced me to thrust him into the limelight in Los Angeles? It requires many minds to become the *Grand Elector*."

Donald turned away. He called to Erika, *"Liebling!"*

"Your German gets so much better," she said, as she broke away from the Novik children to join him.

"Erika," Donald whispered, "can you and I break away for a while?"

"Of course, darling. But why?"

"Just to walk around the block, get some air. I couldn't live through another Papal scoop."

"Of course, *mon cher,* we go ... for a few minutes. I guess they have been talking about De Cordoba being not so much the surprise everyone imagines . . ."

"By 'they,' I guess you mean Uncle Erich."

"Of course, *liebling*. He and *Padre* Morelli are very proud and happy. They have—what do you call it—vanquished the enemy. Torriani, Rossi, that Gentille man. I knew they would."

Donald wondered if he would ever get used to Erika's amazing inside knowledge. "You knew about De Cordoba?"

"Sure, months ago, the Mexican Ambassador to the United Nations was curious about the sudden interest in De Cordoba, who told his aide, who told his . . ."

"Secretary . . . who told you. And I suppose the others who requested information from the White House about Cardinal Riccordi were the Arabs and the Israelis."

"Of course, liebling, how *klug* you are! I love clever men. That's why I love you."

"You never said you loved me before."

"I know, *liebling*. I wanted you to finish this story first."

"I suppose some U.N. secretary told you that it was going to break."

"No, *liebling*," Erika said in a sure, quiet voice, "It was the Holy Spirit."

About the Author

David Hanna was born in Philadephia and began his international career as a journalist in Hollywood, covering the Golden Age of the movies, the 40's and 50's for the *Hollywood Reporter* and the *Los Angeles Daily News*. He began travelling in 1952 and for 20 years covered the International Scene, Jet-Set Society and the entertainment world for the *London Daily Express, New York Times, Herald-Tribune, Coronet Magazine, Cosmopolitan, King Features* and many others. His articles have been translated into a dozen languages. He edited *Confidential, Whisper* and *Uncensored* and now lives in New York City.

In the past five years, Hanna has written more than three dozen paperback books, covering Hollywood personalities, the underworld, and politics. His biographies have included works on Elvis Presley, Henry Kissinger, Jacqueline Susann, Mae West, Robert Redford, and profiles of John Wayne, James Steward, Henry Fonda and Gary Cooper.

He is also the author of *Second Chance,* a study of alcoholism and the famous personalities who have come out of the "closet" to help others with the same problem.